Together, Again is her twentieth novel.

Milly Johnson

Together, Again

**SIMON &
SCHUSTER**

London · New York · Sydney · Toronto · New Delhi

First published in Great Britain by Simon & Schuster UK Ltd, 2022
This Paperback Edition published 2023

3 5 7 9 10 8 6 4 2

Simon & Schuster UK Ltd
1st Floor
222 Gray's Inn Road
London WC1X 8HB

Simon & Schuster Australia, Sydney
Simon & Schuster India, New Delhi

www.simonandschuster.co.uk
www.simonandschuster.com.au
www.simonandschuster.co.in

A CIP catalogue record for this book
is available from the British Library

Paperback ISBN: 978-1-4711-9906-6
eBook ISBN: 978-1-4711-9905-9
Audio ISBN: 978-1-3985-0120-1

Extract for *Ten Steps to Nanette* © Hannah Gadsby
used by permission of Atlantic Books Ltd

Typeset in Bembo by M Rules
Printed and Bound in the UK using 100% Renewable
Electricity at CPI Group (UK) Ltd

MIX
Paper | Supporting
responsible forestry
FSC
www.fsc.org   FSC® C171272

For my mum, in her ninetieth year. For the home cooking, for the warmth and love she gave me, for the fun times we've shared and for the memories of a lovely, safe, happy childhood.

'There is nothing stronger than a broken woman who has rebuilt herself'

HANNAH GADSBY

Eleanor

If you are reading this, then I am gone and you will probably be wondering why I have done what I have.

I need to explain everything, I owe you that.

I will entrust the delivery of this letter to Sally. I will stress that it is for your eyes only and I hope that curiosity will not overcome her. That would be a great shame because I have to write the truth, all of it and I can only guess at her reaction.

I have had a lot of time on my hands in widowhood to reflect and I have learned so much about myself from doing that. I never realised I had a conscience, but I suppose I must have to feel compelled to write this. Whether that is a blessing or a curse, I have no idea. It feels like neither.

Why now, you might ask, after all these years? Because I am frightened. Not of death – it will visit us all. But of meeting my maker with a heart burdened with so many unsaid words. I have had a warning that our meeting is closer than I anticipated and so it is imperative I act before it is too late. I must be at peace.

Daughter, you must believe me when I tell you that I have tried over the years to feel like 'normal' people but it will come as no surprise to hear that outside your father, I am incapable of love . . .

Chapter 1

The girl they all knew as Mai walked down the stairs with her rucksack, carrier bag and pet transporter. There was a crescent of women waiting there, in various stages of upset ranging from silence to crying.

'Aw, no,' she said. 'I wanted to slip away quietly.'

'Not from us lot you're not,' said Denise, her boss of seven years, but also so much more.

'We'll miss you, Mai,' said Velvet, one of her colleagues, tall, stunning, black with long blue hair, handing her a card in an envelope. 'We've all written on it.'

She opened it. There was a daiquiri cocktail on the front with a dodgy-looking half a banana stuck on the rim of the glass, two cherries at its base. It looked very genitalia-esque; deliberately, she thought.

'Will you come back and visit?' said Shirley. 'Or at least Zoom us?'

'I wish I could do my bloody job by Zoom,' said the redhead, Ginger, at the side of her which set off a ripple of laughter.

'You remember us with smiles,' said Velvet. 'That's all we ask. Come here, you.'

She was passed from one to another, squashed, hugged, kissed, an assault of perfumes, every one as sweet as the next. Then she picked up her pet basket and Denise poked her fingers through the front grid to touch the large brindle rabbit sitting inside it. 'Goodbye John Abruzzi. Don't you forget your Auntie Denise, you know, the one that gave you all her best carrots.' She made a face. 'He's got his back to me, I'm talking to his arse. Which is typical working in this place because all I do is talk to people's arses.'

She and Mai walked outside slowly, as if delaying the goodbye, then sat on the wall waiting for the taxi which was on its way, according to the phone app.

'I'm glad to get rid of you. I thought you'd never go,' said Denise.

'You should have said before,' came the reply.

'You know what I mean. I've been waiting since you landed for you to tell me you were moving on.'

Mai smiled. 'I've been thinking for a long time what I should do with my life and now I have plans.'

'Finally,' said Denise, raising her hands to heaven in grateful thanks. 'But promise me that you'll go and make it up with your mum.' Her tone was soft, because she wasn't one to give lectures.

Mai made no comment on that; there was no point. Denise had a planetsworth of life experience packed inside her, but it was beyond her comprehension to accept that any relationship between a mother and her child could not be salvaged. Plus it was too late for that now, but she hadn't said as much.

Denise took the tall, reed-thin woman's face in her soft, fat hands.

'Think of us occasionally, like Velvet said, my little Mai Tai.'

She smiled, looking far younger than her seventy years, partly helped by a recent facelift, a top-up of Botox and foundation applied as thickly as cement.

'Of course I will.'

'But don't look back too much. The past is the past for a reason.' Denise shoved a small roll of money fastened with an elastic band into her hand, and overrode the protest. 'It's for the train.'

'I could buy a blinking train with this wad.'

'Don't be cheeky.'

'Thank you, Denise. For everything.'

A car with 'Steel Taxis' emblazoned on its side rounded the corner.

Denise batted away the emotion that was filling the air between them. 'I'm not sure if I should be thanking *you* though. Giving that lot ideas. Go on, get your taxi and good luck. I hope you make it happen; if you can't, no one can.' Her voice was gruff but there was a telling break in it, not that she'd ever admit to being upset. The line between her work and personal life was bold and definite and yet this beautiful young woman had managed to bridge it. She hated that she'd miss her, but she really had better not come back.

'Mai' had never belonged here; but she'd belonged here more than she'd ever belonged anywhere, which said it all. Denise hoped this was her finally finding the place that fitted her. She waved once, turned, and went back inside.

Chapter 2

Jolene hadn't smoked for years but the yearning came on her as soon as she'd walked into her mother's house. She'd last been here only the previous week and yet the house seemed to have aged abruptly since then. She'd noticed the faint smell of old damp before, but now it whacked into her olfactory nerve as soon as she'd closed the front door behind her. It seemed to smell of abandonment as well as age, tempered with a little sadness. It might sound bonkers had she told anyone this of course, but she'd always felt that this house had the architectural equivalent of a soul, and as such she'd wished better for it than to have the Vamplews as its inhabitants.

It was a good job she didn't have a packet of twenty in her bag because she would have chain-smoked the lot. And done it in her mother's parlour just because she could, in a blatant act of defiance. Funny how those closest to you could stir up such polarised emotions. Past and present.

The house was eerily silent, apart from the slow tock tock of the grandmother clock on the wall marking the time. She hadn't appreciated how much the atmosphere of a house absorbed the essence of people who lived in it until she'd moved into Warren's new-build home on the outskirts of Leeds, ten years ago, just before they married. There were no layers of lives lived within its walls, no depth or dimension to the flat, bland air. Warren was the first person to press himself into it, like a weak watermark, to be added to by her and those who came afterwards. It had two hundred years to catch up on all that Fox House had slyly stolen from its residents.

The Vamplew family home had three floors, six bedrooms, a magnificent dining room and four reception rooms – one of which had been utilised as a study, another as a lady's parlour. The ceilings were high, the period features intact; previous owners had not sought to rip off the dado and picture rails, chip off the cornices and ceiling roses, tear out the elegant fireplaces. She knew that her mother had decided to buy this house as soon as she saw the staircase, an elegant curl and sweep of wood. She had to own it. But that was her mother all over, coveting things for the sake of it. Once she had them, her job was done, her passion for them sated then withered to nothing, which explained much. Probably why the lovely staircase was the most neglected part of the house now.

The most cherished was the study where the ever-present cigar smoke had lingered for months after Julian Vamplew's death, as if the aroma had become every bit a physical characteristic of the room as his burr walnut partner's desk, the massive antique glass cabinets and his bookshelves crammed with textbooks. It had eventually faded away, although her mother had reported that sometimes, when she went in there, it seemed to her as strong as it ever was. She said she found that manifestation of her husband's presence comforting. Jolene suspected it was more imagination or hope on her mother's part but if it brought her comfort, who was she to argue against her fancies?

Jolene had been crying for hours now and was amazed she had sufficient moisture in her system to produce as many tears as she had. Her only explanation was that maybe she'd been storing it up, like a squirrel storing nuts for hibernation, because she couldn't remember the last time she'd cried real tears; she tended to cry inside, implode rather than expode. But now, her cheeks were raw from salt burn and sore from tissue wipes and the worst of it was she didn't know if she was crying for the mother she had, or for the one she wished she'd had but never did.

Glenda, the cleaner, had been very recently because the kitchen of Fox House was immaculate enough to be photographed for a glossy magazine; even the silver kettle shone like a mirror. Jolene filled it up and switched it on. She took from the cupboard the mug with the poppies on it, the one she always used when she came here. It was part of a set of four that Sally next door had bought as a present. Only this last one remained: her mother thought they were tacky and said she'd been glad when they'd been broken.

Jolene had slammed that same mug down on the table last Tuesday and stomped out, intending not to come back for a long time. Her mother had a gift for saying words that acted like a needle pushed under the skin, bang-centre into the heart of a nerve.

'Things that don't bend tend to break, Jolene. Maybe you need to give Warren a little . . . space.'

There was only one interpretation of 'space' from the way she'd said it. That was so rich coming from someone who would have clawed out her husband's eyes if he'd asked for some *space*. She shouldn't have asked for her mother's opinion; that just revealed her desperation and really – what else did she expect? She'd been more angry at herself for being so stupid and opening up to her than for the useless advice she received. She'd overreacted in her response, boiled over for the first time ever, asking her what on earth she could possibly know about this sort of problem, then stormed off and had not been in touch since – and now that could never be repaired. Jolene had held her mother's chilled, dead hand in the hospital and sobbed a rain of apologies, but it didn't count when they were neither heard nor accepted. She might as well have been railing at the moon, which she'd done enough times by now to know how ineffective that was.

She was an orphan: the realisation hit her hard, like a slap. There had been a girl at school who was an orphan; her parents had both died in a car crash when she was seven and the word 'orphan' was rightly applied to her because she was a child, not a peri-menopausal woman with the first showings of permanent frown lines between her brows. She was in a void at present, even more so than usual because emotions were never good go-to places for her these days. She had the sudden urge to run through the rooms until she found her mum and could bury her face into her dress, feel herself pulled into a warm, Calèche-perfumed embrace. Not this *mother* who had just passed, but the warm and pliant one that Eleanor Vamplew had once been, before her sisters had come along, when Jolene had her all to herself. She had changed along the road, hardened, like the objects which hung in the petrifying well near Mother Shipton's cave. Once soft teddy bears, now stone. A double knock-on effect of drip-drip deposition and evaporation, although Jolene had never been able to pinpoint what process her mother had undergone to calcify her.

Jolene's text alert went off: Marsha, her younger sister.

I've finally got a flight. I'll keep you posted. ETA Thursday early morning.

None of that kiss nonsense at the end.

They were strangers more than sisters – all three of them, the seven-year gaps between each birth gaping like a grand canyon, although she and Marsha were positively conjoined twins compared to how they both were in relation to Annis, the baby of the family. The spoilt and beautiful one, the renegade. There would be no text from her saying she was on her way. If she hadn't been there when their father had been desperately ill and died, she certainly wouldn't turn up for her mother. She hadn't been at their father's funeral, not even as a shadowy anonymous figure at the back, hiding under a black veil. Odd, that, because up to the point she had buggered off, aged sixteen, on the coldest night of the year, she'd been the daddy's girl of all daddies' girls. He didn't have favourites, he'd say, but nevertheless he had bestowed the crown on Annis's head without her even trying that hard for it.

Jolene sat at the table cradling the poppy mug. She was bone-deep frozen, but then this house never seemed to retain any warmth at all, though they'd got used to that when they were kids. Even if some had built up from the central heating chugging out its best, open a door for a second and it ran out as if chased by a serial killer.

Her ear flagged a noise, metal grating against metal and her nerves twanged. When she'd lived here as a child she never thought twice about all the noises this old house made, they just *were*: the cracks during the night as wood expanded or contracted; the bathroom door shifting in its frame as a rogue draught toyed with it. Marsha was convinced she'd seen a ghost once, an old lady sitting on the chair in the corner of her room and smiling at her. The fact that she, the most sensitive of them all, hadn't run out screaming onto the landing would intimate that it was a lie, although Marsha had argued it was because she wasn't scared at all, even though the temperature of the room had dipped so much she said she could see plumes of her own breath in the dark.

The noise again: someone was trying to get in using a key, but Jolene's own key in the hole was stopping them. Jolene headed quickly down the hallway and snatched open the front door to find their neighbour Sally Lunn there, key in hand ready to attempt entry again. Sally made a squeaky noise of shock and patted her chest as if steadying her heart rhythm.

'Oh, Jolene, I didn't know anyone was in. I'm sorry, I should have knocked. I didn't see a car.'

Jolene hadn't seen her close up for a few years. She'd aged a lot. Her hair, once a Lego helmet of brown, was now an unbrushed frizz of white and her slight frame was even smaller. She looked not unlike a fresh chick that had fallen out of its nest.

'I parked at the side,' replied Jolene. Force of habit. Her mother didn't like to look out of the window and see cars in the front.

Jolene knew Sally had a key in case of an emergency, but she did wonder why she was trying to get into the house now.

'Is there something you want, Sally?' she asked.

'No, no ... I, er ... just wanted to pop in and see that all the plugs were out and ... everything was okay.'

It was what Sally would do, Jolene knew.

'Do you want to come in?' she asked.

'Yes, yes I will, please but I can't stay long because of Norman,' Sally twittered, stepping over the threshold as if it was an honour to be asked. If she'd been wearing a cap, she would have doffed it.

Jolene's one abiding memory of Norman Lunn was of him trying to stem the blood from his nose, of it dripping off his chin onto his pale green Bri-Nylon shirt, a froth of grey hair visible on his chest where the top two buttons were undone. Crazy what unimportant details the brain remembered when it could have retained things of much more value. He had dementia now, so her mother had told her. He was a shadow of a shadow of his former self, which was quite an achievement seeing as he had only ever been a shadow of a self in the first place.

'I'm so sorry about your mum, Jolene. I haven't stopped crying. We were friends for a long time. Since she moved here, in fact. Forty-one years ago. We hit it off from the start.' Sally smiled fondly; her small eyes were like grey glass, full of tears like clouds full of rain. Even after such a long association, Sally hadn't worked out that they were never friends. She was useful, convenient. Eleanor Vamplew would have considered Sally Lunn as a sort of confidante lady's maid at best, one who might have been under the illusion she was more but division of class would have always made that impossible.

'You were just a little tot then,' Sally went on, now having to bend her head right back to look at Eleanor's oldest daughter's face.

Jolene vaguely remembered living at another house

before this one, a much smaller building and less grand. Her mother had inherited her namesake's fortune which had enabled her to buy Fox House, but she had alienated her family in the process. Not a great loss by all accounts.

'Thank you for all you did for her, Sally. We're very grateful to you.'

'Did they say what it was that . . . took her away?'

'No,' said Jolene. She couldn't remember what they'd said at the hospital, there had been too much to take in.

'I told the ambulancemen everything. I'm sure her face had dropped a bit on one side, as if she'd had a stroke.'

'Like I said, Sally, I don't know.'

There were questions crowded behind a door in Jolene's head but if she opened it too soon, they'd drown her. They'd wait, the answers couldn't alter anything now.

'You'll have a lot to do. So much paperwork. If you wanted any help, you just have to ask. I had to do it all for Norman's parents so I'm a dab hand at the formalities.'

'Thank you, Sally, but we'll manage between us.'

'I'm not sure if you know where your mother kept her documents and . . . things,' said Sally, smoothing down the front of her checked nylon tabard. It was hard to think of Sally Lunn without one of her tabards. Jolene had a stray thought about the pink one she'd had on the day when her husband's nose had splattered blood over everything within a half a mile radius; she wondered if she'd ever managed to get the stains out of it.

'She has a file in the parlour in a cupboard, I know,' said Jolene.

'Her new will isn't in there though. You'll need to contact Wragg and Cripwell. The Regent Street branch. They came out to the house to do it for her just after Easter.'

'Oh.' Jolene hadn't even thought about wills yet. It didn't seem decent to. But still, the fact that her mother had revised her will was a small shock. And at Easter, when she'd had that small health niggle but refused to go to the doctor.

'The will has all her requirements for her funeral listed.' Sally sounded quite anxious now, like someone who had no place to insist on something, insisting all the same. 'She told me to stress, when the time came, that her instructions should be followed to the letter.'

'They will be, don't you worry,' Jolene nodded. She expected nothing less of her mother, who made control freaks seem anarchic.

'I don't know what . . . what's in her will. Just that she told me to make sure I said all this to you,' Sally twittered on.

Jolene didn't really need this now. Her mother had died only hours before and her head was cabbaged. She needed some sleep before even thinking about what came next.

Sally's pocket made a buzzing noise. She reached into it and pulled out a phone.

'Sorry, I have to go, Norman's stirring. I have a camera on my phone that alerts me when it detects movement.'

'How is he?' asked Jolene, a polite ask.

'Oh, you know, good and bad bits, like the curate's egg,' said Sally with a small flash of smile. 'Not great at the moment if I'm being honest, but I couldn't put him in a home so' – she threw her hands up in the air – 'what can you do but carry on carrying on?'

'I'll take the key back now,' said Jolene at the door, smilingly insistent. 'I don't suppose you'll have need of it any more.'

'Oh,' said Sally. 'I, er . . .' She failed to finish the sentence and sighed as if forced to give up something precious. She wrestled it off her keyring and dropped it into Jolene's wait-ing hand from a height that suggested pique.

'Eleanor promised me her locket. I'm sorry to have to mention it now, but I would like it. Something of hers. If not that, just something else that I could wear. I don't mean to be pushy, but she did say—'

'I'll look it out for you,' said Jolene, a wave of weari-ness washing over her. She would have promised Sally the sitting-room carpet if it meant she left. A little of Mrs Lunn was always enough, especially today.

'Thank you,' said Sally and hurried off in that strange skittering way of hers.

Her father used to call Sally Lunn 'the mouse next door'. He would laugh and say no one with the same name as a bun could be taken seriously and they'd all laugh with him at that. There was a steely determination disguised in all that timidity, though, thought Jolene. In fact, Sally Lunn with her meek, mousy ways had to be built of rock to survive what she had.

Jolene closed the door, locked and bolted it and made straight for the staircase. She needed to sleep, she was exhausted. She never slept well when her husband Warren was away, and only marginally better when he wasn't. It was just after seven a.m., 9 August, which would be forever ingrained now in her memory as the day when her mother died, sitting there beside 30 November, the day when her father breathed his last. Coincidentally the exact date when Annis Vamplew had walked out of the house eight years before and never returned.

Chapter 3

Marsha took a sharp right and pulled into the large drive in front of Fox House. She'd last been here three weeks ago. A duty visit; they always were, she didn't get any pleasure from them and she was pretty sure the same was true for her mother, who seemed to endure her presence as she would endure a persistent ache. She couldn't even remember what they talked about, not much probably – banalities as per usual, long silences punctuated with comments about the garden, bridge club, neighbours, world news. This family wouldn't have won any prizes for its common ground.

She parked her red Mercedes next to her sister's sleek blue Jaguar in the front drive. Hadn't they done well for themselves, the Vamplew girls, driving such cars, Marsha imagined Sally Lunn next door saying aloud to Norman, because there was nothing surer than that she'd be glued to the window, spying on any comings and goings from behind that net – the neighbourhood witch, one of their father's nicknames for her; he had quite a few. It had always been her hobby, being a nosy cow. Shame she hadn't been so observant about what was happening under her nose though until it was so rudely pointed out to her. Marsha's shoulders gave an involuntary shudder. Of all the memories she had of her childhood, that one was as sharp and bright and multicoloured as it was possible to get. The pink tutu-like swimsuit with the flounce which someone had bought for teeny Annis; the fierce, bright sunshine, the smell of newly mown grass; the buns with the icing and Jelly Tots topping, the paddling pool with the sun-warmed water.

She got out of the car and the heat of the day hit her after the coolness of the air conditioning. She zapped the lock and walked towards the house. It was by far the grandest structure in the area. Move it from its midway position between Penistone and Barnsley and transplant it in the Home Counties and it would be worth at least a few million pounds more.

There were fourteen houses on the avenue, each one different from the next, a hotch potch of architecture but it was the solid, stone Fox House that was its oldest inhabitant – and king, looking as if it had been there forever and would stay there for even longer. Behind the high brick walls and black iron gates which were almost always open, was a large gravel parking space, enough for ten cars easily, flanked by lawn and rose beds. The house itself had a wide frontage with a huge central stone porch and two massive west-facing bay windows at either side of it which served to let light pour into their father's office and the dining room in the afternoons. There were five large sash windows on the first floor, three of them serving the master suite alone.

Once upon a time there had only been four houses on the street, all with a mass of land that had been carved up and sold off over the last hundred years. The other three were long gone; the Lunns' detached house next door was now the second oldest, designed in the 1930s by an architect with an apparent aversion to windows. The result was that the rooms, even the south-facing ones, were dark. The gardens belonging to the houses on this side of the avenue were enormous, stretching right down to Maltstone Beck and the railway line; they were much smaller and more manageable on the other side.

Fox House looked different in every season. Prettiest in spring, Marsha thought, with the crowded borders of snow-drops, daffodils, hyacinths and crocuses, artfully planted not to look too arranged. They'd employed gardeners to do the lawn and the bulk of the weeding, but it had been her mother, until the arthritis in her hands had prevented her from doing so, who dead-headed the roses, grew the seed-lings, nurtured the exotics in the greenhouse. She'd given her moonflowers and sapphire orchids the sort of intense attention she'd never given to people.

Now in high summer, the house looked stunning, like a jewel set in a verdant mount, the lawns so lush and green they'd acquired an almost artificial colour. There wasn't a dandelion allowed to push out of the ground without an immediate death sentence being imposed on it. The gar-dener was good, she had to say.

She saw a figure in the window and waved; it waved back. She hadn't seen her sister since Christmas and that was more or less in passing. She envied people who said they were going out shopping with their sister or taking a family trip with their sister and mother – all girls together. It was part of the reason why her maternal button had never been pressed, in case she had a family that ended up like the Vamplews: dried crumbs that would not bind, however much they were pressed together.

She twisted the octagonal iron doorknob that she could barely grip in her small hand and pushed open the heavy front door that was so much bigger than normal doors. Everything about Fox House was bigger, though – the widths and lengths and heights, as if it had been built on a larger scale for a giant. It was the sort of house that occupants moved on from but looked back on with fondness. Well, maybe previous occupants because Marsha had very few happy memories of the years she'd lived here. She'd been eleven when Jolene left home and she hadn't really known her enough to miss her. If anything, she was excited because it meant she might eventually have her older sister's bedroom with its two large windows framing the view of the back garden like a matching pair of pictures. She herself had left eight years later, gone off to London to lose herself in people and noise and anything that distracted her. She'd felt the pull to return here only to see her father. When he died, that pull died with him.

She called Jolene's name.

'In the kitchen,' came the reply.

The hallway was long, a worn carpet runner lying over the dark wooden floorboards that were smooth and ridiculously slippy without it. She remembered them rolling it up once and she and Jolene sliding and skidding, having a ball, until she went thudding into the wall and gave herself an egg-bump on the head. She remembered Jolene pressing a cold cloth to it, trying to push it down as if it were a big button before their mother got home. She remembered running to her mother crying, hoping for a cuddle and being told off instead. They were both sent to their rooms and Marsha couldn't remember them playing together any more after that.

Jolene appeared in the doorway. Both sisters embraced, unable to recall when they'd last done so but each felt the other's reluctance to extend it beyond the protocol of politeness.

Jolene put a coffee down on the table for her: milk, no sugar. She had no idea if that was how her sister took it, which spoke volumes, she thought.

Marsha scraped back one of the chairs from the table, hearing her mother's voice in her head, tutting at that, never missing a chance to disapprove. She flopped down on it, her bones weary.

'Have you just come from the airport?' asked Jolene, sitting down next to her.

'Yes. The plane was delayed for four hours. It felt like a very long drive here.' She rubbed her eyes and yawned.

'You look dreadful.'

'Thanks.' Marsha smiled, batting back her sister's apology before it was even offered. She knew she did. She'd been crying quietly in Jakarta airport and on the plane, tears seeping out of her for hours, washing away her make-up and turning her eyes into two pink snooker balls.

'I wish I hadn't gone away. It's not as if I personally have to be touring Indonesian factories to look at their bloody promo merch, I've got buyers to do that for me.'

'Why did you, then?'

She was too tired to go into the whole truth of it: that someone was sniffing around her business wanting to buy it, so it was in her best interests to make sure everything was running tickety boo. But she had no life outside of work and she was frightened of the emptiness that might await her if she let it go.

'Occasionally it's good to see things at first hand again.

Plus I had no reason to suspect that my perfectly healthy mother, give or take a bit of arthritis, was going to ... you know. When did you last see her?'

'Last Tuesday.' Jolene would forever beat herself up that she didn't bob over the day after, make amends. She hated that they'd parted on sour terms. She'd been tempted to scream and run out of the house so many times over the years but had always kept a lid on it, until this once, when it counted.

'She wasn't ill?' asked Marsha.

'No. She complained about a tightness in her chest a few months ago but she refused point blank to let me make an appointment at the doctor's for her. I noticed she'd bought some indigestion tablets but she told me to stop fussing when I asked about them, said it was just a bit of acid reflux, that was all.'

Marsha recognised that look on her sister's face: self-recrimination. She could pick out the expression in a pitch-black room.

'You know what she was like, Jolene. If she believed it was indigestion, it was.' Until it was no longer possible to believe it because the facts were battering her around the head, Marsha added to herself. There came a point when not even her mother's force of will could overcome cold hard reality.

'It might have just been that though,' said Jolene, hopefully. 'I hope they don't do a post-mortem.' She half-whispered it as if she was afraid her mother might be listening, because she would not approve of that at all.

Marsha nodded; for a few moments, there was a silence between them that bulged with words unsaid. Then Marsha sniffed and reached into a bag for a tissue.

'It doesn't feel real, does it?' she said, her throat clogged with tears. 'When Dad died we were sort of prepared for it, and even then it was a shock, but this … suddenness …'

Her face crumpled and for a moment Jolene thought that she looked very much like Annis, which was odd because they were all so different. Jolene was clearly her father's daughter: tall, brown-eyed, big-boned, a darker skin tone to Marsha who took after their pale, blonde, grey-eyed, petite mother. Annis had been skinny and stringy, impossibly long legs, her face a perfect oval. Stunning blue eyes, an alien shade of reddish-blonde hair, full lips to envy; tall like their father, fair-skinned like their mother, but that was all she'd taken from them. Obviously a throwback to some beautiful ancestor who had saved her precious genes to bestow upon the family fuck-up. What a waste. Jolene could have done with those genes and put them to good use. Beauty might have been skin deep, but you needed honey to attract the bees in the hope that one of them might stay, one of the nice bees who realised what a gift he'd been given, not one of the bees for whom his hive queen wasn't enough.

Jolene didn't know which was worse, seeing someone you loved wither away to nothing or be cut off without warning. As contests go, they were both up there on the first place misery podium.

'Has there been a lot to do so far?' asked Marsha. 'I'm sorry it's fallen to you to have to do it all. You've been lumbered with the lion's share as usual.'

Jolene had long accepted the position of primary 'carer', not that their mother needed caring for; she was perfectly capable still, plus she had Glenda the cleaner here for five hours every week and she could always call on Sally in a crisis. But still she worried more than anyone else did about her mother, especially as she was ageing, prematurely Jolene thought, and slowing down, even if Eleanor Vamplew was determined to resist the passage of time.

'Don't worry about it,' said Jolene. She knew how hard her sister worked, she rarely gave herself a day off. Jolene was more flexible, plus she could handle her mother better than Marsha. She'd had longer to learn how to brush off her infuriating idiosyncrasies, she took things less to heart. 'It's all pretty straightforward. They give you a checklist at the hospital. Idiot-proof, apparently.'

When their father died seven years ago, their mother insisted on doing everything herself. She didn't want any help, wouldn't delegate a single thing and the sisters knew better than to try and persuade her.

'I haven't done much so far, I'll be honest. I haven't had the headspace,' Jolene added. She certainly hadn't after getting hold of the copy of her mother's revised will.

'Any news from Annis or is that a stupid question?' asked Marsha.

'It's a stupid question.'

'Thought as much.'

'She read my texts, even if she doesn't pick up the phone.'

'That's something, I suppose,' said Marsha.

'Will you go and see Mum?' asked Jolene then.

Marsha gave a definite 'no' shake of the head. 'I can't. I regretted going to see Dad. I thought he'd look peaceful and asleep but he looked like a waxwork dummy in a suit.' She'd had dreams afterwards that he'd sat up stiffly, that his head had swivelled to the side and he'd started talking like a ventriloquist's doll.

Jolene nodded in agreement. Their father hadn't looked like himself. The undertaker had done his best to pinken his yellow skin but he'd been hollowed out by his illness and the suit their mother had picked was too big for him in his shrunken state. Marsha had held his hand and been repelled by the coldness; she could not equate her larger-than-life father with his handsome maleness and energy that hung around him like the brightest aura with this person lying still in a hideously shaped box. It screwed with her head for many months and still would if she let it.

'Tell me again what happened to Mum. I didn't take it all in.' Marsha took another sip from the mug and grimaced. Her mother was a curious mix of extravagance and economy. She would waste hundreds on items she neither needed nor used, but coveted; yet she'd penny-pinch on things like coffee that she mainlined. And she wouldn't pay extra for free-range eggs because she said those from battery chickens tasted exactly the same.

'Sally next door found her. She was out in her garden in the very early hours and noticed all the lights still on in the house,' Jolene told her, 'so she came over and let herself in and found Mum not well in bed.'

'What the hell was she doing in her garden at that time of the morning?'

'Something to do with her hedgehog village,' replied Jolene. 'When she rang me up she was rabbiting on about that more than about Mum.'

The words sounded mean once they were out of her mouth. Jolene shook her head at herself and tempered her next statement. 'She must have been in shock. She'd tried to give Mum CPR.'

Marsha tried to think of how Sally might act in a crisis and couldn't. She didn't imagine she managed too well.

'So, what ... she found Mum having a seizure or something?'

'I think that was the gist of it, I couldn't take it in properly. She was all over the shop, very upset. By the time I got to the hospital, Mum was gone. They let me sit with her for a while so I could say goodbye. Then I came straight here.'

'Don't you want to be at home with Warren?' asked Marsha.

'He's away on business. I told him not to come back, there's no point. He's busy.'

'I'm here now to help. You go home for a couple of days.'

'No, it's fine. I'm okay.' Jolene was insistent.

Marsha rubbed her eyes. They felt gritty and sore with exhaustion. Adrenaline had propped her up on the drive here, but now it was no longer needed to perform a task and was whooshing out of her system, letting tiredness rush into the vacated space.

'I think I'll have an hour, Jolene, I can't see straight.'

'Of course, but—' she broke off abruptly.

'But what?'

'Nothing. Go and have a sleep. All the beds are made up. I parked myself in my old bedroom but you can have it back if you like.'

'I don't care where I sleep,' said Marsha with a yawn. 'I'll take the blue room.'

Jolene let her go without saying anything else. It would wait another couple of hours, this news she had to give her sister about what their mother had done: an enigma to the last.

Chapter 4

Sally moved away from the window. So both sisters were now in the house. And very well they'd done for themselves with their big posh cars. Eleanor used to brag about their achievements: Marsha liking the promotional products she sold so much that she bought the company, making her out to be the Victor Kiam of her age. And Jolene, a novelist with her books in the *Sunday Times* Bestseller charts, although she never actually bragged about her daughters themselves; there was a subtle difference. She never mentioned Annis, the one Sally didn't want to think about. What happened wasn't her fault, she was only a child, Sally knew that deep down, but if she hadn't been there, none of it would have happened at all. That which had led to all this. What a blithering mess.

Sally loved this room, it was her favourite in the whole house and the one she frequented most of all. That's why she'd had a bed put in it for Norman. It was a heavy one so she could fasten him to it if she had to pop out to the post box or the corner shop. She never left him for long; she was practical, not cruel.

It should have been her own child's nursery, but it wasn't

to be. She used to dream of bathing a child, watching it gurgle as she scooped warm water onto its plump little body, threading its arms and legs into brushed cotton pyjamas, answering its call in the middle of the night to comfort it with a cuddle. Now she had to do all that for Norman. He wouldn't have anyone else do it. They'd tried with carers, but he kicked up such a fuss and she didn't want him being taken away, so she did everything. There wasn't much weight to him these days so that made it easier. He didn't eat much, dribbled most of it. He wore a bib. She'd bought one from the internet with his name embroidered on it, soft white towelling with blue stitching.

She'd envied Eleanor Vamplew so much over the years, envied her as much as liked her, as if her emotions were perfectly balanced on a see-saw. The differences between them had become polished away by a mutual respect and a true meaningful friendship. Except that wasn't the case at all; Eleanor Vamplew had been feeding her a diet of lies.

The truth was in the fat letter she'd entrusted to her. Sally had been beyond curious to know what it contained but it had sat sealed on her dressing table since Easter. But there had been a weakness in her in the early hours of last Tuesday, full moon madness, and she'd taken the letter and steamed the flap open with the kettle. She hadn't expected to find what she did and she had never been as angry in her life. The worm turned at last – and how.

Had things been different and she hadn't read it, she wouldn't be panicking now because lying didn't sit well with her, she got flustered and forgot things. She'd said that she was out tending to her hedgehogs at three in the morning because she couldn't sleep: lie. She said that she'd noticed all the lights on in Eleanor's house: lie. She said that she'd found Eleanor poorly: lie. Eleanor had been sleeping peacefully in a darkened house when Sally stormed round there. She'd flicked on the light and screamed in her face, hot angry tears rolling down her cheeks. Eleanor hadn't said a word, just sank back in her pillow and closed her eyes and Sally thought she'd gone back to sleep. But she hadn't. And that's when Sally swung into action to try and reverse what she'd done, because she had caused the shockwave that had killed her one and only friend.

Chapter 5

Fifteen years ago, it had taken Eleanor Vamplew over two weeks to tell her elder daughters that her youngest had left home.

'We thought she'd be back, so there was no point in saying anything,' she said.

'Have you rung the police?' asked a horrified Jolene.

'Of course we have,' snapped Eleanor. 'But there's not a lot they can do when someone is determined not to be found.'

'She's sixteen,' Jolene had returned.

'My great-grandfather had been working down a mine for several years at the same age,' was Eleanor's reply.

'Dad, we have to do something,' said Marsha. 'What the hell made her run away?'

But it was their mother who answered.

'What makes Annis do anything?'

It was the only time Jolene had ever seen her father cry.

Annis had left a note, apparently, to say she was leaving home of her own volition and did not want anyone to look for her. Her mother said she had thrown it away, putting it down to dramatics and insisting that Annis would be back soon enough with her tail between her legs. She'd been in trouble at school, but then she usually was: nothing major; just playing up, not doing her homework, cheeking teachers. She didn't have any friends: girls either envied her to bitch-level or felt she was out of their league.

Jolene and Marsha, independently of each other, had been to the police but were disappointed at their response. Most runaways came back, they said. She wasn't vulnerable and they filled out a missing person report. Then, six months later, Eleanor told them she'd had a call from Annis to say she was alive and well, but confirming that she would not be back under any circumstances, so they really should stop looking for her, if they still were. And as they had no other choice, that's what they had to do.

But Jolene had been consumed with regret that she hadn't had much to do with her youngest sister growing up, and Marsha with shame that she'd treated her as an annoyance. Their mother point-blank dismissed her as a rotten apple, a bad seed. Jolene, more than once, wondered if this was her attempt to offset her hurt but she refused to talk about the matter. Eleanor Vamplew was a puzzle that defied solving, even by those supposedly closest to her.

Annis's leaving changed their father; he was ... *reduced*, was the only way Jolene could put it. His natural ebullience had gone but he finally gave the share of himself that had been reserved for Annis to them. They felt, after so many years, they were getting to know him as a dad rather than a distant patriarchal figure. By the time he fell ill, he was the dad they had both wanted him to be when they were children, and it was going to be cruelly snatched away from them just as they had secured it.

Seven years ago, the sisters had revived their efforts to find Annis, to give her the chance of reconciling with him before it was too late, and Jolene stupidly mentioned this to their mother who had flown into a disproportionate rage, even by her standards. She didn't want Annis coming back and upsetting their peace, she said. The bed she had made for herself was the one she wanted to sleep in and there was an end to it.

Marsha defied her by putting succinct notices in regional and national newspapers and *Private Eye*. '*Annis Vamplew – please phone this number urgently – J and M.*' Weeks passed, then Marsha happened to be in her parents' house when a number she didn't recognise rang her mobile and she picked up.

'Dolly?'

'It's Marsha,' she said quickly, before her brain registered the name.

'Ah, Mashed Potato.' That unmistakeable naturally husky voice, though slightly age-deepened. She'd called her that as a child, and Jolene 'Dolly' after Dolly Parton.

'Annis?'

'Yep.'

'Thank goodness.' The relief weighed heavy in Marsha's tone. 'We've been trying to trace you for god knows how long.'

'So I hear.'

'Can we see you?'

Annis answered the question with one of her own.

'Why did you want to speak to me urgently?'

Marsha didn't want to tell her this way. There was a long silence as she thought how best to phrase it, though Annis jumped in and did it for her.

'Father's dead, isn't he?'

Marsha swallowed; she wasn't used to the juxtaposition of 'father' and 'dead' in the same sentence and it knocked her. 'Yes. Two days ago. He's been very poorly. We hoped we'd—'

Annis interrupted her. 'Right. I guessed it was about either him or her. I had a feeling it was him.'

Her tone was frozen, unemotional; not even mum or dad, but *him* and *her*.

'Mum's fine,' said Marsha.

'Someone I know saw your message in an old *Private Eye*. I always wondered how many people were actually traced that way,' Annis said, ignoring the condition of her mother.

'It's so good to hear you.' There were a million questions cued in Marsha's throat.

'Okay.' She did not return the sentiment.

'Are you calling from a number I can contact you on in future?' Marsha expected a no, but was flabbergasted to hear 'Sure.'

'I'll text you Jolene's so you have both,' said Marsha. 'I'll let you know the funeral arrangements.'

'I won't be coming.'

'Mum would love to hear from you,' Marsha tried.

A small hard laugh. No accompanying words were necessary.

'I'd like to see you again,' said Marsha.

'Who are you talking to?' asked her mother, appearing in the doorway.

'You'd better go,' said Annis. 'Tell her I'm a wrong number. That's what she's always thought of me anyway.' And with that the line went dead.

They'd rung the number back, left voicemails but Annis

never picked up or returned the calls, nor answered the texts. Not even the Happy Birthday and Merry Christmas texts, but they were read. The door was ajar, wedged open, even if only a little, by hope.

Chapter 6

Four hours later, Marsha walked into a kitchen full of the aroma of omelettes. Jolene was standing by the hob and at the sight of her sister, she slid the omelette out of the pan and onto a plate.

'I thought you might be hungry,' she said. 'I heard you stirring upstairs.'

'Thank you,' said Marsha, then she noticed the omelette was stuffed with cheese.

'If you want this one, I'll take the next one without cheese,' she said.

Jolene gave her head a shake, a gesture of self-annoyance. 'Sorry, of course, you can't eat it, can you.' A picture loomed in her mind of her mother and Marsha having a stand-off in the dining room. Marsha refusing to eat the sandwich, her mother saying she couldn't have suddenly stopped liking cheese, Marsha replying that it made her feel sick so she wasn't eating it any more. Her mother telling her not to be so stupid. Her father ending the argument: *Don't make her eat something she doesn't want to, Eleanor.* Marsha's beaming face that her father had come down on her side, her hero.

A tidbit of his attention, his support was the equivalent of a banquet to them.

Jolene poured the rest of the whisked eggs into the pan.

'I've got a cheese intolerance. That's why I kept having cramps and feeling ill whenever Mum tried to force me to eat it,' explained Marsha. 'When I lived in London, an allergy testing company was looking for paid volunteers so I jumped in. I can't tolerate cheese but I'm fine with milk; that's why Mum never believed me, I suppose.'

'Oh, that's tough,' said Jolene, who loved it. She flipped the plain omelette over in the pan.

'Not really. I never liked it much anyway. One of the girls who works for me loves strawberries but they make her tongue swell up, so you just wouldn't, would you?'

Jolene shuddered at that thought. She brought her plate over and sat at the table.

'I can't believe I slept this long,' said Marsha, before pushing a forkful of the eggs into her mouth. She hadn't eaten for over twelve hours and, for a simple dish, this was on feast level. 'You like cooking?'

Jolene gave a small laugh. 'I've only fried up a few beaten eggs, Marsha. Any idiot can do that.'

'I like to cook,' replied Marsha. 'I'd do a lot more of it if I had anyone to cook for.'

'There's no one ... special in your life, then?' asked her sister.

Marsha gave a humourless laugh which answered the question without the need for words. She loaded her mouth again and chewed.

'How's Warren?' she asked eventually.

'Fine,' nodded Jolene, quickly amending that to, 'Well, he lost his own mother in April and we've had that to deal with.'

'Were you close to her?'

'Not really.' But not for the want of trying. Initially Pamela Cattrell had come across as warm and welcoming, but Jolene learned over the years that she was tolerated merely as an extension to her beloved son. She had wanted to find in Warren's mother what she hadn't in her own; but Pamela's sun only really shone for him, despite what he'd done to her. Then again, she would have forgiven her perfect boy anything. Jolene had been on the brink of telling her who she'd raised too many times to count, to puncture her balloon of condescension, but it would have been cruel and there was already too much of that quality in Jolene's life. It was lucky Pamela had died without learning a quarter of it.

Warren had insisted on doing all the paperwork himself. Jolene wondered what he was trying to hide and so she poked around when he was out one day. Pamela had taken loans out all over the place; the pittance she'd left barely covered the repayments. She'd been comfortably off when Jolene first met her; she'd had no need to borrow unless it was to bail out her son after he'd bled her savings. It was an easy conclusion to draw, because bailing him out was what the women in Warren Cattrell's life did. He'd given the mother he supposedly thought so much of a basic frill-free funeral, with not so much as a cuppa afterwards for attendees. His mother wouldn't want him to waste money on sausage rolls, he'd said, but Jolene knew she would have expected a fancy send-off.

He'd then taken full advantage of his loss to 'take some time out', as Jolene knew he would. Not that he needed to ask for permission. He did what he wanted and she put up with it because she was a weak fool trapped in the aspic of her own stupidity.

'I don't suppose you've heard from the hospital about Mum?' asked Marsha, breaking Jolene's thoughts away from Pamela Cattrell and her son.

'No,' replied Jolene. 'I expect they're checking things with her doctor. I'll be on it in the morning. I have to make a start.'

'*We* have to. I'm here to pull my weight for once.'

'Don't beat yourself up,' said Jolene, who saw the irony. The woman who won gold medals for beating herself up advising others not to.

'I'm going to set up base from here until the funeral at least,' said Marsha, then she scooped up the last of the omelette while wishing there was more. 'I've got a good set of people I can rely on at work.'

'Mum looked very peaceful when I saw her. I sat with her for ages in the dark.' *And I spoke more openly and easily to her than I ever had before.*

'I never thought she'd die,' said Marsha. 'I thought she'd last forever. Seventy isn't old at all. And to have nothing wrong with her but to suddenly go like that, it's scary.' Her voice began to waver. She was having real difficulty absorbing the facts. 'And for Sally to be out in her garden at stupid o'clock and see all the lights on. And then go into the house at the exact time when Mum is having a stroke or whatever it was, don't you think that's odd, Jolene?'

'Of course I do,' said Jolene, 'but then again, that sort of weird stuff happens all the time, doesn't it? The night Warren's mother died, my bedside light turned itself on. It hadn't done that before or since.'

'Have you seen her? *Sally Lunn, Sally Lunn . . .*' asked Marsha, slipping into the rhyme their father used to recite.

'*Face of mouse, name of bun,*' said Jolene, picking it up.

They'd thought it was hilarious at the time, but really it was unkind of him to be so merciless behind her back when he was so charming to her face.

'Yes, she came round on Tuesday, not long after I got here. She was trying to let herself in with her key, obviously not realising I was here.'

'Was she now?' said Marsha, less than impressed.

'She said she was just making sure things were secure. Then again, Mum had promised her the gold locket and she may have wanted to come and take it in case we forgot.'

'Cheeky sod.'

'As it happens, it's mentioned in Mum's will as a disbursement and we would have honoured it of course, though maybe she didn't want to risk that we wouldn't.'

'I hope you took the key off her,' said Marsha, picking up the plates and taking them over to the sink. 'I wouldn't like to wake up and find Sally hovering over me and checking to see if I was still breathing because she's had psychic messages from her hedgehogs to suggest otherwise.'

'I did, but I have to say, it was a good job she had a key when it came to it,' Jolene answered.

'Unless they discover Mum was murdered and Sally is prime suspect.'

Jolene shuddered. 'Don't joke like that. There's not a harmful bone in Sally.'

Marsha started to clean the work surface with a cloth. 'People get greedy though at will time,' she said. 'Remember what happened when Mum's mum died.'

Jolene was all too aware how deaths and ensuing inheritances had a tendency to drive an axe into a split and cause irreversible damage. Their maternal grandmother had died before she had cut her daughter out of her will, so her sons

Milly Johnson

had tried to do it posthumously. There was a court case and they lost and had to pay nearly as much in costs as they inherited.

'I do. It didn't do well to cross Mum, did it? Marsha, just come and sit back down will you.'

If ever there was a perfect time to tell her sister what she must, it was now.

'What's up?'

'It's about Mum's will.'

'She left everything to the local donkey sanctuary?' It was only half a joke but Jolene's expression was telling her that she might be more right than wrong.

Jolene reached into the bag looped over the back of the chair and pulled out a tri-fold clutch of papers. 'Best you read it for yourself.'

Marsha took the will from her, unfolded it, eyes scanning the archaic legal language, the executors named as herself and Jolene but if either of them did not want to take up the role, the sole duty would fall to the other. If both declined, then the duty would fall to Sally Lunn. A gold locket was to be given to Sally, five hundred pounds to the cleaner Glenda Price, an equal amount to the bridge club and the Holy Mother and Child church fund, plus two hundred pounds to the gardener Eric Granger. Her husband's books were to be bequeathed to Leeds University library.

Then Marsha got to it. Jolene could tell she had by the look on her face, by the way Marsha flipped the page back to see if she'd missed anything. Finally she spoke, more breath than words.

'She's left everything to Annis?'

'Yes. Give or take a percentage from the proceeds of the sale of the house,' replied Jolene.

'What the fuck . . .'

It was the first time Jolene had ever heard her sister use the word. Incidentally, exactly the same word she'd used when she got to the same part of the will.

'This is a joke, right?' asked Marsha, reading it again to make sure, but the words stayed in the same place and didn't miraculously shuffle to make any sense.

'You know it isn't.'

Marsha smashed the papers with the back of her hand.

'Why would she do this?' asked Marsha. 'Was she going mad?'

Jolene gave a small laugh, a hard, hollow sound.

'It depends what your definition of insanity is. But if you're asking me do I think she knew exactly what she was doing then yes, I absolutely do. She clearly wasn't being unfairly influenced or coerced by Annis and it's not fraud.'

'It doesn't make any sense,' said Marsha, wearing a mask of incredulity. 'Does she know about this? Annis?'

'No. I left a voicemail to tell her about Mum and followed that up with text messages asking her to get in touch. As usual, she reads them but doesn't respond. To clarify, we don't get anything until the house is sold. The empty house, because Annis gets all the contents as well.'

'Blimey, they must be worth as much as the house.'

It was an exaggeration but not a wild one. There were a lot of antique pieces: the furniture in their father's office had cost over twenty thousand pounds alone. And there were paintings and dreadful bronzes all over the place that her mother was so fond of collecting. She had bought some early pieces by up and coming artists and sculptors who were now established on the circuit. They were worth a hell of a lot more than she paid for them. She definitely had an eye for picking good investments, even if they were bloody ugly.

'So, you and I get ten per cent each from the sale of the house and that's it,' said Marsha, doing a quick calculation in her head. Fox House was worth about a million and a half, though she didn't know if the government would take a big lump of that in inheritance tax. She hadn't even thought about it until this moment. Like her sister, she'd presumed that having to carve up the estate would be years off.

'In a nutshell,' replied Jolene.

'What a bizarre thing for her to do,' said Marsha. 'And it's unfair on you, Jolene. You did so much for Mum, more than I ever did, so this must feel like a proper slap in the face to you. Thank god neither of us needs the money but if you think we should contest it, I'll back you up.' Marsha was getting more annoyed with every passing second. Their mother really did have to go out with a bang.

'When Sally came round to tell me that Mum had written a new will and how to get hold of it, she said that Mum wanted us to obey her requests to the letter,' said Jolene.

'I bet she flaming did. But she can't exactly stop us if we don't.'

Marsha's voice wobbled; a combination of upset, confusion and disappointment. Even from the other side Eleanor Vamplew was still managing to pull their strings and make them dance to her twisted tune.

'I'm not fighting it. It's her money to do with as she wanted,' Jolene said. 'Keeping any discord to the minimum is all we can do to disarm the bomb she's thrown in the middle of us. Maybe she thought that Annis would need it more than either of us. Maybe it's her way of . . . oh, I don't know . . . sending a message to her.'

'Because she couldn't just send a clear message, like a normal person?'

'Well that's it right there, isn't it?' Jolene replied to that. Her mother and 'normal' had never sat well together.

She stood up. 'I'll put the kettle on.' It was far too early for gin, otherwise Jolene thought she just might have bitten the top off a litre bottle with her back teeth and drunk the lot in one gulp.

As Jolene was boiling the kettle, Marsha looked through the rest of the will. Her mother's requests for her funeral were all laid out in bullet points: what clothes she was to be dressed in – already waiting in a box in her wardrobe; four limousines, a solid oak coffin, the shape and make-up of the floral tribute; instructions that she was to be cremated and her ashes cast to the wind in the same spot that her husband's ashes were dispersed, on their next wedding anniversary. No stone had been left unturned, but that was her mother to a tee – a control freak. Over the years, Marsha wondered if she was like that because if she gave an inch, her whole fabric would blow. Like a dam, it had to be complete or it was nothing.

Father Gerard Bannen was to conduct the service and he already had a draft copy of her requests. As Marsha's eyes travelled over the name, she went hot and cold at the same time, as if she had been simultaneously deluged by water from two buckets of differing temperatures.

'Father Gerard?' she said aloud, tasting the name in her mouth. She hadn't said it for a long time, tried to give nothing away as she did so. 'He's still around, is he?'

'He is indeed. I rang him from the hospital and he said he would go up there and say a prayer for Mum.'

Marsha had long since stopped googling him, not that there was ever much to find. She'd had to overcome the urge to type his name into search fields because even his name conjured up a toxic cocktail of emotions within her, ranging from aching despair to volcanic anger. She wondered how he looked now, nineteen years on and if he still wore that French lavender cologne; then she stopped wondering because her thoughts were in danger of being pulled down a rabbit hole with Alice, the white rabbit and Lewis bloody Carroll.

'He's quite the silver fox these days. You had a bit of a crush on him when you were younger, didn't you?' Jolene flashed her sister a teasing smile. 'Then again who didn't. He even melted Mum, which says it all.'

'It wouldn't have been him though, would it?' Marsha threw back. 'It's what he could do for her that did any melting. In other words absolving her of her sins, except he couldn't do that anyway, could he, because she'd have to be contrite for that to happen.'

Jolene poured water over the economy coffee granules and made a mental note to go and buy some decent stuff.

'He can still pull a crowd. The church must be the fullest of any in the area. I remember when he went on leave, it emptied.'

Marsha fought hard against blushing; any change of colour showed easily on her pallid skin.

Your hair is the colour of moonlight. The moment when it all changed. She had kept that breath-taking moment for twenty years, wrapped up in tissue paper in her heart: the tingle in her scalp when his hand lifted up her hair and let it fall through his fingers, the small explosions that were triggered in every part of her body, how she felt for the first time like a woman rather than a girl. She had played those words over and over in her head thousands of times. Even after she learned that priests were as capable of bullshit as ordinary men.

'Thinking about it, he went away from the parish for a couple of years not long after you'd gone to live in London,' said Jolene, bringing over the coffees. 'I seem to remember someone in church asking Mum if there was any connection and getting quite a mouthful in response.'

'How pathetic,' said Marsha, feeling her face grow hot. She got up and went to the loo, giving her perfidious blood time to drain back from her cheeks.

Chapter 7

It had been a big mistake having an early night because Jolene was awake before six a.m. the next morning, turning in bed, attempting to bash the too-firm pillows into some sort of submission. This was the second largest of all the bedrooms, but the nicest by far was Annis's much smaller room. She had a huge doll's house in there that their father had had made for her one Christmas and she spent the following year decorating it and using her pocket money to buy furniture. Her fingers were so nimble and precise, everything to scale and no attention to detail missed. She'd even made tiny plates full of food out of clay and painted them. It was a masterpiece. Then, before she left, she had destroyed it, left it crushed like a statement.

Jolene checked her phone to see if Warren had texted. He hadn't. Something pinged hard against her heart like an elastic band. She had to do something about this situation, it couldn't go on. Then again, she was trapped in a room with no door, no means of escape. And the worst of it all was that she had been the one who had walked right in there, willingly.

She threw the covers back, crisp white sheets and a quilted bedspread; their mother only ever bought top quality bedding. She'd also kept the beds made up in four of the five unused bedrooms: god knows why, because Eleanor never had any visitors over to stay but it didn't do to try and work out what her reasonings were. The house, big as it was, didn't get dirty at all with only one inhabitant moving around in it, and only frequenting a few rooms. She used the kitchen and her parlour and the sitting room for watching TV and the downstairs bathroom; upstairs, the main bathroom and her bedroom. Glenda Price didn't have that hard a job to keep it all spick and span. Her mum Beattie had been their first cleaner; Glenda had taken over when it got too much for her and had been working there too many years to count. Five hundred pounds didn't seem that much of a thank-you for all she did. Jolene decided she'd talk to the others, if they ever got hold of Annis, about giving her some more money. The gardener too – two hundred pounds was a pittance, what was their mother thinking?

Her parents had used the same firm since they moved in here, though it was the original gardener's grandson Eric who now did the bulk of the upkeep. He worked like an SAS operative: keeping out of the way, doing what he had to and then leaving. She'd seen him sometimes, driving the ride-on lawnmower and thought what a great job that must be, hands deep in nature. She'd put him at mid-twenties, dark hair, body toned from hard graft. The sort of man horny housewives would have had a ball salivating over while he tipped a can of Diet Coke into his mouth, or they might hide the lawnmower so he'd have to use a scythe.

Jolene got dressed and walked downstairs, almost taking a tumble as the toe of her shoe caught in a hole in the carpet.

Whoever bought this place had a task and a half on their hands if they wanted to restore it all to its original grandeur. The house was a neglected animal, it had always deserved better than the Vamplews.

A text alert pinged.

Are you all right? X

Warren. Finally. It took all Jolene's reserve not to fire back a sarcastic reply. *What do you care? No, of course I'm not bloody all right. My mother's dead and you're goodness knows where because I don't believe a word that comes out of your sodding mouth any more.*

She rang him but after eight frustrating rings he still hadn't picked up. Another text came through.

Can't talk. Just text me

She wanted to ask why he couldn't talk at this time in the morning. She had a picture in her head of him awake in bed, *her* asleep at the side of him. What other reason could there be? That he'd just shoved a sausage and egg McMuffin in his mouth and was chewing on it? *Damn him*, she thought as she felt the hot sting of tears in her eyes. He had made her totally paranoid, jumping to the conclusion that would hurt her the most every time there was room for doubt. He said it would burn out quickly and he'd be all hers again, but someone was shovelling coal on his affair and keeping the flames alive.

She shouldn't reply, put the worm of unpredictable behaviour in his head for a change but she was weak and she despised herself for it.

As much as can be x

She chose her words carefully, not wanting him to charge her with any emotional blackmail and have him scurrying back to silence.

Can I do anything?

She typed in:

Yes, come here and stop screwing your mistress or fuck off for good.

Her finger hovered over the send arrow, just to take her to the edge of where she should be in this situation, calling the shots. She deleted the message then, wrote instead:

No, it's all straightforward enough x

He replied immediately:

Take care x.

She'd worked out over the past years that when that full stop appeared, that was the last she'd hear from him for now. No doubt an attempt to clarify where they stood and if that wasn't a joke, nothing was.

She padded down the hallway and into the kitchen where she made herself a slice of toast and got out a second plate for when Marsha got up. This was the longest they'd been together in years. She wished they were close enough to talk, really talk because she needed a friend. She'd never been very good at making them, never trusted anyone enough to open up to them and share. Maybe she'd just been unlucky with her peer group. Then she had to go and pick a profession where she was alone with a keyboard for most of the time. Marsha hadn't fared any better at school and from what she'd gleaned, neither had Annis. They'd been like three 'only children', unsociable islands, invisibly marked as 'to be avoided' like Midwich Cuckoos.

She sat down and crunched on her toast. Cheap bread, a day out of date; she wasn't even hungry. Maybe her body was just trying to feed her in a subconscious effort to comfort her. She gave a laugh at the idiocy of her thoughts. No wonder people tended to steer clear of getting to know her.

'Laughing at yourself is the first sign of lunacy, did you know,' said a voice behind her, making her jump.

'Sorry,' said Marsha. 'I thought you'd heard me. It's not as if this house doesn't make enough announcements that anyone is moving around in it.'

'I must have acclimatised and become ear-blind,' said Jolene.

'I couldn't sleep properly,' said Marsha. 'I'm jet-lagged. In my head I've just missed my lunch.'

'There's eggs and toast if you want some breakfast. And smoked salmon in the fridge, well within date.'

'I'll just have a coffee I think. You?'

'If you don't mind.'

Marsha opened the fridge for the milk and looked at the contents: three bottles of champagne and smoked salmon, potted Stilton and Iberico acorn-fed ham. She imagined her mother at the table, linen napkin on her lap, partaking of them all. She could make Princess Margaret look common by comparison.

'How long are you staying around?' asked Marsha.

'I don't know. I'm a book in front, so I can afford to take time off. I'll probably stay until the funeral, like you.'

'How's it going? I see your books in shops and magazines all the time. Funny to think that Kate Logan is you – my sister. What made you pick that name?'

'Kate after my old English teacher, she inspired me to write. I think she would have retired by the time you moved up into the seniors. And Logan after a boy I had a bit of a crush on when I was about thirteen. His parents owned the newspaper shop. He had bright ginger hair and a smiley face and always wore football tops. He became a professional footballer, he coaches now.' She smiled absently. Kate Taylor had been a wonderful teacher, giving her a love of literature; even the starchy classics came alive when she discussed them. And sweet Logan Burns who used to grow beetroot cheeks whenever she went in to buy a comic from his dad's shop and he was serving. As one of the Vamplew girls in the big house, she would have been out of his league then, as he would be out of hers now.

'I think I prefer Jolene to Kate,' said Marsha, weighing it up. 'It's more unusual.'

'I hate Jolene,' came the reply. 'I wish I had a penny for every time that bloody song has been sung at me.'

'Why did they pick it for you?' Marsha had never known.

'Mum's way of trying to replicate the trick of naming a child after a rich relative in the hope of financial recompense,' Jolene replied. 'Josephine Eileen, otherwise known as Jolene, younger sister of her great-aunt Eleanor. Except it didn't work because she ended up leaving everything to a parrot rescue charity and I was left lumbered with the name of a man-stealing tart.'

'Parrot rescue?' repeated Marsha.

'Or cockatoo or parakeet, I can't quite remember which. She had one for about thirty years and never got over it when it died. She had it stuffed and then it was buried with her.'

Marsha sighed. 'I'm not going to laugh because that'll probably be me in fifty years. Me and a stuffed budgie or ferret sharing eternity. How many books have you written now?'

'I'll be releasing number twenty at Christmas.'

'Twenty – wow. That's a lot. I should have more time for reading, I never do. But I've read at least three of yours.'

'Have you?' That surprised Jolene.

'Yes, I enjoyed them. There's a lot of . . . us in them, isn't there?'

Jolene's brows dipped. 'Is there?'

Marsha could recognise them all in the books she'd read so far, even if Jolene didn't realise what she was writing. The larger-than-life fathers, the glacial mothers. There was even, in one, a spinster cousin who was dried up and miserable and Marsha wondered if that was how Jolene saw her now.

'Lost women, lonely people, dysfunction a-plenty,' she answered. 'Were we dysfunctional, or just odd? Certainly not like other families. Not close. Though we should have been, shouldn't we? Three sisters, a brilliant father, a beautiful house, money, a mother who . . .' Her words tailed off.

'I think she did love us. In her own way,' said Jolene, remembering the mother who chased her around the garden, who drew pictures with her at this very table. Jolene had had the best of her, she was sure. The weird thing was, she could remember the fun, smiling mother and the unsmiling, cold matriarch, but not the slide from one to the other.

Just as Jolene was getting all the contents out of her mother's large box file to make a start on the paperwork, her phone rang – a no caller ID number. Marsha listened to Jolene's side of the conversation and deduced easily what it was about.

'That was the coroner's office,' said Jolene, when the call had ended.

'I figured.'

'They're doing a post-mortem on Mum. They've spoken to her GP and with her having no documented history of heart problems they can't presume a cause of death. The pathologist will be next in on Tuesday. We'll have to wait to arrange the funeral.' She rubbed her forehead, a gesture to bring comfort. The words 'post-mortem' had acquired a terrible weight now that they were firmly in her arena.

'Crikey,' said Marsha, for the want of anything more constructive. 'Is it really necessary?'

'Well they can't just guess why she ... passed,' said Jolene, thinking of her mother and her indigestion pains. She really should have doubled her efforts to force her to see a doctor. Maybe they wouldn't be here now if she had.

'It's so intrusive though, isn't it?' said Marsha with a sad shake of the head. Like her sister, she was now facing what that would entail and it was macabre and brutal.

'But we can't stop it,' replied Jolene. 'The man sounded very nice on the phone. They must know that people don't want this for their loved ones.'

Marsha could hear her mother's voice in her head: 'No, I refuse. You have to make them change their mind,

Marsha.' And she prepared for the guilt to slam into her that once again she would disappoint her mother by failing her.

The front doorbell sounded just after eleven, loud Big Ben chimes befitting this grand house. Jolene went to answer it and as Marsha continued to make notes on a pad, she heard the dreaded words drift down the hallway, *Come in, Father*. Her heart leapt in her chest like Red Rum landing on terra firma after Becher's Brook. There was nowhere to escape to, unless she hid in the pantry which would have been weird. She took a breath and tried to prepare herself as best she could but as soon as her eyes framed him, all her intentions went to pot.

The years had been kinder to him than he deserved. He had matured like a fine communion wine; his once almost black hair was artfully striped now with white and grey which added to rather than detracted from his attractiveness. Sunray crinkles at the corners of his eyes, lips still full and soft and at the sight of her they stretched into a smile that radiated up to his eyes that were, as she remembered, bright and hazel, the colour of the autumn.

'Dear Marsha,' he said, in his soft southern Irish accent that had never been ironed out by his years in Yorkshire. He came from Blarney – the irony had never been lost on her. He strode to her, took her hands in his. He felt them chilled and stiff; she would give him nothing – no pliancy, no warmth.

'Coffee, Father? It's horrible stuff, I'll warn you,' asked Jolene.

'Yes, I'll take a quick one with you,' said Father Gerard, his attention temporarily leaving Marsha to answer her sister.

'Sit down, Father,' Jolene invited him. The doorbell rang again.

Marsha stood up to answer it, but Jolene held up her hand. 'I'll go,' she said.

Please don't leave me alone with him, thought Marsha. Her treacherous heart was quickening, old feelings surfacing.

'It's good to see you, Marsha,' said Father Gerard. That seductive voice again, that Baileys-smooth tone.

'How are you?' she asked, switching on a smile of politeness, her back straightening in defiance: she would not be seen to melt in any shape or form in front of him. He belonged to the first half of her life, she didn't want him pushing his way into the second.

'I'm good,' he said.

Dear lord, his eyes. She couldn't look at them, they burned her with their intensity. Her own eyes fell to his hands and she remembered again his fingers brushing against her neck as he nudged her hair over her shoulder. Her pale moonlight hair.

'I've been so glad to hear how well you've done for yourself. Your mother always enjoyed telling me of your progress.'

He hadn't lost his gift for deception then, Marsha thought.

His chair was too close to hers. He was leaning forward, she was leaning back with her hands clenched into tight fists. A body language expert would have a field day here.

'That's nice to know, thank you for telling me that.' Her tone was clipped. A voice expert would be having a ball as well.

'I've wondered so many times if I'd ever see you again. I'm sorry it has to be under these circumstances.'

She thought she would have seen him again when her

father was ill, but she had managed to avoid him. Not that Julian Vamplew would have taken any comfort from prayers, being a pronounced atheist. Apparently he'd been around to say soothing religious things to their mother but Marsha 'just missed him' every time. It happened so often that she began to wonder if God himself had a hand in the orchestration.

The funeral service for their father was stupidly extravagant. A humanist celebrant had conducted it at the crematorium. It didn't sit well with their mother that it was so devoid of artefacts and religious ceremony, but that was what he wanted and she honoured his wishes. There was no Mass, no communion, no hymns, no priest.

'You're looking as if life is agreeing with you,' Father Gerard said.

'It is,' she replied.

He hesitated, as if searching for words, and then went on: 'It's been a long time, Marsha. You went away so quickly all those years ago.'

Wonder why, she said to herself. Then to him, 'I took a chance and it paid off. They do sometimes.'

He looked at her in the same way he used to, as if there was nothing in the world of more importance. Then he said:

'You meant a lot to me, I never lied about it. That has been sitting inside me waiting to be spoken ever since.'

Marsha lifted up her chin, raised her verbal sword and prepared to smash it down on those silky words curling out of his mouth.

'How's Bronwen? Do you still see her?' she asked. She saw his body stiffen as if bracing against the impact of the question.

'Marsha, I—' Her name a sigh.

'Sorry about that.' Jolene bounced back into the room with some letters in her hand. 'The postman wanted to give us his condolences. Now, coffee or tea, Father?'

'No, it's all right,' said Father Gerard, standing up. 'I won't stay. I can see you have a lot to do. I, no doubt, will be liaising with the funeral home shortly; Basil Thompson, I presume?'

'Yes, that's who Mum's asked for,' Jolene answered him. 'She's got to have a post-mortem so there'll be a delay. If it's straightforward we'll be able to start arranging the funeral next week.'

'My sympathies. That's hard for a family to digest,' said Father Gerard, genuinely upset at that news. 'I'll wait to hear from you then, but you must ring me if you need anything.'

Jolene was about to ask him if he was sure he wouldn't stay for a cuppa, but her voice had to follow him down the hall because he was already striding towards the front door, as if he were a vampire escaping the effect of a crucifix.

'What on earth did you say to him?' asked Jolene when she came back into the kitchen. She was only half-joking.

'What do you mean? I said nothing,' replied Marsha. 'He remembered he had something to do, he said,' she lied.

'He's still got the power to make you blush.'

'Give it a rest, Jolene.' Marsha was cross, furious in fact that a door she had nailed shut, boarded up and cemented over could be pushed open with such little effort by him, even after all this time. When he had rushed off, he had left his scent in the air, the lavender that awakened a dangerous dormant place in her brain. In her heart.

Jolene was surprised that her teasing comment had struck such a raw nerve so she didn't say any more. Even though it was she who wrote love stories for a living, Marsha was the more romantic, the softer and more emotional of the two of them. She wondered, not for the first time, if Father Gerard had somehow broken her young impressionable heart once by being so available and unavailable at the same time, and those feelings had left such a long tail that it reached into the present day.

Eleanor

Of course I went to university. My brothers had gone and it was expected that I'd follow suit, given my academic abilities. My chosen subject was mathematics: I enjoyed the truth of it, no grey areas; definite, real, absolute. Julian Vamplew was one of my lecturers. What a cliché we fell into: nubile young blonde, tall, dark handsome, strong in body and mind older man. Could it be any more textbook? At least on the surface.

I think my mother was glad when I was gone. I frightened her. She knew I wasn't like the rest of them, that I had no background noise from emotions, no complication of empathy. Professions such as surgeons and barristers are teeming with people whose brains are wired more for logic than sentiment, as you would want them to be. Love, to people like us, I have learned over the years, is less about ridiculous chemicals making us obsess about someone else, without foundation. We have the advantage of choosing whom to pair with, whom to invest our time and effort into, 'want' foremost rather than 'need'.

He found my disinterest in him fascinating; my value to him was much increased by my dispassion. I was not the low-hanging fruit he was used to, girls who validated him with every blush and stutter. I think he must have thought that if he could seduce me, he could seduce anyone.

I succumbed initially because I was intrigued by the effect he had on me. It would have been hard even for me to resist the intensity of the light that he shone on me, hoping to thaw or blind me. I respected his intellect, I enjoyed his lectures; I liked his company, his savoir faire, his manners and popularity and I began to feel something for him, like the gentlest of flutterings in dead nerve endings. It was intoxicating, a glimpse through a portal into an alien world. It made me want him for that effect. It was like being near a power station.

He had won. I had allowed him to.

I let him take me in his study in my final year. You do not need feelings for good sex and it was very good. I was determined to keep him because I doubted I would ever meet anyone like him ever again. We were special together. He chased me until I caught him.

Chapter 8

Maltstone was a pretty village four miles from the centre of Barnsley. Those in nearby Higher Hoppleton, with its inflated house prices, viewed it as a poor cousin but there were few residences there that could compete with the grandeur of Fox House. It had a small centre served by a variety of shops, a village pub, tiny library and garden centre with café which was a popular place to meet. There was no reason for Eleanor Vamplew to ever go into the town and so she never did. When she shopped for clothes, she did so in York which she enjoyed. If she could have uprooted Fox House and transplanted it there, she would have done so in a breath.

The hospital was on the outskirts of the town and like so many had grossly inadequate parking facilities. So when Jolene said that she had arranged to see her mother that afternoon, Marsha volunteered to drive her there, wait for her and then drive her back. Jolene didn't want to visit after the post-mortem, she didn't think she could bear seeing her mother not whole.

Marsha parked up on a side street and waited for Jolene to

ring, her head full of things it shouldn't have been. Gerard bloody Bannen. She had wanted him to take her virginity, she had wanted to take his. He had made her feel beautiful and blossoming, not like an invisible middle child, the one who should have been born a boy.

She used to think it was funny how women acted in front of Father Gerard, like he was a film star, getting all breathy when he placed a communion wafer on their tongue. He was gorgeous with a dreamy voice and he always had a nice word to say to Mrs Vamplew's middle child, the one with the ghost hair, pale skin and arse the size of Slovenia. He must have sensed she had a hard time at school and his kindness was like a raindrop on a thirsty flower. He asked her if she would like a Saturday job, helping to clean the church, polish the wood, tidy up the hymn books.

When she studied *Jane Eyre* at school, in her head Edward Rochester was black-haired and Irish with eyes like autumn leaves; when she read *Sense and Sensibility* she imagined him as the Brandon to her Marianne. Her Heathcliff, her Sergeant Troy, her Lancelot du Lac. He was her secret love and though she couldn't do a thing to stop blushing in front of him, his kindness validated her, the knock-on effect of which was that the ugly duckling girl dropped her dull brown feathers and started to grow swan-white ones. It would have been impossible for Marsha Vamplew not to have fallen in love with Gerard Bannen. And though he fought it with all his might, his thoughts of the eighteen-year-old, innocent, ethereal blossom that Marsha had become grew to be far more temporal than they were spiritual. He took it to the line but would not cross it; they hugged, he stared into her eyes, held her hand and stroked her face. He told her she was beautiful, that her eyes were the colour of mist, he would run his thumb along her bottom lip as if testing its softness in preparation for his own to meet with it, though they only did so once.

It happened in the sacristy of the church. He had told her after Mass on Sunday to come to him tomorrow morning at twelve because he had something he had to tell her. Her heart had been beating so loudly since, she had no idea how it had not broken out of her chest and bounced into the Lunns' garden. He had sounded serious; whatever he wanted to tell her was important and she was thrown from excitement to trepidation and back, like following an exhausting rally at Wimbledon.

When she arrived at the church the next day, he looked big and crow-black with his dark hair and dark attire and dark, intense expression, safe and dangerous at the same time. He held out his arms towards her and she ran into them only for him to put on the brake before she thudded into his chest.

'Marsha, I have something to tell you,' he said. 'I'm leaving the Church.'

Leaving. He was leaving. The. Church. They could be together. Her heart swelled to twice its size, she could feel it suffusing with joy more with each hurried pump. She knew she must have smiled because he responded to it.

'No, you don't understand.' A deep breath, one that filled his lungs to capacity. 'I'm going to be married.'

Confusion closed up her smile.

'Married?'

'Yes.'

She felt prickles of panic as if her blood was crystallising in her veins.

'How can ... what do you mean ... I don't ...'

He let her go, dropped his head into his hand, rubbed his brow.

'I never meant for this to happen,' he said, his voice low, pained.

'What?' she asked.

'To love you, Marsha.'

The words rang like his church bell. But the sweetness of them was tainted with a sourness that made her wince, like a putrid worm wriggling in a summer apple.

'I don't understand,' she said, feeling the tickle of tears sliding down her cheeks. None of this was making any sense. He loved her, he'd just admitted it, but she had known that since he lifted up her hair, compared it to moonlight a full year ago. That's when the change had occurred. That's when she knew he was seeing her as a woman now and not as a lost girl. He told her that she was an angel, that he imagined her lips would taste like ripened strawberries. He had held her in this room so many times, so closely that not even a breath could have fitted between them, only then to snap to his senses and wrest himself away. Push, pull, push, pull for a whole year, a torturous sizzling foreplay and she knew that if he had touched her anywhere that crossed the decency border she would have exploded with passion. No wonder someone coined the expression 'sex bomb'.

'Married?' she repeated the word again, barely able to speak. 'Who to?'

'It doesn't matter.'

'WHO TO?'

He sighed and looked upwards as if seeking strength or guidance from above. 'You don't know her, her name is Bronwen.'

'Bronwen,' Marsha repeated the name, in a mocking

tone. 'How old is *Bronwen*?' When no answer was forthcoming she screamed the question at him.

'She's thirty.'

'She's ancient.' Marsha's body was filled with a horrible energy that had nowhere to go.

'She's the same age as I am.'

'She's a slag.'

'She's not. Come here.'

'No.' This couldn't be true, there was no warning of it. When, how, where had all this happened?

'It's not like what I feel for you, it's different, more solid,' said Gerard. 'I've been struggling with the celibacy side of things. You awoke in me something that would not sit still.'

'Then marry *meee*,' said Marsha, her tone imploring, desperate. She threw herself against him, lifted her head to him. There was too much of a height difference for her to initiate a kiss, it had to come from him. She felt his hands tight enough on her arms to bruise them, attempting to hold her off, then the strength left them and instead, they wrapped around her and his lips came to press against hers for the very first time without pulling away at the last. She felt his tongue enter to explore her mouth, felt hers respond. She felt his hand stroke down her neck, further, and she prepared for him to touch the soft swell of her breast. He wouldn't be able to stop then, she'd make sure of it. But he did stop: he took a long step back from her as if she were some sort of demon tempting Christ in the wilderness with a picnic basket of goodies he'd regret partaking of.

'I'm sorry. I should never have done that. I can't have you.'

'Why can't you have me?' she cried. 'You can. I'm yours, Gerard.'

'You're nineteen,' he said.

'Nearly twenty,' she threw back. Twenty sounded so much older. 'I'm a *woman*.'

'It would kill the magic,' he said with a loaded sigh. 'I have to settle for less. I can do that with . . . with her. I can't see you again, Marsha. You'll thank me one day for letting you go. Find someone your own age . . .'

She had run home crying before he'd stopped spouting his altruistic bollocks. She desperately wanted, *needed* to talk to someone but she could only offload to her diary. Or the priest in the confessional booth – the irony. She couldn't tell her father and risk him doing to Father Gerard what he'd done to Norman Lunn. And she certainly couldn't confide in her mother who wouldn't have taken her side against a man of God, even if she'd walked in on him bonking her daughter on the altar. Her older sister was a stranger she rarely saw and she had no friends that she'd dare trust to keep her secret.

She remembered writing, pouring out her heart into her precious diary and Annis knocking on her door. Beautiful daddy's favourite Annis with her grade A stars and her perfect face. Even at twelve she had it all together, was confident and self-assured. She'd never hate herself so much that she'd have to stuff herself with chocolate, get fat and then hate herself some more. Annis had walked in tentatively, asking if she was okay. Marsha told her to go AWAY and so she had.

She applied for a job in London and was living there within a fortnight. The week after that she lost her virginity to a man she met in a nightclub. It had hurt, there had been no foreplay, he had grunted as he came. Gerard Bannen would never have the gift of her first time now. It was gone forever and she was glad.

There had been no mention of the colour of her hair or how her lips had tasted of soft, sweet fruit when the man zipped up his jeans and said they must do this again sometime.

Chapter 9

Jolene waited for tears to come as she sat with her mother but they didn't; she was bone-dry inside and yet she felt an overwhelming sadness because talking to her mother, dead as she was, was so much easier than talking to her when she was alive. It should have always been easy, they were mother and daughter, blood, but she'd felt tolerated rather than loved and wanted and over the years she'd come to terms with that because she knew her mother was wired up differently to them. And Jolene was terrified she'd inherited that coldness. Warren levelled that insult at her once and it burned.

She wouldn't come again and as she said goodbye to Eleanor she had a powerful urge to throw her arms around her, bury her head in her shoulder. She might have been forty-five years old, but inside she was still a child wanting a hug from her mum.

Jolene suggested they have a Chinese takeaway later and watch some TV so they ordered in and ate it on trays in the sitting room, even though both sisters said it didn't feel right.

They were only ever allowed to eat from the table in the kitchen or the dining room on more formal occasions. Even now their mother was pulling their strings. Marsha hoped the next people who lived here would encourage such wantonness. She'd always thought that the house would have liked its occupants to have more fun. It had been as stunted as they had this past forty years.

Jolene sent Warren a text before bed.

Goodnight x

He replied with a single kiss fifteen minutes later, followed by a full stop. She lay in bed wide awake, thinking that any normal husband would be here with her, helping her through this. Normality was a gift she'd never been bequeathed, though and she wondered if she ever would be.

Marsha also lay in bed wide awake, cross that Gerard sodding Bannen was occupying so many of her thoughts again after years of shutting him out. She was eight years older now than Bronwen was back then and yet at nineteen, thirty had sounded ancient for a woman. She wondered if Bronwen ever knew that she was so much less than Marsha Vamplew with her eyes of mist and moonlight hair.

Both women were awoken by the same sound, a different one to the standard noises of a building settling. Both women brushed it off, closed their eyes and tried to find their way back into sleep, but the noise happened again. Someone else was in the house.

Marsha grabbed her phone, pressed three nines into it, to save time if she needed to connect to the emergency services. She slipped on her tracksuit bottoms and trainers and then quickly looked around for something to use as a weapon, selected a poker in the companion set at the side of the fireplace. None of the fires had been stripped out of the house; each bedroom still had a working one in it. She opened the door ultra-carefully to avoid any noise, which was impossible; stepped out onto the landing to find Jolene in her pyjamas holding one of her mother's arty bronze sculptures of a horse, or a ballet dancer, they could never work out what it was supposed to be.

They both moved down the stairs as quietly as they could. Muscle memory kicked in; they both remembered that edging down the side nearest the wall gave rise to less sound. There was light coming from the kitchen, then the microwave beeped an alert that it had finished its job. Then the scrape of cutlery against plate, the position of a chair being adjusted at the table.

With her finger on the connect button on her phone, Marsha was ready to march in first, but Jolene barred the movement with her arm. As elder sister, as the bigger and stronger of them, she insisted on putting herself at prime risk. She refreshed her grip on the statuette, prepared to – hopefully – scare the intruder out of the house the way he, or they, came in. She held up her fingers and counted down from three, then she, with Marsha a mere step behind, ran shouting into the kitchen like Mel Gibson in *Braveheart* launching an attack on the army of Longshanks.

'Bloody hell,' said the woman sitting at the table, tucking into leftover noodles and chicken fried rice. 'You nearly gave me a heart attack.'

Jolene's arm dropped, her heart rate didn't.

'Jesus Christ,' she exclaimed, patting her chest with her weapon-free hand.

The woman at the table smiled. It was the same smile she'd had since childhood, the one that made the two large dimples in her cheeks show.

'Close but no cigar. Mash, Dolly. Lovely to see you. It's been too long,' said Annis Vamplew.

Chapter 10

Sally went to the drawer and took out the letter which she had pushed in there as if it were a poisonous spider. It was, in a way, because its venom had ruined her life, as if it hadn't been ruined enough as it was. And all roads led back to the Vamplews. The compulsion refused to go away: *Go on, read it to the end. It can't be any worse. There can be nothing left to hear. You must.*

So, when Norman was asleep, she had taken it out and unfolded it once more, her hands fluttering with trepidation about what she might learn. She needed Eleanor's pen to be vile, unkind, for that would give her all the validation she needed for having acted as she did. She had to know how Eleanor's letter to her daughter ended.

She found the place where she had left off, the words which had made her lose her reason, and then she read on.

True to her nature, Eleanor Vamplew had been horribly unpredictable. Sally Lunn read tender words about herself, probably the most that the woman was capable of writing. *No, no, no.*

Tears dripped from her eyes, stinging and dreadful, though it felt more as if her heart was leaking from being broken.

Chapter 11

'How the hell did you get in?' were Marsha's first words to her younger sister, who had carried on eating the Chinese food without missing a beat.

'Hope you don't mind, I'm starving,' replied Annis, poking back a beansprout that popped out of her mouth as she spoke. 'And to answer your question, same way I always did when I sneaked out and back in again. Downstairs toilet window. They never did fix it did they? Can't imagine I've got that many years of pliancy left, it was a struggle where it used to be so easy.' She lifted up her hand. 'Don't worry, there's a real technique to opening the window and only I know what it is. And I kind of figured that there wouldn't be a burglar alarm in operation. She always said she'd be on constant high alert waiting for it to go off.'

Marsha and Jolene both registered the 'she' instead of 'mum'.

The moment did not present itself for any of them to attempt a hug and none of them felt comfortable initiating one. Marsha sat down at the table, after putting the poker on the floor and stared across at this woman she both recognised and didn't. Grungy, with hair that looked as if it hadn't seen a comb for a year, no make-up and still she looked as if she'd just jumped off a catwalk.

'I'll put the kettle on, shall I?' said Jolene.

'Got anything stronger?' said Annis, through a mouthful of rice. 'I did notice those bottles of champagne in the fridge but would that really be appropriate?' She smiled from one corner of her mouth.

'There's some cognac in the cupboard,' said Marsha. 'Where the cereal used to be kept.'

Jolene bent down and opened that cupboard door. There were also bottles of various liqueurs, gin and other spirits all unopened because her mother didn't drink any of them. Presents, presumably because the gin had a gift tag on it: *To Eleanor, from Patricia and John at the Bridge Club.*

She handed out three generous measures in heavy crystal tumblers and then sat down at the table also.

'You two have aged,' said Annis with a full-on grin that stripped the years from her. Before the others could comment she added, 'in a nice way. Have I?' Now thirty-one, she could easily have passed for someone in their mid-twenties. Clear skin, lips full and naturally plum-pink, eyes bright, beautiful and blue. She was thin, though, like a girl whittled from matchsticks.

'Just a bit,' replied Jolene, watching her tip the rest of the noodles from the carton onto the plate and shovel them up with a fork. 'Then again, you're still as I remember you.' And it was true, despite the passage of time.

Marsha lifted the glass with both hands, she was still shot through with adrenaline and didn't trust herself not to drop it.

'Where have you been, Annis?' she asked, after taking a heavy sip. 'I never thought I'd see you again.'

'I didn't think you'd come.' Jolene almost reached over and gave Annis's hand a squeeze but she didn't. It wasn't what they did in this family.

'I didn't either,' came the reply.

'Why in the middle of the night though? Why not during the day like a normal person?' asked Jolene, though she knew what the answer to that would be. And it was, after Annis had finished her mouthful.

'Normal,' she repeated flatly and the word was weighted with boulders.

'What's that?' asked Marsha, pointing to an animal carrier by the sink, resting there with a rucksack and a bulging 'bag for life' from Morrisons.

'John Abruzzi,' replied Annis. 'He's a giant rabbit. I rescued him from a neighbour's cramped, cold outdoor hutch. Bastards.'

'Rescued?' queried Jolene, suspiciously.

Annis's head jiggled on her shoulders. 'Okay, I nicked him. He's an indoor boy now, he prefers carpet to grass. He's litter-box trained and he knows his name. Amazing what a bit of care and kindness can do for a damaged animal. I taught him to fetch.' She smiled proudly. 'He's getting on a bit and he has a few problems but he's still my number one guy. He'll have a ball in this house. I'm presuming it's okay to stay.'

Marsha and Jolene shared a secret glance. Little did their younger sister know that her rabbit could have the master bedroom if he wanted. Too late an hour to go into all that, though.

'Stay as long as you like,' said Jolene instead. 'We'll both be here until after the funeral at least.'

'When's that?'

'We don't know yet. We're waiting to hear.'

'Any hot water? I could do with a bath,' asked Annis.

'There's plenty of hot water,' said Marsha. One of the good things about this house was that there was always loads of it.

'So what happened, then?' Annis put the fork down on the plate and sat back in the chair. 'What killed her? Silver bullet?'

'Annis.' Jolene's tone was full of reprimand.

'Don't make me pretend I cared,' came the reply.

'Sally next door found her having a seizure. Mum's having a post-mortem to determine what caused it.'

'Ha. Guardian Sally. That was another reason I came when and how I did, so she wouldn't see me. I presume she still sits in her window watching all the comings and goings. The *neighbourhood witch*. It'll be a lovely surprise for her when she knows I've turned up. The five-year-old who did so much damage to her life.'

'No, you didn't,' refuted Marsha.

Annis flashed her an *I-know-better* smile.

'As I was saying,' continued Jolene, 'Sally found her in trouble and called the ambulance, but Mum had died by the time I met them at the hospital.'

'At least she wasn't alone at the end,' said Marsha.

'Is that so important? I wouldn't want my loved ones around just watching me with sad expressions on their faces, but really wanting me to hurry along so they could get on with grieving. And carving up what I'd left in my will.'

'Is that why you came back?' asked Jolene. It would be the most obvious explanation why Annis had turned up now: for her share of any inheritance. She certainly didn't look as if she was rolling in spare money.

But Annis spluttered her response to that. 'You are joking. As if.'

'Then why did you?' asked Marsha.

Annis mused on that for a few moments before answering. She nearly hadn't come back. She'd been staying in a Travelodge for a couple of nights, wondering if she should. Her bravery button had been depressed just after midnight and she knew if she was ever going to act, it had to be on the spur of that prize moment. She wasn't sure there was one overriding reason why she was now sitting here in a house she hadn't missed with sisters she barely knew: the need for change and answers, timing, curiosity. It had been instinct that forced her hand in the end, an instinct which had been sharpened and refined over the past years, serving her well, so she'd acted when it spoke, even at such a stupid hour. Anything but for money. Even if she were, her mother would have made sure that she wouldn't get a penny, so it would have been a pointless exercise.

'A few reasons. Mainly, I've been restless where I was for a while, and needed to do something else. I've been playing with an idea, but I just didn't know how to go about it. Then, when you told me about *her*, I thought maybe the end of the era should mark a new one for me. Time to take stock and get on with things.' *Time to find out what to bury with my mother and what to salvage*, she added to herself.

'What's the idea?' asked Jolene, but Annis waved the question away.

'I'll tell you when it's more fully formed. At the moment it sounds on the edge of insane.'

Marsha yawned. 'Let's talk more tomorrow, shall we? This is all a lot to take in at three o'clock in the morning. Annis, the bed in your old room can be made up.'

'No thanks,' came the reply. 'I'll take the yellow room if that's all right. That'll do Abruzzi and me nicely. Is there a newspaper anywhere? I didn't bring his litter tray but he'll use that until I can get one.'

'Are those the extent of your worldly possessions?' asked Jolene, pointing to the small heap.

'Well, the ones I need. I tend to shed the unimportant things like a skin,' Annis replied, yawning in her turn.

But they knew this already, because she had shed all of them like a skin fifteen years ago.

Eleanor

I was naïve at best, stupid at worst to believe that a man like Julian Vamplew was cut out for monogamy. My adoration was not enough for him, no single person's would be. Julian needed a church.

He had a type of worshipper: drippy girls with starry eyes, who would enjoy what he had to give and then, like fledgling birds, let him cast them off into the sky with a heart full of good memories. They'd sigh over him for years to come, this passionate man who needed more than his wife to satisfy him but who would stay with her nevertheless (how honourable).

Hilde Faulkender was a mistake on his behalf, a sticky, clingy mistake. She was incredibly beautiful, like a fawn with her dark eyes and long dark hair. It was not flattering that she was, physically, my opposite. She was a prodigy, a pure Cornish maid, doing a Masters at sixteen. Her father kept a tight rein on her, but not so tight that she did not find a way to slip it to meet with her wet-dream lecturer in private.

To skip over the gory details, she became pregnant. She came to our apartment to glory in the revelation. She told me that she would give Julian the child he wanted, the child I refused to give him. She told me things about my marriage she could only have known if he had told them to her, this stupid, destructive Lolita. If she intended to break my heart, she was to be sadly disappointed, but I was furious that she threatened my stability, this life we had carved out for ourselves. And I would not be losing Julian to her.

He was contrite of course, begged me not to leave him, and he was very afraid for his career. His vanity, his idiotic hubris had reduced him to rubble and it was so very disappointing to see him weak. Logic will always trump emotion and I knew then that I would always be the stronger in our relationship because of it.

It was an ectopic pregnancy. She almost died. I was glad.

It wasn't so romantic for him dealing with the aftermath of that, with her furious family and his reputation tarnished. He decided that life with his wife was infinitely smoother. Especially a wife in line to inherit a small fortune from a cancer-ridden aunt.

It wouldn't happen in this era of course, but the indiscretion was painted out as if it had never taken place, although he was no longer the god-like creature to his students: he was flawed and that he could not bear.

So we moved north. Julian accepted a post at Leeds university, who were only too pleased to have a man of Julian Vamplew's calibre on their faculty.

And I let him get me pregnant because if anyone was going to have his child, it would be me.

Chapter 12

John Abruzzi snuffling woke Annis up. He often jumped up onto the bed and pressed himself into her face as if enjoying her warm breath on his fur, and she put up with it, even though it disturbed her sleep. She had a *'Where am I?'* moment before the fog cleared. She was in her favourite room in the house, the walls snug around her.

Small as this room was, it out-sized many of the others she'd slept in since she left Fox House fifteen years ago. She'd headed for King's Cross station and had barely set foot off the platform when she'd been approached by a friendly, plausible woman with a lanyard round her neck who offered her a room and some food a bit too insistently for her liking, so she'd refused. Instead, she'd gone into Burger King where she'd bought the homeless woman sitting outside it a meal for her and some chicken nuggets for her dog and she'd ended up hooking up with her for a while. Comfort was relative, she soon came to discover. Two nights of sleeping on a thin blanket on a cold pavement, and a discarded, stained sleeping bag on the third felt like a feather bed. Looking back, it all seemed like a story that had happened to someone else. So she didn't look back if she could avoid it; only the here and now was relevant.

She dressed and left the bedroom, passing her old room, and she wondered if the doll's house was as she had left it or if someone had mended it or thrown it away. She guessed it remained a wreck, a shrine to her final act of defiance. Her mother would have gone in there and stared at it often to refresh her relief that she was gone.

Her parents' bedroom, or rather suite, was at the other end of the landing. She headed for that before the staircase. She twisted the doorknob and walked in and a faint scent drifted by her and took her back years. Her mother's Hermès perfume; an earthy tang of cigar smoke. Likely imagination for the latter, unless the walls had absorbed so much of it that there was a residue stored within them that the house distributed in small puffs like gifts. The room was exactly as she remembered it: there stood the mahogany four-poster, monogrammed initials carved into the bedhead. The colossal his and hers wardrobes with their mirrored middle doors. Every piece of furniture, heavy, large, dark, but it was the bed that focused Annis's attention the most, the bed her mother had likely died in, with its high thread-count cotton sheets and heavy damask bedspread, regal as a monarch's.

The massive windows in the room ran almost floor to ceiling and one of them afforded a view of their small orchard. It was the sort of window that the second Mrs de Winter stood at with Mrs Danvers behind her hoping that she'd fall forwards through it and break her neck. As children they were not allowed in this room unless invited, and they were never invited. Annis was the only one – she presumed – brave enough to ignore the veto and sneak in, sit at her mother's dressing table and pat her face with the large feathery puff that sat on the black box with the gold writing on the side, *Glamour Powder*. Sometimes she would use the large brush with the embroidery on the back on her hair, and study her face in the matching hand mirror, while applying some of her mother's plum lipstick. She was always very careful to put everything back exactly where she found it and pull off any of her red-blonde hairs from the bristles. Sometimes she'd hold up the perfume bottle with the round, soft pump and pretend to spray her neck. Her mother never knew she did this; she would have taken her sternly to task about it. It was probably the only thing she never got into trouble for.

Annis sat on the stool and stared at herself in the triple mirrors, three identical sisters. They threw back a reflection as far from her mother as it was possible to be; they shared no characteristics other than their pale skin. Even now, with her mother gone, Annis felt a quiver in her veins as if she were doing something illicit, something not permitted under any circumstances, something punishable. The room didn't have a friendly vibe at all. When she left, the door seemed to close on her harder than she had pulled it to. It wasn't her imagination.

She walked downstairs, considerately taking the side nearest the wall so she set off as few creaks as possible and marvelled that she'd remembered that. Her mother had bought this house for a song because it needed some renovation and thousands had been knocked off the original asking price to tempt a sale. She could still have afforded it even if she had paid top whack for it, thanks to her great-aunt Eleanor snuffing it and leaving her a small fortune, though if what Annis remembered hearing about her was true, the old woman had stunk like an ancient haddock and was abysmal to everyone except her darling namesake. She supposed they'd sell it now, hopefully to people who would make it their own, strip out the dingy, dark wood and apply lots of bright paint. But then it wasn't the dowdy wallpaper and the drab carpets that had made this a miserable home.

She opened the door to her father's study, the finest room in the house. He'd spent a fortune on his intellectual den, with its dark blue walls which were the perfect compliment to the beautiful burr walnut furniture. It was just as it always was, that magnificent desk, the cabinets full of his books, his research, his interests. Professor Julian Morley Vamplew, eminent, accomplished, gifted, renowned not only for his brilliance but for being a proper looker as well. Mathematics was his primary field but he also lectured in economics, which was more his passion. Numbers and market trends flooded his brain, production, consumption, distribution. There was nothing that could not be reduced to a formula, he said. Not quite. Not how one family who had everything on paper had nothing in reality.

She saw herself sitting on his knee at this desk, feeling his strong arms tight around her as he showed her how to do long division, feeling loved and special and even at that young age bloody smug because she knew that behind the door, Marsha would be sulking that she wasn't in here with Daddy. She adored him, loved him with all her being, was jealous when one of the others got his attention more than she did, which wasn't often. Marsha made it clear that she had no time for her and was always locked away in her bedroom being solitary; Jolene was so much older and sophisticated and she never felt related to her at all. She only had her father and she wished she'd had a pound for every time she wished her mother would find another man and bugger off like Sophie Weston's mum in her class had done.

There wasn't a film of dust in the study, it showed no sign of abandonment. The cleaner must have had instructions to keep it up to standard, as if he had just stepped out of it briefly for she would have bet John Abruzzi's pelt on her mother not saying goodbye easily to him. He was all she ever cared about. It felt like a room still alive, still functioning. It did not feel like the study of a man who had been dead for seven years. Funny how seven years had come into play again, seven years between the deaths of husband and wife; seven years in between each daughter's birth. If his soul could be confined to anywhere, it would be here with his books and his desk and his chair and his pens. Something ached in her heart for the man he had been when she was little. Safe and strong.

Denise always said the dead didn't hurt you, only the living. Thank god for that. There was nothing in his house to hurt her now that the old regime was gone. It was just bricks and mortar and it was a crazy notion to say she felt sorry for the house, but she did. It had been as unloved as they had.

She headed for the kitchen and was surprised to see Jolene there, already up and dressed and having a coffee.

'Kettle's just boiled,' Jolene said.

'Cheers.'

'Sleep well?'

'I always sleep well.'

'Wait until you're peri-menopausal, you won't take that pleasure for granted.' Although Jolene knew Mother Nature's cruel manipulation of her hormones was only part of her insomnia problem.

'That sounds like something to look forward to – not,' said Annis, dropping a teabag into a mug before pouring hot water on it.

'You really are staying around for a while, aren't you?' asked Jolene, watching her sister poking the teabag with a teaspoon. From the back, she looked like a stringy teenager, one who had just got up and who had ignored the call of a hairbrush.

'Yep,' said Annis. 'Unless you have any objections. And I'd understand if you did. Not exactly a part of the family any more, am I?'

'Don't be daft,' replied Jolene.

'True, though. I don't know you, you don't know me.'

'Then maybe it's time we addressed that,' replied Jolene. She'd been half-convinced she would have found Annis gone when she woke up and that was partly what interrupted her sleep. She wasn't sure she quite believed the reason Annis had given for coming back; her gut instinct told her there must have been more to pull her here, but it was both strange and good to see her again and she wanted to make amends, for being too distant a sister, for not being the sort of person that the secretly troubled sixteen-year-old Annis could have confided in.

'I'll be here for the funeral if that's what you're asking. Cross my heart.' Annis drew the shape on her breast.

The stairs announced that Marsha was on her way down. Annis got out another mug in readiness and was holding it with a questioning pose when she walked in.

'Just a hot water please,' said Marsha, sitting at the table.

'No point in asking you if you slept well, is there?' said Annis then with wry amusement. Marsha looked shocking, extra pale – if that was even a possibility – her eyes red and swollen.

'No, I didn't. I kept thinking about Mum,' said Marsha. 'The fact that she died and none of us were with her.' A fresh tear plopped from her eye onto the table where it sat like a silver bead.

'She had saint Sally with her though, didn't you say?' said Annis, putting the mug down in front of Marsha. 'So they made up. How nice. Although maybe not so much for Sally.'

Jolene didn't say anything, but the shake of her head radiated disapproval.

'Oh, come on,' Annis responded to that. 'Don't tell me she turned into Julie Andrews after I'd left because I won't believe you.'

Jolene shifted forward in her seat. 'Annis, there's something we need to tell you' – she stole a look at Marsha – 'about Mum's will.'

Annis held the flat of her palm up. 'Look, it's cool,' she said. 'I don't want anything, that's not why I came back. So if you're going to tell me that everything is split between you two and I don't get a look in, save your breath because—'

'Shh, a moment,' Marsha told her.

Jolene let it out, there was no point in pussy-footing around it.

'Mum left you everything. More or less.'

The words left a clear, long echo in the air, like a tuning fork hit on its optimum spot. Annis's face was split by a grin, as if she was waiting for a killer punchline.

'She did. It's true,' said Marsha, reading her disbelief.

Annis's jaw dropped open. 'Get out of town.' But her sisters' expressions were telling her this was not a joke. The grin disintegrated. 'What?'

'It's absolutely true,' said Jolene.

'Why on earth would she do that?'

Marsha shrugged. 'It was her money to do with as she would.'

'We will get a minor percentage of money from the sale of Fox House and there are a couple of very ... meagre disbursements for other people which we should talk about, but the bulk is yours. Investments, jewellery, bank accounts, house contents,' added Jolene.

Annis let that sink in and when it did, all she could manage was a whispered chain of expletives.

'It's not the sort of thing you put on a text or leave as a voicemail, so I'm glad you're hearing it in person,' said Jolene.

Annis's eyes travelled from sister to sister and back again. 'You must be hurt.'

'I think we all know not to expect the expected in our family,' said Marsha. 'Maybe I'd be more hurt if I were reliant on that money but both Jolene and I have made our own. If that's what Mum wanted, then so be it. She obviously thought about it carefully and must have had her reasons.'

They weren't hard to guess at: managing to drive her youngest daughter away, alienating her so much she didn't even want to come back to say goodbye to her dying father. The guilt *must* have weighed heavy on their mother's mind, even if she had pretended otherwise, and in the end, this gesture was all she could offer by way of recompense. Both elder sisters had worked out as much.

Annis nodded slowly as she tried to make sense of the situation. 'Didn't she leave a letter or anything to explain why?'

'No. All I know is that she changed her will a few months ago,' Jolene replied. 'She had a health niggle that must have caused her to reevaluate things.'

'What did the previous one say?' asked Annis.

'No idea. Not that it matters.'

'She was just the gift that kept on giving, wasn't she?'

Annis blew out her cheeks, rocked to the core by this revelation.

'Mum wouldn't have given us the luxury of seeing into her mind,' said Marsha.

'I often wondered if my adult brain could have worked her out more than my childhood one did,' said Annis. 'I'm guessing not.'

'Do you want to go and see her?' asked Jolene. 'The coroner said that we still could, before the post-mortem on Tuesday. I'm figuring you'll say no.'

But Annis surprised both her sisters by saying:

'Yes, I will go and see her.'

Chapter 13

'Where will we even start packing up this house when we have to?' asked Marsha, opening one of the kitchen cupboards to find a plate for some toast. There was a lot of crockery in it. She remembered her parents holding many dinner parties. Eleanor had been an excellent cook, and when they invited people round, they'd often rope Glenda in to help her and do the washing-up. Eleanor liked to show off her faded-elegant house and her cuisine. The guests were a mix of acquaintances, colleagues of their father's, business people, useful people in whose circles they had drifted; and friends who amused them and who enjoyed being in their orbit, although the Vamplews didn't let people get too close. In fact, the more Marsha thought about them, the more of an enigma she realised they were.

'I'm presuming you don't want to make this your home?' Jolene checked with Annis.

'That's a joke, right?' replied Annis with a snort of laughter.

'Then we'll do it slowly and surely,' said Jolene. 'It would be decent to wait until after the funeral, I think.'

'It would, but we could make a start while we're all here in this limbo of waiting,' replied Marsha. 'Of course, it's your call, Annis. You own everything.'

'What, you're asking for permission to help me?' That amused Annis. 'Why not just tell me to do it myself?'

Both Jolene and Marsha turned to look at her.

'Why would we do that?' Marsha checked the date on the bread and then decided not to bother with the toast.

'Just seems a bit . . . generous in the circumstances. Then again, I suppose, the sooner the house is sold, the sooner you get your cut.' As the words left Annis's mouth, she realised how hard they sounded. 'Sorry, I didn't mean that the way it came out.'

'Don't worry about it,' replied Jolene. 'No offence taken.'

'What she said,' added Marsha.

'You're too good to be true,' said Annis with a wide grin. 'Well, I don't want anything from here so how about you take anything you want and we give the rest to charity?'

'There are some valuable pieces in the house, Annis. I can show you which they are,' said Jolene.

'This is the time when most families scrap.' Annis slurped her tea. noisily.

'Then let's not be those families,' said Marsha. 'We've only just got you back.'

'I didn't leave because of you,' said Annis.

'Why did you really—' But Jolene was interrupted by the doorbell sounding.

'Ooh, Sally,' said Annis with some relish.

'How do you know that?' asked Jolene.

'She always rang the doorbell twice. Used to drive Dad mad. *As if you can't hear it when it's rung just the once*, he used to say. Should I jump out at her from behind the door, do you think?'

'What I think is that you should be kind,' replied Marsha. 'She's lost her friend and her life isn't exactly a bed of roses. Norman's got dementia and she's nursing him herself. It must be hell.'

So Annis braced herself for meeting the woman again. The one who had blamed a five-year-old for everything that came after.

Sally stood on the doorstep like a wizened Uriah Heep. She was only in her mid-sixties but looked so much older, whittled away at by a life that hadn't been that kind to her.

'Sorry to disturb you, Jolene,' she said.

'It's fine, Sally. Do you want to come in? If it's about the locket, I haven't had time—'

'No, no,' Sally waved that away, mumbled something about it not mattering. 'I just came round to see if you needed anything doing. Norman's cousin has come over to give me a break, so if you wanted any shopping . . .'

'Thank you, you're very kind, but I think we're managing.'

'I've been reading your book. I find reading such a comfort.' Jolene then saw that Sally had it in her hand. *The House at the Edge of the Sea*. It was about a woman who had fled an unhappy marriage. She'd written too many books about unhappy women, but then she had accumulated a scrapbook of experience that would have fuelled a thousand books on the subject.

'Did you want me to sign it for you?'

'Oh, oh. Would you? That's not why I came, really. I was just showing you—'

'Of course I'll do it for you,' said Jolene, cutting her off mid-twitter or they could have been there all day. 'Come through.'

Sally followed Jolene down the hallway and into the kitchen. She hadn't been expecting the third sister and her eyeballs rounded as if the sight of Annis was too big for them to take in without expanding their surface area to max.

'Hello, Sally,' Annis smiled at her, a smile that locked her lips but didn't extend to her eyes. She knew that Sally hated her, that Sally had shifted everything that happened on that midsummer day onto her five-year-old shoulders.

But Sally surprised her.

'Oh my goodness, Annis, you're home,' she said, completely knocked off-balance by the sight of her, but without the merest trace of hostility in her voice. 'I'm so sorry . . . for your loss.'

'I'm sorry for your loss too,' returned Annis. 'You knew Mum for much longer than I did.'

'Forty-one years.' Sally's tone was weighted with sadness. She turned to Jolene then. 'Do you have a date for the funeral yet? A few people have been asking.'

'We don't yet, Sally. Mum has to, er . . . have a post-mortem.'

The effect of Jolene's words on Sally was immediate and dramatic. She groped for a chair, looking as if a tap had been turned on in her heel and all her life blood had gushed out of it in rapid pints.

'Sally, are you okay?' asked Jolene, charging Marsha with fetching her a glass of water.

'I'm all right,' said Sally, batting back the fuss. 'Oh my, that's awful. Poor Eleanor. My poor, dear friend.'

'Luckily she won't know anything about it,' said Marsha,

pressing the glass into Sally's little hand. 'We can't stop them, I'm afraid.'

'Why are they doing that to her? It was a stroke, I know it was. Her face was all lopsided,' said Sally, as if trying to convince a doctor and not a daughter. Or herself. She'd gone over it so many times, nudging it into a frame that she could live with, that she couldn't remember what the truth of it was any more.

'Did you say that you saw the lights on and came over?' asked Jolene.

'Yes, it was very late,' said Sally, after gulping at the water. 'I was just checking on my hedgehog village. I've got babies in Woodland Cottage, that's the biggest of the huts, and not all hedgehog mothers are good ones. They sometimes leave them or attack them. I wondered why all the lights should be on, downstairs and up. I don't sleep very well, I have to get up to use the toilet and I'm always on alert for Norman stirring. Going outside and checking on my hogs seems to reset my clock.' She put her glass down on the table, her eyes averted from those trained on her in case they saw the lies in them. 'I got my key, I keep it in the hall cupboard with all the others, and I let myself in. I called, I thought she must be downstairs but she wasn't in here or her parlour or the bathroom so I went upstairs. Her bedroom door was open. She was lying down and her mouth was all droopy, I'm sure of it. I thought she'd had a stroke and she was cold, but then she never put the heating on and this house is very cold. She didn't look as if she was breathing but she was, so I rang the ambulance and then I gave her mouth to mouth, you know, positioning her head back and pinching her nose and breathing into her. The ambulance was very quick. A woman paramedic took over. Then I rang you, Jolene.' She let loose a long breath, as if it was a full stop on her account of things.

Jolene picked up a pen and wrote in Sally's book:

All my very best wishes, Kate Logan X

She added a kiss which she didn't usually do. She really wished she were Kate Logan, a woman whose name was made up of two people who had always made her smile to think of: that wonderful teacher and the flame-haired boy. Looking back she knew he must have fancied her as much as she fancied him, because he was so awkward when she went into the shop. If only wisdom would come when it was needed instead of having to stew in a slow cooker and then present itself years later, when it was usually only useful for passing on to someone else.

'You'd be very welcome to go and see Mum when she gets to the chapel of rest.' Jolene handed Sally the book and saw how trembly her fingers were. The woman was even more of a nervous wreck than usual.

'You will be using Basil Thompson won't you? That's who your mother wanted to look after her,' said Sally.

'Yes, we will do just as she stipulated,' replied Jolene, though she wasn't going to swear to it because she reckoned a couple of tweaks would be in order.

Sally rose from the chair, though she had to make two attempts to do so.

'Thank you, Jolene, for signing the book. Will you let me know what they say? The people doing the post-mortem?' Her voice went as wobbly as her legs. 'I wish I could have brought her back. I feel so guilty.'

'You shouldn't be feeling guilty, Sally,' said Marsha in as

soothing a voice as she could. 'Because of you, she didn't die alone.'

Sally nodded, little jerky nods like a bird would make. Julian Vamplew had likened Sally to a bird sometimes too, a cat-ravaged sparrow; always something verminous.

'Blimey, she's taken it hard, hasn't she?' said Annis to Jolene, after she had shown Sally out. 'Then again, have you ever watched those programmes where suspects are being interviewed and body language experts rip them apart? They nearly always go into ridiculous levels of detail to appear personable and throw you off the scent. I'm amazed we didn't get to find out what the hedgehogs were called and how much the babies weighed at birth.'

'Don't be horrid, Annis,' said Marsha. 'It's just how she is. She's . . .' She was going to say Sally was an old lady now but she wasn't at all. Then again she had been so much older than her years for as long as Marsha could remember. There was only a slightly larger age gap between Sally and Norman than there was between her mother and father, but marrying an older man had not turned her mother into a frump, and marrying a younger woman had kept their father dapper, rather than rushing for the knitted brown waistcoats.

Jolene finished the sentence off for her. 'She's Sally, and that's just how she is. She adored Mum, and watched out for her.'

'Wouldn't be surprised if Mum had a bloody heart attack seeing Sally at stupid o'clock in her bedroom,' said Annis. She shook her head; something just didn't ring wholly true about Sally's account to her, but she moved on. 'So Norman isn't too great then?'

'The last time I saw him he was sitting in the garden and Sally was tying his arm to a deckchair,' said Marsha, taking Sally's glass over to the sink. He looked frail and nothing like his younger fleshy self. She'd always had the suspicion that Sally married the first man who paid any attention to her, and had ended up being lumbered with the lowest-grade fruit of that particular harvest. She looked out of the window, her eye catching some movement on the back lawn.

'Bloody hell, who is *that*?'

Jolene looked over her shoulder.

'It's the gardener. Haven't you seen him before?'

'I think I'd remember if I had,' said Marsha. 'What happened to the old bloke who wore the cowboy hat?'

'Vernon retired yonks ago, that's his grandson Eric.'

Annis came over to see what was causing all the excitement. Like Jolene, she could easily see over Marsha's shoulder at their respective heights.

'Nice,' she declared.

'One of us should go and tell him about Mum. He obviously doesn't know,' said Jolene.

'I think that job should fall to Mashed Potato,' said Annis, patting her sister on the back. 'One of us should have a little sunshine.'

Marsha stepped carefully across the ready-for-a-cut grass, hoping she didn't trip up in front of the demi-god who was about to climb onto the ride-on lawnmower.

'Eric,' she called and waved. He looked round, shielding his eyes as she had a strong sun behind her.

'Hi,' he said, with a nod of greeting.

'I'm Eleanor's daughter, Marsha,' she introduced herself to the young man with the brown-black eyes and summer-tanned skin. He was gorgeous and he would age beautifully, she thought; become even more of a hunk in middle-age than he was now. Life would simmer him on a low heat and keep him ripe for years. Her father had been the same.

'I know,' he said, 'I used to come here with my grandad when I was little. I remember seeing you.' He smiled and Marsha wondered what image he had retained of her. Probably one of her lying on a sunbed like a beached Beluga whale trying to get brown, except she only ever got red and sore. That teenage self wouldn't have bothered to commit to memory any small boys trailing behind the old gardener who wore the leather cowboy hat.

'I don't know if you know, Eric, but … Mum died on Tuesday.'

'Oh my, I'm so sorry.' His smile closed up. 'I, er … I'll put my gear away and—'

'No, please,' Marsha placed a hand on his forearm and registered the feel of his warm skin against her fingers. 'I came to tell you to just carry on as per normal, whatever that is.'

'I, er … usually come weekends, weather permitting. At this time of year, maybe once during the week as well to keep up with the weeding.'

'What about payment?'

'I write down the hours I've done and post it through the letter box and she – Mrs Vamplew – usually leaves it in an envelope in the front porch.'

His voice didn't fit with the rest of him, thought Marsha. It was too deep, too mature. Rich like a Christmas cake. This thought momentarily distracted her and she had to force her head into gear to continue talking to him.

'How much is that approximately?'

'Twelve pounds an hour. Maybe sixteen ... eighteen hours a week at this time of year.'

'Blimey, you're cheap,' said Marsha, comparing that with what she was charged by her gardener for doing the lawn. She apologised immediately, but Eric chuckled.

'To be honest, it's less than we charge anyone else but we've been doing this garden for so long and wouldn't want to lose her custom.'

Marsha guessed that her mother wouldn't have entertained a rise. She'd have rebuffed any attempt to increase what she'd been paying for years with the threat of moving elsewhere. She wouldn't have appreciated the notion that loyalty worked both ways.

'I'll carry on of course,' he continued. 'Will you be selling the place eventually?'

'We will, yes. But we'll still need the grounds upkept till then.'

'I'm sorry for your loss,' Eric said with feeling. 'If there's anything I can do ...'

It was just what people said, but she appreciated it all the same.

'Thank you, that's very kind,' she acknowledged. 'My sisters are staying here with me. I imagine we'll have a lot to do in time.'

'It's a big house to have to empty.'

She looked back at it along with him.

'Oh, yes. A Herculean task.'

'If you need anything lifting, I'm stronger than I look.'

A joke, obviously, because he looked very strong. Strong enough to throw someone around a bedroom, came a rogue thought that she battled back before it could be accompanied by a rogue blush.

She smiled. 'I'll bear that in mind. Can I get you a drink or anything?'

'I always bring plenty with me to see me through,' he said, and she thought he meant by that remark that her mother never offered. It would have been in keeping. She remembered being mid-teens and the house being decorated and one of the painters asking her on the quiet if she could give him a glass of water. She'd made all three decorators some tea and her mother had asked her what she thought she was doing when she found the cups on the kitchen table. Eleanor had been born in the wrong era. She belonged to one where there were clear delineations between upstairs and downstairs.

Marsha walked back to the house, but she felt a strange kind of warmth upon her as if eyes were following her. She made a quick turn at the bottom of the steps and found Eric dropping his head as if he had indeed been staring at her the whole way.

Annis was in the kitchen setting out two bowls of food and water in the corner. John Abruzzi was reposing on a blue furry mat, both hind legs out to the same side.

'You don't mind if I put this here do you?' she asked Marsha. 'John Abruzzi likes to be near me.'

'I don't mind,' came the reply. 'Who actually is John Abruzzi?'

'Fave character in *Prison Break*,' said Annis. 'Seemed appropriate as I broke him out of his prison. I need to take him to a vet's, any thoughts on who might be the best one around here? I ran out of his arthritis medicine.'

'Poor little soul,' said Marsha. She would have loved a pet but she worked such long hours it wouldn't have been fair. Not even on a goldfish. She wouldn't have taken on an animal for it to be lonely.

'I can tell you the closest,' answered Jolene. 'There's Vetman two streets away. Can you remember where Burns newsagents is? Well, it's next to there.'

'Cool,' said Annis. 'I'll find their number and give them a ring.'

She took a mobile out of her pocket which had a cracked screen and was held together with Sellotape.

'You'll be able to buy yourself a new swanky phone,' said Marsha, pointing at it.

Annis sniffed. 'This one works just fine.'

Jolene was looking at her phone too, a much more up-to-date model. Warren was home and had just texted to ask her when she'd be back as if all was normal between them and she felt like throwing it at the wall to stop herself responding. Sometimes she hated herself for being such a wet lettuce, a pushover, the most readable book on the planet. How had she turned into this?

'So what's the deal with Adonis then?' asked Annis, nodding towards the back garden.

'We leave an envelope of money in the porch for him every week and he does his gardening thing and goes,' replied Marsha.

'You'd have beautiful children together. Wonder if they'd be pale and interesting like you or dark and brooding like him,' said Annis, her eyes glittering with mischief.

Marsha answered with a look that held all the disdain she could manage. She and men went together like pickled cockles and pineapple on a pizza. Best avoided. Best left to those who wanted that sort of complicated head-fuckery and heartbreak because it was never, never simple where she was concerned. Men had it so much easier in relationships, she thought. She wished she'd been born male, life would have been so much more straightforward. She would have been wanted, for a start. Even now, twenty-eight years on since she'd been told that she 'should have been a boy', the memory still had the power to sting, every bit as much as hearing the actual words had then.

Eleanor

Pregnancy was hell. I was sick from the moment my egg was fertilised. Morning sickness — ha! I vomited at most points of the day, but in the mornings least. I prayed for a miscarriage. I didn't want this intruder growing inside me, taking over my whole body, stretching it, changing it, leaving nothing of me for myself. I wasn't the first person to have a baby and I wouldn't be the last, said my mother. I think she was secretly pleased that I was so horrified by the experience. Mothers and daughters should be so much closer than that. I did try.

The birth was horrendous. Julian was annoyingly upbeat, desperate to see what he had pushed inside me to grow. As the instrument of nine months of discomfort was placed into my arms, I waited for a wave of emotion to overtake me. I was sure it would, because I wanted it to so much. But there was nothing.

I gave up my job, a low level position in the university. Julian was to be the one who shone and I was to be the housewife and doting mother. He had wanted this child but he didn't actually know what to do with it. Five minutes fuss was enough, he wearied quickly of things that gave nothing in return.

I went through the motions, the mother and baby club where I learned to ape how mothers reacted to their children. It would be easy to be devoid of feelings, so much less complicated, if one lived on an island. But in social circumstances one has to fit in; so one must emulate and feign and it is exhausting. I read stories and fed ducks, I baked and smiled, I splashed in the bath and walked hand in hand with my child. But I was bored, bored, bored.

Chapter 14

'I feel like I'm in limbo,' said Marsha, swinging her arms as she waited for the kettle to boil yet again.

'We are, that's why,' Jolene said to that. It had been the same when their father died, that horrible time before the funeral, when their feelings wouldn't be herded into any order. Their mother would not let them help her organise anything in any way. It would have helped them if she had, focused their attention on something constructive. As it was, Jolene had made a few lists and then had a nap. Marsha had sent off some emails so that everyone at her company knew what they were doing while she was away. Annis had sat on the kitchen floor reading a book with her rabbit at her side. None of them really knew what to do with themselves.

'Anyone fancy a pizza?' asked Annis. 'My treat.'

'I can't remember the last time I had a pizza,' said Jolene.

'I worked with a woman who lived off them,' said Annis. 'Every night she ordered one from the place down the road and what she didn't finish, she'd warm up for breakfast. Every night, without fail – no lie.'

'Bet she was healthy,' said Marsha to that.

'She seemed it,' replied Annis. 'She was always buzzing with energy. Maybe carbs suited her.'

'Where was that then?' asked Jolene, hoping for any insight, however small, into the missing years. She'd fought against interrogating her sister as if she was in the big black *Mastermind* chair with the specialised subject of herself; she didn't want to scare her off. A couple of times both she and Marsha had asked her questions that dipped into her life and she'd swerved them, and they hadn't pressed, but she was madly curious to know what Annis had been up to for all this time.

'Sheffield,' Annis replied, to Jolene's surprise.

'You lived in Sheffield?' asked Marsha, also shocked that her sister had been living so near to them.

'Yep. For the last few years I have.'

'What were you doing there?' asked Jolene.

'I was working as a waitress in a cocktail bar . . .' Annis sang.

'I can't believe you were living so close.' Jolene was still shaken by that and a little annoyed if she were honest. 'I just wish—' *Careful*, warned a voice, but she overrode it, '—I wish that you'd let us know that you were okay.'

'Did you worry about me?' Annis tilted her head and smiled at her sister.

'Of course we did, Annis. We went to the police, we went to see girls you were at school with, your teachers. Even when you rang Mum and told us to stop looking for you, you were always on our mind. We couldn't find you on social media, the police said they couldn't do anything if you didn't want to be found . . .'

Even when you rang Mum . . . Annis had never phoned her. She had walked out of the house without a backward glance and left them to work out themselves why she had gone. But she didn't say this. She said instead, 'So, back to food, does anyone fancy a pizza because I'm bloody starving.'

They ordered two between them. Annis rang it in and asked for a Margherita and one with everything *and* the kitchen sink on. And while they waited for them to be delivered, Annis and Jolene ventured into the wine cellar which had been their father's pride and joy. It had been packed to the gills once upon a time. Not so much now, but there were still a lot of bottles left in the racks.

'White or red?' asked Jolene.

'Not fussed,' said Annis.

'I suppose you know all about wines if you worked in a bar?'

'I know a bit, yes.' Annis pulled a bottle from the rack and read the label. A Chianti. She put it back. 'I like the New World wines best: Chile and South Africa for reds, New Zealand for whites. Wines have to fit food, company, occasion, even the time of day. Sometimes they're background accompaniments, sometimes they're centre stage. I used to like to recommend them based on what people wanted from them.'

Jolene raised her eyebrows. Her sister, who looked as if she'd foraged in a skip for clothes, did not seem like the sort of person who would know her way around a wine list.

'One of the regular customers knew a lot about wines. We'd sit and talk sometimes. He liked to wax lyrical and I was interested.'

'Ah.' Jolene put a French wine back in its slot. 'My husband is the wine buff. He usually chooses if we go out for a meal. I don't have a very discerning palate.' Not only for wine, she added to herself. 'Sounds a friendly place.'

'It was more of a club really,' said Annis. 'There was a bar of course, and a lounge for gentlemen and ...' Her voice tailed off. She didn't go into detail about what else there was. She wiped the dust off a bottle with the cuff of her sleeve before reading its label and deciding it was also a no. A third bottle met with her approval.

'A club?' repeated Jolene.

'Yeah, like the Groucho only shit.'

They both jumped as a piece of plaster fell off the wall and hit the stone-flagged floor. They were united in the same thought.

'Shit, shit, SHIT,' Annis shouted with increasing volume, as if to antagonise an affronted spirit.

'There's obviously a bit of damp, look, there's a pile of dropped plaster over there,' said Jolene going over to the offending part and taking a look. *It's not mother making a statement.* When Annis spoke next, it was as if she had heard her unsaid thoughts.

'You don't think she'd approve that all I've done with my life so far is mix up a few Mai Tais and pour out some Pinotage then?' She cocked her head and looked about fourteen again. Jolene remembered her as a teenager, when she was too awkward for her long limbs. Girls at school had given her a lot of gyp because she towered over them apparently, highlighting what they saw as faults to disguise their petty jealousies. Really, they would all have killed for her endless legs, her long neck, her beautiful oval face, her red-blonde hair that looked like spun sunset. Vermeer would have sold his kidney to paint her if she'd lived in his timeframe.

'Does it matter?' Jolene asked her.

'Not really. She wouldn't have approved if I was running NASA.'

Jolene didn't say anything to that. She didn't want to bad-mouth her mother but Annis was right. If she'd known that her daughter was a barmaid, she'd have slow-blinked like a disinterested owl, giving nothing of her opinion away and yet giving all of it away at the same time. She could heap on disapproval with the merest twitch.

'This will do, or rather these,' said Annis. 'A Pinot Noir and a Chenin Blanc. We can start with those.'

'Start?' queried Jolene.

'Start,' Annis confirmed.

Marsha had taken some money from her mother's cash box under the sink, slid it in an envelope and headed down the garden as she could see that Eric was putting some things away in the shed, although it was more of a working summer house really. At one end were tools, at the other a table and couch and store cupboards and a small sink and there was an old outside toilet next door to it. Eric was brushing some dried mud off a spade. She noticed the dark patches of sweat on the front of his T-shirt and had an absurd desire to press her head against his chest and inhale. She was having a mid-life crisis too early, she reasoned. Either that or she'd read too much D. H. Lawrence. She'd studied *Lady Chatterley's Lover* at school, though they'd only been one-third into the book when some miserable goat of a parent had complained and they'd had to change it and switched to *Jude the Obscure*, which was the most depressing book on the planet. Jude was a total drip, not even Sally Lunn would have fantasised about him. But she'd sneaked a copy of *Lady Chatterley* home and read it under her cover at night by torchlight as if it were porn. She couldn't remember how it ended, but she could remember how it made her feel. Her hormones must have been changing at the time, her body tuning itself to the realisation that there was a world of Dionysian pleasures beyond innate innocence. She had carried with her two quotes from that book which had embedded themselves into her. The first was 'She was always waiting, it seemed to be her forte', and she concluded years later that the only reason that must have stuck with her was because it was a portent of her life to come. Waiting for Gerard Bannen to turn his back on the Church; waiting for the love bee to come and visit her flower, though it visited every other sodding bloom in the garden and totally ignored hers. Waity Katie had nothing on her; she wrote the manual on waiting. The title of her autobiography would be *Time Waits for No Man, but I Wait for Every Bleeder*. And she was still waiting, invisible as air.

The second quote she carried with her was tucked up in her heart, like a secret sweet: 'We fucked a flame into being'. That's how she had felt about Father Gerard and she had *known* that if they ever did have sex, it's what it would feel like. He would have loved her too much to have turned his back on her, once he'd tasted her. She'd believed that then, at any rate. How many times had she been in the sacristy and imagined that he would reach for her, press his lips on hers with such ferocity that she would feel them bruise instantly. Their clothes would fall off as if by magic and as skin found skin they would both gasp with the intensity of the sensation. He would breathe in her hair and kiss her face and he would slide his hardness between her legs, transporting them both to a whole different planet of emotions.

That's what her first time should have been like. As it was, there hadn't been enough flame to attract a freezing moth and she'd had more emotional intensity eating a bag of prawn cocktail crisps. Gerard Bannen had cheated her, made her give herself away to punish him, but she had punished herself more and she would never forgive him for that.

'Hi,' she said as she neared Eric. 'I've brought you the money for today. It didn't feel right just leaving it out in the porch.'

'Thank you.' Eric took the envelope from her.

'Do check it. I've rounded it up.'

'You didn't have to. And no, I trust you.'

'Honest face?' she smiled and then a censuring voice in her head told her she was flirting. Any internal reprimanding voice always sounded like her mother's.

'Nice honest face,' he said, adding in an adjective that made her cheeks begin to tingle with warmth and she blamed the weather.

'My, it's hot, isn't it?' She patted her burning cheeks. 'I didn't realise, being inside. The house is quite chilly.'

'Never been in it,' said Eric.

'What, never?'

'Nope. Not even stepped over the threshold. I've always wondered what it was like. I have an idea though, my imagination has built it up over the years.' His smile extended. He had a lovely smile, nice teeth. He cared for himself, that was clear.

'Well, I'll give you a guided tour sometime if you like,' said Marsha. 'It's probably not half as grand as you imagine. It's very dark inside, dull. Even with the central heating on full blast it struggles to keep warm.'

'Thanks for bringing this,' said Eric. 'The old system has been pretty reliable for forty years so you can leave the money in the porch as normal. No one's ever taken it yet. And I'm sure you'll have enough to do at the moment.'

'To be honest we don't know what to do with ourselves. It doesn't seem right boxing things up before the funeral.'

'Why?' said Eric. 'Who's it hurting? And it's got to be done, surely?'

He was right of course. There was no point in them all floating around inside the house knowing there was so much to do but not doing it in case they offended the god of common decency.

Eric wiped the back of his neck with his palm and Marsha saw the sweat marks under his arms too. Clean, musky, sweat from hard toil, very different from Gary in the warehouse whose BO announced itself five minutes before he entered a room.

'If it helps, I, er ... know someone who buys vintage furniture, good stuff. Dave West. He won't rip you off, but never accept his first offer would be my advice. Trades in quality pieces. I've got his business card at home, I'll look it out for you.'

'Thank you.' She couldn't think of anything else to say and he wasn't making any attempt to extend the conversation so she said goodbye. He had too much of an effect on her for comfort. *This is what being dangled on the end of emotional strings for all your life must do to you*, she thought. *Make you into a dried-up, frustrated predator.*

Chapter 15

Sally knelt down at the side of the bed and prayed. She always felt when she needed to pray seriously, when gravitas and respect were in most demand, that kneeling was essential. It was the position she used to assume as a child, when she'd pray that her father would stop getting drunk and her mother would stop antagonising him, because if she didn't then he'd lamp her one and she'd be making breakfast for them in the morning with her hair parted a different way to disguise the lump or the bruise on her cheek. Usually Sally prayed as she lay in bed, mainly asking for a good night's sleep to fortify her for yet another rubbish day ahead. She prayed a lot that Norman would stop breathing, just drift off with no pain. This wasn't a life for him and it wasn't a life for her either. Especially now that the only bright light in her existence had gone, and she had snuffed it out.

Since Eleanor died, she'd prayed a lot in this position rather than whispering into her pillow, prayed that she'd have news that there was some underlying health issue that was undetected like a bomb inside her and it had chosen that moment to go off. Surely shouting at her couldn't have killed her, even if it was the middle of the night when Eleanor would be in the arms of a deep sleep, not expecting someone to barge into her bedroom, throw on the light and scream such terrible things at her.

Sally knew she was a good woman, loyal, with no real harm in her. And she knew that Eleanor Vamplew had never seen her as her equal but as a pet, like a cat; although not one to climb on her lap and be pampered, but to use for catching rats and be given scraps on which to survive. She'd given her tidbits of what she considered friendship over the years, but they weren't that at all. They were small hallucinatory drugs designed to make her think she was a friend; but having read to the end of the letter now, she realised that wasn't a choice on Eleanor's part, it was just all she had to give. If she'd had a pound for every time she wished she hadn't read the letter she would have been a rich woman, but life had no rewind button, and knowledge, however unwelcome, could not be unlearned.

She'd loved Eleanor, she loved her grace and her class and her unattainability. She'd worshipped at her altar, loved being in her orbit and basking in the shine from her attention. She'd hoped that when Norman passed away, Eleanor would tell her to sell up and move into Fox House with her, so they could be together having coffee every morning in the kitchen as it flooded with sunlight. It was a strange kind of love, she wasn't queer or anything like that, but it had devastated her to the core when they had fallen out and when their friendship had been reconstituted, she had felt whole again.

Now it would never be, and she was not only heartbroken but terrified. What if the police came and got hold of some CCTV from across the street or from the next house down?

They'd see the lights weren't on at all to alert Sally to something being wrong. They wouldn't see her in the garden tending to her hedgehog village because she'd marched straight round there from her own house.

If only she'd stayed at home, expended her anger pacing up and down the floor instead. She would have forgiven Eleanor in time, she would have rationalised away what she knew, ignored the doubts because she was good at that, a lifetime's practice. If it meant they remained friends, she would have done anything.

She had gone to confession and wanted so much to tell Father Bannen about it but when she opened her mouth, she had chickened out at the last, told him instead that she had snapped at Norman and he had been kind and told her that she was under a lot of strain and should forgive herself for momentary lapses of patience. He might have been understanding if she'd told him about Eleanor, but the human man part of him would have judged her differently and he would always see her stained as a murderer. He might even ask her to go to the police and then what would happen to Norman? All she could do was pray that God would be merciful to her and mete out some secret punishment that befitted the situation. As if she hadn't been punished enough in advance of it.

Chapter 16

'So, tell me then,' said Annis through a mouthful of pizza, 'what you've both been doing for the last fifteen years?' She was stuffing it into her mouth as if she hadn't eaten for a month. Jolene had rescued an old dog like that once, and even though he had no competition for his food, he still wolfed it down as if he had, right up to the end of his days.

'You first, as oldest,' Annis said, pointing at Jolene.

'Well, as you know, I went to uni, got my degree, didn't really know what to do with it. I did a PGCE but teaching, in practice, wasn't for me. I fell into a job doing accounts but I wasn't great at it. I just hopped around other various jobs, none of which fitted me because I only ever wanted to write books, not that I ever said as much to anyone. I didn't want them to laugh.'

Jolene had been the least academic of them all. Bs and Cs more than As and A stars and she'd really had to put the work in to get those. She felt the pressure of being the daughter of such an illustrious professor because she hated maths and sciences, struggled terribly with them. She could break out in a sweat now thinking about presenting her yearly school reports to her mother, watching her face scan the grades, looking for the distinctions that were never present. The disappointment was so thick in the air, Jolene could have sliced chunks of it and buttered it.

'Dad wrote books,' put in Marsha.

'Research books, sensible fact books. The sort of books I wanted to write wouldn't have been seen as on the same planet,' replied Jolene to that. 'Anyway, I'd do the crap jobs, come home, write, send my manuscript off to an agent, get the reject letter and that cycle went on for years until I gave it one last shot, took a fresh hold and wrote a book about a shop in a Yorkshire village. I got a deal and it was so successful that it turned into a series. I was about four books in when I was able to afford to write full time.'

'How many have you written now, Dolly?' asked Annis.

'Twenty.' Jolene snatched a moment then to bite down on her slice. 'Well, I've written twenty-one, I'm one in front. Twenty is coming out at Christmas.'

'Are we in them?' asked Annis with a cheeky grin spreading over her face.

'No,' said Jolene, in a perish-the-thought way.

Marsha stayed quiet.

'What's the hubby like?' asked Annis.

'Warren. He has his own business, water filtration taps.'

'Sexy. Is he doing okay?'

'Yes, okay.' Jolene didn't sound convincing and she realised that, so added, 'Well, it was great in the beginning but he's high-end quality apparatus and there's a lot of cheaper competition so he has to play the long game and build up a strong clientele, let his reputation speak for itself.'

If his reputation spoke for itself it would say 'I am an incompetent twat', she didn't add.

Neither did she say how much money she had loaned him to keep his business afloat, though loan was a stretch because she wouldn't get it back. She didn't say that they had already remortgaged the house, and he must have gone through the meagre amount he had inherited from his mother faster than a dodgy oyster goes through a digestive tract because he had asked her yet again for another 'loan' and she really didn't want to give it to him because it was the last of her savings. She knew he'd get round her because he always did, rolling out that they were a partnership, that he was doing this for them both and other such platitudes. He was like a dog with a bone when it came to getting his own way.

'Where did you meet him?' asked Annis.

'On a course in Leeds, about promoting your own business. We were split into teams for activities and he was in mine and we clicked. It was quite the surprise. I thought I was set for spinsterhood.' She'd dated of course, but no one who'd blown her away, at least not until she'd encountered Warren's charm offensive.

'She got married within the year,' put in Marsha.

'Marry in haste,' said Annis with a snort. She was joking but Jolene was only too well aware how close she had skimmed to the truth.

'We're still together,' said Jolene. 'It's our tenth anniversary on the twenty-sixth.' She realised she was playing with her necklace again and stopped herself because it was like a nervous tic and she could see that Annis had noticed her doing it too. It was a silver moon on a long chain. It was nearest she could find to one she had lost a couple of years ago that Warren had bought her for their fifth anniversary. A gold crescent moon with a tiny cat sitting on the lower curve. She'd been gutted, she'd been so certain she'd put it back in the box, as she was always so careful with her things. He'd been furious. It was just one episode in an *annus horribilis* that made the Queen's look like Disneyland.

'No kids?' Though Annis had already deduced that.

'No children. Never really got the maternal urge thing,' said Jolene. That much was true. And she was glad she hadn't the way things had turned out. 'Anyway, that's me in a nutshell: married, mid-forties woman prickling with the first stages of the menopause, writing books about romance and doing very well at it. Now, let me eat the rest of my pizza before it goes too cold.'

'Mash?' said Annis, turning the light of her large blue eyes on her sister.

'Hardly anything to tell. Left home, went to London, had a few jobs, found one I really liked and stuck with it: sourcing and selling promotional goods. Worked my way up the ladder, moved with the company when it relocated to Bakewell. I became a partner, then the owner sold up and I bought it . . . that's about it.'

'So you own a whole company then?' Annis whistled. 'You must be loaded.'

'I'm okay financially.' Understatement. Marsha had grown and expanded the business into market leader shape and was reaping a more bountiful harvest with every passing year.

'What about romantically?'

Don't even go there.

'I'm happily single.'

She didn't sound as if she was; her tone had a bitter note in it.

'What, no one?' asked Annis. She found it hard to believe. Marsha was beautiful, she always was. When they were young girls, Annis thought her elder sister looked just like a fairy with her small frame, white-blonde hair and shining grey eyes. She was still petite, her hair long and pale, her skin creamy and clear. She looked so much younger than her thirty-eight years, but then they all looked to have beaten the clock. That was probably down to their mother's genes. They all thought she'd be immortal.

'I don't have time, too busy,' Marsha said with a sniff. 'And I've never met anyone that made me want to make time.'

Had she been Pinocchio at this point, her nose would have shot across the kitchen and broken the glass of the window.

'I did try a bit of internet dating once.' Marsha volunteered this information, in case she was giving them the impression she had borderline nun status and was about to burst into 'Climb Every Mountain'.

'And?' asked Jolene.

'It was a free site and I got what I paid for,' said Marsha, deadpan, taking a long slug of wine. 'Let's just say on jollity levels, it was steps down from a disembowelling.'

'Such as?' asked Annis, smiling at her sister's turn of phrase.

'Maybe another time.'

'No, now, come on,' Annis urged her with a slice of pizza stabbed in her direction.

Marsha sighed. Where to begin ...

'Mart from Harrogate. Looked a magnificent specimen on his profile pic, obviously taken fifteen years previously. We went out for dinner and it was going fine until the bill arrived and he said that I had two choices, going half or if he paid he wanted something for it. And that he was all ready because it didn't take him long to get revved up.'

Jolene's jaw dropped open so low the pizza she was chewing almost fell out.

'Then there was someone whose name I can't even remember. I decided not to do the meal thing again, just have a coffee, then I could make a quick exit if I needed to. Oh yes, Eddie.' She clicked her fingers as the name came to her. 'He smelt of dog and he had dog hairs all over him and scruffy fingernails and swore a lot. Said before we went any further that he needed to know if I was pro-abortion or anti because my answer would determine whether we went on a proper date or not.'

'What?' asked her sisters together.

'The fact that I wouldn't commit to an immediate answer made his mind up that I was the devil incarnate so he told me I was a … C-word, and he left.'

'Lucky escape,' said Jolene, who hadn't heard any of this before. But then she'd never asked.

'Johnny was a breath of fresh air. I really started to fall for him, then his pregnant wife and two kids rolled up at the house looking for him. Two Daves: one let me pay for everything once too often, the other blew hot and cold and I never knew where I was. Billy wanted to blame me for everything his ex-wife had put him through; Stephen ghosted me, made up with me and then did exactly the same again. There were a couple of others that I wish would just piss off out of my memory, but you get the gist.' Then Marsha bit down on her pizza with a ferocity that suggested she was biting down on those bad memories in the hope of severing their jugulars.

'Wow,' said Annis. 'No good ones to report?'

'One nice one, ticked every box except I didn't fancy him and trust me, I really tried,' came the reply. 'Now you, Annis, because I think we're overdue.'

Annis trilled an oh-so familiar riff of laughter. 'I can't tell you it all, we'd be here for days. But I met a nice woman called Scottish Shelagh, slept on the streets for a while, then I got a job washing up in a hotel and the manager there let me stay in one of the rooms that wasn't being used while it was being refurbed.' She omitted the part about how one should beware of Greeks bearing gifts, even if he wasn't Greek, he was from Swansea and he was a creep. She woke up with him on top of her and she kicked him in the balls and got out of there. 'I went back on the streets with Shelagh for a while. Then Shelagh moved into a hostel, but she had to give her dog away because they didn't take animals and she was heartbroken but her arthritis was so bad she couldn't bear the cold any more. I learned who I could trust out there, who was safe to club together with. Occasionally I stayed in squats, night shelters and an abandoned tent, although someone set light to it while I was away getting some food, which was pretty devastating.' She skipped a chapter then, because she didn't want to relive it through the telling. 'I moved to the coast hoping to get summer jobs and I did, in bars and amusement arcades. Then in the winters I came back and stayed on Shelagh's floor. Then someone I got to know was coming up to Sheffield for a job in a club and asked if there might be one for me and by chance there was.'

She smiled then and a painful ache bloomed in both Jolene and Marsha's hearts. It sounded awful, a million miles from soft beds and security. Jolene couldn't hold back from addressing the elephant in the room any longer.

'Annis, why did you go?'

'Oh, you know what it was like here.' Annis stared at her, deep into her eyes as if she was looking for an answer that was buried there.

'Yes, I do; it wasn't great growing up with parents who

had us and then didn't really know what to do with us, but ... was it that bad that you had to run away and stay away? Surely you must have wished to be home when you were lying on a pavement somewhere?'

'No,' she said, which was true. She hadn't, not once. The freedom was worth it all. Being able to breathe without feeling there was a hand clutched at her throat at all times, a feeling of dread that wouldn't go away. She had felt cleansed of anxiety and stress and anger, because she had been very angry and she'd lumped them all in the mix together. It hadn't occurred to her young self then to reach out to her elder sisters because they'd grown up here too, they'd have known it all and they'd never reached out to her. That's what she'd thought then, but the years since had made her rethink her theories.

'Can you imagine what my life would have been like if I had come back,' Annis went on. 'I acted on an urge to go without really giving myself that much time to think it through, and then it just felt easier to stay away.'

She'd met so many people on the streets who had done the same thing. There were too many who had left because of the pressures that lay within their own four walls at home, because their families were not the safe castle keep of life they should have been.

'I didn't fit. Anywhere. I didn't have any real friends at school, they all thought I was a bit of an oddball, and a rich bitch because I lived here.' Annis picked up some pizza and then put it down. It was cold and the tomato topping was congealing.

'I feel bad that you couldn't turn to me,' said Jolene. 'I have done for too many years to count. If only I'd known you were so unhappy.'

Marsha stayed silent because she had been too busy look-ing inward back then. Too concerned with her own misery to be sensitive to anyone else's. She couldn't have turned to Jolene either. She was trapped by her oath to Gerard Bannen to say nothing. When she upped sticks and moved to London, albeit with some plan of what to do when she got there and somewhere to stay, she'd gained an insight into what had triggered Annis into running away, leaving everything behind her so that she didn't have to face it, see it, deal with it. The fresh space was the equivalent of a cleansing shower. It was the best move she ever made.

Annis gave a small shrug. Blessed hindsight showed her that she had other options, back then she felt she had just the one – and she had to take it.

'Mum and Dad thought you'd be back. We all did,' said Jolene.

'That's why I wasn't,' said Annis.

'So you ended up in a club in Sheffield?' asked Marsha.

'Yep.'

'Is that where you were when we tried to get hold of you when Dad fell ill?'

Annis nodded. 'It was, Mash. It was a job that suited me. The woman who owned it was rough around the edges but she had a soft spot for me.'

Denise Riley saw her staff as just that and nothing more but she'd taken to Annis and vice versa. She'd felt protec-tive towards the young woman who'd worked hard for her, never letting her down. That's why she'd stepped in when she'd had a problem.

'I felt settled there for a long time, stable, you know. The people were nice – mostly.' There'd been one who definitely wasn't and made her want to run off again.

'We put ads everywhere,' said Jolene. 'We even hired a private investigator but it was as if you were invisible.'

It was Denise who had seen the advert in *Private Eye*. She knew Annis's real name. Annis didn't want the past creeping into her life again, though it had never really gone away because it was part of who she was. But eventually the curiosity had become too much for her to resist. She found out that her father had died and she felt nothing. It was only later when she was plagued with memories of how much she once loved him that she had a minor breakdown and cried so much that Denise made her take some time off before she drowned them all.

Annis's lips stretched into a smile, too wide and stiff to be genuine. 'But you found me eventually, and here I am.'

'But not in time,' said Jolene. 'Dad thought he could see you in the room at the end. He kept getting distressed that you wouldn't come to him. He said he was sorry.'

Sorry, repeated Annis to herself. One of those words that came free with the aroma of bullshit. It was a cloth on a wipe-clean board, except you could always see the ghost of what it had tried to erase. It never quite went away.

Chapter 17

Sunday was a dull day, devoid of sunshine with on/off showers of rain, as if someone mischievous were playing with a tap in the sky.

Jolene went to Mass. She thought she should go and hoped the others would accompany her. Annis just laughed at the suggestion, while Marsha refused on the basis that she didn't want to face all those 'sorry for your loss's, besides which she hadn't been to church for many years. She didn't admit why she was the most lapsed of all lapsed Catholics: that she had taken umbrage with the whole religion because one of their priests was the male equivalent of a prick-teaser. Her excuse stood up well enough because Jolene was besieged with a whole host of 'sorry for your loss's. *Such a generous woman. Such a sad shame. She was so young still, and wonderful.* Their mother had a refined gift for making strangers feel as if they were intimates, and vice versa. She only gave away what she had to spare and yet it felt like so much more.

Sally was there and joined the line of people wanting to pass on their condolences, a watery smile flickering on and off her face.

'I've lit a candle for your mum,' she said, taking a handkerchief out of her pocket which was the size of a duvet cover. As she lifted it to her eyes, Jolene spotted the embroidered 'N' which triggered a flash of memory: Norman Lunn trying to stem the bleeding from his nose with a large bright-white handkerchief ripped from his pocket. 'I still can't believe she's gone.'

Sally kept repeating those words, as if some inner mechanism was stuck and Jolene seized the first gap in their one-way conversation to extricate herself. At the church door, Father Gerard took her hands between his. He had soft, narrow hands for a man of his size, Jolene thought. They didn't fit with the rest of him.

'How are you, Jolene?' he asked her, sympathy heavily weighted in his eyes.

It was a question Jolene was already tired of. Her answer all morning had been a hundred variations of, 'Oh you know, bearing up.' She had a ridiculous impulse to say, 'Never happier'. Instead she plumped for the standard, 'Just getting through it all.'

Jolene saw him glance behind her.

'Are you by yourself today?'

'Yes. My sisters are at home.'

He picked up on the plural immediately. 'Both?'

'Yes, Annis is back, too.'

'Oh my goodness, that's ... that's wonderful. Really good news. Well, I'm here if any of you need me. You or Annis or ... Marsha must ring if you just want me to pop round and lead you in prayer. It can be very comforting at these times.'

Jolene had noted the fractional pause before he said Marsha's name, as if he was afraid to say it in case he gave something of himself away. It stood out like a sore thumb and she wondered what it signified.

'Thank you, Father. I'll be in touch about the funeral as soon as we have clearance.'

'I mean it. I'm here any time for all of you. Lapsed or otherwise.' He smiled as he let her hands go and they chilled instantly in the air of this cold but beautiful church.

There were plenty still behind Jolene in the queue to have a word with Father Gerard, she saw as she briefly turned around. The line had never been so long before he came, when Father O'Rourke was in charge, a wheezing mountain of blubber who exuded an odour of damp clothes. He never sent regular heartbeats off-kilter like Father Gerard had. What a heady mix, being unattainable while being available for anyone who asked. She wondered if Father Gerard was aware of his power and if so, whether he fought against getting a thrill from it or secretly enjoyed being adored and fantasised over.

When she got back to the house, Annis had taken John Abruzzi to the vet's and Marsha was catching up with some work on the kitchen table.

The heavy flash showers seemed to have turned the grass a more vibrant shade of green. The garden looked as if it had been photoshopped.

'I don't think the gardener will be here today, do you?' commented Jolene.

Shame, thought Marsha.

'I think I'm going to nip home for a day or so,' Jolene went on. 'I need to get some clothes and bits and bobs. You don't mind, do you? I mean, we can't really do much until after the results of the PM, can we?'

'I found some flat-pack boxes in the garage. I can

construct those and at least make a start on putting clothes in to go to charity,' replied Marsha. 'There are a hell of a lot. And all of Dad's clothes are still in the wardrobes too.'

'Father Gerard asked after you at Mass today,' said Jolene.

'Oh, did he?' was all Marsha said, hoping she'd given the right reaction even though her heart beat a stupid fast tattoo at the thought of her name in his mouth.

*

So far Annis wasn't so impressed by The Vetman, but then people did tend to judge institutions by their receptionists and the horrible mousy-haired minger behind the desk with the attitude problem wasn't a great representative of the 'We Care About Your Pets and YOU' poster plastered on the wall behind her. She'd been chatting to the other receptionist for ages, letting the phone ring so much it tired and stopped and Annis bet herself that whoever was on the other end of the line wouldn't have been ringing to pass the time of day. She thought about Denise back in Sheffield and how furious she would have been if the phone in reception hadn't been picked up immediately with a warm and welcoming greeting: 'Cocktails, how can we help you?'

Mouse-minger had tried to be a bit funny with her when she said she wasn't registered with them and didn't want to register with them because she wasn't living around here for very long.

'Who did you speak to? Because we only see registered pets on Sunday.'

'No idea, didn't get a name,' replied Annis, with one of her smiles that didn't set her dimples dimpling. 'I just rang and they gave me this slot, said there had been a convenient cancellation so here I am. I only need some tablets for my rabbit's arthritis.'

Mouse-minger reached into a drawer and rustled around in it.

'Fill in this form,' she said.

'Please,' added Annis, not quite under her breath. She couldn't abide rudeness; she'd found so much less of it with the people she'd been mixing with over the past few years than she had with 'respectable' people like mouse-minger here. She half-wished that Denise had been here with her; she'd have reached over the counter, pulled the receptionist over it by her shirt and shouted in her face to have some fucking respect for how she spoke to customers.

Annis filled in the form and handed it back.

'Take a seat,' said mouse-minger. Annis locked eyes with her and the look in them got what it demanded. 'Please.'

She sat on a bench, put John Abruzzi's basket on it next to her and poked her finger through the holes in the front so he knew she was there.

A man behind her was called through. His bulldog was the canine version of him, stocky and solid. He pulled on the lead gently, 'Come on, mate' but the dog wouldn't, or couldn't budge. The man stooped, picked up the dog gently and carried it into the vet's room.

A shivering German shepherd pup weed on the floor and mouse-minger had to mop it up. She didn't tackle the duty with gusto but Annis was delighted, silently willing it to do a big sloppy poo for good measure. She was called through eventually. The vet was a woman who didn't look old enough to drive, yet she had an efficient manner, instilling confidence.

'He's gorgeous,' she said, when Annis had tipped her rabbit out of the basket. 'How old is he?'

'About eight, I think,' she replied.

'Good age.' The vet seemed impressed.

'He's arthritic, though. He doesn't move as much as he used to. I've run out of his meds but he's due an annual check-up anyway.' Annis pre-empted the next question. 'I've moved away from our usual vet.'

The vet felt around John Abruzzi's body, concentrating as she did so; looked in his mouth, which he wasn't happy about but tolerated. She looked in his ears and then stroked him. 'He's so sweet, isn't he?'

'Yes, he's lovely,' said Annis. 'It wasn't in my plans to have a rabbit but he was a rescue.'

She didn't say that she'd climbed over a six-foot wall and pulled the door off his far-too-small hutch to rescue him, then broke up the hutch with a house brick to discourage the neighbours from getting another.

'His teeth are good, his ears are clear, inflammation around the joints as you say but that's pretty normal for a boy his age,' the vet said as she started tapping into a computer. 'If you go back into the waiting room, I'll have some meds sent down. You can get rabbit food with glucosamine which might be beneficial.'

'He's already on that,' said Annis. She liked this vet; enough to put up with the cock of a receptionist if she had to come back.

She sat and waited for the medicine. The man who had taken the bulldog into a treatment room came out without him, just holding a lead. He didn't take a seat, just loitered by the reception desk as if disorientated. Then, he dropped his head into his hands and broke into a sob, then as quickly he stopped himself, threw his head back as if to drain away tears from his eyes.

'John Abruzzi Vamplew' called the second receptionist. Annis thought they must feel proper tits sometimes having to call out pets' names.

At the counter Annis paid her bill while mouse-minger was dealing with the man with the lead. He looked felled.

'You do know that euthanasia isn't likely to be covered by your insurance,' she was saying to him. He couldn't answer, he just stuck his card in the machine. Then he was given his receipt and he left as quickly as he was able.

Annis couldn't stop herself. When she'd been handed her medicine, she leaned over the desk and said, ever so sweetly, to mouse-minger. 'You know when you get sacked from this place because of your shitty, heartless attitude to customers, love, whatever you do, don't shift careers into bereavement counselling.'

Then she picked up John Abruzzi and was out of there.

The man was sitting on the wall. He looked too big and hard to be crying his eyeballs out, not caring who saw him. Annis had passed him by about twenty steps when she felt compelled to walk back.

'You okay?' she asked.

The man half-raised his head. 'Yeah, I'm fine,' he said, grinding his fists into his eyes, embarrassed now at being forced to converse.

'She didn't help. That miserable cow in there,' Annis said. 'I had to have a serious word.'

The man shook his head slowly from side to side.

'I have no idea what I'm going to do without him,' he said. 'I got him from the animal shelter. We took to each other from the get go.'

He had wrapped the lead tight around his fist. The collar

was attached and a silver bone-shaped tag inscribed with the dog's name.

Annis parked John Abruzzi's basket on the ground and sat down on the wall beside him.

'What was he called?'

'Paulie Walnuts,' came the answer. 'It's a character in—'

'—*The Sopranos*. I know,' Annis interrupted him. 'No explanation needed.'

The man shared a small smile. 'It was a good idea at the time. He looked like a little bag of walnuts when I first got him.'

'I've always liked bulldogs,' said Annis. Denise had one when she first went to work for her. The ugliest bugger Annis had ever seen and didn't in the slightest match her name of Angelina. She was docile and sweet and the customers would pet her while they waited to be served with drinks or otherwise. Old Jonjo always brought her a custard doughnut when he called. Both of them gone now. She didn't want to think about death, there was too much of it around her at the moment.

'Never gave me a minute's bother,' said the man. 'Not until these past couple of months. I only brought him in for his yearly jab, that's when they found it.'

She didn't ask what 'it' was. It didn't even matter, but 'it' was the thing that had led the dog to his end and to the man sitting on a wall pouring his heart out to a stranger.

A fresh flurry of tears, for which the man apologised. He growled at himself.

'I know it's only a d—'

'Oh don't,' said Annis. 'They're never "only an animal". Don't finish that sentence. If anything happened to my boy here, I'd be just the same.'

'Cat?' asked the man with a sniff, glancing at the basket.

'Rabbit,' said Annis. 'John Abruzzi.'

'*Prison Break*?'

'Yep.'

'We have the same taste in TV programmes,' the man said with a little laugh. 'Is he okay?'

'Arthritis,' replied Annis. 'He's more flop than hop these days.'

'Poor lad.'

'I'll be a wreck when his time is up,' she went on. 'They take a piece of you with them, don't they? Maybe that's the point, they're saving it so they can give it back to you when you get up there too.' She pointed to the sky and smiled and the man smiled back.

'That's a nice way of thinking about it. I'll remember that.'

She stood up; the intensity of the present shower was increasing. 'I'd better get him home or I'll be having to share his arthritis tablets.'

'Can I offer you a lift?' asked the man.

'Cheers, but we've just got a short walk,' she replied. As if she'd get into a car with a strange bloke, however affable he appeared. 'Take care. It's really hard, I know. Time is the only healer I've come across that's of any use.'

She dreaded John Abruzzi dying. She knew she'd cry harder for him than she ever had for any person. Even the thought of it was enough to make her eyes blur.

As she turned into the drive of Fox House, she didn't notice the blue Jeep passing by and taking a glance at where she was going.

Chapter 18

Jolene headed for home after Annis got back. It was only a forty-five minute drive but in every one of those minutes her mouth grew drier with anxiety. Warren was going to be furious when he found out how little she'd been left in the will. No doubt he'd come out with some bullshit about how unfair it was on *her* and urge her to contest it. And if she didn't, he'd take matters into his own hands.

She wasn't sure if she loved him any more. She thought there must be some vestiges left and that would explain why she was still with him, still sharing his bed and wearing his ring, even though he was an arsehole of the highest order and every sense she had was screaming that she should leave him. She'd have to be the one that went because they lived in his house and she didn't know how that left her financially if they divorced. She'd been on the brink of telling him it was over too many times to count but the enormity of it, the actual process of splitting seemed horrendously complicated, too much, too big. And now was not the time to do it, with everything else that was going on; it really wasn't.

It would be easy if he was Mr Hyde twenty-four/seven,

but he wasn't and his Dr Jekyll side was personable and magnetic. In company, he sparkled, was witty and funny. He brought flowers and presents for her. He should have been a politician, sliding like a greased eel away from anything that didn't suit him and he was a first-class silky manipulator. He could have convinced her that the sun came out at night and the moon during the day and her counter-arguments wouldn't have held water.

He'd been charm personified when she first met him; she'd had romantic twinges as soon as they'd been pushed together in a team on that business course. They were lumped with two other people who were taking it all so seriously it was comedy gold. Then later he'd come and sat with her on a coffee break. The conversation at first had been banal: *So, how are you finding it? What line of work are you in?* The professional niceties. Then the questions began to highlight a more personal interest in her. Where was she based; was she married; did she have any children?

Their relationship had gone from zero to sixty in a day. She'd never met a man more tailor-made for her. He liked everything she liked, they laughed together in and out of bed. Their sex life had been normal, sweet, lovely. Her father had liked him, dispensed business advice to him and Warren would give him his whole attention whenever they spoke as if he was a cobra charmed. She thought her mother had warmed to him – as much as she was ever able. She'd remarked that he resembled Rock Hudson in his prime, though she did once let it drop in passing that she found him glib.

She hadn't wanted a big wedding, but Warren had insisted. Surely she wanted all the bells and whistles? There had been an embarrassing dinner at Fox House where Warren took every opportunity to bring conversation back to the wedding, however far it strayed. He might as well have saved them all two hours, dropped to his knees and begged her father to pay for everything. Of course it was inconceivable that Jolene would have a cut-price wedding. It was all about appearances, that shiny, thin veneer of respectability and show. But her mother had been of the mindset that if they paid for it, they'd have 'some' say in it and that was the problem, because suddenly it wasn't Jolene's day any more. Her mother picked the venue, the menu, the church, the hymns. It was a beautiful, classy wedding, but she hadn't chosen any of it and she'd felt alone on her side of the battle lines. Warren was in complete agreement with her mother's dictates. Only afterwards did he say that if she wasn't happy then she should have spoken out, even though she had but not loud enough to be heard; and she was angry at herself for not claiming her day, but she had felt outnumbered. She'd had a quiet word with her father, asking him to intervene, but he had been as weak as dishwater, arguing that her mother's tastes were impeccable and she should let her have her way. He had changed after Annis had left. If their mother said jump, he would ask how high. She had always worn the trousers, but by that point she was wearing the underpants, socks and braces as well. So in effect, it was her mother who was central to the celebrations, and not the bride as it should have been.

Warren's mother wanted whatever he wanted because he was her life. His father hadn't been around since he was a small child. Maybe that's why he had no male role model to show him how not to be a dickhead. And maybe why he expected women to bend to his every want and need because his mother was as pliant as a damp reed where he was concerned.

Jolene switched on the radio. Driving gave her too much time to think. She sometimes understood what had led Annis to load a rucksack and just bloody disappear.

Warren was in the kitchen. She wasn't sure if he'd be home. She wasn't sure if he'd taken advantage of her being away to bring *her* here. He said she'd never been in the house, but then again when trust was broken, one never took any statement paraded as truth at face value.

'In here,' he called, as if everything was fine. As if they were a normal, happily wedded couple. As if their marriage was a field of beautiful daisies.

She walked in, tried to smile but it sat precariously on her lips as if expecting to be kicked off at any minute.

'I didn't think you'd be here,' she said.

'Yes I'm here. Coffee?' He smiled, turned to the kettle.

Once upon a time she would have walked over to him, put her arms around him and pressed herself to his back. Now she daren't, in case she smelt an alien scent or he pushed her off.

'Please.'

She put down her bag on the table, the one she'd stuffed haphazardly the morning Sally rang, unzipped it and then loaded her clothes straight into the washer.

Warren put a coffee down on the table for her.

'How's you?' he asked. 'How's things?' He leaned over, kissed her on the cheek.

'Okay, under the circumstances.' She was aware that she sounded glum, as if subconsciously playing an emotional manipulation card and tried to counterbalance it with a more upbeat tone. 'We're in limbo really at the moment. But we're coping. How are you?'

'Sealed the deal on a great order on Friday. Buzzing about it.'

Buzzing. Appropriately he had on a polo shirt she hadn't seen before with a bee motif at the chest. Dior. Expensive. She didn't bother to draw attention to it, he would only have lied that it was a second or an end of season piece.

'Very influential customer, worldwide distributor,' he went on, beaming like a doped-up Cheshire Cat.

He will have celebrated, she thought. He always used to celebrate a big deal with a big meal. Roll out the champagne. He wouldn't have been alone.

'That's good.' She nodded encouragingly but she'd stopped getting excited about his supposed deals a long time ago. They always seemed to fall through at the last minute, however 'sealed' they were.

'Was Marsha staying with you?' He sounded concerned for her welfare. As if he wouldn't have wanted her to be alone in that big old house.

'Yes. And Annis.'

Warren's head jerked. 'Annis? She came back?' His eyebrows rose to the perfect height for surprise. 'I'll finally get to meet her then, will I?'

Of course he never had. He'd just heard a little about the sister who left home one November night for no plausible reason that anyone could think of and hadn't been seen since.

'Yep.'

'Too little, too late. I can't imagine your mother has left her anything in the will after her behaviour.' He gave a brief smug smirk that infuriated her. He smirked a lot, but then he was living the life of a man with two working dicks. She wanted to wipe it off his face so very much but if she told him, he'd be furious, he'd fly into a rage. Then again, she wanted to puncture his balloon of self-satisfaction, watch him suffer. And this would make him suffer very much.

She couldn't stop it coming out. 'On the contrary, Mum's left her almost everything.'

You shouldn't have done that, said a too-late voice inside her. He froze. At that moment, in his designer polo shirt and sweatpants, he looked not unlike a model posing for an old clothes catalogue.

'What did you say?' he asked, even though it was obvious he'd taken in the words. She saw him swallow and knew what emotion had formed the obstruction in his throat.

'I said, she's le—'

'I heard you. Jesus Christ, well, you'll have to contest that, won't you?' he said with a small burst of laughter that had no humour in it whatsoever.

'I don't think I can. Mum has it all sewn up.' She didn't know that for a fact, but she would bet it would be so.

Warren mumbled something that didn't sound very nice as he grabbed his phone, scrolled, rang a number.

'Hi, Dan, sorry to bother you at a weekend but is there anyone at your gaff that deals with contesting wills?'

Jolene mouthed 'No' at him, but it was like everything she did that he didn't agree with: overridden by his force-fulness. Warren turned away so she couldn't distract him.

'Right . . . and could he give me a call? Soon as . . . great, yes, and you? . . . Cheers, Dan, appreciate it.' He ended the call, chewed on his lip for a few seconds before speaking. 'After all you did for Eleanor, you more than anyone else and she did this to you?' he said. 'Absolutely we are checking this out. We are not taking it lying down.'

She noted the 'we' which should, by right, have been a 'you'.

*

In bed she heard his breath even and deep. He never had any trouble sleeping, he could always shove things into a 'to be dealt with' box in his head for the morning. She wished she had his ability. She was lying here awake enough to fly a plane with a brain whirring, trying yet again to make sense of this mess of a life she was living.

She *must* love him if she was jealous of his other woman and still wishing that he would turn around and hold her so she could stamp ownership on him. She wasn't sure whom she had lost most respect for – him or herself, because an aerial overview of her marriage would show her stuffing the crumbs from his table into her mouth as if they were a dine in meal for two from M and S.

He said that he saved her for best, she had no worries that he would ever leave her. He said he loved her and only her. Then again, he also said that he understood the money she gave him was just a loan and he'd pay her back.

He made a contented snuffle and she wondered what he was dreaming about; overturning her mother's will, probably. He'd manage to sleep soundly if he'd just murdered her and had to lie down in the bloodbath. She, however, stared at the ceiling, cursing herself for her weakness but more than herself, cursing the other woman who had made him into this man who couldn't be turned back to the way he was before.

What woman with any pride would put up with this shit?

Chapter 19

The next morning when Annis opened the front door to take out a bag of recycling, she found four bunches of flowers on the doorstep. She gathered them up and took them through to the kitchen.

'It looked as if there'd been an accident in the porch with all this lot,' she said to Marsha, who was filling up John Abruzzi's water bowl, though he shied away from anyone who wasn't Annis and made a *back off* growl when they came too close.

Annis took out a stick from the first bunch which had a card fastened on the end. *'RIP Eleanor, from Mary, Peter and Graham (church).'*

'I don't know how many vases people think an average household has,' said Marsha, knowing it was probably rather ungrateful to say as much.

'This one's from . . . no idea, can't read the name.' The scratchy handwriting of an old person. There was an envelope in the third bunch, a clutch of sweet-smelling freesias. The woman at the vet's with John Abruzzi the rabbit' was written on the front. An apology from mouse-minger perchance, thought Annis for the splittest of split seconds. She took out the card inside.

> Hello there, this is just a very small thank-you for taking the time to talk to me yesterday. I was just on my way home from the vet's when I noticed you turning down this drive. I wasn't stalking you, honest. But you were kindness itself when I needed some and it really touched me.
>
> If you fancy a coffee sometime ... Or lunch – I work just around the corner from the church in Millspring. Meynell's garage, down Rock Lane. I really hope this isn't coming across as a bit weird. If it is, ignore it. If it isn't, my number is on the other side of this card. But thank you anyway.
>
> Daz Meynell.

'Who's that from?' asked Marsha, seeing the slow smile spread across her sister's face and setting her dimples to full.

'A man I met yesterday in the vet's,' said Annis, turning over the card and looking at the number. 'His dog had just been put down and I talked to him for a bit and now he wants to take me for lunch.'

'Creep,' said Marsha, looking in the cupboards for anything sizeable enough to act as a vase for tall flowers.

'No, actually he wasn't at all,' said Annis. He was nice, but still, she didn't like that he'd sought her out and found her. She didn't like that at all.

Marsha found some brown tape in her father's office. She still had the urge to knock before entering and it still didn't feel right looking in his desk. The drawers were full of stationery, his pens and drawing pins, stapler and staples, unused quality-paper notepads. He had a pencil sharpener clamped to the corner of the desk that Marsha remembered using, turning the handle slowly so the long point didn't break off. She remembered the disproportionate amount of pride that swelled her heart whenever she achieved the perfect point on her father's pencils. But then a crumb was a feast to the starving.

He was always too busy for them until his last years, either working or doing things in his study. Their mother was around but equally unavailable and intolerant of small beings asking questions. Or breathing the same air as her.

She remembered pushing open the door one day and seeing Annis sitting on her father's knee, reading a book. She remembered jealousy rising through her like magma in a volcano, her father asking her what she wanted, and her stuttering an answer that she hadn't prepared because she didn't want anything, she just wanted to find him. He made time for Annis in his busy schedule and she resented that her younger sister had so much of him. Marsha felt like the Elizabeth to his Henry VIII, his great disappointment, his promised son born as 'a boy without a winkle', as Nursey said in *Blackadder*.

'Here, let me help you with those,' said Annis, seeing her struggling up the stairs with the flat cardboard boxes.

'Thank you,' she said, as Annis took half of them from her.

They went into their parents' room and began to construct the boxes.

Marsha opened her father's wardrobe and even after all this time, his smell drifted out with the trapped air, something that always smelt harsh and bitter in the bottle, but on his skin was akin to Christmas spices. It was very expensive and came from Harrods in fancy packaging.

Annis whistled at all the suits, hanging there so precisely, like artwork.

'What a waste,' she said. 'Someone could have been wearing those.'

'It's hard for some people to let things go though, isn't it?' Marsha answered. This was her mother's attempt at keeping hold of their father.

'I bet she cleared my room out pretty fast,' said Annis with a huff of amusement.

'Haven't you been in to see?' asked Marsha.

'I'm not one for trips down Memory Lane.' Annis got down on the floor and dragged over some cardboard. 'No point in looking back, you can't change anything.'

'Would you, if you could?' asked Marsha. 'Would you have still run off?'

Annis didn't answer those questions directly.

'Everything that happened to me has led me to this point where I am an heiress,' she said and then she laughed. 'Now, I suggest that we give these clothes to a charity near to where I used to work in Sheffield: Olive's Animal Welfare. I know they take clothes donations for definite because a few of the girls I worked with used to buy them from there. They'd be glad of this lot.'

Marsha lifted the first suit from the wardrobe. She pressed it to her face and inhaled her father.

'He always looked so smart, didn't he?' said Marsha. 'Can you remember? Dapper. I imagine his students thought he was the coolest dude.'

'What was he like with you?' asked Annis, tilting her head at her sister.

'Well, he was just busy all the time, wasn't he? More available for others than he was for us.' People, she had often thought, would have been surprised by that. He had the air of a family man, someone who doted on his children equally, who made space for them all in his life, his three beautiful daughters. All part of the grand illusion of life within the impressively well-appointed Fox House.

'After you left, he started to change,' said Marsha. 'He was different, softer. He'd ring me up and see how I was. When I came round we'd sit and chat in the garden and he gave me some great business advice.' She smiled. 'I just wish he'd been more like that when I was growing up.' Because by then she'd been fully formed, from a little girl who felt like the world's biggest letdown.

'Right.' Annis nodded as if thinking about that.

'I didn't have *that* father for long enough,' said Marsha. 'As soon as I'd found him he started to get ill.' She coughed a wobble out of her throat.

'Did he talk about me ever?'

'I think it upset him too much to,' replied Marsha.

Annis opened up her mother's wardrobe. She took a long dress from it with a dry-cleaning label still pinned to the shoulder. She didn't do as Marsha had with their father's suit because she didn't want her olfactory nerves tickled into action. The dress was ice-blue with what looked like a million pastel sequins and beads weighting it. She folded it carefully and put it in the first box. It was a size eight, she noted.

'What size was Mum at the end?' she asked.

'She stayed the same size all her life,' said Marsha. 'I wish I'd had her genes. I have to work at staying slim.'

'Yeah, I remember you being a few different sizes when you were young,' said Annis, thinking back to the fairy-like young girl and the much rounder teenager. 'At one point it was as if you lost half your body weight overnight. You couldn't have done, but that's what it seemed like.'

'Thanks for the reminder I was a porker.' Marsha laughed.

'You had knockers. I was so envious. Even when you lost the weight, you still kept those.'

Marsha had been the first girl in her class to wear a bra. She hadn't liked to stand out for any reason but nature had dealt her a crap hand there with hair that was almost white and ghost-pale skin and teachers telling her to wipe off her lipstick when her lips were naturally so dark a pink. Then she had to go and blow up like a barrage balloon and endure fat-shaming as well.

'Didn't feel like a blessing at the time, being the only girl in my year group to need a bra,' said Marsha.

'Neither did being the last.' Annis put her hands over her small breasts. 'And sorry, but I have a confession to make. I found the chocolate box under your bed.'

'You did what?' said Marsha.

'Oh, come on, don't tell me you didn't snoop in Jolene's room,' Annis gave a wry chuckle. 'That's what younger sisters do.'

'No I bloody didn't,' said Marsha, quickly amending it. 'Not snoop as such. I might have borrowed the odd comic and put it back without her knowing.'

'I couldn't believe you didn't seem to notice when your stocks went missing,' said Annis. 'You mustn't have counted them.'

'I didn't because I didn't think I needed to.' Marsha sounded aggrieved, which amused Annis even more.

'I think I saved your bacon once without meaning to. I ate three Flakes on the bounce, cleared the box. We'd argued over something and I was cross so I robbed you. And then

I remember Mum stomping upstairs and you running after her and lots of noise coming from your room.'

'That was you?'

'Yep.' Annis grinned proudly.

'Mum had put me on a diet because of my weight and she was convinced I must have a secret stash of sweets hidden.'

'Well you did have a secret stash. And thanks to me she didn't find it. And I got away with it because you never even asked me about it.'

Marsha couldn't remember what conclusion she'd come to about the chocolate, only that she'd been so gobsmacked to find the box under her bed had just her diaries in it. She knew her mother would have told her father and his disappointment in her would have been so much worse than her mother's anger, but a miracle had saved her. It had been enough to make her more careful in future though, and hide her treasure box behind a short broken piece of skirting board.

It was then that Father Gerard had started to be nice to her, because she had been the class fatty. She'd thought about it over the years, wondered if he'd moved in to groom her but she was certain that wasn't the case. His motives were purely altruistic, although it must have played to his vanity that his attention would give her some validation. Funnily enough, having him shine his light on her dissipated her need for the chocolate to make her feel good and the weight dropped off. Father Gerard was the Pygmalion to her Galatea. He had carved her with his kindness and then had fallen in love with his creation. Her diaries had told of every suspicion she'd had about his attentiveness, every moment when she'd imagined his eyes lingered on her a smidgen longer than was decent and all of it being wishful thinking, until the day of hairmoonlightgate.

That brought a thought that made Marsha's cheeks burn.

'I kept my diaries in that box. Did you ever read them?'

Annis shook her head. 'Can't remember anything else but chocolate, that's all I was interested in. I was like Black Ops: in, nick, out. I didn't hang around.'

She was lying. She'd read them, of course, hoping to find something juicy to use against the sister who tried to pretend she didn't exist. She'd found loads of ammunition, but also there was a lot of sadness in those pages and so she knew she would never try and hurt Marsha with it.

Annis lifted a fur coat from the hanger and wrinkled up her nose. She hated the sight of real fur, wondered how anyone could wear it, though she remembered how elegant her mother looked in this piece, like a princess with her pale-gold hair piled up on her head and pin-heeled Cinderella shoes. Their mother walked on heels as if she'd been born to them.

'Did you keep any friends from school?' asked Annis.

'A few, though they all fell by the wayside eventually. The ones I didn't lose when I moved to London, I lost when they had kids. It can be a bit of a divider.'

'Do you think you'll ever have them? You've still got time, if you get a move on.'

'I doubt it,' replied Marsha. It was a sore subject. She got broody sometimes, seeing babies on Instagram, and she could have gone it alone, but babies were all part of that happy family picture she craved. She wanted the whole husband and two point four children caboodle. She reckoned by the time she landed Mr Right, her ovaries would have shrivelled to old olives.

'What about you?' she threw the question back at Annis.

'I'd love kids,' Annis said, surprising her. 'But I'd be terrified of getting it as wrong as they did.' She'd questioned for years why people had children. She'd certainly questioned why the Vamplews had them. From reading Marsha's diary though, she knew the reason why she'd been born. She wondered if the pain of finding out was still deep-seated in her sister. Some stains just couldn't be washed away.

Eleanor

The child – Jolene – was three when Aunt Eleanor died. The timing was serendipitous because Julian and I were on the brink of breaking up. I was resentful that I was the one expected to give everything up to look after something that drained my patience and energy, however much I enjoyed our intellectual repartee, his illustrious company, the reflected glory, the sex.

She left me far more than I expected. She was a frightful old harridan but my swollen coffers made me feel quite cordial towards her memory. And maybe not so strangely, my marriage had a renewal of sorts. It's easier to be happy when you have money to burn.

Fox House had been on the market for a long time. No one wanted the upkeep of such a large and expensive residence. So I bought it, in my name only. A string to bind him to me. All that was missing from our perfect life was a son, he said. He wanted a son so very badly. I was sufficiently carried away by my circumstances to fall pregnant again. When I was ready.

I carried the second child differently from the first, I knew it was a boy, I felt it. I bought blue clothes for it, I painted the room blue. It was a golden period for us. Julian was feted, loved, revered. The house was perfect, befitting a family of our status. We were good.

They told me at the scan it was a boy. It was a boy. Congratulations, you are having a son, Mrs Vamplew.

I knew I would love this child. He would touch my heart. His father's boy.

The chances of an error with an ultrasound are five per cent. I gave birth to a girl. Pretending I felt something for this albatross was beyond weary. I was diagnosed with postpartum depression, but it wasn't that that was the problem. It should have been a boy, and it wasn't.

Chapter 20

Half an hour later, Annis broke off to go and see her mum in the hospital morgue, as Jolene had arranged for her. She let Marsha give her a lift there but said she'd find her own way home. With every step from the car to the hospital entrance, Annis had an increasing dread and she cursed whatever had decided this was in her best interests; but she had been a creature of instinct for years now and so she went with it.

She'd obviously been watching too many crime dramas, because she'd expected someone to lead her to a giant room with loads of chrome fridge doors, pull out a drawer and for her mother to be lying there, naked and half-frozen under a sheet. Instead she was directed to a room with a viewing window and a closed curtain which a member of staff drew back for her. There lying peacefully was the woman who had carried her for nine months and two weeks and whom she hadn't seen for fifteen years. She looked frail, the pale golden hair she remembered white-silver now, longer than she recalled, not quite combed to standard and she wondered if those thin lips, now pressed together, were capable of stinging right to the end. Her eyes were closed, shrunk back. Her skin looked paper-thin, stretched tightly over sharp bones.

Annis wasn't sure what her reaction would be on seeing her again: maybe that was why she was here; a test set for herself, by herself. All sorts of thoughts were dive-bombing her like birds drugged out of their avian minds, junk thoughts, spam thoughts ranging from the mildly nostalgic to the hateful. She could make proper sense of none of them because they zoomed at her and away at breakneck speed before she could catch them to pin down and analyse.

She found herself asking the mortuary assistant, 'Can I hold her hand?'

'Yes of course, just give me a minute or so to prepare her.'

She would have liked that, being 'prepared' as if she were Cleopatra. Annis was called through and sat at the side of her mum, the assistant waiting discreetly behind. She reached out, her fingers curling around a hand that she couldn't remember touching ever. Had her mother ever held her hand? She supposed she must have, but she couldn't recall it. Not even on the day when Norman Lunn's nose was spraying blood everywhere and at an odd angle to the rest of his face: she could only remember being dragged off by her wrist, when her mother could have held her hand, or picked her up and carried her away from the carnage. No wonder she had felt, even then, that somehow what had happened was her fault. The only person she could remember holding her hand was Marsha, begrudgingly having to take it as they walked to school and gladly letting it go at the steps to the Primary Girls' entrance.

Her mother's hand was beyond chilly. A different sort of cold, a point-of-no-return cold. However much she should chafe and rub this hand, it would never warm up.

Why did a dead body look so different from a sleeping one, she thought? Even if you couldn't see the chest rise and fall with breath, there was something missing, something had let go, lifted itself out of the flesh and left, never to return. This was her mother and yet it wasn't and it never would be again. Annis didn't realise she was crying until she felt the itch of a tear slide down her cheek.

She wasn't alone in the room, the mortuary assistant was at the back, giving them as much privacy as was possible, even though ears couldn't be averted like eyes could be. It wasn't enough for Annis to send words silently; she needed to say them, even though they wouldn't be heard.

'Did you leave me everything as your way of saying sorry, Mum? Is that why? Because I can't think of any other reason why you would.' *It had to be that, didn't it?* A glimmer of light through a cloud that had always been so dense and black, the smallest sliver of contrition, a hand finally reaching out to her. It meant everything.

What did she expect? A confirming twitch or squeeze, however slight?

'We all loved you. Even if you couldn't love us back, you could have just been nice to us,' she blurted out then, the words followed by a flurry of tears. She had loved her, but she'd been so afraid of the consequences of seeking her love in return, of being hurt by the lack of it, that she had always been in a defensive crouch where her mother was concerned. It had been so much easier to cut free, and no longer try and rationalise her betrayal.

It would have been impossible to make anyone understand why she should feel anything for this woman whose lifeless hand she was holding and did not want to let go of. Annis didn't even understand it herself, but the final words she spoke to her mum were true and from her heart: 'I love you.'

For once there was a plausible excuse why Eleanor Vamplew did not return the sentiment.

Annis sat on the wall outside the bus stop. She had intended to walk into town but she just didn't feel as if she had the strength. And she was perished, chilled through to the bone. The sun was having a duvet day, letting the rain play in the skies. She had considered warming herself up in the hospital coffee shop but it was packed to the gills when she passed it.

She had leaned over and kissed her mother's forehead before she left and wished she hadn't because the coldness against her lips was a sensation she couldn't shake.

Annis had been embarrassed at yet another outpouring of emotion she couldn't stop. The mortuary assistant had given her a tissue; she should have grabbed a clutch of them and not just the one which was now in wet bits in her hand. She couldn't staunch the flow: tears and snot. How the hell was she supposed to get on the bus with her face exploding like this?

Someone walked past and her eyes flicked up slightly to see a man's leather trousers and boots pass by; then they walked backwards, as if a rewind button had been pressed, and stopped in front of her.

'Hello, are you all right there?'

'Thanks, but yes, I am all right,' she answered, on the polite side of 'just piss off will you'.

'Hello,' said the voice again.

She lifted her head to give the bloke short shrift. One glimpse of a face that looked as if she'd been zapped by Spiderman's gack glands should chase him off. She found herself looking up at the owner of Paulie Walnuts and leaver of flowers.

'I thought it was you,' he said, pinching his nose; a nervous gesture, she thought. 'What are the odds? I'm not tailing you, really I'm not.' He pointed in the general direction of the hospital. 'I've just been in there to visit a mate.' He fumbled in his leather jacket pocket. 'Here,' he said, presenting her with a full packet of tissues. 'Take them all, I don't need them.'

Annis outstretched her hand, aware it was glistening with mucus. Embarrassing. She tore into the packet and did a quick repair job on herself, blew her nose, wiped her hands.

'I've left my bike at my mate's house just down the street there. You can never get a parking spot here.' He thumbed behind him. 'There's a café a few doors up from it if you want a cuppa. You look frozen. I'm sorry if the flowers were a bit much.'

'They weren't, they were very thoughtful,' she said, sniffing back more snot. God, she must look a proper scuffer.

She got up from the wall because going with him seemed, at that moment, like the better thing to do, rather than fob him off with an 'I'm okay thanks' when she clearly wasn't.

Chapter 21

Marsha went downstairs for a coffee and to tweak up the thermostat on the central heating. Her hands were freezing. It was as cold as her bedroom used to get on the occasions when the old lady used to turn up and sit smiling in the corner of her room. No one believed her, so she didn't mention it after the first time. It wasn't a dream and no, she wasn't scared, if anything it was a comfort, it made her feel watched over as if by a babysitting grandmother. As an adult, it made her think that nice people had once lived in Fox House and imprinted their happiness upon it and the old lady was one of them. She picked up the newly delivered local free newspaper from the front door mat and dumped it on the kitchen table before switching on the kettle. She'd have to go and get some shopping in if she was to be staying here. Her mother's freezer was full of food which had 'best before' dates on that went back years and, though it was probably fine, she didn't fancy eating an eight-year-old piece of salmon and veg that had been covered in ice crystals.

She opened up the thin newspaper hoping to find five minutes' entertainment to pass the time. There was a report on some of the summer fairs which had been held and there, taking up half the page, were two brightly-dressed women on stilts and between them, Gerard Bannen in his black priest's garb. The man was haunting her. The instant effect that even a grainy photo had on her was pathetic. How come he still had the power, after all this time, to make her feel so much for him? And how dare he get more handsome with age with his white-striped hair and George Clooney lines radiating out from the corners of his eyes, his Cary Grant mouth.

'Leave me alone, Gerard Bannen,' she shouted at the page.

She got up from the table, paced up and down to expend some excess energy and then wondered if she was going slightly mad. Her eye fell on her mother's cognac bottle left out on the work surface. She pulled the cork stopper from it and poured a measure into a cup – less of a finger and more of a giant hand. She glugged it back, feeling the burn in her throat; the fiery aroma made her cough. Jesus, it was nice when sipped, but taken at this speed, it was vile. She wasn't drinking it for the taste, though, but for its numbing effects.

Marsha, don't.

She heard her own weak voice protesting against herself as she reached for the bottle again. And then again.

Annis remembered this café as a shop when she was younger. She could see herself waiting with her mother in the queue, drawing a face on top of a dusty tin of fruit and being told to *stop that*. So many instances of reprimands, so few of praise. If any, because she could remember none.

The café seemed much larger than the shop and Annis, with her short kilt and bright red Doc Martens and Daz Meynell, with his shaved head and leathers, drew a few wary looks from the more soberly dressed clientele taking tea, eating Battenburg and toasted fruited teacakes. Daz walked to the back table in the corner and Annis followed him.

'You could have saved yourself a bunch of flowers, if only you'd known we'd bump into each other again so soon,' she said, settling herself on the seat.

'I've never done that before in my life,' said Daz, stroking his clipped beard as if it were a small facial pet. 'I put them there at six this morning and I've been worrying about them ever since.'

The other bunches must have joined his afterwards, she thought, or he would have passed comment.

'It was very kind of you, thank you.' She flashed him her best grateful smile. She'd kept the accompanying card, even though she probably wouldn't have rung him. Or maybe she would and that's why she hadn't thrown it away.

The waitress arrived at their side. Annis ordered a pot of tea, while Daz ordered the same plus four toasted teacakes. 'They're only small,' he commented when the waitress had gone.

'So, do you bring all the women here that you find waiting at bus stops?' she asked him.

He opened his mouth to protest then realised she was joking.

'You're the first,' he said. 'Trial run. I haven't been up at the hospital for a while, touch wood—' He patted his hand down on the table '— my pal came off his bike. We're getting too old for them. It's not us at fault though, it's the stupid bloody car drivers who don't check their mirrors.'

'Is he okay?' asked Annis.

'Fractured hip and a broken Harley Davidson. I don't know which one is making him cry more.'

'Ouch,' she replied with a sharp intake of breath.

'Why were you there? Visiting?' asked Daz.

'Sort of.' Annis wondered how best to phrase it because it was a bit of a conversation killer. There was no great way really though. 'My mother died last week. I was just saying goodbye.'

'Oh ... oh,' said Daz. 'I'm so sorry to hear that. And there's me ... mither— ... bothering you, asking you to go for a ... and—'

She raised her hand, pushed it towards him to stem the flow of his stuttering response.

'It's fine, honest. We weren't close.'

'Yeah, but it's still your mum isn't it?' He gave her a sad variation of a smile. 'Me and my mum didn't see eye to eye but it hit me like a ton of bricks when I lost her a couple of years ago. It brings a lot of crap to the surface.'

What an understatement, thought Annis.

The waitress arrived with a pot of tea, sugar, milk and mugs and a tower of toasted, buttered teacakes which weren't at all small. The smell stirred an emptiness in Annis's stomach and made it grumble with a hunger she didn't know she had.

'Tuck in,' said Daz, leading the way. 'I can order more.'

'How are you doing? After yesterday,' asked Annis.

He shook his head, shaking the question away in the process. 'Can't go there,' he said, his voice barely above a whisper. 'I'm taking a couple of days off to—' He coughed away the emotion in his throat.

'I get it,' she nodded, understanding. 'Sorry, I shouldn't have brought it up.'

'Gawd, what a pair,' said Daz.

'What do you do? For a living?' asked Annis, in an attempt

to move them onto jollier ground. 'You said on the flower card that you worked at a garage. Do you mend or sell?'

'I'm a mechanic first and foremost.' Daz spread the butter around on his teacake because it was dry at one end and loaded at the other. 'It's my own garage, which is why I can take a couple of days off, though I can't remember the last time I did that. Paulie used to come to work with me. Not quite ready for walking in without him.' He coughed again, stamped his foot. 'I'll give you mates' rates if you ever need a service.'

Annis smirked and Daz realised what he'd said.

'I didn't mean I'd give *you* a service. I meant . . .'

The waitress appeared at that inopportune moment. 'Everything all right?' she asked, expression half-polite, half-*WTF?*

'Yes it's fine, it's great,' said Annis, still grinning.

Daz rubbed his forehead in despair. 'The ground really needs to rise up and swallow me whole.'

'You're very kind,' said Annis, 'and of course I knew what you meant. If I had a car, or a bike, you would from this moment hence be assured of my business, but I don't have either. I've always just walked or used a train, a tram, a bus . . .'

'I see,' Daz raised a pair of impressed eyebrows. 'That's unusual in this day and age. Mind you, cars get more and more expensive to run as time goes on.'

She nodded and wondered if he thought the reason she didn't have a vehicle was because she was skint. She didn't look like she'd soon have well over a million pounds to her name, to be fair. Probably much more. She couldn't even think what investments her mother had and how many thousands squirrelled away in bank accounts. She used to spend a lot of time poring over stock markets, buying and selling and she was shrewd. *The queen was in her counting house, counting out her money.* She'd coveted artworks and antiques and of course, her biggest extravagance – Fox House itself. The biggest house on the street, the biggest house in the village. The status symbol.

'Bloody Gerard Bannen,' Marsha thought for the umpteenth time, staring at his photo, reading the editorial underneath. *Father Gerard Bannen in between High and Mighty, stilt performers at the recent fair held at the church of the Holy Mother and Child, Penistone.* She felt her scalp begin to prickle as if someone were pouring very cold water on it from a great height, pins and needles creeping into her fingers and toes. If she hadn't been sitting down, she would have needed to have sat down. She felt like scribbling out his features with a pen, or tearing him out of the newspaper altogether, but she didn't. It frightened her that she felt like that; she hoped it was the cognac talking and not her. Tearfully, she lifted up the bottle to her lips, cutting out the middleman of a cup now. She drank from it as if it were an antidote to his happy, contented, gorgeous, bastard face.

She wondered if he'd ended it with the mysterious Bronwen because he had realised she wasn't a patch on her. She wondered if he'd ever bonked Bronwen but closed his eyes and imagined her beneath him. He still felt something for her, she'd seen that in his eyes, and as for herself, she clearly wasn't over him at all. Would she ever be? The truth was, no man she'd ever had in her bed lived up to her fantasy of what she and Father Gerard would have been like under the sheets.

*

'Why is your mum still at the hospital if she died last week?' asked Daz, after they'd just ordered another pot of tea. 'If you'd rather not talk about it, just say,' he added quickly.

'I don't mind,' said Annis. 'She's having a post-mortem tomorrow. The cause of death isn't crystal clear.'

'Ah.' Daz nodded. 'That's an extra pressure you could do without, I suppose.'

Annis made a small sound of agreement.

'Lovely house. Do you live there?' Daz asked.

'Not now. I was brought up there, but I left when I was sixteen. I haven't been back since.'

Daz opened his mouth and then closed it again. The question he was going to ask would have led on to about five thousand others.

'Sorry,' Annis immediately apologised. 'That sounds intentionally enigmatic and I didn't mean it to be. I left home, I never regretted it. Don't be fooled by the house. It was big and spacious and full of expensive things but it never felt like my home.'

He didn't ask why, which she appreciated, even though he must have wondered.

'Are you dealing with everything yourself or have you got brothers and sisters? Or maybe . . . a partner? I . . . I didn't even ask if you . . . were with someone. The chances are that you are, of course.'

'Why?' asked Annis.

'Because you're lovely,' Daz said, no stuttering this time, no hesitation.

Annis took a drink. 'You don't know me. My mother thought I was the anti-Christ.'

'She sounds like mine,' said Daz. 'My brother could do no wrong, I could do no right.'

'I'm not sure my sisters pleased her that much either,' said Annis. 'I have two and we're all together again in the house at the moment. My eldest sister is fourteen years older than me. I never really got to know her. I was only four when she left for uni and she didn't come back that much. My middle sister is seven years older and she considered me a royal pain in the butt, so I never had much to do with her either. We're all very different. Jolene's a romantic novelist and Marsha runs her own company. Like I say, nothing like me – the deadbeat.'

'And what do you do to merit the title deadbeat, then?' Daz wiped his fingers with a serviette. The butter to teacake ratio was virtually evens.

'I've been working as a waitress and receptionist in a club for a few years,' came the reply. 'I reached the end of that particular road though and I was looking for pastures new when life dragged me back here, to the fold.'

Or rather death, but she didn't say that because it sounded a bit dark.

'Important job, a receptionist,' said Daz, nodding and that made Annis smile, because he was dressing it up. It made her think, *this guy has a kind soul.*

'The woman – Sandra – who works the front desk in my garage used to be a doctor's receptionist. She's a proper force to be reckoned with.' Daz blew out his cheeks. 'I wouldn't cross her.'

She still wouldn't have had to deal with the rough sods I've had to deal with sometimes, thought Annis. In saying that, there had only been the one time that she'd felt truly intimidated and out of her depth with a customer. And that once was enough. Annis gave an involuntary shudder.

'Someone walked over your grave?' said Daz, then

immediately apologised. 'Gordon bloody Bennett, me and my big mouth. Sorry. Can I get you anything else to eat?'

'Thanks,' said Annis, 'but I've left my sister packing up clothes and there's a lot to do so I'd better go soon.'

'Of course, of course,' said Daz. 'I've taken up too much of your time. I bet you just wanted to sit on the bus and think, but I came along and . . . and . . .'

'. . . forced me to eat delicious teacakes,' Annis finished his sentence off for him. 'Trust me, the last thing I wanted to do was think. You did me a massive favour.'

He smiled; actually he beamed and she found her own lips curving to mirror his expression. He was a nice guy. She was glad that fate had forced her hand and thrown him her way again.

The cognac tasted like something that could melt metal pipes but Marsha kept topping up her cup until the bottle was empty. Whatever she was trying to drown was floating like a polystyrene Michael Phelps with water wings on. She was *not enough*: an evil voiceover was playing those words on a continuous loop in her head. Not enough for Gerard Bannen, not enough for her parents. She should have been a boy; she even hacked all her hair off once to make herself into one, and all she got for her efforts was slapped legs. She couldn't even get that right. And the school bullies had yet another field day with her about her convict cut.

She reeled towards the kettle. She needed a black coffee because she was already getting the stirrings of a hangover. As she waited for it to boil, she loitered by the window, looked out at the garden, saw Eric the gardener walk into the shed as the rain started to pump out of the clouds. In her brandy-addled brain, it seemed a really good idea to take him a coffee too.

'You never said if you had a partner,' said Daz, about to drink the last of his tea. It was cold, but then he'd eked it out for as long as possible.

'No, I don't. I presume you don't either.' He didn't seem like the sort to invite women he'd just met out for a meal or a coffee via flowers if he was attached.

'No,' he said, as if the suggestion was preposterous. 'I haven't had a date for years.'

'Why's that?' she asked.

'I've been too busy,' he said. 'I can't turn work down and . . . you'll laugh.'

'I promise I won't,' said Annis, her promise already making her face crack.

'I'm in a tribute band. You have to guess who it might be. There are four of us, all male. And we look nothing like the people we're imitating.'

'Well that narrows the field down a bit,' said Annis.

'And we're retro.'

'I'm good with retro,' said Annis. 'Sixties, seventies, a smattering of eighties.' She studied Daz's face.

'It's no good you staring at me, it's not a clue. Oh and it's not the Beatles.'

'The Who?' she tried. 'You have a look of Keith Moon.'

Daz tipped his head back and laughed. The resemblance did not exist, not even under the influence of strong hallucinogens.

'Ever heard of the Monkees?' he asked.

'Of course I've heard of the Monkees,' she replied. 'I love the Monkees.'

He eyed her sceptically. 'Yeah, course you do.'

'I really do.' She drew a cross on her heart. One of Denise's favourite groups. She played a lot of retro music in the bar area. Most of the guests were retro, so she liked them to feel at home. On pensioners' day, the music went right back to the forties. 'Which one are you?'

'Micky Dolenz,' he said and ran his large palm over his scalp. 'If I didn't shave this, I'd have his hair. Grows like a bush.'

Annis hooted.

'You finished with these?' said the waitress, ready to swipe away their crockery. She was keen to see them off if they weren't ordering anything else.

Annis and Daz got up, made their way outside.

'What do you call yourselves?' she asked.

He pulled on her sleeve, led her to the side window of the post office two doors down where there was a poster. Four men in double-breasted red shirts and bright blue trousers, one wearing a green bobble hat. Daz on the left, clean shaven but with a mop of brown hair, presumably a wig.

'The Hunkees' she read. 'Clever.'

'We used to be the Chunkees,' said Daz, 'but then we got buff.' He pushed out his chest and grinned.

'What made you decide to do it?'

'Well, we were four ex-army mates and one of the lads was struggling a bit, PTSD, so we came up with something to bring him back from the brink. He was in a bad place and this, believe it or not, seemed like a really good idea. We didn't expect to be a success, we were just mucking about.'

'What made you pick the Monkees?' asked Annis.

'Well, Shah's a proper guitarist, the rest of us could just about manage Chopsticks on a keyboard or banging a triangle so we needed something pretty straightforward, easy chords, and there was already a Status Quo on the circuit, Status No, so we went full-on retro. Si's missus made the costumes, Keith's sister started touting us around, Shah's cousin gave us crash courses in playing our instruments on a need-to-know basis. We did a show for charity and then we started to get bookings. Then we all decided to lose a bit of weight and turn ourselves from a joke into ... a bit less of one.' He pointed to the poster. 'That's the next gig right there on Friday the twenty-sixth. Come if you're doing nothing. It's nearly a fortnight away so you've got plenty of time to think up an excuse if you didn't want to.'

'I can't make any plans at the mo,' said Annis, a regretful smile on her lips.

Daz shook his head, presumably at his own stupidity.

'Course you can't,' he said. 'Idiot. I'm sorry.'

Annis smiled. 'If I'm free, I'll come, I promise.' She looked towards the bus stop. 'Well, thanks for the tea and teacakes.'

'Do you want a lift? I've got a spare helmet and I'm safe on the roads. Or at least let me get you a taxi.'

Annis shook her head. 'I'm good with the bus, honestly. I have nicer things to think about now.'

'Can I see you again?' Daz blurted it out, as if he'd found a brief window of confidence and had to use it before it closed on him.

'Yes,' she said.

From the expression on his face, she knew she'd stunned him with an answer he probably thought he'd have to work harder for.

'Great. I know your circumstances, I'll be respectful, but I've really enjoyed talking to you.'

'Give me your phone,' said Annis. Daz couldn't get it out of his pocket fast enough. He nearly dropped it in his haste to unlock it before handing it to her. She tapped in her number, thumbs a-blur with speed.

'There. It's under Annis. I'm not sure I ever told you what my name was.'

Daz's face segued from incredulity to a smile of embarrassment. 'I didn't ask, did I? God, I'm rubbish at this. No wonder I haven't had a date this century. Annis, that's such a beautiful name.'

'Thank you.'

She'd captivated him, she could tell. She wasn't vain but she knew she had a few qualities on the desirability list: big lips, dimples, large blue eyes with cat-lifted corners, model-slim, tall. She'd scooped the lottery win with looks, not that they were particularly useful; they could even be a hindrance when someone had a fixation on you. Especially someone who made the hairs on the back of her neck stand up just to think about them.

Chapter 22

Annis walked into the house to find Marsha's forehead resting on the kitchen table and yet her hand was outstretched, holding a glass of water at a most graceful angle. It would have been funny had it not been so odd. There was vomit in the sink and an empty bottle of cognac on the draining board. She extricated the tumbler from her sister's hand, which woke Marsha up and she began talking as if she was picking up a conversation she'd had only a moment's pause from.

'. . . you were a bit of a prick then and I bet you still are.'

'Cheers, sis,' said Annis, though she was pretty sure the insult wasn't levelled at her.

Marsha lifted her head. 'Oh, Annis, hi.' She grinned horribly, then her features went through a series of formations as her brain foraged for the perfect sober face. Then the grin was wiped away as her body began to pulse as if she were a cat priming to get rid of a giant hairball. The much stronger Annis pulled her petite sister up by the material at her shoulder and jerked her towards the sink, just in time for Marsha to throw up a large splatter of dark liquid with a primeval sound effect. It kept coming in mouthfuls of watery stink.

Annis smoothed back tendrils of Marsha's soft, pale hair. She'd envied her sister's hair when they were younger. She looked like a princess from one of her story books, the one her mother had bought for her that she was almost afraid to read in case she creased a page. In the story, the princess had been surrounded by everything anyone could desire, but she broke away to live with a poor Gypsy boy with whom she found happiness. She suspected her mother hadn't reviewed the contents for such subversion before she'd given the book to her.

Marsha pumped out the contents of her stomach and another three people's as well by the volume. It was like a scene from *The Exorcist.*

'Mashed Potato, what have you done to yourself?' asked Annis. When the flow had subsided and Annis reckoned she was spent, she led her sister back to the chair, then ran a tea towel under the cold tap, wrung it out and pressed it to Marsha's forehead. From the sigh Marsha made, it was clear it hit the spot.

'I tried to shag the gardener,' said Marsha, pushing herself as far into the tea towel as it was possible to get.

Annis laughed and thought, *Just when I didn't think this family could get more fucked up, it tries to bed the hired hand.*

'Please don't be disgusted with me, Annis.'

'Come on, tell me the full story.'

'I can't, I just want to sleep,' said Marsha.

Annis pulled her bag over and searched in the side pocket for ibuprofen. She popped two out and put them down in front of her sister with a large glass of water.

'I suggest you take those before you lay down your purrty head, otherwise it will be your worst enemy in a couple of hours. Make sure you drink all of it.'

Marsha obeyed, sipping at the water and trying to swallow the tablets.

'I need to lie down,' she said, attempting unsteadily to stand. She had about as much chance of getting up the stairs unaided as Sally next door had of climbing the north face of the Eiger in her fluffy slippers.

'Come on then,' said Annis, hoisting her to her feet and guiding her rubber legs towards the staircase. For such a slight woman, Marsha was ridiculously cumbersome in this state and had the situation been reversed, Marsha wouldn't have had a chance at manoeuvring her sister up to her bedroom. Marsha face-planted onto the single bed with relief and buried her head into the pillow. Annis lifted her feet up and then tucked the satin eiderdown around her. She was asleep in seconds. Through the window, Annis could see the gardener calmly putting some tools away so he couldn't have been that traumatised by whatever Marsha had tried to do to him.

She closed the curtains. Blue, because this was the room her mother had painted for the new baby, the boy she was sure she was having. Poor Marsha had tried so hard to be the child her parents wanted. She'd asked Santa for toy cars and train sets, hoping that surrounding herself with stereotypical boy things would make her into one; Annis knew this from reading her diaries. And how terrified she was when their mother became pregnant again that she'd have a real boy.

As Annis walked down the stairs, she thought how little it took to warp a child; a thousand small cuts could do more damage than one deep gaping wound. The only way she'd managed to untwist herself was fleeing this damned place. She hoped it wasn't too late for her poor sisters.

*

As Annis was cleaning the sink, there was a knock at the back door. It was Eric, the gardener, carrying a poppy-painted mug.

'Hi,' he said. 'I'm just returning this.'

Annis held out her hand to shake. 'We haven't met. I'm Annis, the youngest daughter.'

'Blimey, you're not alike, are you.' Eric's grip was firm, big gardener's hands.

'Nope,' said Annis. 'Not in the slightest.'

'Is your sister okay?' He sounded concerned, for someone who might have been sexually manhandled. 'Only she was, er . . . she looked . . . slightly . . .'

He said 'upset' at the same time as Annis said 'rat-arsed' and they both laughed.

'A bit,' said Eric.

'She's off her face,' said Annis. 'I'm sorry if she did or said something she shouldn't. Let me apologise for her, but no doubt she'll be horrified when she wakes up and want to do that for herself.'

'It's fine,' said Eric. 'It's an unsettling time. People do mad things, out-of-character things.'

'Marsha isn't predatory normally,' said Annis, though she didn't know this for sure. She never used to be, she was always far more likely to hurt herself than anyone else, but that wasn't to say that in the intervening fifteen years she hadn't become a voracious cougar.

'She only tried to kiss me,' said Eric. 'It wasn't anything more than that. We were just talking and she may have misread the signs.'

How gallant of him, thought Annis, to shoulder the blame.

'I wouldn't want it to add to anything she's going through. She was clearly very . . . distressed,' he went on.

'It's because Mum died suddenly that—'

'No, it wasn't your mum she was talking about, it was someone called Gerald, I think,' Eric interrupted her. 'That's what she was in a proper loop about.'

'I see,' said Annis, taking the mug from him. Though she didn't really see at all.

★

Warren walked in from work as Jolene was getting some carrier bags out of the cupboard for a supermarket trip. She would take some things to Fox House, but they needed bread and fresh milk here too and it was *her* job to stock the cupboards. Warren wouldn't think of doing a shop, he was far too busy with his executive lifestyle. He was swinging the beautiful Mont Blanc document case she'd bought him for Christmas. He hadn't spent half as much on her, but then he had two women to buy for. Out of her own money, if that wasn't adding insult to injury. She hadn't seen what *she* had bought him, there was no new watch or pen, as far as she was aware. She didn't know what sort of competition she had, whether the woman was rich or poor, so in Jolene's mind her rival was horribly fluid, better than the reality would ever be. She imagined this woman outdoing her at every turn, like her namesake in the song but in reverse because this time it was Jolene who was being shafted. And Jolene didn't know how much time Warren devoted to her either. When he said he was working late or on a business trip, she tried not to presume he was lying, but the uncertainty had made her paranoid.

At least he hadn't spent Christmas away from home; he was here, being the perfect host as they catered for friends, or were catered for by friends. They were more his friends than hers. The sort where the female partners made tentative plans to meet up without the men: 'We must do this or that' but it never happened. They weren't really her choice of women anyway so she wasn't disappointed. They were Botoxed up to the ceiling, self-obsessed and vacuous. She wondered how many of the men knew about his mistress. They must, they probably egged him on, the lucky bastard. And because of that, she couldn't quite warm to them, even if she had wanted to. But she didn't want to: one was smug, one was a snob, the other a complete bore. In her head she had grouped them as 'The Three Tossers'. And all of them were decidedly sniffy about her career. It wasn't as if she wrote proper books with substance; she could almost hear their brains churning that one out. Silly books for silly women with silly romantic ideals. They might have taken her more seriously if they realised how much she earned and how it was she who brought home the fat bacon to prop up CATT Water Filtrations and stop it going under until it found stability enough to survive without her cash injections. In their eyes Warren was the big I AM and she was the hobbyist.

'I'm going to need to get hold of a copy of your mother's will,' said Warren before he'd even said 'hello'. She knew it would have occupied his mind all day. 'I spoke to Dan's colleague today for over half an hour.' Dan was the worst of the three tossers. 'There could be a way—'

'I'm not contesting the will, Warren, and that's final,' said Jolene with some rare steel in her voice. She'd been thinking about it too, building up the courage to be adamant because her husband was strong-willed and dogged. If a problem couldn't be solved one way, he would come in at it from another angle and another until he had smashed it into not being a problem any more. But this was a problem she did not want solving.

Warren threw his hands up in the air. 'What the actual fuck, Jolene?'

'It's clearly what Mum wanted.'

'What is that supposed to mean?' He was looking at her as if she were an idiot.

'It means that it will be watertight because she'll have made it so. She was sane, not manipulated in any way, it isn't forged and Annis is the one who most needs the money, which must have been uppermost in Mum's mind. I'll receive my share when the house is sold—'

'Which isn't enough,' said Warren loudly as he poured himself a neat bourbon from the decanter. Just himself.

'Well, it just has to be *enough*,' said Jolene. 'It's hardly a small amount.'

'It's not your fair share though, is it? You're the eldest daughter. You went round there every week, you were at her beck and call if she needed you, you cared for her more than either of *them*.' The way he referred to her sisters left no doubt as to his opinion of them. 'I was . . . hoping that . . .' He waved it away but he didn't need to finish the sentence. She knew very well what he was hoping. She even wondered if that's why he hadn't left her yet. Because he was waiting for her mother to die so he could get his hands on what she'd inherit – the *motherlode*.

'Are you in debt?' she asked, about to tag 'again' onto the end but leaving it off because for a small word it had a mighty and insulting weight.

He made a sound of weariness. 'It's not debt, Jolene. It's speculation for accumulation. Most businesses don't break even for a few years, then they fly. You have to ride the losses in the beginning. This is just one of those that takes a longer time to get off the ground. But it will all be worth it, trust me.'

Trust me. She did once, but it trickled through her fingers until there was none of it left. He would start talking about blue-sky thinking and getting his ducks in a row in a minute, plus other corporate twattery. She'd long stopped being blinded by his science. She just wanted the money she had ploughed into his filtering tap scheme returned to her but it was locked away at best, lost at worst. The only way she would ever get it back was by giving him more first. If she didn't, she could wave goodbye to it all.

She paid all the household bills; their flash, fancy cars were leased. They were supposed to split the mortgage, although what she put into the joint account every month was way more than he did. Sometimes she felt as if she were paying him to go to work and lose their money.

It had all been so much simpler when they met and his first business was solvent and turning a decent profit, before he gave it up for ambitious pie-in-the-sky ideas. Before he had the affair and discovered the door into another universe and became Billy Big Bollocks.

'Maybe,' said Jolene, sweeping up the carrier bags and her car keys, 'you should ask *her* to give you a director's loan for a change.'

★

Annis took a bowl of pasta into her mother's parlour and had the sudden urge to smear passata over the pale green velvet curtains, the cream carpet, the mink sofas. She sat her meal on her mother's desk. This was the desk that a lady might write letters at. This was the desk from which the unnamed heroine in *Rebecca* might have scooped up all the 'R' branded stationery to dump into Mrs Danvers's hands and declare 'I am Mrs de Winter now.'

Her mother had almost become a Rebecca de Winter in her head over the years; an enchanting, enigmatic creature with surprising depths of cruelty and hidden seams of darkness. No one who didn't live in this house could ever understand what it was like to have been brought up in it. You had to be here, as she and Marsha and Jolene had been, bonded by this common experience without being bonded at all. She had carried so few memories of her childhood forward, which said everything really, and all of them soured with sadness at best.

Annis could feel her mother's disapproval pushing through the membrane that separated the living from the dead. The impudence of her bringing food into her sanctum. But her mother was no longer here to slap her thighs until they stung to wipe off that look of insolence. It always hurt enough for her to concede defeat and drop her eyes in submission, but inside something was hardening like rock.

They were never beaten with red-hot pokers or sworn at, or starved – quite the contrary, they ate very well. They were sent to their rooms a lot, with their soft beds and velvet furnishings, toys and books, luxurious solitary confinement. They were given games as Christmas presents, but denied friends into the house to play them. They were never given compliments by their mother, could never achieve her exacting standards at anything. She knew that Marsha in particular strove to achieve the A stars, just to force her mother into acknowledging them, but she never did.

Their father, so strong and dominant outside the house, deferred to his wife within it. Her house, her money, her rules. She had true power over him.

A text message sounded, cutting off her thoughts just before she dropped into an abyss she had crept too close to. She put down her fork and picked up her phone.

> Hi. Just to say thank you for a lovely afternoon.
> I hope you're okay. I'm just testing the
> communication channel between us is open. Here
> if you need anything like heavy lifting or a drum
> solo. That's it. Goodnight, Annis. It's Daz btw x

Again she smiled. Kindness poured out of such a short text. She'd discovered kindness only in the second half of her life and found it was a much underrated commodity.

★

In bed that night, Warren pulled Jolene towards him, buried his jawline into the hollow of her shoulder.

'Is this okay?' he asked. 'If you'd rather not . . . I thought it might take your mind off things.' He kissed that place on her neck that had always turned her to jelly. She made the appropriate sounds, but she was play-acting as much as he was because she knew this was his attempt at getting her onside for fighting the will. As much as she wished she were in the arms of the old Warren who made her feel like she was made of gold, she was beginning to wonder if he'd ever existed and she'd been manipulated from day one.

She let him 'make love' to her, because it was less complicated than saying no.

Chapter 23

'Well, good morning,' said Annis cheerfully and full of beans as Marsha slid into the kitchen paler than usual. Any whiter and she could have stood in front of the fridge and no one could have told where she ended and it began.

'Morning,' said Marsha, sounding as if she'd just been dug up and swallowed half the soil on the grave in the process.

'How do you feel?' Annis asked her as she stood by the hob, stirring something in a pan.

'Still half-cut,' said Marsha. It wasn't a lie, she felt disorientated, light-headed and shivery-cold.

'Coffee? I went to the mini-mart and bought some decent stuff that tastes of actual coffee and not shit, lots of eggs, free range, lovely orange yolks. I'm just scrambling some but I always make too much so you're welcome to share. Sit, I'll serve.'

'Thank you, more than I deserve,' said Marsha.

'Why?'

'I can't imagine what state I was in yesterday. I keep getting flashbacks and all of them are grim.'

'You got pissed. Understandable, your mother has just died and you're in a weird no-man's land.'

'Thanks,' said Marsha with a thin smile, as Annis put down a coffee in front of her.

'And drinking brandy plus grief is bound to make you want to try and shag a gardener. I must say Eric is incredibly good-looking close up so who would blame you?' Annis laughed as Marsha put her head into her hands.

'God, no,' Marsha said under her breath. 'It really happened.'

'It's fine. He didn't go to the police, you'll face no charges for sexual assault. What did happen was that he brought his mug back to the house and asked if you were all right. You only tried to snog him, apparently, and he rather chivalrously took the blame. He said he might have given you wrong signals. Boy does he deserve a seat at the round table.'

Marsha picked up the mug of coffee and let it warm her hands. She needed that warmth to sink into her and defrost her bones.

'He didn't give me any signals. I just told him he was gorgeous and looped my arms around his neck while he was sat on a box. That much I do remember, in glorious technicolour. And he unlooped them far more politely than I deserved. After that it's a blank.' Marsha groaned.

'Don't deserve a lot, do you?' said Annis, putting four slices of fresh, thick-cut granary bread into the toaster. 'You don't deserve scrambled eggs or coffee or young gardeners being gentlemen.'

'I don't behave like this. It's not me,' said Marsha.

Annis wondered what her sister did behave like. She had a great curiosity to know this present version of her.

'You were proper sick in the sink. I'm surprised you didn't throw up a lung,' Annis said with glee.

'Oh, please don't.'

'How's your bonce?'

'Better than I—' She cut off what she was about to say to avoid the risk of sounding like a stuck record. 'I don't know how I escaped a hangover.'

'I made you have some ibuprofen and water,' said Annis. 'That's how.'

'Did you? Thank you.'

The toaster popped and Annis buttered then spooned a golden mountain of egg onto each slice.

'Here you go,' she said, bringing the plates over. 'That'll be either kill or cure.'

It smelt like cure. The aroma of buttery eggs curled up Marsha's nostrils and hit her 'oh yeah' nerve.

'Eric said you were upset,' said Annis, through a mouthful.

'It's nothing.'

'Must be if you drank half a bottle of Mother's best cognac.'

Marsha had her head down but Annis saw the single tear slide down her sister's cheek before she dashed it away.

'If you want to talk . . .' Annis offered.

'I don't.' It came out as a snap and Marsha apologised immediately. 'I'm sorry.'

'It's cool. Eat.' Annis had no right to demand secret-sharing, though she'd wondered if Eric had misheard *Gerald* for *Gerard*. Surely he wasn't still a tenant in her sister's heart?

'Tell me about Jolene's husband,' she asked after she'd swallowed a few mouthfuls. 'What's he like?'

'He's got his own company, water filt—'

'I know, she told me but what's he *like*?'

Marsha chewed on her breakfast but Annis could see the cogs behind her eyes whirring.

'I don't really know him. I've only seen him a handful of times.'

Annis pressed her. 'And what did you think when you did see him? Presumably you went to the wedding.'

Marsha humphed. 'I think the whole county went to the wedding. It was huge. Total waste of money. Jolene didn't even look as if she was enjoying herself. Mum had a hat the size of a satellite dish and her outfit cost more than Jolene's dress. Loads of people she didn't even know went because they were friends of Mum and Dad. Country house reception, grey suits and top hats as far as the eye could see.'

'Were you a bridesmaid? Did I miss out on a pink satin frock?'

'Aquamarine,' Marsha came back. 'One of Jolene's friends at the time refused to be one because there was a strictly no child stipulation and she took umbrage. And Mum wasn't budging on it.'

Annis weighed that up. 'Didn't Jolene have a say in her own wedding?'

'Not if she wasn't paying for it. That's the impression I got anyway. It was the perfect day – for Mum, at least. Even the sun came out as commanded.'

'Did Mum and Dad like Warren?'

'They must have or I'd have heard. I think he thought they liked him anyway. He was very charming and disarming. Although ... Mum once dropped a comment about him being *glib*, I think was the word she used.' Marsha tried to think back. 'Yes, that was it. I was here with Jolene for Mum's sixty-fifth birthday, even though she insisted it was just another day and we shouldn't have bothered. Out of nowhere Mum said that she'd always found Warren terribly glib. Jolene was rather hurt, as I recall.'

'So, what you're telling me is that she hadn't changed.'

'No, I don't think she had. I don't think age mellowed or worsened her. But then she saw things logically and not emotionally, didn't she? There was no hoodwinking her, she was putty in no one's hands.'

Annis nodded. Very little got past their mother because her sight was not hampered by sentiment. She was, by nature, a creature with pure basic instincts: survival and self-preservation being uppermost.

'She maintained her ability to be caustic right to the end. And if I'm being honest . . .' Marsha paused as if she was in two minds whether to say her next words or not, then decided she would. 'I don't like Warren and I don't know why. There's just something about him . . . He's polite, smart, he dresses well, he's tall, fifties film star look if you know what I mean. But . . . but I just get the feeling he's . . . hiding behind himself, if that makes any sense. That he's a lake that runs very deep.' She waved away such nonsense. 'I'm being unfair, I don't know him well enough to judge. I do know that a few years ago Jolene lost a load of weight and looked terrible. I have no idea what that was about; she wasn't ill, but she changed, in the same way – and this is going to sound odd I know – but in the same way Dad changed after you left, as if something had been ripped out of her. I'd bet anything they had marriage problems. She's never quite been the same since, there's something . . . *missing* in her. Just like Dad.' She shrugged, held up her hands. 'I could be talking out of my bumhole of course, it's just a feeling.'

'Didn't you ask her?'

'Yes, but we aren't very good in this family about giving ourselves away, are we? Too afraid of coming out of the kennel in case we get kicked,' replied Marsha. She lifted her shoulders and dropped them heavily. 'If it was a blip, they rode it out and are still together. Maybe my imagination is too overactive. They've got nice cars and a big house, successful businesses. She's gorgeous, he's a dish. As a couple, they have it all really.'

Annis carried on eating, but as she knew only too well, some men had it all and still wanted more. They never quite got to the stage where they were satisfied.

Chapter 24

Sally darted out of the house as soon as she saw Jolene's car pull up in the Vamplews' drive. She ran over with her little mousy scuttle, waving and shouting.

'Is it today when your mum has the ... the ... post-mortem?' she asked.

'Yes, Sally,' replied Jolene.

'When will they tell you the results?'

'I presume in a couple of days,' said Jolene, popping the boot to get out her luggage and the shopping. 'I'll be sure to let you know. And we've made a start on boxing things up, so I'll bring you the locket when I find it.' It had slipped her mind until that moment; she must get that sorted.

'Thank you,' said Sally. 'I hope you don't mind me asking, I don't want to be a pest.'

'Of course not,' said Jolene.

Sally's brow creased. 'It's quite early to be packing things up, isn't it?'

That needled Jolene and it showed in her tone.

'It's a big house, Sally, and we—'

'Oh, I didn't mean anything by that. I'm so sorry if I caused offence. I really didn't mean to.'

Jolene cut her off before she went on ad infinitum. Sally looked on the verge of tears and she wasn't in the mood for her histrionics. Her brain was overloaded as it was.

'You didn't, Sally,' though the tenor very much insinuated that she did.

Sally pointed to Jolene's large suitcase and the two bags of shopping. 'Looks like you're planning to stay a while.'

'Yes,' said Jolene. 'For as long as it takes.'

'Up here,' called Marsha, when she heard Jolene's 'Hello, hello.'

'I'll just put this shopping away first,' Jolene shouted back. She saw that someone had already bought coffee and eggs. Nice eggs though, large free range, not the small, cheaper ones from battery farms that her mother bought. She'd had an omelette at home before setting off; Warren had made them. They'd sat at the dining table together and he'd said, 'Well, this is nice, isn't it? We don't do it enough, do we, having breakfast together.' And she'd wanted to ask him how often he had breakfast with *her* and if he cooked her fluffy omelettes in the morning after making love to her at night and telling her he loved her. But instead she'd smiled and said, 'Yes, it is nice,' and wondered which of them would win the Oscar for best acting.

He might have been telling the truth; he was good, credible but the doubt was always there and worms begat worms. Had he been unfaithful before he had confessed? Or were the first five years of her marriage a solid oasis in the middle of a quicksand that was waiting to engulf her?

He hadn't mentioned the will again, but only because

he'd retreated in order to regroup, decide on his next offensive. She didn't know what it would be, only that he hadn't given up, because that wasn't how he rolled and Warren didn't like things not going his way. They tended to because he made it so. When things *really* upset him, he imploded, internalising the problem to transform it into a fuel.

The last time it had happened was about three years ago. She'd tried to prise out of him what was making him crunch his teeth as he slept, but he told her in no uncertain terms to stop asking because she wouldn't like the answer. She knew what that meant; it was something to do with his 'other life', the 'outlet' she'd agreed he could have in a weak moment and he'd told her that she could not change her mind once she'd given him her permission to 'do what he had to'.

The irony was that it was he who needed her onside, his golden goose. The way they both behaved in this marriage would suggest otherwise. If she left him, he'd be up shit creek without his paddle. Maybe he'd be the one to leave her, now that her inheritance wasn't what he was expecting. That should have made her elated, that he might finally make the decision she was too scared to make. But he had whittled at her confidence with sly scrapes of his knife for years; she'd barely noticed her self-esteem being peeled away bit by bit, letting him convince her that no one else would have her and that she would never survive alone. Then again, her success was growing with every book and he wasn't going to untether a cash cow with a bounteous supply of milk. She prayed for something to make her find her backbone and act.

She knew if she'd had a friend to confide in, she might have been supported enough to break away. Friends had dropped off over the years, they'd moved to places new or had families and their boats, once moored close to hers, had drifted off to other seas. Writing was no longer the lonely profession it used to be thanks to social media, but some authors embraced it more than others. She didn't like it, found it intrusive. She used it to share posts about her new books, but nothing more than that. She found it false, all those shiny lives, all those tweaked photographs. She could almost smell what lay underneath their public image. *Appearance is everything.* It was so important to present that perfect face to the world. She'd had enough of all that to last her a lifetime. Especially as one who had left the frying pan for the fire.

In her books women said to other women, *How can you put up with this? What are you getting from it?* The women in her stories picked up a suitcase and walked out, shedding their dysfunctional lives like old snakeskin because they knew they could rebuild once they were out of there, from nothing if needs be. They stopped being moths burning their wings against the flame just because they were too used to doing it. They didn't care that they'd be crucified financially; their happiness was more important, as was their survival.

Jolene put the shopping away and bent down to give John Abruzzi some flat-leaf parsley from a packet she'd bought for him. He gave it a tentative sniff and then dived straight in. He was a lovely creature; she would have liked a cat or a rescue dog keeping her company as she wrote, but Warren was allergic – or so he said, anyway; she had no proof of that. She tried to stroke the rabbit but he shrank back from her. She couldn't even befriend a flaming bunny, she thought as she made her way upstairs.

A lot of their parents' bedroom was in boxes and black bin liners now.

'Goodness, you have been busy,' said Jolene. 'What else have I missed?'

'Marsha tried to hump the gardener,' said Annis.

'You did not!' exclaimed Jolene, but Marsha's horrified expression said everything.

Annis broke into laughter. 'Don't you think it's about time this place had some merriment in it?' She sighed and looked around the room. 'It's such a shame, it's a beautiful house and yet we've all made it very unhappy.'

'What do you mean?' asked Jolene.

'I mean it's a family house, meant for kids to play hide and seek in all the nooks and crannies and have music and noise. It always felt like a different house when Mum and Dad had their parties; it warmed up, as if it liked having people in it.'

Jolene gave a small start. 'I thought that was just me who felt that.'

Marsha had felt it too. She'd written a poem about it in one of her diaries. She wished she'd kept them, but she'd burned them after reading them and crying again at the sad girl she was, pouring out her unhappy, mixed-up, mangled heart onto the pages.

'I felt like an only child growing up,' Annis confessed.

'I *was* an only child for the first seven years,' said Jolene.

'Then I came along and ruined it,' said Marsha.

'I was so looking forward to having a little ... sister,' said Jolene, not meaning to leave a pause before the word, but Marsha leapt on it.

'Brother, you mean. You can say it.'

Jolene sighed. 'She told everyone she was carrying a boy. I think maybe she thought if she believed it enough it would happen. That was usually the case. I was all hyped up for a brother. The thought of a sister would have put me on edge, I'd have seen you as a rival.'

'She once told me that I should have been a boy,' said Marsha. 'I can't remember the circumstances, but I do remember her saying it quite coldly and it cut me to the bone. _You should have been a boy._ I knew exactly what she meant: that I was an abject disappointment, not what she'd wanted.'

'Is that why you once cut all your hair off?' asked Jolene.

'Did you?' said Annis, though she knew this from reading Marsha's diary.

'Yes,' said Marsha. 'I thought she would love me more if I became one. She didn't, I just got slapped really hard for being stupid.'

'She liked to slap, didn't she?' said Annis, recalling the sting of her mother's whip-like hand. 'She once slapped me so many times I think she forgot how to stop. I had hand-prints all over my legs. She kept me off school the next day. I think she was afraid I'd bruise.' Even at that age, Annis had realised her mother was slapping at something other than her behaviour. But her physical punishment didn't hurt half as much as her words could.

'I made her ill because I wasn't male, she told me,' said Marsha.

'She had post-natal depression. It was medical. It was nothing to do with the fact that you weren't a boy.'

Jolene said it for her sister's sake, but she didn't believe the words coming out of her own mouth. And Marsha didn't believe them either.

'If I _had_ been born a boy, would it have made that much difference? I often wonder.'

'You should stop wondering.' Annis taped shut a full box of clothes. 'Dad would have been too busy for him and

Mum would have got pissed off with him. She couldn't love anything or anyone. Whatever connection she had with Dad, it wasn't love.' She wrote LADIES WEAR on the side with a thick pen.

'I remember you coming home from the hospital,' said Jolene to Marsha. 'After the initial horror, I was fascinated by you. You were just perfect.'

Marsha gave a hoot of laughter. 'That's the first and last time I've been called that.'

'Beattie Rogers warned me that sometimes ladies who had babies got a bit sad and I was to be a good girl,' said Jolene, remembering the pep talk.

'Who's that?' asked Annis.

'Glenda's mum. She was our cleaner back then and our childminder. I vaguely remember a couple of live-in nannies but they never stayed very long – surprise, surprise – so Mum used Beattie quite a lot when we were little,' explained Jolene.

'She was a lovely woman, soft, quite bouncy.' Marsha smiled. The few memories she had of Beattie were of a kind and caring woman with a gentle, Welsh voice. 'When they had dinner parties she'd help Mum with the cooking and tidying up like Glenda did.'

They all remembered the dinner parties, hearing their parents entertaining friends, laughter drifting up the stairs, their father on top form, their mother reaping the praise for her cuisine, their dazzling personas to the fore. Their veneers.

'I loved Beattie,' said Jolene. 'She taught me how to play patience and solitaire and knit.'

As soon as she said it, she expected a sarcastic response from Annis, who surprised her.

'I knit. One of the girls I worked with taught me. We'd sit and knit in quiet times.'

'It doesn't sound like your traditional cocktail bar,' noted Marsha.

'My boss didn't mind, the customers didn't mind.'

A picture came into her head of her perched behind the bar, knitting a lime-green jumper on huge needles, talking to their regulars. Barry had worked on the royal yacht, *Britannia* and Arthur had been a boxer in his youth. They had fascinating stories and funny anecdotes and she enjoyed listening to them. Such full young lives drained to empty old lives.

Annis picked up another blouse to fold. It was beige chiffon and she thought she remembered her mum wearing it, or certainly one very like it. As in all her memories of her, her mother was either standing or sitting with a disapproving countenance. She couldn't ever recall her mother smiling at her once.

Glenda the cleaner arrived just as they had finished for the day, carrying a long box with a drawing of flowers on the side.

'There's a vase as well. You can never have too many at times like this,' she said. She was visibly upset and wouldn't come in. 'End of an era,' she went on, after blowing her nose on a tissue. 'When you're ready to sell, I'll do the place top to bottom for you. No charge. It's the least I can do for your mum giving me the job for all these years.' She smiled tearfully at Jolene and Marsha, a smile that closed by degrees when she spotted Annis.

'You came back, then,' she said to her, adding pointedly, 'for this one.'

'I did, Glenda.' A smile from Annis in return, but one of her smaller, polite ones. 'It's nice to see you again. Hope you've been keeping well.'

Glenda snapped her attention away from Annis and back to her sisters. 'Right then, I'll not keep you. You will let me know when the funeral is, won't you?'

'Of course,' said Jolene.

When they shut the door on her Annis pulled a face.

'Goodness. If looks could kill,' she said. 'Mind you, Glenda always did see me as the spoilt brat in constant trouble. Then I go and give my parents all that hassle by running off, the ingrate that I am.'

'Why did you go really, Annis?' asked Marsha. 'It was impossible not to worry about you when there was no trace of you.'

'It's not that hard to fly under the radar when you want to. Cash-in-hand jobs, and I have no desire to share pictures of my dinners with strangers on social media sites.'

'You were always on my mind, Annis,' said Jolene. 'If only I'd known life here was so sad for you that you had to run away.'

Annis batted her concern aside. She didn't want to go there. 'It's done, I'm back.' She didn't say that it wasn't sadness that had made her pack a rucksack, but anger, bitterness, panic.

Marsha headed towards the kitchen. 'I'll put the kettle on.'

'Sod the kettle, let's raid the cellar,' said Annis.

Marsha went downstairs to pick a bottle and as her eyes roved over the choices, she wondered how hard her parents truly had tried to find Annis. It was a question to which she wasn't sure she wanted the answer.

*

'I've never enjoyed Beaujolais much before but this isn't half bad,' said Marsha, appraising the wine in her glass. Then she addressed Annis specifically: 'I won't be knocking it back, so don't worry.'

'I wouldn't leave anyone in a pool of their own sick. Well, maybe one or two,' replied Annis.

Jolene laughed. 'You have such a way with words.' She barely knew this woman who was her sister but she liked her. She was so different from the pouty teenager she remembered. She'd envied her confidence, thought that it must have come from being loved so much more than either she or Marsha had been. At least by their father. He'd doted on her, maybe even been somewhat over-protective towards her. She recalled hearing how furious he'd been when she went to the pictures with a boy without asking permission, when he hadn't worried about his elder daughters doing that at the same age. But still Jolene felt the guilt of envying her young spoilt sister who had clearly been deeply unhappy under all her brazenness.

'In actual fact, you could barely walk but you still managed to get to the sink to vom without spilling a drop on the floor. Most impressive.' Annis chuckled.

'Please don't,' said Marsha, still burning from the consequences of her over-liquidation. She tore into a garlic naan bread. They'd ordered in an Indian banquet for three and the table legs were almost buckling with the weight of food that was laid out on it.

'This is nice,' said Jolene suddenly, feeling a glow as if someone had turned on a halogen heater inside her for a second. 'Us talking and being together.'

'That's always been the trouble in this house,' said Annis, as the others looked to her for enlightenment. So she enlightened them. 'No one ever talked. We were all afraid of showing a soft underbelly because it might be used against us. I've thought a lot about it over the years.'

Marsha tried not to look back but the past bled into her present life all too often. Jolene didn't think she did, but her memories crept out onto the page and pretended to be fiction.

'You were the only child for seven years,' said Annis, poking her fork in Jolene's direction, 'then along comes Mashed Potato here and I'll bet there was no gentle introduction, only a feeling of *Get off the stage, Jolene, you're banished to the wings now.* So the little sister who you probably want to love becomes your enemy, the competition, there's a barrier between you. Then along I come, the *baby*. Another girl, another rival.' She rolled her eyes heavenward. 'Need I go on? Oh, did you know that I was a mistake? I grew quietly inside her, giving her no symptoms and she only knew she was pregnant once it was too late to flush me out. Otherwise I wouldn't be here now, soaking up all the inheritance. I bet she spent loads of time in hot baths drinking gin.'

'Who told you that nonsense?' said Jolene, though she knew it was true because she'd heard her mother say it; but it hurt her to think that Annis was aware of it.

'It's fine, I'm over it. She told me to my face I was a mistake. Right after she'd been dragged into school by Miss Houstell for something I hadn't even done. But that old cow had it in for me. I'm only surprised she didn't try and blame me for the Iraq war.'

Miss Houstell had had it in for Marsha, too. There was obviously some element of jealousy in play because she made a few sly digs about being privileged and rich. But

Marsha had taken it lying down while Annis had retaliated. Then again, at their school you could be hanged for a curled lip of insolence. She wondered if Miss Houstell ever thought she just might have contributed to Annis Vamplew's disappearance.

'What made you get so drunk, Marsha?' asked Jolene softly, expecting her sister to mutter something to close down that conversation.

'Just being back here, it's bringing a lot of memories to the surface. I didn't know I had so many stored,' was the reply. It was true, she didn't. Sometimes she was astounded at how few memories she had of her childhood, as if she'd stuffed them all in cupboards so as not to think about them, but some of them had managed to break free this past week nonetheless. And she wanted to put them back, but they had expanded too much for that. How sad and lonely she'd been, sitting in her room scoffing chocolate to make her feel better, then getting plump and feeling worse and buying more chocolate. A dreadful cycle she couldn't break.

Jolene reached over and gave her hand a fleeting squeeze, as if her head had suddenly grown transparent and her sister could see her pain and wanted to take it away from her. A small, sweet gesture that spoke of great understanding.

Eleanor

You read in the newspapers about women who only learn they are pregnant in the second trimester, without any symptoms or visible signs before then. I always thought that was nonsense. With the first two, I was sick almost from the moment they came into existence but with you, you crept up on me by stealth. An accident. You sat inside me growing, like a tumour; waiting, like a bomb. And when I did find out, you made your presence known with every negative symptom you could muster. I was so sick, so ill, so limp. Like a portent of the havoc you were to cause in my life. It was as if you hated me from the off, resented your coming into being yet ironically, you would not leave my body (and yes, I'm afraid I did try to be rid of you) and had to be cut out. Screaming and long, they were going to place you in my arms but instead your father held you first. Another girl. But you bewitched him from the off.

Chapter 25

They were all up early the next morning, checking out the massive attic which was thankfully clear of everything but a few large cardboard boxes and a large wooden trunk that looked like something a pirate might have. Annis remembered it as being much fuller, with storage bags of summer clothes when it was winter and vice versa, boxes of their father's book drafts and papers, things her mother had grown tired of and wanted out of sight but wasn't quite ready to permanently discard.

'I used to come up here and dress in Mum's shoes and gowns and parade in front of that huge cheval mirror,' said Annis. 'She had long strings of pearls in the drawer at the bottom of it and all those hats in boxes.'

'So did I,' said Marsha. 'Then she caught me once and slapped my legs and I didn't do it again.'

Annis laughed. 'She caught me and slapped me too but I kept coming back.'

'I never came up here because I was told not to,' said Jolene.

'Goody two shoes.' Annis grinned at her.

'In fact,' Jolene went on, 'when Dad died and Mum decided she wanted to clear it, it still felt weird coming up here.'

'What did she keep then that was so important? Let's see,' said Annis, pushing back the lid of the trunk to find, carefully wrapped in black tissue paper, a black dress and jacket. Shoes and a bag wrapped separately, a hat with a veil stored there too, all black.

'It's what she wore to Dad's funeral,' said Jolene, recognising it immediately. 'Most of this is Chanel. It must have cost her a fortune. She wanted to say goodbye to him in style.' They'd have to sell the ensemble rather than donate it to charity: it was worth thousands.

'I wonder if they loved each other,' said Marsha suddenly. 'I mean I only ever saw them being affectionate to each other when they held their parties. I never saw them kiss, though I suppose they must have.'

'We weren't immaculate conceptions,' said Annis.

'I think Mum was a narcissist. That's why she had all the parties, because she craved admiration. And it sounds really bad' – Marsha dropped the volume of her words as if she felt ashamed of what she was about to say – 'but I sometimes wonder if it was the love of the lifestyle that kept them together more than affection. He had the kudos but she had so much more money than Dad did, and this house, all in her name.'

'Do people really stay together for money?' asked Annis.

Jolene didn't answer.

The other boxes yielded more clothes, gowns both elegant and glittering, never worn. It was as if their mother had an obsession, like a magpie, coveting beautiful dresses. Jolene wondered if buying them was like a drug, giving her mother a high of short-lived pleasure to offset unhappiness, because her husband had died or her daughter would not come home – an attempt to fill up an emptiness within.

'Oh my, look, the dressing-up box,' said Marsha, taking the very dusty lid off a large container. 'Why on earth did she keep this?'

'She didn't, I did,' said Jolene. 'I couldn't quite bring myself to throw it away so I left it up here. I meant to come back up and have a proper look in it but I forgot all about it.'

Marsha took the top item out, a white satin dress and shook the folds from it. All three girls had played with this old wedding dress. Jolene seemed to remember that Sally had found it in a church jumble sale and brought it home for them.

'I married Dad in this once,' said Jolene. She smiled, then remembered how keen she was to secure his affections after Marsha came along. No one had bothered to tell her that hearts expanded to include new babies without having to eject anyone to make way for them, but she wasn't sure that was true in her case anyway. She was simply banished to a cold, lonely hinterland where seeds of resentment grew like Japanese knotweed, fed and watered by emotional starvation.

'I can't imagine Dad playing those sorts of games with us,' said Marsha incredulously.

'I can only remember that one instance,' said Jolene. 'The hallway was the aisle and I'd positioned him by the front door. I walked up it slowly humming the bridal chorus. I remember him laughing at me.'

The memory was dipped in rose-coloured paint, she knew this, but it was still precious because it was rare for their father to give such intense attention to her and it came at a time when she really needed it. The new baby was so delicate and angelic fair and she felt big and gawky and so ordinary by comparison. Her new sister had the same colouring as their mother and so by deduction, their father was going to love her the best. She could taste the tang of desperation again in her mouth, bitter and metallic.

'Apparently women use their fathers as a template for picking their mates,' said Marsha. 'Is that what you did with Warren?'

'Maybe,' replied Jolene. Both tall, dark, handsome, charismatic. Then again she'd been drawn to him mainly because he showered her with affection. Maybe she'd always known, on a subconscious level, he would withdraw it and she'd be on the begging end of that relationship too.

Annis also remembered wearing the dress. Remembered wanting to marry her father and leave her mother behind.

We can go away together. Some place no one knows us. Just the two of us.

She cut off the memory before it consumed her and pushed the dress into a bag destined for the dump.

'Dear god, why did she keep this?' asked Jolene, opening up a small plastic carrier bag, taking out something small and pink.

A strange silence fell upon them; they all knew what it was. The sight of it dragged them all back through a wormhole: Jolene to her bedroom, writing a university assignment; Marsha and Annis to Sally's garden. Annis had the pink costume on; she would have been five at most. No one could remember what Marsha was wearing, because she was incidental to the story. Sally had made buns for them with Jelly Tots on the top, and there was a jug of over-diluted orange squash. There was a small inflatable paddling pool with sun-warmed water in it set on the grass, which looked strange and wobbly through the haze of heat rising from the ground. Then the clouds drew across the sun and it was time for the fun to stop.

Jolene couldn't remember why her father was up in her room but they were looking through the window at Sally's garden, at Norman drying Annis with a towel, her wet costume on the ground beside her.

Jolene remembered her father thundering down the stairs and outside, and following him, picking up their mother in the stream who had been alerted by the alacrity of her husband's pace. She remembered how he broke through the low conifers that separated their gardens. She remembered the expression on her father's face as his fist flew back. She remembered the blood, Norman pleading, Sally screaming, Eleanor Vamplew trying to take control of her husband as he bellowed at the man crouched on the grass, '*Don't you ever so much as fucking look at my daughter again.*'

Annis remembered her mother dragging her by the arm across the grass when she should have picked her up and carried her.

As if all three had been watching the replay on a screen, Jolene sighed and said, 'What a weird day that was.'

'I'll say,' added Marsha.

'Do you think Norman was ... odd like that?' Jolene didn't say the word that came first to her mind, but her meaning was clear.

'Dad certainly did,' replied Marsha with a small humourless laugh. 'He despised violence, so he must have had a reason for posting Norman's nose in an easterly direction.' A snake of revulsion wriggled down her spine. 'I have no idea why Mum kept this but let's throw it away, shall we?' She stuffed the small pink costume in the dump bag and wished she could stuff the accompanying memories in there as well. She'd been totally freaked out by what she'd witnessed: a part of her father she couldn't recognise, because it didn't fit with the father she loved. It had scared her enough to have nightmares for weeks.

Life had changed for them after that incident. The gardener was instructed not to cut the tops of the conifers any more but to let them grow up, Sally was tarred with the same brush as her husband and her friendship with Eleanor came to an abrupt end. Her calls were not answered, her attempts at doorstepping to make amends ignored. The children were no longer to go round there to bake or paint or play with all the toys and games she had bought in for them. Norman and his broken nose stayed out of their way.

'Do you think Sally knew? Is that why they never had kids of their own?' asked Marsha.

'I don't know if there was anything to know,' replied Annis.

'He was quite creepy, though, wasn't he. That dyed combover and his horrible criss-crossed teeth.'

There were worse monsters, thought Annis. The ones without the warning flags of bad hair and dodgy dentristy. They were the ones you had to watch out for.

They were just heading down the stairs when Jolene's mobile rang: Ian from the coroner's office.

'We have the results of the post-mortem back and I thought I should let you know right away, because it's a worrying time and I appreciate you are waiting.'

'Thank you,' said Jolene. 'I've got you on speaker so my sisters can hear.' Her jaw felt tight with tension, her mouth dry.

'We have the cause of death now: a cardiac arrest.'

'A heart attack?' said Jolene.

'Not quite the same,' said Ian. 'We didn't find a clot or build-up that would prevent blood from passing through to the heart. Who knows why they sometimes just stop beating without warning; it's rare, but it happens. A shock, an accumulation of stress, maybe it just stopped working. We can't pinpoint a specific reason, alas.'

'Right,' said Jolene, her head spinning.

'You are entitled to a copy of the full post-mortem report if you would like to receive it. I would warn you that it could be upsetting and may contain things that you wouldn't wish to read.'

Jolene looked to her sisters and noticed the unconscious shaking of their heads.

'Thank you, but I don't think we need to see that,' she answered him.

'I'm very sorry for your loss. You will be able to arrange a funeral now. I'll send the form electronically to the registrar so you can register your mum's death and get the certificate. I'll do that today and they'll be in contact with you. I'll forward them your details. Are you having your mother cremated or buried?'

'Cremated,' said Jolene without hesitation.

'Okay. Then you can go ahead and arrange that.' Ian's voice carried kindness and sensitivity in it. 'Are you clear about what to do next?'

'Yes, I've made a list,' Jolene answered.

'Is there anything else I can help you with?'

'No, that's ... that's all. Thank you for letting us know so quickly.'

'I don't like to keep people hanging around,' said Ian. 'I

know first-hand how even the small periods of waiting can feel torturous.'

'Thank you, Ian.' Jolene disconnected the call, then she gave a heavy sigh. 'Well, that's that then. Cardiac arrest.' She felt tears rise inside her and pushed them down.

'*Was* she stressed?' Marsha asked, doubt heavy in her question.

'Maybe she was worrying about those pains she'd put down to indigestion and created a self-fulfilling prophecy. I should have rung the doctor and spoken to him about it.' Jolene growled at herself.

'Stop that now,' Annis's voice was firm.

'She'd have gone bonkers if you'd done that,' said Marsha. 'And the doctor probably wouldn't have spoken to you anyway. Patient confidentiality and all that.'

'I totally agree,' said Annis, hoping their two-pronged attack would wipe that desolate look from Jolene's face.

'I hate to play devil's advocate, but what if Sally walking into her bedroom in the middle of the night was what did the damage after all?' asked Marsha.

'Oh no, we can't load her with that. Especially if we don't know it for sure,' said a horrified Jolene.

Marsha looked deep in thought. 'I thought she said that Mum's face was all twisted up.'

'Mash, she was obviously in a state of panic. Her brain must have been playing tricks,' Annis said. 'The bottom line is that we don't know and we'll never know what caused it. Maybe, as the coroner said, there was *no* reason for it and her heart just stopped like a broken clock.' A fitting end for their mother, a mystery to the last.

Jolene's hands were in prayer position at her mouth. 'I promised I'd tell Sally as soon as I heard.'

'It can wait,' said Annis. 'Let's digest all this ourselves first.' At that moment, she sounded the oldest and wisest of them by far.

Chapter 26

Jolene wanted to get on with the funeral arrangements now they had the results of the post-mortem. Marsha thought she'd nip home and check everything was all right with her house and pick up some things now it was full steam ahead. And Annis rang Daz Meynell's number and asked if he had time for a visitor bearing sandwiches. The tone of his voice said that even if he'd been in the middle of having his appendix out, he'd have said he was free. Daz said the Sarnie Shop on the High Street did nice ones so Marsha dropped her off there and she loaded up with lunch. Daz's garage was easy to find and was a bigger place than she'd been expecting. There were a couple of cars for sale in the front and a youth, yet to grow into his gawky limbs, was washing them with a sponge and a bucket.

On her approach she could see Daz through the large front window leaning on a reception desk, talking to the woman behind it. As she walked in, the woman flicked her eyes quickly up and down the tall, slim visitor with the short shock of red-blonde hair and the lips which *surely* had been puffed up with injections by someone who really knew what they were doing. Annis was used to being assessed. So long as all they did was look.

Daz's face split into a grin. 'Annis, come through,' he said, marshalling her forward and behind reception to his office. He had a little gold plaque on the door with black writing saying simply 'Daz' and she thought that might be as corporate as he got.

'Sorry about the mess,' he said. There was none, but she would bet his office wasn't quite so tidy up to half an hour ago.

'Hope you don't mind,' she said. 'I just felt like a break from ... things.'

'I don't mind at all. How's it all going?' he asked.

'We've been waiting for the post-mortem result and it appears Mum died of a cardiac arrest.'

'Ah, I'm sorry.'

'I didn't realise she had a heart if I'm honest.' She immediately apologised. 'Sorry, that's not really appropriate, is it.'

'You don't have to pretend with me,' said Daz. 'I've always been a say-it-as-you-see-it bloke and I like it when other people are the same. Saves having to wade through bullshit.'

Annis reached into her rucksack and put all her purchases on his desk.

'Cheese and red onion, beef and horseradish, egg mayo, BLT; I didn't know what you liked.'

'All of them.' Daz whistled. 'And crisps, too.'

'And drinks.' She put four different bottles on the desk also, along with the four packs of crisps.

'Are we expecting visitors?' asked Daz and smiled.

'I'm not sure I have enough here for me, never mind you,' she replied. 'I eat like a horse. I may not look as if I do.'

'I love a girl who can put it away,' said Daz. 'You choose first.'

Annis picked up the cheese, unwrapped the cling film, bit down hard on the sandwich.

'I joined the army to please my mum,' said Daz. 'She said I'd never amount to anything. I wanted to prove her wrong so much. I'm not sure I did. Then again, I don't think I'd have made her proud if I'd turned up on her doorstep as a Field Marshal. Some people only get pleasure from not getting any pleasure.'

Annis stopped chewing. She cleared her mouth and said, 'That's it, that's just what Mum was like. What makes someone like that?'

'She was only like that with me though. My brother was on a pedestal so high, he had a permanent case of altitude sickness,' quipped Daz, unwrapping the beef.

'What's your brother do?'

'He's a reporter with the *Daily Trumpet* now. She used to buy every newspaper he ever wrote a piece in, just to show off his byline to everyone and their dog.'

'That the paper that's always apologising for goofs?'

'The very same.' Daz nodded. 'They're not deliberate either, which goes to show what calibre of reporter they go for.'

'You close?'

'Not any more. He raided the house when Mum died, took anything of value so I wouldn't get my hands on it. I was choosing her flowers at the undertaker's and he was unscrewing the lightbulbs. That's the sort of relationship we have and I cannot get my head around that level of greed. We haven't spoken since the funeral. I was quite surprised when Mum left everything to be split between us. He and I both thought he was copping for the lot, as golden bollocks. Not that she left a lot. Mum made me sole executor of her will, so she must have trusted me more than him. I took a bit of comfort from that. Money and wills. People really show their true colours where they're concerned. One minute they're crying their eyes out that their so-called loved one has gone, the next they're scrapping over who's getting the spatula.'

Annis gave a small laugh, though she was yet to witness the fallout in her case. It had all gone smoothly for her so far but it couldn't last. The bomb in her family was just sitting there too stunned to go off for now, but it was bound to make its presence known in due course. Her mother had surprised her as much as Daz's mother had surprised him, it seems; made some effort at reparation without being quite brave enough to do it when they were still alive. The parallels between them were mounting up.

'I hope you took off what he owed you for all the stuff he swiped,' she said.

'I might have made a slight adjustment, mainly because he'd been such an arse,' said Daz. 'We used to be good mates. Inseparable as kids. I don't know what happened.'

Opposite of us then, thought Annis. It was early days, of course, and there was still plenty of time for her sisters to resort to dirty tricks; maybe they'd already been to see a solicitor about contesting the will behind her back. There was a lot of money at stake after all.

'The garage was my second stab at making Mum think that maybe I would amount to something after all.' Daz opened up a packet of crisps.

'And did it?'

'She never said so. Maybe if she had, I wouldn't have worked so hard to make a success of it.'

She got that, because her sisters had been exactly the same, pulling out every stop to earn the parental approval that would validate them.

'So you're rich, are you?' said Annis through her sandwich.

Even with a gobful of bread she looked classy, thought Daz. He felt not unlike his teenage self when the school 'It' girl had turned her light on him at the disco, even if it was only for the penultimate dance to a Whitesnake number.

'I'm doing all right,' he replied, careful not to brag. He'd been stung before by a woman liking his bank balance more than she liked him, not that Annis gave out the slightest vibe of being a gold-digger. He couldn't guess what her financial position was, but she dressed as if she could only afford clothes from a charity shop's bargain bucket and she still could out-beaut any woman he knew. This was only the third time he'd seen her and he was already in trouble.

'Are you and your sisters getting on okay? I think you said that you didn't really know each other all that well.'

'We are, strangely enough,' said Annis. 'But . . .' She jiggled her head, unsure of how best to say it, 'I don't think we quite trust each other yet. It's as if we're three mines and we're just tapping on each other's facework at present.'

'And what's buried in your mine?' asked Daz, reaching for the second half of his sandwich.

'I'm an open book, me,' said Annis. Probably her biggest lie to date.

Eleanor

You do remember that day, don't you? You wouldn't even begin to guess the fallout. I don't mean that Sally was no longer invited into the house. She was a kind woman, if vacuous. Norman, I'd never really liked. He was full of his own self-importance; he puffed up like a balloon in front of Julian, in the hope of being his equal, this silly little man who rooted out those defrauding the DSS while believing he was some sort of government spy. We used to call him James Bond behind his back. I remembered the binoculars he showed us once, how rabidly excited he was about them. I began to view everything through a different prism from that day onwards, as if the floor of my world had tip-tilted and I had to adjust madly to regain my equilibrium.

You may have found the pink swimming costume and wonder why I kept it. I didn't know at the time. And then again maybe I did.

Chapter 27

Jolene hadn't knocked on Sally's door for over twenty-six years. After the paddling pool incident, Norman and Sally were cancelled. Sally had written a letter to Eleanor saying that it was all a misunderstanding and Norman loved children, he would never harm them and could they put their friendship back on some footing, whatever it took to do that. But it seemed that Eleanor had taken the opportunity to divorce her too and did not respond, not even when Sally knocked on the door to sort it out between them. Christmas cards, birthday cards, Easter cards were not acknowledged, much less reciprocated. The Lunns were *personae non gratae* and they were lucky to be only that.

Sally had left Norman the year after and the house had gone up for sale. Their father stopped doing his skits about them in front of friends, his abhorrence of Norman visceral. Then, surprisingly, the *for sale* notice was removed and Sally was once again in residence. At some point, though, Eleanor and Sally must have reconciled, a secret coffee here and there probably. Jolene wondered if it was round about the time when their father was ill. That would have made sense, when her mother was in need. Sally had come to the funeral, though Norman didn't. He was starting to get ill himself then.

Their front garden was now all concrete flags, easier to maintain, though weeds were growing wild through the joints. The bench outside the lounge window looked like wood washed by the sea, grey and fragile. Once upon a time Norman had stained it every year and she had no idea why she remembered that. One of those bits of flotsam and jetsam that the mind retains, when it could remember so much more of value. The window frames, always pristine and white, were no longer kept to their once exacting standards. The Lunns were merely surviving, and as such their priorities had changed.

She knocked on the door because the bell button was hanging off and didn't look as if it was connected any more. She heard Sally's voice from the belly of the house shouting, 'I'm coming, I'm coming.' The door opened as far as the chain would allow, giving Jolene a slice of her, one eye widening as if she were a debt collector armed with a hammer. The door shut immediately and then opened again, freed from the chain.

'Hi Sally, I just came to—'

'Come in, Jolene, please,' Sally was out of sorts, doing that twitchy, twittering thing she was too renowned for.

Jolene didn't really want to but Sally was already heading down the hallway towards their kitchen so she had no choice but to follow. The house looked unaltered, a step back in time. It was always drab, in shades of browns and mustard, and dark thanks to its small windows. There was a faint air of fustiness, and a smell she associated with an old people's home.

Norman and Sally had been a source of much amusement to their parents. She remembered creeping down the stairs to listen to the conversation at their dinner parties drifting from the dining room. *What's the latest on the couple next door, Julian? Do tell us more about Lame Bond; has he caught any Russians forging their giros?* They'd all guffaw, fuelled with wine and cognac as their father would reenact a scene with the affected accent Norman used to put on when talking to them as if he were a lesser man bulling himself up to be an equal, and their mother would flutter around in the background doing an impression of Sally as a bird with too-fast moving wings, unsure of which direction to flit.

'Sorry I had to rush in then,' Sally explained. 'I can't leave Norman when he's in his chair, he rocks backwards if he gets agitated. And if you could sit out of his eyeline here, that would be good.' She was entirely made up of little tics and twitches and spasms. Jolene perched on the end of the seat at her kitchen table to be polite.

Norman Lunn was sitting in what could best be described as an adult, and lower, version of a child's high chair. A Tommee Tippee mug, in boy blue, sat on the tray in front of him next to a teaspoon and a small bowl of something pureed. He was dressed in a shirt, slacks and a cardigan. Norman would have had clean clothes on every day, pressed and aired, Jolene knew, and Sally would be doing her utmost to keep him clean through the day which was why he was also wearing a protective bib. His once-brown combover was white now, his eyes dull and flat, staring at the wall.

'He's having a good day today, aren't you love?' said Sally, giving his hand a rub. 'He's eaten well; he doesn't always.'

He and Julian Vamplew were the same age. Jolene momentarily wondered if it would have been better or worse to have her father still here, but like that, or gone. She felt the loss of him so acutely sometimes she thought she would have taken him any way as long as he was breathing and she could put her arms around him. She missed him so much. She missed the father he was at the end, the one he'd admitted that he should have been all her life. But no, she wouldn't have wanted him to be like this. Not a husk, a shell with nothing of him left inside.

'I won't stay, Sally, I've got a lot to do.'

'Of course you have.' Sally smiled and Jolene noticed the puffy bags under her eyes and the bubbles of angry spots all over her nose. She looked in a worse state than her husband.

'I just came to tell you that we've had the post–mortem and Mum had a heart attack, well cardiac arrest to be precise. Apparently there's a difference. It wasn't a blockage; her heart just stopped.'

Sally's body locked, as if a clockwork mechanism inside her had ground to a sudden halt. She sank onto the chair next to Jolene as if all the rigidity had left her bones.

'Oh my, did they say what caused it?' she asked.

Be careful, Jolene, warned an inner voice. Sally was the type to see blame where none was intended and absorb it, make it her own. The woman had enough on her plate as it was.

'Do you know if she was ... stressed about anything? I thought you'd know if anyone.'

'No, not that ... I'm aware of.' Sally started pulling at the long pointy collar of her blouse. 'I can't think ... of anything at all. I really can't. Do hearts just stop like that?'

'Apparently it's quite rare, but it happens. We'll never know why Mum's did. It could have been any number of factors I suppose.'

Sally nodded slowly. The blood seemed to have drained

from her face; she was as white as the nets that hung at her window. Jolene could almost see inside her head, trying to fathom out if she had any part in what had happened. That, they would never know. All she was sure of was that Sally would never do anything less than her best for her friend.

Norman made a noise and Jolene hoped that he wasn't a cognisant being trapped in that shell of a body, like the driving soft inner of a Dalek.

'He gets a bit ruffled when his peace is interrupted,' said Sally in a tone that suggested her initial welcome had run its course.

'Of course, Sally, I didn't want to take up your time. I just wanted to tell you about Mum. I'll let you know about the funeral. We can arrange one now.'

'Thank you,' said Sally, getting up to herd Jolene out.

'You know,' Sally said at the door, 'Norman was a good man. He would have made a lovely father if we'd been able to have children.'

Even after all these years, Sally was scarred by the accusation, still protesting his innocence into the wind. It was a savage charge to level at a man if other people believed it and it wasn't true. She had to have believed he was a man much maligned or she could never have stayed with him, could she?

Sally closed the door on Jolene and had to fight the urge to slide down it and stay there until she dissolved in a pool of her own tears, sank through the carpet, through the floorboards and evaporated into thin air. Eleanor's heart had stopped because of her and though no one could ever prove it, she *knew*. She had shocked her so much with the terrible words she had levelled at her that it had caused the switch to click to the off position in her heart. If only she'd read on to the end of the letter, where, on the last page, Eleanor said that Sally must have the locket, that it was a small gift compared to the gift of loyalty and friendship that she had so freely given. She knew the truth now, but what a price she and Norman had had to pay for it.

Chapter 28

'Why is it so much easier to talk to strangers than people you know?' Annis asked Daz.

'I was just thinking the same,' said Daz. 'You're very easy to talk to, Annis. Where did that name come from? It's so unusual.' It suited her perfectly, because she was unusual, confident without being self-absorbed, and beautiful. The name sounded like a flower. Something white with a soft scent. She would have thought he was a dick if he'd come out with that line so he kept it to himself.

'No idea,' she said. 'They must have just liked it. I didn't. When I left home I called myself other names. I was Annie for a while, then Red, then ... Mai, when I worked in the cocktail club. We were all named after drinks there; I was Mai Tai.'

'I'd really love to take you out to dinner,' said Daz then, without letting caution hinder him. 'If I can afford it. You seem like a girl who'd have all the courses and then cheese afterwards.'

Annis didn't answer immediately, but mulled it over.

'That sounds suspiciously like a date.'

'Not really,' said Daz with a shrug. 'Okay then, maybe it is. A little one.'

'Don't jump into the abyss, you're too nice,' said Annis, popping a crisp into her mouth.

'It would just be dinner. Somewhere chilled, a bistro maybe.'

'Can I be honest, Daz? I'm not the dating sort. I've been a fuck-up since the day I was born. I've done too many things that I'd end up having to hide or apologise for.'

He felt her slipping through his fingers, just as his hands were closing around her.

'Like what?'

She prepared to fire at him. 'Shoplifted some socks.'

'I shoplifted some Airfix paint from the toy shop in town once. I was sick with guilt. Never did it again. And when I was twelve, I got a stern telling-off from a bobby when me and my mate Gary Plunkett got caught scrumping apples.'

Annis smiled a smile that pulled her dimples deep.

'I lived on and off the streets for a few years.'

'Did you? Wow. That must have been hard.' He seemed genuinely shocked by that. 'Why did you—' he cut off the question. 'Sorry. Not my business. Unless you wanted to tell me.'

She didn't. 'Despite this cool, calm, collected exterior, I'm not the sort of woman men take home to their mothers.'

'Thank god for that,' said Daz, holding out the two remaining sandwich packets for her to choose from.

★

Marsha's house was nowhere near as big as Fox House, but it was still a mighty construction all the same, she thought, as if viewing it through a fresh pair of eyes after pressing the entry code to clear the gates. There were three houses in this gated community and hers was the largest, queening it over the other two from a slightly higher vantage point. It was modern and airy and new but it had no living energy within its walls, that was yet to be made. She dreaded to think what she was imprinting on the place as its first inhabitant; her loneliness, probably. For years she'd thought Fox House was a vacuum but it was quite the opposite. There was too much emotion in it, too many layers of sadness and unrequited need coating the air so thickly it almost clogged up the lungs when it was breathed in.

There were five bedrooms to this house. What had she been thinking when she bought it? That it was a basket ready to fill with a husband and children? Well that hadn't worked, had it? She wanted to make a family so much, prove to the world that she could break a mould, redraw a pattern, have a house filled with light and laughter. She had considered going to a sperm bank and ordering a baby with characteristics totally opposite to the men who'd so far littered up her life. She'd pick a donor who wasn't emotionally unavailable, was an atheist, wasn't a lying, using arsehole. She wanted to marry someone like her dad, tall and strong and intelligent and handsome, who'd turn into Lennox Lewis if she was ever threatened, but whose heart wasn't secured behind barbed wire. Or a pulpit.

She checked all was well, emptied her suitcase, filled it with clean clothes and then left and locked up. Maybe she should get a pet that she could take into the office with her, a rabbit like John Abruzzi. The sight of him lolloping after her sister whenever she moved cheered her. It would be lovely to have something that wanted to be around her and didn't judge, that didn't promise what it couldn't deliver.

She should get some shopping, she decided on the drive back; call in at the farm shop by the park. Her mother liked the quality of their goods; Marsha always took something for her from there when she visited as she very much enjoyed their game pie and their farmhouse pâté, their choices of cheese and home-made crackers. It had always been hard to please her mother – only their father seemed to be able to manage that particular feat with any skill. He bought her wildly expensive jewellery for special occasions, huge bouquets of flowers, showy and decadent. She in turn bought him cufflinks, watches, first edition books. Sometimes Marsha felt as if she had spent her whole young life trying to hack through the ice wall surrounding her mother. She remembered the Mother's Day card she had made at school for her, with an egg box segment for a daffodil trumpet and inside she had written 'I love you' so many times there was barely any white space between the letters.

'That's very nice, thank you,' was all her mother had said, after giving it a cursory once-over. She'd put it on the dresser with Jolene's shop-bought one and then she'd carried on with whatever she was doing. They were both in the kitchen bin the next day. It would have taken so little to mend Marsha's heart, as it took so little to break it.

Marsha pulled into the farm shop and put some herby sausages, tiny button mushrooms, porterhouse steaks, pearl potatoes, an olive loaf and some salt-crusted Yorkshire butter in her basket. She was just about to add some long slim carrots with their flourish of ferny green tops, 'Bugs Bunny' carrots as she thought of them, when she felt someone at her shoulder, a *hello* said too closely to be for anyone else. She turned to find Eric the gardener there. A halogen light turned up to full under the skin of her cheeks.

'Hello,' she said and dropped the carrots on the floor. She bent to pick them up, he bent, they clashed heads like two rutting elk, and both heard the awful clunk of her cheekbone and his brow connecting.

'Oh god, I'm so sorry,' he said, 'are you all right?'

'Yes, I'm fine,' Marsha said, but she wasn't. She'd have to buy the carrots at her feet now. She went to pick them up again and staggered. His arms came out to right her, then he bent down to get them.

'Thank you,' she said, stuffing them in her basket.

'I'm so sorry,' said Eric again, a wincing expression. 'I've hurt you, haven't I?'

'No, really, I'm okay.' She wasn't. She was embarrassed, dizzy and there was a heartbeat in her fast-swelling cheek.

'Maybe you should sit down for a bit, you look very red,' said Eric.

Course I'm red, I got rat-arsed and tried to shag you in my parents' bloody shed and now you've just nutted me in front of a million people, she thought. Her face was really painful.

'Come on,' his hand was on her back, steering her towards the farm shop café. 'You can take the basket in with you, unless you've got ice cream in there.' He took a quick look in it to check. 'It's my brother's place so you have my assurance that no one's going to tell you off.'

She found herself being guided to a table for two by the wall. A waitress came straight over.

'Coffee okay?' Eric asked her.

She began to protest. 'Really, I'm fine . . .'

'You might as well have a drink while you're sitting. You're all wobbly, you can't drive in that state. I won't let you,' he said, making the decision for them. 'Two Cappuccinos, please.'

She could see her swollen cheek with her left eye. This

was torture. She should have just dropped the basket, legged it to the car and never come here again without a wig and dark glasses.

Across the table, Eric was staring at her so intently that she had no chance of any blushes subsiding. In fact her head was in danger of blowing clean off her shoulders from overheating, which would solve the problem perfectly, as oblivion would be a preferable state to be in.

'I think you need some ice on that,' Eric said. 'I'll get—'

She cut him off. There was something more pressing to discuss than how to stop her face from doubling in size.

'Eric, I am so sorry about what happened ... at the house. That's not me, I'm not some sort of cougar woman. I hadn't had anything to eat, I got upset, I stupidly threw some brandy down my neck, really idiotic and not like me and—'

He held two hands up, pressed at the air between them. 'Just ... take a breath. I know, you don't have to explain. Your sister—'

She interrupted back. 'It wasn't down to my sister to apologise for me. I was waiting until I saw you at the house again. I'm appalled.' She shook her head.

'Please don't beat yourself up, Miss Vamplew.'

He made her sound like a teacher, which made it slightly worse as that put into her head an image of herself in a classroom trying it on with a pupil.

'Marsha, please call me Marsha.'

'Lovely name,' said Eric with a nod and a smile. 'Like marshmallows, soft.'

He was cut off from continuing on the theme of her being edible and squashy by the Cappuccinos arriving.

'I was named after Cantona,' said Eric. 'Dad was a big fan.'

'Oh my goodness,' said Marsha as the realisation hit her. 'You look like him as well.'

Eric laughed. 'Yeah, I know. So did my dad. Used to get people double-taking at him all the time. He played up to it mind, wore his hair the same. And I'm the spit of him.'

He really did look like a young Eric Cantona, with his dark stubble, heavy black brows and strong nose, even though he was smilier, less brooding. And his accent was very different.

'I imagine it did you a lot of favours with girls.' Then she added hurriedly, 'Or boys ... whichever you ... er ...'

'It did me some favours with *girls*,' Eric emphasised for clarity, 'but it doesn't make for a strong basis on which to build a relationship. Can I get you something to eat? I'm going to have to insist you get some ice on that cheek before it hatches.'

Marsha pressed her fingers against her face where there was a fine lump forming indeed. Her eye felt like a slit.

'I'll be okay,' she said, nudging some hair over it. 'And thank you, but no, I'm not hungry.'

'How are you getting on with ... everything?'

'Oh ... we're working our way through it,' said Marsha. 'We made a start on packing things up in the house for something to do really, while we're all there.'

'Ah.' Eric wagged his finger as if reminded of something, reached into his back pocket and brought out his wallet. 'Dave West's business card; you know, the one I said I'd find for you. The furniture guy. I was going to give it to you tomorrow because the weather forecast is good and I was coming up to put a few hours in. Everything grows so fast at this time of year.'

The swelling on her face certainly was.

He slid the card across the table and she noticed how nice his hands were, large and square, with neatly clipped nails. He had a ring on his third finger, but it was his right hand.

'Thank you,' she said.

'He's really fair,' said Eric, then after sipping his coffee he asked, 'Do you have a funeral date yet?'

'My sister is sorting that out today. Mum had to have a post-mortem and we just found out that she had a cardiac arrest, which apparently is different from a heart attack – who knew? They think it just stopped beating, for whatever reason.'

'I'm sorry,' said Eric.

She noticed the dark hair on his arms resting on the table. Man's arms, not youthful boy's arms.

'It must have been very sudden. I'd like to think that she wouldn't have been in any pain,' said Marsha.

Their father's end had been protracted and it was hard to watch him wither and shrink as if he was a punctured balloon. But at least she'd had a chance to prepare for his going and tell him that she loved him, even though she would have felt stupid saying it in normal circumstances.

'Did you get on with Mum?' asked Marsha then, curious to know. Eleanor was good at charming strangers, though they didn't realise she wasn't really giving them anything of herself.

'She never missed a payment,' said Eric.

'That's quite a diplomatic answer.' Marsha picked up her cup and drank from it, then dabbed her top lip so she wasn't wearing a moustache as well as a face like Rocky Balboa.

'If you want me to be honest, I always felt as if she was like an electric substation. One that gives out a current that says "stay back",' said Eric.

Marsha nodded. His observation was right on the nose.

'My grandad used to tell me to keep out of her way when I was a kid because she didn't like children. Your dad was quite chatty to me though whenever he came to talk to Grandad. But, I have to say, when I took over from him she was very polite, and very clear about what she wanted me to do in the garden and she never complained, so I took that as being a good indication that all was well.'

'She left you something in her will,' said Marsha. 'I can't remember what it was, but we'll make sure you get it.' She could remember but it was an embarrassingly small amount and they needed to up it.

'Oh, that's kind. There was no need for her to do that.' He sighed, shuffled in his seat. 'I can't profess to knowing your mum at all, even after all the years of working on her garden, but I feel very sad that an era has ended. I always enjoyed it. Whoever originally landscaped it did it very well, everything was balanced and there was an abundance for each season. As the spring flowers faded, the summer ones began to grow, the snowdrops gave way to the blue-bells. There are hundreds of those down by the stream. It's beautiful in April.'

'I never went down that far,' said Marsha. 'I thought it was just a dribble anyway rather than a stream.'

'When there's been a lot of rain there's quite a flow. I've seen ducks and geese swim past. A swan once. Think he must have put the wrong postcode in his satnav.'

Marsha chuckled. Her awkwardness with him was fading. He'd forgiven her, she should forgive herself but she'd always been very bad at that. She took the last drink from her cup. There was only froth left in it now that was holding reso-lutely to the bottom.

'Thank you for the coffee,' she said.

'Ice on that when you get home,' said Eric. He reached across the table and placed his thumb on her cheek, pressed it slightly and the lump seemed to shift from her face to her throat.

Don't be so bloody silly, Marsha, said her heart, warning itself.

Jolene contacted the funeral home and Father Gerard, who said he would pop over tomorrow and then she sat at the kitchen table with her checklist. She'd rung the banks, but not the building society. And she should really set the wheels in motion regarding probate. She probably could fill out all the forms herself, she wasn't daunted by paperwork, but her head was crowded as it was. As she understood it, they could put the house up for sale but they couldn't complete without it. It would take months before she got her share of the money, which was good. She both needed it and didn't want it. At least not until she'd grown a pair of female bollocks.

Her marriage was dead, she knew it deep down. It couldn't be brought back to life with a super-strength defibrillator. The more she lay awake in her old bed, analysing, from a distance, the toxic waters in which she was floundering, the more she was convinced she'd been played like an old spinning top from their first meeting. He'd been so interested in how novelists earned their money, the sources it came from and she'd been secretly delighted in impressing him that she'd been able to drop the day job because her writing life supported her needs adequately. No wonder they enjoyed so many of the same things: he'd designed himself to fit her, he'd moulded exactly to what she wanted, what she couldn't resist. He'd open doors for her, he'd buy her gifts, he'd make sure she was pleased in bed. And when he'd landed her hook, line and sinker, he'd weakened her will, whittled away at her confidence, a nip here, a slice there, so skilfully that she hadn't realised the losses. The little digs at how she wore her hair, he made them sound like compliments: *Don't wear your hair like that, darling, it makes your ears look big, wear it down, it's lovely that way* . . .

He'd even convinced her that his having a mistress strengthened their marriage because it protected her, kept the unsavoury part of himself away from her so she didn't have to accommodate it. What he had with the other woman wasn't love, *this* was love, he'd say, grabbing her hand, rolling her wedding band between his fingers.

She hurt inside. Sometimes she felt as if she were made up mainly of pain and there was no one to talk to about it. Pain and unspent reserves of love. She wanted to love so very much, and be loved. She wasn't sure she ever had been.

She picked up the gold locket that she'd found on Eleanor's dressing table. She would give it to Sally as promised. She pressed it in her hand, trying to extract something of her mother from it because she wore it all the time and if anything had absorbed her essence, it would be this.

Photos of a young Eleanor and Julian sat inside in matching ovals. Her father, athletic and dashing in a V-necked cricket jumper, his face lineless and slim, his brown eyes reading a book just visible at the bottom border; and on the right her mother, perfect skin, large bright eyes, shoulder-length fair hair, hand at the base of her throat, looking left as if she could see her husband in the adjoining frame. It summed them up really – her father's world was his books, his work and her mother's world was him.

Eleanor

There are lessons you learn in life that you never expected to. Read in a textbook they seem absurd, but when you experience them you acquire a different perspective. You have to learn to bend, because those who don't will break. Sometimes you have to learn to unsee. Sometimes you have to accept the unacceptable. Sometimes you have to rationalise away your greatest fears, resist giving in to your suspicions, swallow lies, deflect, block, fight. You have to do some or all of these to survive. They say you can fool other people but not yourself, but that is not how it is in practice. We all try to fool ourselves and make our own truth.

Chapter 29

'What happened to your face?' asked Annis when Marsha walked in with a bag of shopping. Her cheek was discoloured by a blue-purple bruise now and though her face hadn't swelled any further, it hadn't gone down either.

'I headbutted Eric the gardener when we both knelt down to pick up some carrots in the farm shop,' Marsha answered, opening the fridge.

'It has to be how it happened,' said Annis to Jolene. 'No one would make that up.'

'Coincidental meeting or planned?' asked Jolene.

Marsha gave her her best look of disbelief. 'Coincidental, of course. But at least bumping into him, literally, gave me the chance to apologise for . . . my drunken interlude. We're good now, so it was well worth the injury. And I have the name of someone who might be interested in buying the furniture if you want that, Annis.'

'Yeah, that sounds good. I'll ring them if you give me the number.' Annis tilted her head at her sisters then. 'You're nice, aren't you? The pair of you. When is it all going to get nasty and money-grabbing between us?'

'It's not,' said Jolene. 'There's no reason for it to be like that.' She wanted Annis to have the money because if it was shared out, Warren would stake his claim to it. Nothing surer. She smiled. 'I'm actually enjoying getting to know you.'

Annis mirrored her smile.

'Ditto,' she said, and meant it.

'Who were you meeting in Millspring earlier, Annis? You said you'd tell me later,' said Marsha, putting the steaks in the fridge.

'I was having coffee with a friend,' she replied and smiled again, enigmatically.

You have a friend?' said Jolene, teasing her.

'Someone I met when I took John Abruzzi to the vet's. He'd just had to have his bulldog put down and we got chatting. He's nice. He owns a garage and is in a Monkees tribute band called the Hunkees.'

Jolene laughed, a tinkly sound that she'd forgotten she was capable of.

'That sounds fun.'

'The one who left the flowers.' Marsha clicked her fingers as she put two and two together.

'He's a really nice bloke,' said Annis. 'I just don't want it to be any more than it is.'

'Why wouldn't you?' asked Marsha.

Annis shrugged by way of an answer and picked up John Abruzzi who was on his back paws, front feet on her legs angling for attention. He reminded Jolene of herself as a young girl with her mother, except Annis didn't leave him hanging but reached down and scooped him up, pressing him close to her so he was enveloped in her scent and her love.

*

Marsha cooked dinner; steaks, peppercorn sauce, baby corn, pearl potatoes, mangetout and the carrots which tasted no less delicious for being dropped on the farm shop floor. They washed it down with a glass of Chenin Blanc from the cellar.

'This is top scran,' said Annis, nodding. 'You got Mum's cooking gene, I see. I certainly didn't. Though I do make a mean Pot Noodle.'

'I loved to watch her cook,' said Marsha. 'Even if I was always getting in the way. She was very good at it, wasn't she? Remember her Christmas dinners?'

Annis felt something pierce her deeply. That first Christmas away from home, her dinner was a turkey and cranberry sandwich, surplus stock donated by a supermarket and a bashed mince pie. The tears had been rolling down her cheeks as she'd imagined the dining room at Fox House with the huge floral centrepiece and all the smells of Christmas food mingling in the air. The roast potatoes would have been crisped to perfection, the sprouts yielding to the teeth, the gravy rich and tasty. But a door had been closed and it could not be opened again. She'd had to go, she'd had to leave the goose down pillows, the beautiful garden, the crowded bookshelves, the antique furniture, the house that people drove past and wished they lived in.

'I used to love Christmas days in this house,' Marsha went on. 'It was the only day of the year when I felt as if we were a normal family. Every other day, we were like five crumbs in a bowl that wouldn't bind. The house always seemed warmer, Mum was usually parading some new jewellery so she was in a good mood, Dad put down his books for once ... it was like a spell that only ever lasted twenty-four hours.'

Jolene nodded in agreement. Yes, the Christmas days

were wonderful here. Almost like an enchantment because their mother defrosted, their father was jolly and invested, and there was always a Santa's sledful of presents. As she'd grown up, she'd realised that few families resembled the Brady Bunch, but theirs was beyond the weird pale. Maybe because to the outsider's eye they had every ingredient necessary to make a happy family, but they just weren't.

'I've made an appointment with Basil Thompson for tomorrow and I rang Father Gerard and he's coming to the house in the morning,' announced Jolene. Out of the corner of her eye she saw Marsha shift her seat position at the mention of his name. His name ruffled her sister, she could tell.

'You need to delegate, Dolly. You can't do it all.' Annis wagged her knife at her sister. 'I don't mind being directed.' She smiled and her sister was reminded of Annis's two grades of smiles: the put-on one and the genuine one that showed her dimples, like this. Something soft brushed against her heart like a current of warm air.

'Mum made her own arrangements, so I don't think it will take three of us to go through it with Basil Thompson, although I'm going to suggest tweaking a couple of her mandates because we don't need the amount of cars she's put down for a start. It's just throwing money away and Basil is minted enough.' She looked to her sisters for confirmation that was okay. 'I'll go by myself if you like and you two can deal with Father Gerard.'

Marsha was going to say that she'd rather throw herself down the stairs and spend the morning in A and E but she nodded instead. She couldn't really avoid him at this time and she might pander more to his ego by trying to.

After their meal they went into the sitting room, taking the rest of the bottle of wine in with them and Marsha brought in a bowl of posh farm shop crisps: buttered baked potato flavour. When she switched on the TV, Jolene noticed all the programmes that their mum had on a series link: art documentaries, a programme about Egyptian deities, a biopic of Coco Chanel, *Question Time*; nothing light or frothy, nor the surprise of a gritty London gangster movie with lots of bashed-in skulls and sawn-off shotguns. Eleanor's recording choices gave her no new insights with which to colour the portrait of her mother.

Jolene had intended to carve up some of the jobs on her notepad, but she was beat tonight. She let her head fall back as far as it would sink in the unrelenting hide sofa and enjoyed the companionable silence that hung between herself and her two sisters, trying not to second-guess what Warren was plotting from their house in Leeds.

Later, in bed, Annis didn't go to sleep immediately but sat up reading one of Jolene's books, the only one she hadn't read. It was about a well-to-do woman who left an abusive husband and had to build up her life from scratch. Jolene wrote a lot about women in need of a renaissance and she wrote about them too well. Annis had met women like them in her own life, so she could sense the ring of truth in her stories and her characters. Quite a few of them were trapped in a cycle of leaving worthless men with every intention of being born again into a new life of freedom, only to have to crawl back with their tails between their legs because sometimes the adulterous bastard you knew was less scary than the unknown. And it never failed to perturb Annis how often power tried to disguise itself as love.

Chapter 30

The next morning Jolene was first up, although she'd been jogged awake in the wee small hours by a germ of an idea for a future book. It featured a heroine who was so much braver than she was. The irony was that readers wrote to her, thanking her for providing templates of healthy relationships in her stories, guiding them to change things for themselves. They must think she was a chick who had her life together. Maybe she should read one of her own novels and follow its lead.

She heard the stirrings of someone getting up as she unlocked the front door, and called upstairs: 'I'm just going to see the funeral director, do we need anything while I'm out?'

It was Marsha's voice that responded.

'Not that I can think of.'

Both of them felt the echo of a reprimand that they should not be shouting to each other from a distance, as that was not what young ladies did. There were so many things that young ladies shouldn't do that neither of them had wanted to be a young lady at the time, because they sounded like proper boring bitches. It felt like the house had heard so many tellings-off, it had retained them and played back faint recordings of them when they were triggered.

Marsha wandered downstairs, hating that she'd made so much of an effort with herself. No jeggings this morning, no loose top, but jeans and a pale lilac shirt – a shade she knew complimented her colouring. A smear of rose-pink lipstick to lead the eye to the feature that fascinated *him*, second to the pale tone of her hair. He said he had never seen anyone with a more beautiful mouth and that had really shocked her because she'd never considered herself anything like pretty before. Bitchy schoolgirl comments about her looking like a ghost had buried themselves deep in her ego like botflies; it never crossed her mind that they might be jealous of her singular looks, her gentle grey eyes and full lips or the fact that her skin was cream-smooth and clear of any of the teenage spots that plagued them. Maybe if she had been able to recognise their jealousy, she wouldn't have been driven to stuff herself with sugar. She thought that Father Gerard had saved her, but she'd just gorged on him instead of Mars Bars and he'd caused her even more damage.

She filled the kettle and waited impatiently for it to boil. Annis hadn't surfaced yet. She was in the room directly above and the floorboards would make a creaky protest even if someone up there so much as turned over in bed.

She'd just taken the top off the milk when the doorbell rang and her heart kicked. Why the hell did he have to come this early? She opened the door hoping it just might be the postman instead, but it wasn't.

She pushed out a smile and said, 'Ah good morning, Father Gerard, do come in.' She led him into the kitchen.

'Coffee? The kettle's just boiled.' She had her Stepford wife face on.

'You can still call me Ged, Marsha,' he said, his voice dangerously low and deep. *Ged*. She really couldn't. That name belonged to a different Marsha, who was a wide-open book full of white pages ready to be written on. And *Ged* had scribbled all over them with a black Sharpie.

He'd thrown her composure to the wolves already. He had kicked her carefully manufactured persona with a single toe and it had given way like balsa wood.

'How do you take it, Father?' *Just a hint of milk and half a teaspoon of sugar.* She wouldn't admit she remembered and she wouldn't call him Ged either.

'Just a hint of milk and half a teaspoon of sugar, please, Marsha.'

She used to lie in bed at night replaying over and over how he said her name.

'Is it just you in?' he asked. She turned to bring the mugs over and a movement out of the kitchen window caught her eye. Eric was in the garden.

'No, Annis is upstairs. She'll be down in a minute,' she replied, hoping it was true.

'The first coffee of the morning always tastes the best doesn't it?' He smiled. Damn him, the years had been so kind to him. He'd been thirty when they'd had their . . . *whatever it was: fling, interlude* and he was gorgeous then but now, at almost fifty, he was more so with his fully-fired up masculinity, his stripey hair, his artful crinkle-wrinkles. He'd aged like the best wine, the finest cheese and other tried and tested tropes. She wished they'd made love, just the once, just so she could have bust the myth; 'kill the magic', as he had put it, and no flame would have been fucked into being as her young heart had envisioned. She saw now that the reality would never have lived up to her *Thorn Birds*-type passionate fantasy; and if she'd been disappointed, she could have let him go so much more easily.

She put the coffee down in front of him and then sat in the chair next to his to show him that she could be near him without spontaneously combusting. Then she opened the file on the table and handed him a sheet of A4.

'These are our notes and Mum's hymn and reading choices. She was very organised, as you might imagine.'

Gerard smiled. 'I do imagine.'

'Jolene would like to do the eulogy.'

'It must be hard for you, Marsha. I know things weren't easy between you and your mother. I remember.'

She'd given up so many of her secrets to him. Not how she used to cram whole Twixs in her mouth, she didn't want him to be revolted by her. But she'd told him that she was the great family disappointment because of not being a boy.

'She was my mother,' said Marsha, 'and she gave what she could of herself. None of us can go back into the past and repair all that went wrong but we'd like to say goodbye to her with dignity and lay her to rest with our love.'

'Did your mother ever apologise to you for the hurt she caused?' he asked.

'No, but then you didn't either.'

She hadn't meant to say that, but it had been bubbling inside her for too long, like a genie desperate for freedom and once out grew too fast, too quickly to be put back in the bottle.

'So, *Ged*, how come you never left the Church for Bronwen, the woman of your dreams?' She knew she sounded like a bitchy teenager and she still couldn't stop herself. Outwardly she was a dignified adult and yet her mouth was pure Tracy Beaker.

'Stop this, Marsha.' His eyes were closing, shutting her out, creating distance between them.

'I think after all these years the least you could give me is an explanation. I'm owed that,' she hissed at him.

His eyes eventually opened and glued themselves to the blue file on the table.

'I didn't love her,' he said. 'I thought I could shift my feelings across to her ... from you. Live as ... a secular man.'

'You mean have sex,' said Marsha.

Gerard winced as if her words burned him, then he admitted it with an almost whispered, 'That was only part of it.'

'But if you loved me, as you said you did, and were going to leave the Church, why wouldn't you have done it for me?' A reprimanding voice inside warned her that her tone was wheedling and she told it to piss off.

Gerard Bannen turned the full force of his gaze on her. 'Think of what the fallout would have been from that. You were a teenager, I was eleven years older.'

'I was nearly twenty, I was a full-grown adult.'

'You were sad and vulnerable and I should not have encouraged your affections.'

'We'd have been happy.' She almost screamed it at him.

'Would we?' he matched her for volume, his eyes drilling into hers. 'There were no guarantees. I'd have damaged you irreparably, with your family, with the community.'

'Do you think I would have cared what anyone thought? Annis walked away from it all, I could have too. I loved you so much—'

He interrupted her. 'You only thought you did.'

'No, I really did.'

'You might have grown to resent me. I might have grown to resent you. We'd have both lost too much.'

'We might not have,' she countered.

Gerard dropped his head as if it was suddenly loaded with a great weight. 'All right, maybe I made a mistake.'

'Thanks a bunch.'

'I didn't mean it like that. I meant perhaps I should have left the Church for *you*,' said Gerard. 'I missed you so much that I knew it was ... you or nobody. A life with Bronwen would have been a lie. But you ran off to London. That's why I was persuaded to stay in the priesthood.'

Marsha held her breath. What was he saying? That if she hadn't taken the job in London he would have thrown everything in for her? That if she'd hung on a bit longer, she could have had him? Her head was a washing machine on a fast spin.

'Marsha, dearest Marsha.' She watched his hand move across the space that separated them, as if in slow motion. He leaned in close and she felt the warm air of her whispered name against her cheek, his fingers brush against her pale moonlight hair.

Heavy footsteps tripped down the hall. How had Annis managed to leave her bedroom and come downstairs without a single noise? Marsha sprang away from Father Gerard just in time as Annis walked in, dressed in her usual charity shop grunge and still looking as if she'd just been rigged out by Vivienne Westwood.

'Oh good morning, Father. How lovely to see you.'

Father Gerard rose from his seat and took Annis's hand between his own, greeting her warmly, asking her how she was, telling her how great it was that she was here. Marsha watched him. He was always tactile, never shied from contact, especially if he thought someone might need a comforting squeeze on their shoulder or an avuncular hug. She remembered him holding her so tightly that she could barely breathe.

'Are you home for long, Annis?' asked Father Gerard.

'No idea, Father,' she smiled at him but Marsha noticed that her dimples were a no-show. 'I hadn't intended to, but even the best-made plans change, don't they?'

'Annis, is there anything you've thought of that you'd like to add to the service?' asked Marsha, trying to appear as if she hadn't been felled by Gerard's revelation, as if he hadn't rocked her world yet again.

'I'll just go with what's been decided,' said Annis.

'It all looks very straightforward,' said Father Gerard. 'I have a lovely reading of my own that your mother asked me to say, when the time came. Is that all right? It's about joining your father in heaven.'

'That's nice,' said Annis, holding the perfunctory smile. 'I'm sure they'll find their way to each other if they haven't already.'

'Well,' Father Gerard waved the sheet of paper in his hand. 'I'll take this away with me and weave my words into yours. And I'll liaise with Basil.' He picked up his coffee and drank enough to make an impact on it. 'Thank you, Marsha, for that. And er ... I'll be touch before the service.'

He stood up to go, and bobbed his head towards Annis first, then Marsha.

'You both look after yourselves, and each other. And if you need me for anything, do not hesitate to ask. Anything.'

He stressed the word, but he didn't mean *anything*. There were limitations and everything Marsha might want from him was outside their barricade.

Marsha saw him to the door but there were no more intimacies, not even a glance, a touch; he had slipped back into his Father Gerard priest role as quickly as he had earlier slipped into his Ged persona, like a mental muscle memory, never quite unlearned. Tears of confusion crept to her eyes as she closed the door on him and she forced them down because she wouldn't be able to explain them away if she walked into the kitchen with them.

Annis was making herself a slice of toast.

'He's got even more better-looking,' she said.

Marsha slumped to the chair Gerard had just vacated, it still retained his heat.

'And he knows he's fit,' Annis went on. 'He always did.'

'What do you mean?' asked Marsha.

'I've learned a lot about men in the last fifteen years. How some of them hide behind their smart clothes and fancy job titles. I bet he's the sort that secretly loves the adoration and he's had plenty of it over the years, looking like that. And he can keep a load of ladies dangling on strings because that moment just before things hot up is always the most intoxicating, don't you think? The line they think he'll cross but he never does.'

Marsha opened her mouth to speak but Annis carried on talking. 'The irony is that it's the unattainable priest part of him that's the most attractive, but if anyone did attain it, they'd see him as a lesser being, a weak man with no will, not a strong one overcome by passion. A man like that could spin a woman a barrowful of baloney and get away with it. He might tell her that he was going to give everything up for her, but would he really when push came to shove?'

Marsha gulped and felt her face growing hot and cursed her own transparency. 'You were listening, weren't you?' she said eventually.

'No,' said Annis flatly. 'I just know men, that's all.'

The toast popped up. She buttered it and then lingered by the window as she took the first bite.

'The gardener's here. I must admit, having read both, I always preferred *Lady Chatterley's Lover* to the *Thorn Birds*. Men do love power, don't they? And it's so often their downfall. Have you ever heard of the Bathsheba syndrome? In short it's when a man begins to believe his own hype and ends up—'

'I think I'll make him a coffee.'

Uncomfortable now, Marsha got up quickly and made for the kettle but Annis grabbed her arm as she passed.

'You can talk to me if you ever need to, you know. I realise I haven't got a lot of proven form in my listening skills with you, but I'm good at it.'

'Thank you,' said Marsha. 'I'll remember that for when I do.'

With every step that Marsha took towards the gardening shed, she got more and more incensed. With Annis for snooping, because if that *Thorn Birds* reference wasn't meant for her, she was Kate Bush. With Father Gerard Bloody Bannen for being Father Gerard Bloody Bannen. And with herself, for letting him get to her still after all these years. If Annis could tell he was spinning her a yarn, why couldn't she? Was it bullshit that he'd realised his mistake and was going to throw in his collar for her only to find she'd sodded off to London? It would certainly shift the blame onto her for her own unhappiness. And talking about unhappiness – what about poor old Bronwen? He hadn't half led her a merry dance – if she even existed. Her head was scrambled.

She reached for the handle on the shed door at the same moment as it opened and Eric stood there, a look of surprise on his face. A nice smiley look of surprise.

'Oh, hello,' he said, sounding genuinely pleased to see her.

'Hi, I just brought you this,' she said, stepping past him and putting it down on the work surface next to a roll of strimmer wire. 'Thank you for the coffee yesterday, I realise I didn't even offer to pay—'

'Whoa, slow down,' said Eric. 'Has someone just put new batteries in you?'

She took a breath, realising how she must be coming across.

'Are you okay?' he asked her.

'Yes, yes, no . . . no I'm not,' she said. She should go, she'd made enough of a fool of herself in front of this man as it was and she couldn't bear to add another episode to her list. She was a walking whirlpool of stripped emotions and rage and confused thoughts and tickled longings and loneliness and regret and bewilderment.

'Let me see your cheek,' said Eric. He placed his hands on her arms and looked at her face; the swelling had subsided and the bruise had been covered with a heavy thud of foundation, although it was still visible up close. His eyes were so brown, dark, and drinking her in with an intensity that she would usually have shrunk from, but it was filling her with sparks and fizzes and obliterating everything else she had been feeling when she walked in. She tried to remove herself from his hold before she made a tit of herself and leapt on him again. But it was he who leaned forward, he who placed his soft lips upon hers. And it was he who did to her everything in that shed that she'd once wanted Father Gerard Bannen to do to her in his vestry.

Chapter 31

Sally had had a terrible night's sleep worrying about Norman. It was taking him longer and longer to go upstairs to bed and he couldn't sleep downstairs because she needed to shower him every morning and there was no bathroom there. Besides there was no room for a double bed anywhere but in the middle of the lounge and that wouldn't do. She wished she had even a quarter of the money the Vamplews had, for a nice new bungalow with all the mod cons and adaptations he needed now. Norman had always told her that his pension pot was overflowing, but it appeared that he'd been exaggerating about that. It was all right, they were solvent but their energy bills were high. She washed clothes every day and they were on a water meter so the cost had really shot up, but she wouldn't have Norman looking any less than his best, it wouldn't have been proper. He was never dapper like Julian Vamplew, even though he had tried to copy his style, at least before they were ejected from his glittering orbit, but he was always clean and shaven and smelt of his old faithful Aramis.

She felt her lip curling at the thought of that high and

mighty clever Dickie, mocking them, making fun of them in his big house with his posh friends. Sally hadn't even thought any swear words until recently; then she'd thought quite a lot of them. Julian used to 'f' this and 'f' that, and it sounded more like 'fack', almost classy, sitting back with his long legs crossed and a cigarette or a pipe to his lips. He thought he was so above them all. She and Norman thought he was too. If only they'd known.

Her shoulder was sore this morning because Norman had bitten it when she'd tried to hoist him up. He didn't mean it, he wouldn't have hurt a fly if he was well. He couldn't, he didn't have it in him, she was sure. What he'd done all those years ago had been naïve, nothing more. Not deviant. Why would he have done it in the garden otherwise? The child was only little, there was nothing about her to make a grown man think of taking advantage. It had been made into something it wasn't, and ruined their lives because there remained that niggle of doubt in her like a dandelion: however much she pulled it out and thought it was gone, over time it had begun to poke out of the ground again.

Surely God would understand why she couldn't have waited until the morning to confront Eleanor when she'd read what she had in the letter?

Basil Thompson was an odious little man; Jolene had thought as much when her father was being looked after by him. His customer service was second to none, his establishment the height of tranquil decorum and he ran his business with military precision. His prices were high, though people were happy to pay them because it was worth it to them for peace of mind. But Basil himself had grown fat and arrogant on his reputation. His politeness, once extended liberally to all, now ran in tandem with how much a customer clocked up in extras. Basil greeted Jolene with so much obsequiousness that she half-expected to find a slug-like trail on the floor in his wake.

She'd brought the clothes in which her mother wished to meet her maker; they'd been stored in a large box at the bottom of her wardrobe. A long black elegant dress, black high heels that hadn't been worn for many years, and Jolene wondered if there was any significance to them. She'd never know. So many questions unanswered when someone died. Maybe she'd just liked them; maybe they were tied to an event or occasion. She'd left black tights out too but Jolene decided not to include them, unable to bear the thought of the undertaker wrestling her into them.

Her mother, apparently, had already sent a letter to Basil some time after Easter outlining her requests, which is why the tweaks that Jolene wanted to make didn't go down well. She said they could not justify a solid oak lined coffin for a cremation, nor four limousines for the cortege. One would be quite sufficient. At her father's funeral, apart from the first car, the others were filled with people they barely knew, because their mother wanted the procession to look grand. No, Jolene was not going to line Basil's pockets with extra thousands of pounds for no good reason.

'But these were your mother's wishes,' said Basil, with an oily, if impatient smile.

She wasn't to be swayed from *her* wishes though, which was quite a feat given Basil's passive-aggressiveness and she emerged from the meeting with renewed faith in herself that she had it in her not to be a pushover all the time.

She called in at the supermarket on the way home to pick up an anniversary card for Warren. Ten years. Tin, apparently, which symbolised the strength and resilience of a marriage. She expected he'd buy her a showy bouquet and she knew they were going out to dinner, because it had been booked for weeks. He was very big on occasions like their anniversaries, it was just the rest of the marriage he was no good at.

She wondered if Warren and his mistress had an anniversary for the day they first met or consummated their relationship or the first time she shoved a courgette up his arse. His other life ran concurrently to their life, a constant low-level buzz in the background, like a mosquito at the far side of the room. You couldn't ignore it and you were always primed to feel it bite.

The cards all had soppy verses, lines about being in it for the long haul and being best friends and she just couldn't put her signature to one of those. Warren would. He'd buy a fancy card with a long poem or with embellishments on the front that pumped the price up and then sign it 'to my darling wife' without even reading what the verse said. It had taken her years to realise he was all bluster and no substance, handsome smoke.

When she got back to the house, Annis was sitting cross-legged on the floor in the sitting room looking at some photos she'd found in a shoe box, John Abruzzi at her side, content on the carpet.

'I'm getting a feel of what I missed in the years I was away,' she explained, looking up at Jolene. 'Not that there are many family photos, are there? Mostly Dad and his students and cronies and Mum dressed up to go out.'

'No, we never really bothered with taking photos, did we,' replied Jolene. 'Where's Marsha?'

'Lady Chatterley took a coffee down to Mellors an aeon

ago and hasn't been back since. I wonder if he's showing her his dibble.'

Jolene cracked a smile and a memory came to her of Annis as a gawky young girl, hanging around her, hoping to be befriended by her chic older sibling but Jolene had kept her at a distance. She shouldn't have done that. She, as the elder, should have made sure they set the foundations of friendship early. She should have ensured the common denominator of blood was merely their starting point.

'She's very fragile, isn't she?' Annis went on, still flicking through the photographs.

'Marsha?' asked Jolene for clarification. 'What makes you think that?'

'Because she always was,' replied Annis. 'What's the story with her and Father Gerard?'

'Oh, he came, did he?' asked Jolene.

'He might have done, if I hadn't interrupted them when I did,' replied Annis with a lopsided grin.

'*Annis.*' A rebuke.

'Just an irreverent joke. Did they have some sort of a fling, I wonder?' She'd been thinking about it ever since, piecing it all together in her head from what she'd heard that morning standing outside the kitchen, before she'd tiptoed back down the hallway and made a second louder approach to warn them she was on her way – and from the snippets of Marsha's diary she remembered, recording every instance the priest had looked at her for more than a nanosecond. Her sister had been infatuated.

'Don't be daft,' said Jolene. 'And what do you mean when you said she was always fragile?'

'She used to gorge on chocolate, that's why she became a bit of a porker in her teens. I found her impressive sweet store under the bed ...' She then added pointedly, 'With her diaries.'

'You didn't read them, did you?'

'Oh come on,' said Annis disbelievingly. 'I was the devil's spawn, of course I did.'

'That wasn't on, was it?' protested Jolene, then couldn't resist asking what Annis had seen in them.

'A lot of hearts drawn around their joint initials.'

'Okay, so she had a crush on Father Gerard. Who didn't?'

Annis knew Marsha had, but until she'd overheard them talking together today, she had never considered it might be two-way traffic.

'I think he led her on.'

'Of course he didn't. Annis, you're talking rubbish. It was natural she found a figure of authority like he was someone to moon over. How many girls do you think fell in love with Dad?' Jolene laughed as she slipped out of her jacket.

Annis bristled. Older men didn't always take the care they should over young hearts. They fooled themselves into believing their intentions were honourable, when really it was their own wants and needs that were paramount.

With their appetites slaked, Marsha and Eric were now in a cringey state of awkwardness as they dressed. It was a task much less exciting than unbuttoning, unzipping, divesting.

'My coffee's gone cold,' said Eric. That was all it needed to reset them: Marsha's tension gave way to a much-needed roll of laughter, amplified when she fell over while balancing on one leg to put on a sock that had somehow come off, even though the other one was still on her other foot.

'Where did all that come from?' said Eric with a whistle.

'I don't know, I'm sorry,' said Marsha.

'You're regretting it already?' said Eric. 'Blimey.' He affected a hurt expression.

'Are you?' Marsha asked tentatively.

'I'm not. Not at all, it was . . . it was fantastic,' said Eric. 'I was just moving in for a kiss and then . . .'

He didn't say it but what he meant was that she took over. And how.

'I didn't think people ever had sex as good as it looks in films but . . .' He whistled and Marsha laughed again, then her lips contracted as quickly.

'This isn't how I usually behave,' she said. 'I'm not—'

'You said that about last time,' said Eric, a teasing smile on his lips.

Marsha was dressed now. 'Shall I make you another coffee?'

'I don't think you should. Look what happens when you do.'

He picked up her hand and kissed her palm and she gasped at the intimacy of it.

'Don't start fretting that you've done something wrong. We're both adults.'

'I'm more adult than you,' said Marsha, wondering how big the age difference between them was.

'How old are you?' he asked.

'Thirty-eight,' she said, wincing.

'Wow, you don't look that at all. I'm twenty-nine. Barely a gap between us. It's nothing.'

It didn't sound nothing. When she was twenty, he was eleven.

She snatched her eyes away from the dark hair poking out of the top of his T-shirt.

'I'd better go,' said Marsha. 'My sister will wonder what I've been doing.'

'I'm pretty sure she'll have guessed.'

He had a shadow of stubble and she had a sudden flash-back to the raspy feel of it against her skin.

'Oh god,' she said, as something warm popped inside her heart.

'It was lovely,' he said. 'You're lovely. Thank you. Now go, because I need to finish my work before the rain starts. It's forecast for this afternoon.'

He held the mug full of cold coffee out towards her. She took it, opened the shed door and tried to walk back to the house without looking as if she'd been riding a Shire horse for a week.

Eleanor

It is a terrible curse to be at the begging end of a man's attentions, especially one who initially turned his light onto you and made you want him, give him more of yourself than you ever thought you could give. He had my heart and he warmed it. But then to realise that you will never be enough . . .

When I met my mother for the last time, she laughed in my face. She said I would never keep him and she was glad. A just punishment for not sharing the inheritance that was mine by rights.

She knew, somehow. She knew.

Chapter 32

'You were a suspiciously long time, Mash,' said Annis, eyes sparkling. 'And why is your shirt on inside out?'

The speed at which Marsha looked down at herself was telling.

'Oh, very funny,' she said.

'I have a date for Mum's funeral,' said Jolene. 'Tuesday August thirtieth. We need to find two photos of Mum for the front and back covers of the order of service.'

'Mum and Dad's wedding photo maybe?' suggested Marsha. 'And what about the one of her on her seventieth? You know, that must have been the last photo she ever had taken.' She turned to address Annis. 'Someone at her bridge club took it of her. She said she didn't want a party but they gave her a surprise one anyway.'

'She didn't want a party?' Annis threw back.

'She said she didn't want to go to anything like that if Dad wasn't there with her. I don't think she enjoyed life all that much after he was gone.'

'I'll fetch the box of photos,' said Annis. 'It's got to be in there.'

She went off to the sitting room and when she was gone, Jolene tilted her head at Marsha and tried to see her as vulnerable as Annis said she was. Marsha misinterpreted the look.

'We were only talking,' insisted Marsha. 'He's very mature for twenty-nine.'

'I believe you,' said Jolene, smile tugging the corner of her lip. 'Of course.'

'Here we are,' said Annis, putting the large box down in the middle of the table.

Marsha rifled through them. When she found it, Jolene wrinkled her nose up.

'You can't use that, she's got her glasses on,' she said.

Marsha nodded. 'Oh god yes.'

Annis let loose a burst of laughter. 'What?'

'Mum has had glasses for years but she's never worn them, at least not in front of anyone.'

'Why?' Annis answered her own question then. 'Don't tell me she was too vain.'

'And she was getting a bit deaf. She had a hearing aid test and would have benefitted very much but she stubbornly refused to even try them. I'm surprised she let herself be photographed in glasses and I'm dumbfounded that she kept it,' said Jolene with a small sigh. 'It's a lovely one.'

Annis took it from her hand and looked at it, looked at the signs of age in her mum, the pale blonde hair turned to silver, the slight sagging at her neck. Thinking about it, she hadn't seemed to change that much in the sixteen years of her life here, but in the fifteen since, it had caught up with her and Annis wondered if she'd been a contribution to that.

Jolene pulled a clutch of photos towards her and began to search through them. She put a black and white one on the

table: three children and a woman standing behind them.
Only the girl was smiling. She had a dark ribbon in her fair
hair, a pretty dress on, socks and buckled shoes. The boys
were bigger, in suits, looking choked in their ties.

Annis picked it up. Her mother was instantly recognisable
as the young girl, despite the smile. She must have played
out, had friends, laughed and cried. They knew almost
nothing about their mother as a child; it was hard to imagine
her as anything but an adult. Annis couldn't even remember
what the brothers were called – her uncles.

'Hugh and Philip,' said Jolene, when she asked.
'Apparently they were a pair of little shits. They got on with
each other but not with little sis.'

'Was she loved?' Annis asked.

'I can't imagine her being ruined with affection,' said
Marsha, remembering the one time she met her sour-faced
grandmother. 'Then there was all that trouble when she
inherited the money from her great-aunt. There was far
more of it than anyone expected and it had always been
presumed that she'd share like a good girl, but she didn't.
So she was cast out of the family, not that it bothered her
in the least.'

'You won't remember this but just after you were born,
Annis, Grandma attempted a reconciliation,' said Jolene.

'Yep. We were rolled out in our posh frocks and taken to
this . . . retirement home that smelt of cheap stew is my overriding memory,' said Marsha. 'And considering Grandma
had been the one to instigate things, she was very hostile.'
She remembered being pushed forward to give this woman
whom she didn't know a kiss, and how papery and dry her
cheek felt against her lips.

'It descended very quickly into disaster from what I

recall,' said Jolene. 'The subject of great-aunt Eleanor's money reared its head again, obviously not a dead and buried subject at all. I think Mum realised quite quickly that Grandma was hoping she'd stump up for a better retirement home, that was her real aim for the meeting. It wasn't going to happen and so Grandma got quite nasty, saying that Mum deserved everything she got, or something like that. Mum just stood up and said, "We're going." Then ...' Oh my, how could she have forgotten how it ended? But then sometimes memories pulled others up along with them, like tissues from a box.

'What?' asked Annis.

'She said ...' Jolene paused as she delved into her memory banks, determined to get it right, exactly as it was. 'She said as her parting shot, something like: *You'll never keep him and you know why*. She had this really horrible twisted look on her face. Mum just pushed me out and grabbed Marsha's arm.' She shuddered. 'Mum wouldn't ever talk about it. We weren't to mention it and so we didn't.'

'Mum was so angry,' said Marsha. 'I had her finger marks on my arm and I remember examining them in the car.'

'She was more shaken than angry, what Grandma said really got to her,' said Jolene, who had a clearer memory. 'And that was that then, the great reunion that never was. Grandma died not long after. Mum had a phone call from Hugh, I think, to tell her and that she wasn't invited to the funeral. Then there was a load of hoo-ha because they tried to stop her from inheriting her share of what Grandma left. There was a legal wrangle and Mum won, all of which made for good family relations.'

'What did she mean, do you think, by "You'll never keep him and you know why"?' asked Marsha, musing on it.

'I don't know. Maybe she was just trying to hurt her because she didn't get her own way. Anyway, what does it matter because she was wrong and Mum did keep him, didn't she?'

'What about Mum's father?' asked Annis.

'God knows,' said Jolene. 'I can't ever remember her mentioning him. I get the feeling he wasn't around, though. I wonder sometimes if she was trying to find a substitute father in Dad; you know, older man.'

'Happens,' said Annis. 'I had a friend at a hostel who fell for someone who volunteered there. Solid, safe, older man. She moved in with him and he changed just like that—' She clicked her fingers. 'He didn't hit her or anything, but he got paranoid that she'd leave him. So he started to lock her in whenever he went out. She ended up climbing out of the window to get away and never went back.'

Something in her voice suggested it wasn't a friend at all, but Annis herself she was talking about, but they let her carry on.

'She said it was a shame because his first face was really lovely. She thought she'd hit the jackpot, but no woman should put up with that sort of thing. Though plenty do.'

Hit the jackpot. That is exactly what Jolene had thought when she met Warren, whose 'first face' as her sister so fabulously put it, was straight out of the 'exactly what I need' shop.

Mark Jarvis was not the scariest man that Annis had met by far, though. She didn't want her thoughts even dipping there. She gave herself a mental shake, shifted her focus back to the here and now.

'So, which photo are we going to use?'

*

Annis cooked that evening, a very simple dish of pasta in tomato sauce with olives and a generous grating of Parmesan and she put a couple of part-baked batons in the oven and the aroma of fresh bread filled the kitchen. In the kitchen behind the bar at Cocktails there was a breadmaker that Denise used to set off sometimes in the mornings when they were all cleaning, getting ready for another working day. Right at the end of the cycle, a delicious, homely smell filled the place and there was always a mad rush to eat the warm end result. The girls would sit at one of the tables, cut thick slices, slather them with butter and talk. Her mother used to bake bread and the kitchen would be filled with a heavenly scent, but there was no breaking into it, putting the world to rights over it.

'This is absolutely delicious,' said Jolene, loading her fork. 'How have you made dried pasta and a jar of sauce taste so good?'

Annis tapped her nose. 'Secret ingredient,' she said.

'Which is?'

'Wouldn't be secret if I told you, would it?'

'I have to know,' pressed Jolene.

Annis leaned forward to impart the classified information and instinctively her sisters mirrored the action.

'Camaraderie,' she whispered.

'Twit,' said Marsha with a chuckle.

But she was right, because it wasn't what they were eating, it was what they were feeling that made the difference.

'Maybe if I'd known we could have got on so well, I would have come home more from uni,' said Jolene, though she wasn't sure that would have been true. She'd secured a job in a hotel and worked there during the breaks.

She didn't miss home that much when she was away from

it and every time the need came upon her to make the trip, it was mainly to see her father.

'So the man you were talking about earlier on ... and your friend,' said Marsha, who'd been intrigued by the story, 'did she ever see him again?'

'She did but she kept her distance. He couldn't understand what her problem was. He said he was protecting her.'

'Blimey,' said Jolene. 'Sounds to me like he was the one she needed protecting from.'

'People rationalise their behaviour, though, don't they?' said Annis. 'They knock the edges off the truth and smooth it down until it's a shape they can live comfortably with. This man had a respectable job in an office, he volunteered helping homeless people, he mowed his lawn, he paid his bills, but something had damaged him so much that he had an irrational fear of losing anyone he got close to. And when his actions drove them away, he became even more paranoid. I'm not the sort of woman that would be persuaded to stay in a relationship like that and try and fool myself that he cared so much about me and that's why he acted like that.' Her pretence had dropped. She was talking about herself and Mark Jarvis and she knew they knew. 'He was a time bomb waiting to go off. He checked my phone, he smelt my clothes, almost as if he was determined to find evidence to justify his behaviour. It was exhausting.'

Marsha let loose a long breath. 'I think that would have put me off men for life.'

'Not at all,' said Annis. 'There are lovely men out there; you have to give people a chance. But you cut and run when your alarm bells go off. I've worked with so many women who've managed to convince themselves that the man they're with slaps them around because he loves them, because he's got a passionate nature. That boys will be boys. That the other women mean nothing to him—'

Jolene swallowed, fiddled with her necklace. She did that a lot, Annis noted. A silver crescent moon on a chain.

'They see the man they want to see, not as he is. They think the one who reeled them in with a charm offensive is the real one and not the knobhead they're lumbered with now and they hang on in there waiting for that first face to come out to them again, but he never does. Because that was never him,' Annis went on.

'But this guy you met in the vet's . . . he's nice, is he?' asked Marsha.

'Seems so, he gives out a good vibe,' replied Annis. 'But he's just a friend. I'm not intending it to develop into more, but if it does and it's right then so be it. And if it's wrong, then I'll walk away and not look back.'

'Not easy to do that when you have mortgages and financial ties . . . and children,' Jolene added that to deflect from the idea she might be talking about herself.

'It's harder, but it can and should be done if you're in an abusive relationship, because it won't get better, only worse,' said Annis. 'Mark didn't think he was abusive because he didn't associate himself with men who hit women. He thought they were scum.'

'Where was this cocktail club you worked at?' asked Jolene.

'Deancliffe,' said Annis, shovelling some pasta into her mouth and chewing.

Jolene raised her eyebrows. She'd driven through Deancliffe on numerous occasions and was glad to get out alive. It was dog rough, with a renowned red light area.

'I wouldn't have thought Deancliffe was the sort of place you'd find a gentleman's club,' said Jolene.

'Depends what sort of gentlemen you mean,' Annis came back.

Marsha tilted her head, like a collie trying to make sense of his master's voice.

'What are you saying, Annis?'

'Why do you think it was called *Cocktails?*' she replied.

Cocktails, Annis admitted, was a massage parlour masquerading as a club. High end for that part of Sheffield, which wasn't saying much. There were rooms off the bar area where clients came for relief, muscular or otherwise. Denise didn't want to know the details, so long as she got her cut. Annis managed the cocktail bar. A few of those who paid their monthly dues just came in to sit, read the paper, have a coffee or an Old Fashioned, enjoy some company, mainly the older set.

'So Denise was a madam, then?' asked Jolene, mouth open so far her jaw looked dislocated.

'Well, sort of. She was a rough old diamond, but she cared about people.'

'But . . . that's immoral earnings,' said Marsha, wrinkling up her nose. She couldn't quite see this Denise as the saviour Annis was painting her as.

'Some girls don't have the job choices available,' said Annis. 'It suited them, plus it was safer for them than being out on the streets. They earned and Denise earned. Don't compare this cosy world against theirs.'

Jolene chewed her lip as she thought on that. Marsha was absorbing the information too.

'And no, in case you were wondering, my duties were

strictly reception, cleaning and serving drinks. We were all named after cocktails. I was Mai Tai. And yes, I did have a room I used, but not for what you might think.'

'I don't know what to say,' said Jolene, who had long since abandoned her pasta.

'You don't need to say anything,' said Annis. 'I don't think Mum would have left her money to me if she'd known all this, do you?' A trill of laughter.

'It sounds very benign,' said Jolene, shaking her head. 'A bit *Pretty Woman*. It couldn't have been, surely?'

'Nothing like *Pretty Woman* I can assure you of that. And yes, there were a few incidents here and there,' said Annis, 'but Denise's son Freddie was resident muscle. He was a nice lad, more brawn than brains and a bit easily led so she set him on working for her. She could keep her eye on him then, and he could keep his eye on any trouble.'

'But . . . the women are being exploited, aren't they?' This from Marsha.

Annis gave a weighty sigh. 'Well, Mash, I'm sure that given the choice, a lot of them would rather have worked in a lovely dress shop or been a teacher, but those options weren't there for them. And do you know what held them back more than anything?' She waited for her sisters to answer, but they didn't. 'Not being able to read. Think how many times every day you read something to get by: the news, instructions, recipes, travel timetables . . . your world shrinks when you can't read. Girls who get into trouble might be full of the best intentions to change their lives, widen their worlds but they're so restricted by not being able to read, so they keep going back to what they know – the same dysfunctional crowd. They keep making the same mistakes and getting into the same sort of trouble, a cycle they can't break. The room I had wasn't big enough for any "business", so Denise let me use it to hold classes in. I taught girls how to read there.'

'How come they couldn't read? Hadn't they been to school?' asked Marsha.

Annis laughed again. 'Remember when anyone played truant from our school and teachers were straight on the phone to the parents? That's your ideal world right there. A lot of Denise's girls were turning tricks for their parents' drug money when they should have been studying logarithms or making cakes in domestic science. And if the authorities got involved, they'd move. Lot of ghost kids around, the system doesn't know anything about them so it doesn't have the chance to care.'

'In this day and age?' asked Jolene.

'Probably more than ever. At least her girls weren't trafficked in, shut in houses, made to perform eight, ten times a day without ever seeing outside. You have no idea what's going on behind some curtains in ordinary towns filled with ordinary people.'

Jolene leaned over the table and squeezed her sister's arm and felt tearful that her wisdom about life had been so hard-earned. She wished she had half her strength.

Chapter 33

Dave West, the furniture man whom Eric had recommended came the next morning to view what they had. He hadn't been expecting so many high-end pieces but he would gladly buy them. He'd have to work out a price, but they wouldn't get better than his offer, he promised them. And, though the pieces of art weren't his thing, he could recommend some galleries and auction houses whom he felt sure would be interested. Much to Annis's amusement especially, Mr West went into ecstasies about the aesthetic beauty of the ugly lumps of bronze and she only wished she could see them through his eyes. She didn't like abstract pieces, she liked paintings and sculptures to look like the things they were supposed to represent. She liked clarity and truth and no pretension or surprises.

She had a call from Daz saying that if she fancied fish and chips, there was a new shop opened up in Millspring – Cod's Gift – and they were doing a two for one lunchtime deal today. Marsha gave her a lift and also a lecture en route about booking herself in for some driving lessons. And then buying a sensible car and not a Porsche with a daft-sized engine, although she would easily be able to afford one. Annis laughed and told her that she sounded like her mum, but it was a figure of speech because she didn't at all. If anything, Marsha sounded like Denise who nagged her like a Mum should, looking out for her rather than only really speaking to her when she had something to criticise.

When Marsha got back to Fox House, Eric's van was parked outside and her heart gave a kick by way of response. He hadn't got as much gardening done yesterday as he'd planned which is probably why he was here today.

She had replayed what had happened in the shed over and over as she lay in bed. It had taken her an age to get to sleep, thinking about what they'd done, where his hands had been, his lips, how tender he was. She wondered if he'd replayed it too when he got home or if any rose-coloured tint in his glasses had completely faded by the time he'd put the lawn edger away. She had to know.

Jolene was on her laptop in their mother's parlour writing while waiting for some phone calls to be returned. Marsha made a coffee in a big mug, gritted her teeth and went to take it out to Eric. At the back door she paused, had a vision of him telling his mates at five-a-side or whatever he was into, *the woman I work for is a right raver. Every time she gives me a coffee, I get so much more as well.*

She looked at the mug in her hand. What was she doing? What fall was she setting herself up for? She tipped the coffee down the sink, picked up her phone to check in with her deputy at work, and let Eric get on with his weeding.

'You really do like your grub, don't you?' said Daz Meynell, watching Annis load chips onto a triangle of bread along with a tail of fish and a spoonful of peas. They were sitting outside on the back patio of the new fish and chip shop, at a metal bistro table for two. It was crowded and they'd been lucky, arriving just as someone was leaving.

'I do indeed,' she said. 'This was a great idea of yours, by the way.'

'I haven't had fish and chips for ages and they always taste better outside. Preferably in a place where seagulls are squawking but this comes a close second,' he said. 'How are things, are you coping?'

'Yeah,' said Annis spitting out breadcrumbs as she spoke and making him laugh.

'They'll be throwing you out of that big posh house for eating like that,' he said.

She chuckled. 'I doubt it. I cooked for us all last night and they were well impressed.'

'My mum was a terrible cook,' said Daz. 'The only time I ate veg as a kid was when I went round to my granny's for Sunday lunch. I learned to cook when I was a teenager and got into body-building. Fish, chicken, steak. I cooked a lot of steak for Paulie when he got ill. The best stuff. He was on fillets and I was eating rump.' He gave a sad smile and Annis knew that his grief was still riding high under the surface of him.

'My mum was an amazing cook,' she said, pulling him away from the subject of his dog. 'She liked to have dinner parties so she could show off her skills.'

'I can imagine that house having a great big dining room with a massive table and loads of throne-like chairs set around it,' said Daz. 'I bet you had some fun growing up in it.'

'Yeah, that's why I ran off when I was sixteen.'

'Why did you?' he asked.

'You'd have had to live with us to understand that one,' she said.

'I suppose I ran away too, didn't I, going into the army, but I worried about my mum all the time, hoping she'd be all right. She was an old bat, but I loved her.'

'This is nice,' replied Annis, not wanting to talk about families. Her head had been full of them since she came back to Fox House. She wanted a break from the subject.

'I've got something to show you,' said Daz. 'I wasn't sure if you'd approve or not.'

He rolled up his sleeve to reveal a tattoo of a bulldog and underneath, on a scroll, the name *Paulie Walnuts*.

'It's not finished yet, I've got to get it coloured in but it's photo realistic, I'm so pleased. I sobbed like a berk when I saw it for the first time. It's just like him.'

'It's beautiful,' said Annis and she meant it. The artwork was amazing.

'I feel like I have him with me again,' said Daz, coughing away a rise of emotion that threatened to claim his voice box. He rolled down his sleeve.

'I get that,' said Annis.

'You got any tattoos?'

'No,' said Annis, 'but if anything happened to John Abruzzi, I'd be tempted for the same reasons you were.'

Daz smiled at her. 'You're a nice person, Annis Vamplew.'

'Shut up and eat your chips,' she told him.

Marsha was on her laptop checking out a rival promo goods site when someone knocked at the back door and a quick glance through the window told her it was Eric. She wondered if he was going to apologise for rogering her and suggesting an official line that it never happened, but when she opened the door he was standing there with a chocolate orange. Her eyes went from it to his face and back again.

'Hi,' he said, hint of nerves showing in his in/out smile. 'I brought you this. A present.' He handed it over. 'To be honest, I was going to buy you a box of chocs but the shop had a really crap selection and ... well, everyone likes these, don't they?'

She didn't have the heart to say that she couldn't stand them.

'Thank you ... that's really sweet,' she said, slightly stunned.

'It seemed like a really good idea but the closer I got to the door, the worse it got.' He was wincing now. 'I thought you'd know I was here and I was ... expecting you to bring me a coffee.' He held up his palms; 'Not that I mean I was expecting anything else with it.' He shook his head at himself. 'I'm a cock, aren't I?'

Marsha's lips melted into a smile. 'You're not a cock, it was a lovely thought. Thank you.'

'I was thinking about you a lot last night,' he said, his voice just above a whisper in case her sisters were nearby.

'Were you?' That surprised her.

'I could actually murder a drink if you've got time to make me one and bring it down,' he said.

'Yes, I ... I'll do that,' said Marsha.

'Okay, I'll see you in a minute then. I'll just ... wait,' said Eric, pointing to the shed.

Marsha put the kettle on and while it was boiling she flew up the stairs to change into sexier knickers.

'Do you think you'll be able to come to the tribute band evening then?' asked Daz, pouring out some more tea for them both from a big metal pot. 'You won't have to pay.'

'You saying I'm a freeloader?' Annis raised her eyebrows at him while swiping the last piece of bread and mopping up the peas from her plate with it.

'If the cap fits,' said Daz and grinned. 'You know, I used to think it was *if the cat fits*. I only found out it was *cap* about three years ago.'

'I worked with someone who didn't realise that the robot dog in *Doctor Who* was called K9 because he was a *canine*,' said Annis. That was Denise's big lumpy son Freddie.

'Never. This is the club bar you worked in?'

'Yes,' said Annis, not missing a beat. 'Cocktail bar, gentleman's club-cum-massage parlour.'

Daz laughed, then realised she wasn't joking and his smile dropped. 'Really?'

'Not quite sure why I told you that,' said Annis, though she knew perfectly well. She was giving this sweet man every opportunity to walk away before he got hurt.

'That's quite a combo,' said Daz. 'I'm presuming when you say *massage parlour* you mean . . .'

'I do. I managed reception and the bar, that was all.'

'I love a Pina Colada,' said Daz. 'Maybe, if you don't succeed in putting me off you, even though you're trying very hard but it's not working, you could mix me one sometime. Heavy on the Bacardi, please.'

Annis smiled. 'I will,' she said.

Marsha put the mug of coffee down on the table and waited for what would happen next, if anything. This gardener's shed with its crumbles of dried mud on the wooden slatted floor and spidery corners was no Gerard Bannen's sacristy but at that moment it was filled with more electricity than his pristine and holy place ever was, and that was saying something.

Eric stood there, unmoving. To an onlooker she supposed they might look like two gunfighters at the OK Corral, each waiting for the other to twitch. The moment stretched so much it began to ache, like skin pressed too close to ice. Then, just as Marsha was going to say, 'Right then, I'll leave you to it,' Eric's hand reached out, cupped the back of her neck and he pulled her towards him, crushing his lips against hers. Her body responded like plasticine, moulding itself to his. He was holding her so tightly she couldn't get her breath and she didn't want him to let go.

'Do you ... would you like ...?' asked Eric, the meaning clear.

'Oh god yes,' she said.

So they did, and it was even better than last time.

'Does it hurt?' asked Annis, as Daz drew up outside her house.

'Saying goodbye to you kills me.' Daz patted his solid chest.

Annis grinned. 'I mean the tattoo. Does it sting?'

'Yes, I'm dosed up on drugs to numb the pain,' Daz answered. 'Bloody well does kill, but it's worth it.'

Annis unclipped her seat belt. 'I'll try and persuade Mash to come with me to your Hunkees evening. I have a funny feeling it's Dolly's – Jolene's – anniversary the same night so no doubt she'll be going home for a romantic dinner. But I'll come alone if I have to. I'd like to see you as Micky Dolenz.'

Daz smiled and she thought again what a nice smile he had. Nice curve, slightly to one side, nice looked-after teeth, if a bit wonky on the bottom. And his blue eyes smiled when his mouth did, sending a spray of fine wrinkles from the outer corners. She didn't trust perfect smiles, the sort that looked as if they'd been bought off the shelf to mask what lurked beneath.

Daz hadn't made a move on her yet, not even a kiss on the cheek. He was scared of frightening her off, she knew; respectful of her situation. So she leaned over and pressed her lips to his. He tasted of vinegar and salt, like the seaside.

'Thank you,' he said, when she pulled away.

'What are you thanking me for?' said Annis with a hoot of laughter. 'You paid.'

'Thank you for your company,' he said. 'And thank you for liking my tattoo.'

'It's really beautiful. Wear short sleeves and show it off,' said Annis, feeling that Daz needed her approval. She recognised a person who hadn't had much of that in their life when she saw one.

This time when they dressed, Marsha was less awkward. She felt empowered if anything and very satisfied. And, in a weird way, cleansed. She hadn't had great sex with anyone in her life before, not much sex at all really: that initial mechanical deflowering; a brief fling with Thomas, a fellow worker with a very off-putting yeast problem; secretly-married-Johnny whose guilt subconsciously impacted on his 'up-ability' and a couple of others who presumed that when they'd finished, so had she, and never cared to check if that were the case. Eric, however, had made sure she was sorted, and sorted again. And again.

Eric lifted his arm and sniffed under it.

'Sorry, I'm a bit sweaty,' he said.

There were different kinds of sweat. Eric's sweat was musky and earthy and bursting with the scent of post-coitus. She could have inhaled him all day.

'Well you were working very hard,' said Marsha, pulling up her jeans' zip.

'I'd like to get to know you,' Eric blurted out.

Marsha wondered if she'd heard him right. 'Pardon?'

'I mean, the sex is great. But ... I'd like to get to know you on closer terms than this.'

She couldn't think of anything to say to that other than, 'Why?'

He laughed. 'Because I do. I would like it to be more. Sort of work backwards a bit.'

She looked at him quizzically, because she thought she knew what he meant, but something rotten was drifting in from left field.

'I know this really isn't the best time to discuss it,' Eric went on, misinterpreting her silence. 'Or maybe this is just enough for you, but I ... I'd like ... more.'

No, she didn't want more. She knew where she was with this. She didn't want to open up and let him in. She didn't want to be at the mercy of emotions tickled into tidal waves and left with nowhere for them to go.

'But if this is all you want, then ...' Eric went on.

'It is,' she said. 'Just this.'

'Right, that's fine,' he answered her. And she tried not to see the hurt in his eyes.

Chapter 34

After days of honeyed sunshine, the clouds could take no more and had to drop their load. They grew grey and lumpen and smothered the sun and then a giant hand began to wring the moisture from them. There would be no gardening done that weekend, no appearance by Eric. Marsha took her disappointment and moulded it into indifference. Habits could be manufactured with some determination and repetition. If she said to herself enough times that she didn't care if he was around or not, that she'd see him when she saw him, it would eventually become true and save her a lot of tears, recriminations and wasted energy.

Marsha and Annis took all the clothes to the charity shop Annis knew in Sheffield, bags and bags of them. The manager was absolutely delighted, in fact she couldn't believe her luck. They had a sister shop in Harrogate, she explained, where there would be more call for clothes like these. There weren't many people around this area that went on cruises or out for dinners where you had sorbet between courses.

'She was happy,' said Marsha, as they pulled away. 'She had a micro sob at one point, did you see?'

'Just turn left here,' said Annis, pointing through the windscreen.

Marsha did as she was asked. It was rough around these parts, depressing and dull, rows of grimy-looking shops, terraced houses with unkempt fronts, boards over lots of windows.

'It looks more like a bombed-out warzone than a city in Yorkshire,' Marsha observed, slowing down to look to either side.

Annis knew it was bad, but she'd seen it only through her own grateful eyes and not someone privileged like her sister's.

'There's the club,' she said, 'coming up on the right.'

'Do you want me to stop?' asked Marsha.

'No,' replied Annis, but a swell of emotion rose up in her heart like a strong wave of sea water. It was eleven o'clock on a Saturday which meant they would be getting ready to open up, cleaning and sprucing. They had a regular with a bad back who came for an hour-long massage at noon every week, with the beautiful Espresso Martini, and then he would sit in the bar and read the paper. Alfred, a retired solicitor, lonely after the death of his wife and son, turned up at three and stayed until eight, drank Rusty Nails and read Dick Francis books. She knocked him up a sandwich on the house if she had time. The cocktails weren't cheap, the cost of enjoying them while sitting on the velvet upholstery was pumped into the price. Bum tax, Denise called it.

'Looks nice,' said Marsha, because it did. An oasis of brightness in a drab landscape with pink and blue signage depicting a cocktail glass complete with red cherry.

Annis switched her eyes to the other side of the road.

'That's where I used to live,' she said, pointing to the upper floor of one of those rundown houses. It was the only one in the row with a pair of curtains; bright yellow with blue flowers.

Marsha didn't say anything because she didn't want to criticise but it looked beyond awful.

'Looks worse from the outside than it was in,' said Annis as if reading her thoughts. 'Denise owns all these flats. I had a bit of trouble with one of the punters and she let me move in there so I was closer to the club.'

'What sort of trouble?' asked Marsha.

'He wouldn't take no for an answer sort of trouble,' was the reply.

Geoff the paramedic, with his heroic day job and seedy alter ego. A shiver snaked down Annis's back. She never wanted to think about him again.

Marsha slammed on the brakes as a squirrel rippled across the road.

'He's lost,' she said. 'What would squirrels have to climb around here except lampposts?'

'There's a lot of trees behind the houses. They flank the railway line,' said Annis. 'They're lovely little things, aren't they?'

'Mum hated them,' said Marsha. 'I remember her once asking the gardener to put down some traps for them. He didn't.'

Annis didn't reply. She didn't have to. There wasn't much she could hear about her mother that would surprise her.

Jolene took the anniversary card out of the cellophane cover and picked up a pen. Why was she even having to think about what to write in it, she asked herself. It should be natural: *To my darling Warren, Happy 10th Anniversary. Here's to the next 10 . . . 20 . . . 30. All my love, always.* She couldn't write a dialogue she didn't believe in. It felt like when she was trying to put words in one of her characters' mouths and they were protesting, '*No, I wouldn't say this.*' And eventually she'd have to bow to the dictates of a fictional being. No wonder she was half bloody insane.

He was taking her out to *their* place, an Italian restaurant on the road to York called simply 'I', although there was nothing understated about their prices. They didn't serve the best food either, too many pretentious twists on dishes that worked better without them. She wondered if the other woman knew it was their tenth anniversary or if Warren kept what happened in their marriage as far away from her as he kept his peccadillo business from his wife.

She heard the front door open and Annis's chirpy voice drift down the hallway. She was a ball of energy and someone who brought light into this dull, staid house. Maybe she and Marsha should have packed up a rucksack and climbed through the window to a new life too. Maybe then, Marsha wouldn't have been someone intent on busting a gut to prove to the world she was someone of worth, better than a boy, and she herself wouldn't be so cold and insubstantial.

'I'm in here,' she called.

Annis strolled in and made immediately for John Abruzzi who was sitting contentedly in the corner on his blanket. She picked him up and nuzzled him.

'Did they want it all?' asked Jolene.

'They were delighted,' said Marsha. 'Over the moon in fact. We even had a little flurry of tears.'

'What are you up to?' asked Annis, peering over Jolene's shoulder.

'I'm about to write my anniversary card to my husband,' came the answer.

'Should be easy for an author to write some suitable mush, surely?' said Annis.

'Are you doing anything for it?' asked Marsha.

'He's taking me to I,' replied Jolene, turning to Annis to enlighten her. 'It's an Italian.'

'Ooh, what a treat.' Marsha was impressed.

'It used to be,' said Jolene, 'but it was taken over by new management who decided to inflate the prices and distort the tried and tested dishes out of all recognition: scallops with a chicken liver jus, prawn cocktail and whelk surprise. Obviously not those, but you get my gist.'

'I never eat seafood, apart from cod and haddock,' said Annis, spooning coffee into three mugs. 'I had a spell living near a grotty bit of coast and once you've seen prawns clinging on to a sanitary towel for dear life it sort of puts you off.'

Marsha gagged and snorted at the same time. Jolene, after a delayed reaction, gave a short burst of laughter and was stung with a sharp pin of regret that she'd missed so many years with this sweet, funny girl-woman. She'd never been allowed to bloom growing up in this house, like a sunflower destined to reach for the sky but kept in a box. But flower she had, physically and mentally. She was by far the strongest and most robust of them all.

'What's he like, your old man?' asked Annis. She'd already had Marsha's opinion on him but she was interested in what her sister thought about her husband. He sounded a bit of an arse to her; why wasn't he here for starters, supporting her?

'He works very hard,' said Jolene, touching her necklace again. 'He's smart, charming, a great raconteur in company.'

'Nice,' said Annis, noticing the missing buzzwords: *kind, gentle, caring.* The words people didn't use to compliment her mother either.

'Did he buy you that?' she asked, pointing to her necklace. 'You fiddle with it a lot.'

Jolene didn't even realise she'd been doing it. 'No, I bought this. He got me one very similar years ago, but I lost it and I could never find the same one anywhere. Such a pity, it was lovely. It had a little cat sitting on it; a limited edition piece.'

'Really,' said Annis. She'd seen a necklace of that description once, but in gold. She'd been given it by Geoff the paramedic and he wouldn't take it back. He didn't take kindly to her rejection. She batted the thought of him away; there had been too many of those today.

Jolene had wrapped her mother's gold locket up in some white tissue paper and put it in a spare jewellery box to make it look like a gift. The turn in the weather meant that she had to avail herself of her father's umbrella which still stood in the antique stand in the hallway, faithfully waiting for its master's usage. It had a black oak handle with a sterling silver collar which should have tarnished but hadn't, suggesting that someone had kept up its polishing. The rain was falling straight and evenly in thick heavy drops as if distributed from a giant shower head above. Jolene skirted the puddles which had formed and had a sudden memory flash of her mother holding her hand as they were walking somewhere in the rain, her tiny self in red wellingtons jumping in puddles, in the days when she was an only child. There must have been more happy things that occurred when she was older, but she couldn't remember them. Maybe one day she'd pay for some hypnotherapy to locate them, bring them to the fore of her thoughts so she could view them like a newly discovered photo album.

She hurried towards the shelter of the Lunns' front porch where she shook the water off the umbrella and propped it up in the corner while waiting for Sally to answer her knock. When she did so, Jolene's mouth dropped open at the sight of her. She looked horribly pale and tired.

'Sally, are you all right?'

'Come in, dear, out of this awful weather,' said Sally. 'Have you time for a cup of tea? Norman's asleep and I've just brewed a pot.'

'Yes, thank you,' said Jolene. Sally wasn't all right and it seemed rude to just cut and run. She wasn't fluttering today.

The kitchen didn't look as tidy as it usually did. There was unwashed crockery in the sink and the table needed a wipe down.

'Are you in pain?' asked Jolene, noting Sally's expression and how she rubbed her shoulder.

'Ohhh,' Sally groaned, a long drawn-out sound of utter wretchedness as she dumped herself in a chair after getting an extra cup out. 'It's at times like this when I wish I had lots of children to help me.' She picked up the teapot that Jolene recognised as once being theirs a long time ago. She poured the tea into the cups, adding a slice of lemon. Something else courtesy of Eleanor Vamplew.

'I always have one of these when I feel a bit out of sorts,' said Sally. 'It seems to calm me right down. I wonder if it's the tea or the lemon, or maybe the *folie à deux* of both.'

'You should have some help,' said Jolene.

'Your mother managed to care for your father and I shall care for Norman,' Sally replied adamantly.

'My father didn't have the same condition that Norman has and he had nurses calling in,' said Jolene. 'This is much harder work.'

'Now, what can I do for you?' said Sally with a watery smile, closing down that line of conversation and Jolene let it be closed down for she had no right to tell Sally how to run things. She reached into her pocket and pulled out the box.

'I brought you this, as promised.'

Sally's face lit up. Her hands came out reverently to receive the gift. She cracked open the box and took out the locket, marvelling at it. Then, with trembling fingers, she opened it to reveal the photographs. Her eyes were shiny with emotion. She put the chain over her head and pressed the oval to her chest. Her voice was almost all whisper when she said, 'Thank you so much, Jolene.'

'You'll have to put your own photos in it now. You and Norman.'

'Oh no,' said Sally, 'it's perfect as it is. My dear friend with me, next to my heart.' She smiled again and Jolene found it pitiful to see how grateful she was. She felt so sorry for this woman who hadn't had the children she craved and who had been tainted by her association with her husband. She guessed that her friendship with Eleanor was akin to a small, insignificant planet orbiting a great sun and the breakdown of their relationship all those years ago would have hit her hard; inversely, so the rekindling of it would have meant everything. Eleanor and Julian Vamplew, responsible for so much emotion when they were barely capable of showing any themselves. And now Sally had lost her friend and the husband she had chosen to stay loyal to was beyond repair. She had nothing, she had no one.

'It's precious to me,' said Sally, curling her fingers around the locket. 'I know it's worth a lot of money and I wouldn't have minded if you said you wanted to keep it, but Eleanor said I should have it.'

'Well, you have it now,' said Jolene.

'I'll make sure that you get it back one day. I don't have anyone to leave it to.'

Jolene swallowed the lump in her throat. What a poor soul Sally was.

'I miss her,' said Sally. 'She was my only friend.'

Jolene noticed a white hair stuck to the slice of lemon in her tea. She couldn't drink it.

'I won't keep you, Sally,' she said. 'Don't get up, I'll see myself out.'

'Thank you again, Jolene.'

The first thing Sally did when she heard the door close was to open up the locket again, take out the photo of Julian Vamplew and rip it into as many shreds as was possible.

Chapter 35

For the next week, the three women concentrated on clearing the house, breaking the back of what they had to do. They stripped their father's bookshelves of his works and sent them to the university as their mother had requested. They filled up boxes of quality bric-à-brac, each one themed – i.e. books, office equipment, crockery. Dave West arrived with four strong lads to take away the bulk of the antique pieces: Eric had warned Marsha not to accept his first offer, so she had bartered a bit before agreeing to a fair price. They took sheets and towels to the local animal shelter. Annis hired a giant skip from one of Daz Meynell's contacts – Tom Broom – for everything they couldn't recycle; the broken and unwanted. They kept the kitchen, sitting room and three of the bedrooms more or less as they were because they needed to live here for a while still and they'd empty them when they had to. They needed tables to work from and eat off, a sofa to sit on, a TV to relax in front of.

Annis's old room was the last to be cleared. She hadn't been in it since she left all those years ago and when she pushed open the door and entered, dust motes stirred in the air as if woken from a long sleep. It was the only bed in the house not made up. The mattress was undressed, the shelves had been cleared. None of her annuals or books or CDs remained, her precious collection of elephants was long gone. She'd heard somewhere they drove away negative energy, which is why she'd started buying them, just cheap bits of tat from discount stores and second-hand shops, but she'd chosen each one with care, placed them near her door to offer protection and on her windowsill to chase away evil.

There was a film of dust over the shelves and the carpet, but not fifteen years' worth so someone had been in and given the place a fettle at some point. Underneath the window stood the giant doll's house she'd so painstakingly transformed from a bare-wood structure into a museum piece, now irreparably broken. Only the room at the bottom had survived undamaged, ironically the family room, with its pile of miniature games on top of the table. Games that no one played. She'd made each little box: Cluedo, snakes and ladders, Monopoly, the Game of Life. She had wallpapered every room, moulded lightshades and food out of polymer clay, made curtains and rugs from scraps of materials bought in assorted bags from Carol's Crafts stall on Barnsley market.

Annis felt someone at her shoulder as she stared at it, remembering her young self dressed to leave, rucksack packed and heavy on her shoulder, the hammer that usually sat in the tool box under the kitchen sink in her hand. It was her final defiant act, sending out the clearest message she could without actually shouting it.

'Why did you do it? I mean, after all the hours you put into it?' It was Jolene.

'It was how I felt,' said Annis.

'A message to Mum and Dad?' Jolene asked.

'If you like. I'm not sure if they got the subtlety of it. You would hope so, wouldn't you, with all their so-called intelligence.'

Jolene gave it a once-over, wondering if it was salvage-able. It really wasn't.

'What do you want to do with it, Annis?'

'This,' said Annis. She snapped open one of the bin liners in her hand. Jolene helped her fill it with the wallpapered walls, carpeted floors, tiled roof, toy games and food, fur-niture, doors and windows – both broken and intact. Then Annis launched it into Tom Broom's skip where it belonged.

Jolene picked up her anniversary card and put it in her bag. She wished she weren't going home. It had been only sev-enteen days since her mother died and she didn't really want to celebrate her anniversary – for more than one reason.

'Go and enjoy yourself,' said Annis. 'Remember to avoid the prawns.' And she winked.

'I wish I could unremember what you said about them,' said Jolene with smiling disgust.

Annis took her hands from behind her back and pro-duced a bunch of white, yellow and pink flowers wrapped in newspaper.

'From the garden,' she said. 'Well, ours and next door's. The white roses were poking through the fence, which I think makes them fair game.'

Jolene lifted them to her nose and inhaled the scent from the freesias. They were her favourites. 'That's so sweet of you, Annis.' Her voice cracked and she referenced it: 'Listen to me. Anyone would think I was about to cry. I'm not sentimental at all, anyone will tell you.'

'Oh, I think you are,' replied Annis. 'You've just split yourself into two and you spend your emotion on the page so you don't have to do it in real life. I've read all your books, so I know.'

Marsha coming up from the cellar interrupted any response to that.

'I found this,' she said, holding up a green bottle with a large 'S' on its otherwise unobtrusive black label. 'You should take it.'

'Bloody hell,' said Annis, snatching the bottle from her and giving it the once-over. 'Champagne Salon. Very nice. I think they start at about seven hundred quid a bottle.'

Jolene shook her head. 'I can't drink that.'

'Don't be daft, course you can,' said Annis. 'Take it. And if you can't drink it, let him pour it over you and—'

'Okay, I'll take it,' said Jolene, anything to shut up that flow. 'I'll be back tomorrow.'

Marsha was still gobsmacked at the price. 'Seven hundred quid? There are a few of those bottles down there. What was Dad thinking of?'

'Speculation for accumulation,' replied Jolene, putting on a gruff man's voice. 'That's what Warren always says.'

'Go,' commanded Marsha. So Jolene did, though she reckoned she'd give the seafood a miss. She wished she could give it all a miss and go out with her sisters to see the Monkees tribute band at the working men's club in Oxworth instead.

When Jolene had gone Marsha asked Annis if she wanted anything to eat before they went out, but had to ask her twice because her head was someplace else.

'What's up?' she asked. 'You look as if you've seen a ghost.'

Maybe not seen a ghost, but heard one. *Speculation for accumulation*. That's what Geoff used to say when he was in the club holding court, regaling people about his dabbles in the stock market, bragging how he'd be able to retire on a lot more than just his NHS pension. He spoke at a volume to be overheard, to impress. Annis felt as if she had stumbled on the wavelength where he was presently residing and she didn't like it at all.

'Jolene's husband, has he a medical background?' she asked Marsha, even though it would be ridiculous to think it was anything more than coincidence.

'No,' came the answer. 'He's your Mr Corporate through and through.'

'Is he very good-looking?'

Marsha laughed at the line of questioning. Warren wasn't her type at all, so her answer was in keeping with her personal tastes. 'I wouldn't say so,' she said, pulling a face. Although, she would, if pressed, have admitted that he had really nice teeth.

'Is it fancy dress?' asked Marsha, as they queued up outside the club, behind some hippies and a lot of people in green bobble hats. She felt overdressed in her smart black trousers and jacket.

'It's sixties garb,' laughed Annis.

'I don't know any of the music except "I'm a Believer". That was them, wasn't it?'

'Yes, it was.' Annis broke off from talking to her to tell the people on the front desk that Micky Dolenz had left her a couple of tickets. Then she bought two green bobble hats for a fiver each and handed one to Marsha. 'There you go, now you fit in.'

Marsha put it on.

'Suits you,' said Annis. 'Goes with your ghost hair.'

'Shut up.'

Annis bought two bottles of Peroni from the bar and they sat at a table quite near the front, sharing with an elderly couple in psychedelic shirts and very bad blonde wigs. There was a tambourine on the table.

'Peter Tork is our grandson,' said the woman. 'Looks bloody nothing like him.'

'Wonder if Jolene will have a prawn cocktail tonight?' Annis asked her sister.

'I doubt it. I don't think I'll ever have one again either.'

'What's happening with you and the gardener then?' Annis asked. 'I mean you don't have to tell me, but I'd love to know.'

'Nothing,' said Marsha. 'He's younger than you.'

'So?'

'So he's okay for a shag but nothing more.' Marsha flashed a humourless smile at her.

Annis gave her head a shake. 'That's not you talking, Marsha. Don't be the sort of person who's done you damage. You know how much it hurts.'

'How do you know he's not a twat?' asked Marsha, picking up the bottle and tipping it into her mouth.

'I don't, and neither do you. Maybe he is and maybe he isn't. People don't come with labels on them, you have to learn about them. Like you're learning about me. Like I'm learning about Micky Dolenz up there.'

A wave of cheering arose as four men in their late thirties to mid-forties with dodgy wigs and sideburns wandered onto the stage and took their positions.

Peter Tork's grandmother leaned over the table. 'They're better than they look.'

'They weren't when they started off,' said his grandad. 'They were crap.'

Annis noted that Daz had shaved off his beard for his role. He looked younger without it, cheekier.

'Good evening, ladies and gentlemen,' said Davy Jones, who must have been about six foot six. 'Welcome to an evening with the Hunkees.'

'What the bloody hell have you dragged me to?' Marsha said to her wildly applauding sister.

They *were* better than they looked, luckily. The audience loved them; they were having fun up there, Annis thought, and they'd obviously worked hard at this. She shone her full beam of attention on each of Daz's bandmates in turn and wondered which one of them had the breakdown that sparked the group into life. They weren't perfect. They'd had to stop during 'Last Train to Clarksville' so that Daz could retrieve his wig from the floor. Everyone cheered when it was back on his head again.

'Well I have to say, I recognised more Monkees hits than I thought I would,' said Marsha at the end, after the encore of 'Pleasant Valley Sunday' where Mike Nesmith could show off his smooth twelve-string guitar skills. She was also on her fourth Peroni and her speech was ever so slightly slurry. She was glad that Annis had persuaded her not to drive and get a taxi instead.

'Good, wasn't it?' said Annis. 'Come and meet my friend the drummer.'

Chapter 36

Jolene's card to Warren sat on the mantelpiece next to his large, glittery, beribboned one with *To My Wonderful Wife* in raised gold lettering. He obviously hadn't read the words inside when he'd bought it because *You are the only one* would surely have struck as irony. There was a showy bouquet waiting for her when she got back, red roses and all. He must have bought it a couple of days ago and forgotten to put it in a bucket of water because a couple of the roses had droopy heads; and as she put them in a vase, scarlet petals drifted onto the tiled floor and she thought of the weeping rose in *Beauty and the Beast*, dying through lack of love.

He'd greeted her warmly when she walked in, asked immediately how she was, how things were going even though he seemed to zone out when she answered. He said he'd missed her and couldn't wait until all 'this business was over and done with' and then she could come home. Jolene found herself wishing that she couldn't wait until *this* business was over and done with – i.e. this date night – and she could get back to Fox House, to the sisters she was learning about. She was enjoying their companionship, their buckling down together and putting things in boxes, sharing their history, dissecting it in a safe, understanding space because only they three could ever know what it was like to have a family dynamic like theirs. She felt, for the first time, that a bond was growing between them, tendrils reaching out from each of them towards the others, connecting in a way they had never been allowed to before and she liked it very much.

She put on a black dress, ruched at the front which made the best of her tall figure, lending it more shape, and what she called her 'indulgence shoes': black patent Christian Louboutins with a spike heel. She'd bought them with her first book royalties; she hadn't even known she had some due. She'd bought Warren a Rolex watch which cost five times what her shoes cost and she'd had pleasure doing it. But that was before. All the good times she remembered were *before*.

He liked her to wear those shoes because Warren was six foot four and with her heels on, Jolene was just below the six foot mark and that was a perfect match for him, he said. He hated to see tall men with small women, especially when they celebrated their difference by wearing flat shoes; he thought they looked like fathers out with their children. That led Jolene to think that his mistress must be tall. She had drawn her own conclusions as to what this woman was like through what little he gave away, like the comment about height.

For the past five years Jolene had been like a crab sifting and gathering any tidbit of information she could find about her, storing, trying to fit the pieces together to make a picture, but she was nine-hundred-plus pieces short of a thousand-piece jigsaw so far. He'd been so very careful, so

thorough and yet sometimes Jolene thought he laid something down for her to find, just to torment her. She'd found
a long blonde hair on his jacket sleeve once, too obvious for
him not to have seen it and brushed it away. Not for someone so hell-bent on keeping his two lives separate.

She looked at herself in the full-length mirror in their
bedroom. Her waist was only slightly bigger than it had
been when she was younger and her breasts had filled out
somewhat as she'd got older but not so much that they'd
drooped with age. She'd twisted her long, dark hair up and
fastened it with a tortoiseshell clip and it gave her some of
the innate, effortless elegance that her mother wore like a
perfume. Jolene knew her mother would have loved to have
been tall even though she relished her prim, neat stature,
her small trim waist and fine bones. She would have enjoyed
matching her husband in height as they strolled anywhere
arm in arm. 'You're very lucky you take after your father in
that respect,' she once said, 'your features would not have sat
well upon a petite girl.' On more than one occasion, she'd
thought her mother might be jealous of her.

She cut the mustard for this evening, she decided, though
there wasn't a lot she could do about the cold sore tingling
on the corner of her lip which felt four times larger than it
was. She got them when she was stressed and she got them
often these days. She was surprised her head wasn't just one
massive cold sore, she thought as she dabbed a thick blob of
foundation onto it and hoped for subdued lighting.

They got a taxi to the restaurant and were seated in one of
the more intimate booths at the back. The waiter lit a candle
between them, next to a bud vase with a red rose in it, one
with a velvety proud head. Warren wore a suit, dark grey
with a crisp white shirt and a grey tie. He'd slicked his hair

back and looked even more striking than he usually did: big shoulders, powerfully built, a face that had only grown more handsome in the eleven years she'd known him. Jolene's heart gave a sad thud to think of the beginning of the arc of their relationship and how different it was to now – for her at least. She would have died for him, she was so very in love and felt it was reciprocated wholly. She remembered what Annis had said when she'd told them the truth about the cocktail bar, about women who were reeled in by a man wearing a charming veneer. It was her to a tee. Her savvy little sister, wisdom earned through experiences she didn't even want to imagine. She wondered how differently she'd turned out to the Annis who would have stayed around. She thought she might have liked that Annis less.

Jolene lifted the menu and looked at the starters, saw the prawns and couldn't stop the smile escaping. She'd give them a miss, she thought. Warren chose a steak for mains, rare with a gorgonzola and wild mushroom sauce; she chose orzo with pesto, prosciutto and cream and asked if it was possible to leave out the salsicciamo because it was one ingredient too many. Of course she could, said the oily waiter. At those prices she could have had her orzo shaped like a spaceship if she'd wanted.

'Seems to be dragging on, doesn't it?' said Warren when the waiter had delivered and poured an expensive red wine. Warren had insisted on tasting it, as he always did, tossing it around in his mouth before eventually swallowing. Jolene always found it embarrassing, knowing it was all for show. Her father always sampled his wine and he knew in an instant if it passed muster. He made the testing of it look almost regal. She still thought of him every day, even if just for a few seconds.

'Sorry, what?' asked Jolene, distracted by comparing the two men, one effortlessly refined, the other an aspiring nouveau-riche dickhead.

'I said it's all taking an age,' Warren paraphrased.

'You mean Mum?' she asked flatly, knowing exactly what he meant but she didn't want the saying goodbye to her mum reduced to 'it'.

'Yes of course that's what I mean. It wasn't this drawn-out with my mother and she died in winter.'

Jolene shrugged. What was she supposed to say to that, other than *it is what it is*?

'How are you getting on with the paperwork?'

She prickled, knowing where this was going.

'I think we've done all we can for now.'

'Has the house gone up for sale yet?'

She raised her eyebrows at the nerve of him asking that. 'Not yet. We're just in the process of emptying it.'

'How far have you got with that?'

'A long way, considering that most people wouldn't want to empty a drawer until some time after the funeral.'

'Probate is working out at around seven months at the moment,' said Warren, taking a sip of his wine and she did the same. It was too weak for her tastes, not heavy enough, no substance.

'Is it?' she answered. He'd researched it 'on her behalf', obviously.

'I should think a house like that might take a while to sell.'

In other words he meant she should push for putting it on the market because the sooner it was sold, the sooner she would get her inheritance.

Silence reigned for a long minute while Jolene buttered her bread roll and Warren planned his next angle of attack.

'When's your next book contract due?' he asked her then, casually, as if he were asking her what the weather was like outside.

'Can we talk about something other than money,' said Jolene, suddenly irritated. She could almost hear the machinations and calculations going on in his brain. Warren feigned shock. 'I wasn't talking money,' he said, 'I'm taking an interest in what's going on in your life, actually.'

He was very good at dressing things up in disguises.

'How's the business doing?' she asked.

'Oh, so it's okay for you to talk about money then?' he cast back.

'I wasn't, I was taking an interest in what's going on in your life.' She gave him her best innocent smile. The sarcasm went over his head.

'It's good actually. I'm meeting a potential client in France on Tuesday.' He sipped and grimaced and she could tell he wasn't too keen on his wine choice either. Not that he'd admit to such a costly mistake.

'What part of France?'

'Near Paris.'

'Nice. Are you taking *her* with you?' It was out before she could stop it.

His eyes shuttered down and his head gave a shake, a duet of annoyance and frustration.

'No, I'm not. I'm going alone,' he said, the words ground out between his teeth.

The starters arrived and the waiter took an age to describe what they were about to eat; which region of Italy Jolene's mozzarella came from, how long the bloody tomatoes were hanging on the vine for, the exact location where Warren's prawns were sourced in Cornwall, though no mention of whether they were fished near any sewage outlets, nor if they went surfboarding on Tenaladys.

They ate in silence, Warren quietly seething that Jolene couldn't just give him a break from talking about his 'other life' on their tenth wedding anniversary. He couldn't believe she was so thoughtless.

Daz was overjoyed that Annis had turned up. He introduced her to the other group members, his old army buddies, Si, Keith and Shah. Shah was mixed race, Wakefield and Bangalore and had puffy black sideburns glued on his face. Even with the green bobble hat on, he looked about as much like Mike Nesmith as Sally Lunn did. Peter Tork was Si, the grandson of the old couple Annis and Marsha had been sitting with. He was built like a barn door and on a constant moan – so the others said – that he'd had to sacrifice his beloved ZZ Top-style facial hair for the whole time he was in this flipping band. Keith – Davy Jones – towered over everyone but his wig was good and someone had done a great job on thickening up and darkening his ginger eyebrows with a make-up pencil.

Daz went off to buy a round of drinks and while Si was giving Marsha a masterclass in how to play the tambourine, Shah pulled Annis away from the others.

'He's told us all about you,' he said with a wink.

'I hope not,' said Annis.

'All good stuff,' said Shah.

'He told me all about you too. You know, why you decided to do this.'

Shah nodded. 'Told you, did he?'

'I think it's wonderful,' she said. 'You're all brilliant.'

Shah smiled and sighed at the same time. 'Who would

have thought four men in dodgy shirts and wigs and these things' – he flicked his right sideburn – 'from Rita's Fancy Dress shop in Penistone would be able to draw a crowd like this?'

They both laughed at that.

Shah's voice dropped. 'I'm just glad it worked, it was a bonkers idea but we were all worried, you know, about him. The Monkees and that scraggy old bulldog saved him.'

And Shah looked across at Daz buying drinks and Annis knew then which one of them had needed to be pulled back from the brink.

The food rolled around in Jolene's mouth, and she swallowed, but she derived no enjoyment from it. How could she. What a ludicrous situation, sitting here opposite a husband whom she had allowed to have a mistress because she either shared him or lost him, that was the deal he put on the table.

'Can we talk?' she asked him, not being able to bear the swollen silence that sat between them like an egg sac bulging with baby scorpions.

'It depends what about,' Warren replied, not lifting his head, cutting his steak with a zeal that suggested he was cutting something else in his imagination.

'Us,' Jolene said.

'We are okay, Jolene. We don't need to discuss *us* at our tenth anniversary meal. I wanted this to be lovely for you in *our* restaurant.'

This was his favourite place, not hers. She liked another Italian, a homely bistro where the service was a bit slap-happy but the ambience was warm and kind.

He chewed, she could see his jaw working not only on

the meat but on their present situation. She was in danger of ruining the whole evening if she said just one more word on the subject. Every time she attempted to pull him close to discuss it, he backed a little bit further away from her. She wanted to bring it to a head now because she was tired of being lonely, swimming around alone in her marriage. Ever since Annis had said what she had about women in abusive relationships, the words had been swooping and diving in her head like a murmuration of starlings. Annis had said she had split herself in two and it was true. Half of her was suffering in an emotionally abusive relationship, half of her was writing templates of them for other women to recognise and avoid. She needed to pull both of her halves together, realign. She just needed a catalyst to make it happen. Just one small straw to break the donkey's back, make the change.

Marsha went to wait for the taxi as Annis had asked if she could just have a quick word with Daz before they went home. Shah had presumed she'd known the whole truth of him. Daz had been the man at the end of his rope, so his friends had put him in a groovy sixties shirt and wig and given him back his reason to live. Kindness was such an underrated quality, outshone by flashier ones, but it was a fundamental of life, of society. Even small kindnesses could grow like Jack's beanstalk and flower and bring the most valuable fruits. Daz Meynell was one of life's good guys, she could see that, even though she'd known him for such a short time. The measure of him showed in his friends, how he loved animals, how he accepted that she was far from a perfect being, how he was trying so hard to register his interest and balance that with respecting her circumstances.

'Thank you for being here tonight, it means a lot,' he said and bent to kiss her cheek.

'You can kiss me properly if you like,' said Annis. 'I might even let you stick your tongue in.'

Daz Meynell smiled and his arms came around her as if she were as fragile as tissue. Only Annis knew that's exactly what she had been, for too long.

They didn't seal their tenth anniversary with celebratory sex. Warren didn't make an approach and Jolene was glad of it. He felt she'd ruined his efforts, it was coming off him in waves and for once she didn't really care. Her calm, composed exterior belied the feelings swirling inside her: a hideous cocktail of regrets, self-recrimination and an ache for a love that had burned out like old stars, but whose fading, illusory light was still visible to her heart.

In bed Warren kissed her goodnight, his lips dry on her cheek. But in the morning, when he woke and turned around to initiate sex, she was gone.

Chapter 37

Sally sat at the kitchen table and sobbed, partly from the pain in her heart but mostly this morning from the pain in her side. She'd twisted something trying to pick up Norman, who had fallen from the bed. She'd felt something give as she made one final effort to hoist him back up. She'd shouted at him, something she was doing more and more these days, and as soon as the words had gone from her, the guilt rushed into the vacancy they'd left. He'd made her promise never to put him in a home and she'd sworn that on the Bible and she considered herself an honourable woman. Look what had happened when she'd broken her promise to Eleanor, not to read the letter she'd left for Annis? She didn't deserve this beautiful locket that sat around her neck – the first thing she put on in the morning, the last thing she took off at night. She'd prayed so many times for forgiveness and she'd come closer than ever this past week to confessing to Father Gerard so that he could absolve her from her sins in the name of God himself. The burden was too heavy, and when she was picking up Norman from the carpet, it was as if it was physically manifested in the weight of him. This is what her soul had felt like every day since it happened. And praying to God, and to Eleanor, for forgiveness so far had done nothing to lighten her load.

Jolene called in at Basil Thompson's funeral parlour before going back to Fox House. She just wanted to sit with her mum for five minutes, she said.

She didn't want the coffin lid opened, in case it disturbed her mother, she explained – ludicrous, but it helped to think of her mum sleeping, cosy, dreaming of dinner parties where she dazzled.

She told her mum that so many people wanted to come to the funeral. She'd had lots of texted and emailed RSVPs. It would please her mum to be popular, even though she gave them the merest morsel of herself, a sample of the person she wanted them to believe she was. None of them knew her at all, but they thought they did. Then she'd told her mum that her marriage was in shreds and she didn't know what to do about it. She knew that her mum wouldn't be able to identify with her situation; but just shaping her feelings into words and releasing them to the air, helped a little, especially as her mother wouldn't come out with any baloney now about bending rather than breaking.

She wished Eleanor had been the sort of mother who took her out for lunch and they'd have a Prosecco and then she'd say, 'Right, my girl, what's wrong? Let's sort it. Let's put the world to rights.' People who'd met their father presumed he would be a great dad to talk to because his students felt able to share their problems with him and he gave them extra time with their assignments and directed them to counselling if they needed it; but he couldn't do that with his own daughters. If only he had pretended they were his students,

Jolene would have taken the illusion over the indifference. But illusion had cost her, pretending had exhausted her, she could see it in her own flat, dull eyes which had once shone like conkers.

'What I wanted to say was that I forgive you, Mum. I don't know why you couldn't love us. Maybe it was something in your make-up. I wish I knew the truth of you. I think you would have if you could. I loved you, though.' Once again she remembered the mother of her early days, the memories she had clung on to, although she didn't know if they made everything worse or better.

Jolene wished she could cry at this moment but she felt dried out and not sure at all what she was feeling. But then, her emotions hadn't fitted into pigeonholes for a long time.

The post brought a clutch of cards to put with the rest of them: *Sorry for your loss . . . In God's Hands . . . With Sympathy.* Also some more RSVPs from those saying they would be attending the funeral, people from her bridge club and church and some people the sisters hadn't a clue about. Eleanor's popularity was surprising, but the same had happened at their father's funeral. So many blinded by their façades.

Annis was desperately trying to find a caterer when Jolene got home, because the one they'd planned to use for the after-service had double-booked with a wedding, and they'd let down the less lucrative of the two customers. She was rounding off a phone call to someone, telling them she'd come back to them. Then she put the phone down and pulled a flabbergasted face.

'Trying to charge thirty quid a head! I told them, "It's not a royal wedding you know". Cheeky feckers.' She drew a dick shape out from her forehead, then smiled at her newly arrived sister. 'How's you, Dolly? Good evening?' She winked lasciviously and Jolene felt something rise in her stomach.

'Yes, lovely,' she said, moving the conversation on quickly. 'Any more RSVPs?'

'Yep. Five more in today's post and no indication if they were bringing a plus one. I wonder how many others will post rather than email or text. And use second-class stamps.' Marsha made a small growl of frustration.

'Old farts not embracing technology,' said Annis. 'That'll bring the numbers up to over fifty.'

'Let's cater for seventy. Mum wouldn't want us to run out of food,' Jolene said. 'If we can find someone at this late hour.'

'Well, I found one woman who was free on the day. She was a bit pricey but it looks as if you get a lot for your dollar. And desserts. Old people like a bit of cake at a do.' Annis consulted a sheet of paper on the table.

'Okay, ring her then and get it booked,' said Marsha. 'I'm so angry at that catering firm letting us down like that. I hope the wedding cancels on them.' The doorbell rang. 'I'll get it.'

'I went to speak to Mum,' said Jolene, sitting down at the table next to Annis. 'I told her I loved her.'

'And was it the truth?' asked Annis.

'I think so but I'm all over the place. I wish I were more like her, not being able to feel so much.'

'No, you really don't,' replied Annis, noticing the painful-looking sore on her sister's bottom lip, as if there was a lot of anguish inside her breaking its way out.

Marsha returned with a large spray of pink blooms.

'Not more bloody flowers,' said Annis.

'These *bloody flowers* are for you, actually,' said Marsha, reading the card. 'Love, Micky Dolenz'.

Jolene and Annis went to the supermarket together because Annis wanted to call in at Pets At Home to pick up some more food for John Abruzzi and she thought she'd treat him to a new carrot home which was basically a box covered in hay that he ate. They'd been gone about fifteen minutes when Marsha heard the lawnmower's engine start and looked out of the window to see Eric driving it. She changed into a nicer top, gave herself a spray of perfume, slicked on some lipstick and took him a coffee. She waved to him when she was halfway down the garden, but he didn't wave back, nor did he stop driving, not even when she held up the mug. She stood there, feeling like a confused lemon, then he turned quickly and headed towards her, his eyebrows low, expression stiff. He cut the mower engine when he drew level with her, but he didn't get off it.

'I brought you this,' she said. 'Do you want to drink it in the shed?'

'Thank you,' he said, holding out his hand to receive it, 'but I'm busy. I need to concentrate on the garden.'

'Oh, okay.' He was turning her down. 'Everything all right?'

He drank, then he wiped his mouth, drawing the back of his hand across his lips. 'No, not really,' he said, tipping the rest of the coffee on the grass before returning the mug to her. 'Thank you.' He went to turn the ignition back on and her hand fell onto his, stopping him.

'What's wrong?' she asked.

'Nothing,' he said, but she wasn't about to shift.

'Okay,' he relented. 'Look, what we . . . have been doing is really nice but I don't want to do it again.'

Marsha felt a squeeze of hurt, a fist in her gut. 'I totally understand,' she said. A voice in her head, sounding like her mother's: *How long did you really think he'd be interested for after he'd got what he wanted?*

'No, I don't think you do,' said Eric with a huff. 'Okay then, why have I just said that? Come on?'

'Because you . . . you . . . think . . . feel that . . . because . . .'

He listened to her stuttering for long enough and then he answered for her. 'I'll tell you why. I don't want to be used, by you or anyone. You've made it quite clear, you aren't interested in *me*. So I think we should just leave it there.'

Marsha swallowed. Was this a line? She presumed she'd only thought that but she must have said it aloud because he answered it, his lips pulled back from his teeth.

'No, it's not a line, Marsha. Look at me. I know your emotions are probably all over the shop at the moment so I'm giving you a really easy get-out, but me – I'm way deeper in than I wanted to be with you. So thank you for some really nice afternoons but . . . it needs to end now before we go any further. I can get a fuck anywhere. I want more than that.' His tone was hard, defensive, in line with his feelings.

He turned on the ignition and she immediately turned it off again.

'I feel the same,' she blurted. 'But I don't want to get hurt either.'

Eric took a big breath. 'If this is about the age gap, I'm twenty-nine, Marsha. I'm a full-grown man. I don't want your money, I've got my own. I don't want your body – well, I do . . .' They both laughed, the tension popped.

'Look, I didn't expect this to happen to me, but it feels good. I think about you all the time and I've never had that before with anyone. Ever. Take a chance on me, will you. And I'll take a chance on you. Let's be gentle with each other. When you've got headspace. I'll wait.'

'Okay,' she said, barely above a whisper, the sound half the volume of her racing heartbeat.

He reached out, booped her on the nose with the tip of his finger and she felt the reverberations of that small, tender action all the way down to the centre of her soul.

Chapter 38

Jolene cooked for them that evening: a hearty cottage pie with buttery mash. She thought that cooking would take her mind off things but it didn't, because she could cook something like this on automatic pilot.

She remembered, as Marsha was setting the table, to take the bottle of Champagne Salon out of her overnight bag.

'We didn't drink it. I didn't want to waste it,' she answered her sister's quizzical look.

The bubbles in that bottle wouldn't have outdone the ones fizzing in Marsha's veins and arteries.

'You wouldn't have been wasting it,' said Annis, returning from the cellar with two bottles of wine. 'Red Italian or white Chilean?'

'Chilean,' said Jolene, making the decision. She didn't want to think about Italians or red wine tonight. She wanted to create as much distance as possible from anything that reminded her of Warren because thoughts of him were bonded to thoughts of her own weakness and idiocy and her brain was sore from self-flagellating.

They ate and drank in a silence that didn't need to be

filled with words other than the odd 'Mmm' and 'This is really good'. And the wine was cellar-cold and crisp. It was a million times more tasty than the pretentious pasta of the night before and Jolene felt a billion times more at ease.

'You do know I'm going to split the money,' Annis announced, a few forkfuls of food from the end of her meal. 'I would never have kept it all, whatever the will said because it wouldn't have been fair. Three ways, don't argue, it's happening.'

Jolene glanced up, a spiral of panic shooting through her. 'Don't. That's not what Mum wanted.'

'No, it's not, but it's what I want. And I can satisfy the terms of her will by taking it all and then dividing it up,' Annis replied. 'Also, I just said don't argue, but you did.'

Marsha's turn to pipe up.

'Oh Annis, that's sweet of you, but—'

'You as well,' Annis exclaimed.

'Don't give it to me, Annis, please,' said Jolene, astounding the others by bursting into a flash flood of tears.

Marsha jumped up to get a square of kitchen roll but she thought she might need the whole thing. Jolene wasn't so much crying as dissolving. Annis looked to Marsha for clues; Marsha gave a mystified shrug.

Jolene started to apologise, picked up her fork and tried to pretend the last twenty seconds hadn't happened, which was hard with tears dropping onto her plate and her face crunched up with distress.

Annis gently took the fork out of her hand and put it down.

'What's up, Dolly?' she said. 'Spill. Whatever it is, just say it.'

So Jolene did.

'The money will complicate things for me. I want to leave Warren and I don't want him to get his hands on it. He's had all the cash I've ever saved. I'm broke. We have debts in joint names that only I'm paying and I feel as if I'm drowning.' Her emotional banks were bursting along with her tear ducts and she couldn't stop them.

Marsha couldn't believe it. She thought her sister was loaded – she should be, with all the book success she'd had. And happy. She'd actually aspired to be as contented as her. And just when Marsha didn't think she could be more gobsmacked, Jolene came out with, 'He's . . . he's got a mistress.'

The revelation landed in the middle of them like a stone in a pond; the initial *thwunk* followed by spreading ripples of revulsion.

'What?' said Marsha.

'Wanker,' said Annis.

'Jolene, how long's that been going on for? How did you find out?' asked Marsha.

'Just under five years.' The cat was now out of the bag and Jolene was no longer in control of it. She couldn't stuff it back in, its claws would catch on the cloth.

'Five years?' Marsha's jaw dropped.

'Who is it? Someone you know?' This from Annis.

'I've no idea who she is. I can't find out and believe me I have tried. He's very good at keeping her under wraps,' said Jolene.

Marsha sat back heavily in the chair, her mouth moving over the shapes of questions but not knowing which to ask first.

'It's my fault. I said he could,' Jolene blurted out. 'I said if it meant he wouldn't leave me, he could see her.' She closed her eyes against the onslaught of judgement to come. But all she heard was Annis saying:

'He must have brought you lower than low for you to agree to that.'

'What happened, Jolene? What did he do to you?'

Marsha had never really liked him. She thought he was up his own backside, cocksure. He certainly was that, if all this was to be believed. She reached over, took her sister's hand in hers and squeezed it. Jolene felt the warmth transmitted, the kindness and understanding. She felt love in that small gesture.

Jolene couldn't have told them the whole truth, it was too ignominious. She hadn't even told her priest in the confessional booth that she wished Warren would suddenly die so she could be released from his grip. How could a virginal man advise her on the vile complexities of her marriage and what had led her to such dark thoughts?

'I knew there was something amiss, there was a strange, nasty tingle in the air as if there was a loose wire in my life leaking electricity,' said Jolene. 'But I never imagined that he'd be unfaithful to me. I mean, I know he worked away a lot. He was always chasing leads or going to meetings, conferences all over the country, sometimes abroad, but I've always been of the mindset that if a man was going to be unfaithful, he was as likely to do it on his own doorstep as at a marketing event in Dusseldorf.' Jolene paused to wet her dry lips with a sweep of her tongue. 'I trusted him implicitly, until I . . . until I started to . . . get this feeling, no concrete clues, just intuition. So I asked him if anything was going on and he just came right out with it. That he'd met someone. It was purely physical – as if that made it more palatable.'

Jolene did not go so far as to tell her sisters that this other woman liked her sex spicy and found in him a willing convert. He'd thrown himself down a rabbit hole of risky outdoor sex, hot wax, ropes and bindings, breath play – and he didn't want to climb out of it. Jolene had tried to accommodate his new tastes, but the first time he put the silk scarf around her neck, she panicked and screamed as the pressure increased. An annoyed Warren made it clear that if they were to stay together, she would have to let him explore his newly unleashed proclivities.

'He said if I wanted to keep him that I'd have to share him. He loved me, he didn't want to divorce. He said he'd keep that part of his life totally away from me and he promised me the best of himself. He'd be the soul of discretion, he said. And my god, he really was because I have no idea who she is or anything about her. Every time he leaves the house, I wonder if he's going to see her. It's killed me.'

'And you agreed to that because you loved him,' said Annis.

'Yes,' said Jolene. She'd wanted her husband back, the one she'd married, not this version of him. She'd hung on, faithfully, waiting and hoping for someone she now wasn't even sure existed in the first place. Just like the women Annis had told them about.

'I've been wondering if he ever loved me. Maybe there was a spark in the beginning,' Jolene went on, 'but as soon as he realised I might be a cash cow, he upped the ante and secured me to a fairground ride that left me dizzy with confusion. He'd buy me flowers, tell me how much he loved me and in the next breath how I should cut my hair shorter because I'm a little too old to wear it this long, and question what I'm wearing, the colour of my lipstick, the height of my shoes. He's only telling me because he cares about me, of course. And I believed that, for a while.' She let out a breath that emptied her lungs. 'I have no pride left, no dignity and definitely no money. *Speculation for accumulation* as he always says. He's certainly speculated and accumulated where I'm concerned. I've been holding off signing a new book contract because I know he'll have the upfront advance from me as soon as it lands in my bank. He's relentless when he wants something, and I'm weak. I don't know what to do.' Her voice squeaked like a young distressed girl's.

'You're not weak, you've been weakened,' said Annis.

Jolene nodded. 'I must still love him, and that's why I hurt so much. But I want to leave him.' She groaned, a sound of real torment. 'I don't know what I feel any more.'

'Sometimes it's your ego that throbs and the pain refers itself to the heart,' said Annis. 'Emotions are never cut sharply, they overlap and they tangle and they defy separating. You might think it's love, but love goes hand in hand with respect and this man does not respect you.'

'I'm to blame, I gave him permission,' railed Jolene.

'You were bullied into giving it,' Annis threw back.

'Clever bastard,' said Marsha, who could have sat an A-level on clever bastards.

'He cornered you and he gave you one chance, one lifeline to hang on to him and you could do nothing else but grab it with both hands,' Annis went on.

Her young sister was right, that's exactly how it was. Jolene was beyond grateful that she was being seen through eyes that weren't judging her as a fool.

'I'll keep your share of the money until you're clear of him,' said Annis. 'It will completely free you and give you a new start.'

'It's yours, Annis. Mum left it to—'

Annis cut her off. 'Shut up, Jolene. And don't you start either,' she twisted her head towards Marsha. This money would be used to unite them, not divide them further. And that was a legacy worth leaving.

Eleanor

I have done plenty of research into my condition over the years. Maybe because it is part of my make-up to be narcissistic. People like me are, apparently, delusional, according to textbooks. We can believe what we want to without the need for solid evidence. Maybe that is why I have chosen to believe in God. But then again, surely, that is the definition of faith?

I am very good at delusion. I chose to believe also that any dalliances my husband might have had were no threat to me. He would not have left this life of privilege we shared; it was too good, too comfortable; I made it so. Chains of silk. But I always knew that if the day came when the core of my marriage was in danger, I would act, I would fight, I would win. And I did.

Chapter 39

The next day, Gerard Bannen came round to go over the running order of the funeral. Marsha opened the door to him and waited for her treacherous heart to start playing a military tattoo, but there was just a small hiccup in its rhythm before it settled quickly to its regular beat. It did not even attempt to leap when he took her hands and said, 'Are you bearing up, Marsha?'

'I'm fine, Father,' she answered him. Nothing of the warmth of his hands travelled up her arms to spread inside her. The intensity of his autumn eyes staring into hers gave her only the merest ruffle of fluttery feelings, then it was gone. She was in a blessed state of indifference, free from the spell of his pheromonal scent, released from the game, and a voice in her brain said, 'thank fuck for that.' Standing there on the doorstep, she saw Gerard Bannen in a new light. He was not a bad man at all, he was a good, solid parish priest, but he had a vanity she doubted even he knew he possessed because it was so established, it was an integral part of him, and that weakened him – and she wasn't going to do weak men ever again. She didn't give him the satisfaction of pulling her hands away from his because they neither burned nor thrilled her. She let him hold her and she knew that something within him was trying to work an enchantment, but he had no chance. Eric was due soon; she'd take him a coffee down to the shed and they'd sit and talk for a while or kiss or maybe more if it happened for them both . . . and she'd tell him she had all the headspace for him he wanted and more because there would be parity. Blessed parity. Hallelujah.

Annis made him a drink. Father Gerard asked if there was any bric-à-brac spare because the church council were having a jumble sale in mid-September and Jolene told him that there were plenty of boxes of it if someone would like to pick them up after the funeral. Their mother would want him to have what she no longer needed to raise some funds for the church if they would be of benefit.

Father Gerard's service sounded exactly what their mother would have approved of: reverent and respectful, with the added feeling of someone who knew her well. Or at least who thought he did. Their mother was a great believer in offloading her sins in the confessional booth and all three of her daughters wondered what secrets of her soul Father Gerard had collected from her and was storing behind the lock and key of his mind.

He asked them if he might visit Eleanor in the funeral home and they said of course he could. It would be good for him to be her final visitor. Jolene had said her goodbyes, Annis had said all she had to say in the hospital and Marsha still couldn't face going.

When he had left, Annis asked her, 'What's the story with you and him, because there is one.'

And this time Marsha didn't deny it and she told them it all, as if the kitchen table and her sisters made her own confessional booth.

Sally stroked Norman's cool brow and she kissed his face. When he was sleeping, she could imagine that he'd awaken and be the Norman of old. The one who said, 'Put the kettle on, Sally, and get out the biscuits.' He always loved a biscuit. She could picture him waking up, rotating his feet in bed and then getting up to carry on doing his stretching exercises on the carpet so he was ready for the day. Retirement had suited him well, pottering about in the garden and they'd often go off to the seaside and have fish and chips on the prom. She'd had a good life with Norman, apart from not having any children. He didn't want to be poked about so they never knew if the problem was with her or him, and she'd been forced to accept it was God's will and sometimes she'd wonder if God was trying to tell her something in not letting them have the gift of a baby. Occasionally a programme would come on the telly about IVF and she got that ache inside her again, that they could have had a child if they'd only tried harder. Even after the menopause, the desire had never diminished to feel a baby growing inside her.

He sighed contentedly as if the old Norman was still in there, like a kernel in a nut. She thought of all those years of wasted energy trying to pretend that there was nothing wrong with Norman in *that way*. The extra lines they'd caused on her face, the anxiety that kept her awake, the bad dreams she'd had with the tablets that helped her sleep.

She'd been right to stay with him, but the truth had

come too late for them to take advantage of it and enjoy their freedom from that awful shadow. They still had their lives though, unlike the Vamplews. If you could call this a life.

Chapter 40

The following day was beyond strange; they all felt it. The hot preceding days had caused so much moisture to be dragged from the ground, from plants and lakes and rivers that the clouds grew pregnant with it. They hung above, dark and threatening, promising rain on their terms.

Jolene was trying to do some work in the sitting room but her brain wouldn't play the game. Likewise Marsha was on the phone to her second in command but her concentration levels were low. If she'd had any doubts that selling her company was the right thing to do, they had all but disappeared. It was much too early, she knew this, to plan to live nearer to Eric, but he had moved pieces around inside her, made her realise she wanted different things from those she had. She'd never felt settled in her large house in Derbyshire. It just didn't feel like a home. She had decisions of her own to make, as much as her elder sister. Thankfully not as traumatic.

Annis was sitting on the floor in the kitchen reading with John Abruzzi on her lap. He was a glorious, warm weight. Her thoughts drifted to Daz and she wondered if he'd get himself another dog because animals fitted into spaces in hearts where people never could. She felt the portent in the air too, but it was nothing to do with the weather. What she felt was within these walls, a sadness, as if it was in mourning for a mistress it had a one-sided relationship with. *Join the club, House,* thought Annis.

Marsha wandered into the kitchen.

'Aren't you uncomfortable down there?' she asked, smiling at Annis's long, crossed legs and the rabbit sitting on her lap.

'Nope.'

Marsha leaned down and gave John Abruzzi a tickle on his forehead. He let her, for the first time. Result.

Jolene came in. 'Did someone mention food?' she asked.

'That's a good call. I'm peckish,' replied Annis, putting down her book and shifting her big rabbit onto his bedding. 'Heinz tomato soup and part-baked rolls, I reckon.'

Comfort food. The smell of baking bread took her back to the club, to Denise and the rough-and-ready girls.

'Sounds good.' Marsha opened up the drawer and got out a tin opener. 'I hope whoever buys this house is happy in it. We could have had a ball if we'd all been kids the same age in it, don't you think?'

'We were three only children, weren't we?' said Jolene. 'I can't believe I'm actually going to say this, but I'll miss it. I think I've enjoyed being here with you these past three weeks more than I ever did in all the years I spent growing up in it. What will you do with your money, Annis?'

'My third share of the money you mean,' corrected Annis, to confirm her word was good. 'I want to spend some on a course so I can teach people who can't how to read. I was thinking of doing it when I worked at the cocktail club but it's not so easy to kick off the ground when you have no cash, no qualifications – a pipe dream really, but it wouldn't leave me alone. I did a pretty good job of teaching, if I say so myself. I developed a system, found what worked and what didn't, but I would like to do it properly. I've seen what a massive difference it makes to people, how it allows them to better their lives. And it's something all of us who can read just take for granted, never realising the power it gives us.'

'Wow,' said Jolene when that had sunk in. She was moved to tears, and blinked them back into her eyes, laughing at herself.

'You could buy a school,' said Marsha.

'I will buy a house to make into my school. Throw in some simple maths. Maybe some basic cooking. A month ago I was adamant I was somehow going to do it and I had no money, so now I have, and lots of it, it's definitely going to happen.'

'I wish I had a clear plan,' said Jolene, taking two ibuprofen out of the cupboard. She had a stress headache and there was no guessing why.

'Bite-sized pieces,' advised Annis.

Marsha stirred the soup in the pan. 'Is he coming to the funeral?'

'Yes.' Jolene washed down the tablets with a glass of water. 'Then I'll go home with him and somehow I'll have to start the process of leaving him. I'm dreading it. You have no idea how manipulative he can be.'

'We are hardwired into taking the easy way to save energy,' said Annis, 'but he's destroying you. That isn't self-preservation.'

'When did you get to be so wise?' said Jolene, smiling at this younger sister she barely knew and yet she felt their blood connection grow stronger with every passing day.

'It's been hard earned,' replied Annis.

'I'll bet,' said Marsha, thinking of the cocktail bar in the grotty street and the upstairs flat with the jaunty yellow curtains.

'Is he violent?' asked Annis.

'No, not at all. I mean he has a bit of a temper and shouts when he doesn't get his own way but ...' Her voice tailed off and an inner one finished the sentence: *he always does get his own way.*

Jolene had always caved in to keep the peace. She knew that as soon as the funeral was done with he would resume his mission to oppose the will; he hadn't given up on it. He *wouldn't* give up on something like that. The only way to stop him would be to leave him.

'Did you encounter many violent people?' Marsha asked Annis.

'Not really. Although I always found the scariest ones were the quietest. The ones who looked harmless, ordinary.' She shuddered involuntarily.

'That Mark bloke, you mean. The one who locked you in his house?' asked Marsha.

'There was one ...' Annis began, then shook her head, silently cursing herself for opening up this closed box, because she never went there. 'He was a paramedic. His name was Geoff. I liked him in the beginning. He was courteous, polite, impeccable manners. He tipped me with every drink he bought and I knew he'd taken a shine to me. He asked me if I was *available* to give him a massage and, of course, I said I wasn't.'

Marsha turned the heat right down under the soup. No one was going to be eating until this story had finished.

'He told us he was a widower and that he was lonely.

He'd been left a large amount of money courtesy of his wife's insurance policy and he started splashing a lot of it at our place. And I mean a lot, champagne at stupid prices, rounds of drinks for people in the bar, double sessions with the girls. But he wouldn't stop hassling me to go out with him, promised me Denise would never find out about it because she wouldn't have allowed that. He said he'd treat me really well, buy me things, take me places. He turned up with presents all the time.' She looked at Jolene, faffing again with the moon on her silver necklace and she remembered the gold one with the small cat on the curve.

'He bought me jewellery, make-up – expensive stuff, a watch and he wouldn't take them back when I refused them. I suppose that meant, in his eyes, that I'd accepted them, but I hadn't. I didn't want them. I put them on a shelf in the stockroom.'

The gold moon with the small cat.

'People must get attached, I'm assuming,' said Jolene. 'Especially if he was missing his wife.'

'Some do. The girls are paid to be nice, to mould themselves to what a client wants and it's too easy when you're a bit lonely to believe that what comes out of their mouths is genuine. Nothing new about that, we all try and convince ourselves that the truth exists where it doesn't sometimes.'

Both Jolene and Marsha were testament to that and they nodded without even knowing they were.

'But Geoff's façade was starting to slip, especially when he'd had a couple of drinks. He was always talking about his money, showing off about how much he had invested and where.'

Speculation for accumulation.

'He was pissing off some of Denise's clients who didn't want to listen to him, but as I say he was spending a great deal, so she kept her eye on the situation. But one day, she wasn't there and neither was Freddie for some reason. And I went down to the cellar for a bottle of something and Geoff followed me.' She took a breath to steady herself, aware that she was feeling the dread in the pit of her stomach all over again. 'He was a big man. And he tried to take what I wouldn't give him. I bit his hand and managed to scream and the girls came to my rescue, and one of the old regulars who had a weekly hot stones and whatever else. Black Velvet smashed a bottle and she would have used it on him, I have no doubt about that. He left, calling me a prick-teaser, horrible names – the worst – threatening that I'd be sorry. We had to lock the door and calm down; all four of us, and the pensioner, were shaking. It was then that Blue Lagoon, the girl he went to most times, told us that he used to pay her extra to let him be rough with her. He'd taken it to the line with her though last time and she refused to have him again. Denise was livid when she turned up and heard what had happened.'

Jolene blinked hard. 'And this man was a paramedic?'

Marsha was horribly fascinated. 'Did you get the police?'

'She wouldn't have pressed charges; Denise and the police ...' Annis pulled a face and her inference was clear. 'We thought that was that. But then I started getting things sent to me at the club, weird things: a dog turd in a box, knickers with the crotch ripped out, that sort of perverted shit. Then he must have followed me because these presents started arriving in the post at my bedsit, then they were hand-delivered through the letter box: a Barbie doll with no head, a sliced-up bra. I was living in a ground-floor place then and I was terrified. Denise moved me into one of the flats she owned across the road. She'd been doing some digging around. Seems there were a couple of people from other . . . establishments who really wanted to talk to Geoff, people he wouldn't want to talk back to. I thought I saw him everywhere I went. He was so normal, respectable, that's the scary part. Those poor girls on the streets, they roll the dice every time they go out.'

'You've had it rough, haven't you,' said Jolene. 'Weren't you even tempted to come home? Surely it couldn't have been worse than that. What was it that really kept you away, love?'

'Too much water under the bridge by then,' was all Annis said by way of reply.

Daz rang Annis in the late afternoon. She saw his name come up on her phone and she smiled.

'Would you like me to come tomorrow?' he asked. 'I mean, I don't know your family but if you want a bit of moral support. I'll just stand at the back and be there if you need me and if you don't, I'll be invisible.'

'Thank you, Daz, but I have my sisters,' said Annis, who said that before she thought about it. But it was true, she did have them, and they had her. They were together again, and it felt good, just as it always should have done.

Warren rang Jolene to double-check the funeral time. He would come to Fox House first and ride in the limo with her, if that was all right. She said it was, of course. He sounded concerned, felt bad that he might have been a bit crotchety on their anniversary and that she'd been gone the next morning when he woke up. He missed her, he said. She'd been away too long from him and he would be glad when she finally came home. He said he loved her and poured more silky words down the phone that she might have fallen for once.

She just had the next day to get through and then the fun would start. She was prepared to hurt at peeling her life from his; but it had to be better than what it was now.

Eric called round to the house and asked if he could have a word with Marsha. They walked down to the shed together, the fragrance of honeysuckle syrupy and thick in the heavy air.

'I just came to see you before tomorrow, that's all,' he said, pulling her close to him in this place they had made their own. She inhaled the scent of him, sweet and honest. 'I wanted to make sure you're okay. The night before . . . it's crap. You won't sleep.'

'I know,' said Marsha. 'I've been here before, with Dad.'

'But this is the woman who grew you inside her,' he said. 'I can't even think what state I'd be in if I lost mine.'

Marsha would have envied him that pain. One day, his grief would be the price he paid for the love he had that would eventually remould itself into happy memories with a thin seam of poignancy running through them. Her grief was the price for nothing other than a cold and unmalleable emptiness.

That night Jolene opened up the bottle of Champagne Salon and they drank it with fish and chips from Cod's Gift in Millspring.

'How long will you stay here?' Jolene asked Annis.

'I have nowhere else to go. I might as well make my base here. Why don't you stay with me, Dolly?'

'Will you ever stop calling me that?' said Jolene, a smile on her lovely face.

'Maybe when I grow up. You'll always be Dolly and Mashed Potato to me. As I will always be the spoilt brat to you.'

Marsha thumped her on the arm. 'If I'd gotten to know you then as I'm getting to know you now, I'd have shared my chocolate with you.'

'Lying cow,' said Annis, making her sister snort with laughter. 'And you definitely wouldn't have shared your secrets about Father Gerard with me.'

'Do you think Bronwen existed?' asked Marsha, taking a sip of the champagne and appraising it. It was lovely but she was grateful her palate was unsophisticated enough not to want to buy more when their five-bottle stocks ran out.

'Yes, I do,' said Annis. 'But I think Father Gerard might have singled her out before she even knew she'd been chosen. And with his arrogance, he presumed he'd be able to persuade her to his way of thinking.' Annis picked up a chip and wagged it at Marsha. 'Could be wrong of course, just a theory.'

'Ah – he went to Rome after you'd left for London, I remembered and meant to tell you,' said Jolene.

Marsha gave a nod by way of reply but she would ask no more questions about him, she decided. Eric Granger was the sunshine who had chased away the long shadow of the past. Time to unhook it from her heel and shrug it off for good.

'Jolene, this house could be a refuge for us for a while,' Annis pressed her. 'Let's try and make up with it and leave it on good terms.'

'Sounds like a plan,' said Jolene. Something to look

forward to. She'd pray really hard this evening for the strength she needed tomorrow. It was going to be a rough one from start to finish.

Chapter 41

They went to bed on a warm, balmy night, so humid that all three women had their sash windows lifted to let in air, and all three had to wake up about two a.m. to close them as the rain was falling in a shushing sheet and splashing over the sills, as if it was trying to gain entry to seek shelter from itself.

They were united in their broken sleeps, memories riding like small ships tossed on a large sea of insomnia. Their mother was still of this earth, but by tomorrow she would not exist in her bodily form any more and that had a significance none of them could decipher. Marsha sobbed into her pillow as she scraped the barrel of her thirty-eight years to find treasured moments of her mum: the lovely food she made, the Christmas days, her elegance, the holidays in the South of France, her mother's head tilted to the sun; but at the edges of each one were black borders bleeding into the scene and those words watermarked through so much of her early life: *You should have been a boy.*

Jolene was anxious that everything go to plan. She wanted

to do her mother proud, part with her finally having done something nearing perfection that could not be criticised.

Annis stared upwards, thinking about Jolene worrying her necklace with her fingers, the silver version of a gold one she'd lost, with a cat on the crest of the moon. Annis thought of the necklace she'd been given that matched that description. Then she thought of Geoff the paramedic who told her they'd have to get rid of her rabbit when they moved in together because he was allergic to fur. She thought of Jolene saying that her husband didn't take too kindly to not getting his own way and she thought of the phrase: *speculation for accumulation*.

She got out her phone and googled the name Warren Cattrell. She had to search hard and deep and it took ages, but just when she was about to give up, she found what she was looking for. The image was grainy, fifteen years old but it was him without a doubt. Warren Cattrell was the man she knew as Geoff.

'I didn't recognise you,' said Jolene, doing a double-take as Annis walked into the kitchen looking the height of sophistication in a long black frock coat, heels and a black hat. She was transformed from the adult street urchin whom she'd found scoffing warmed-up Chinese food less than three weeks ago. Was it only that? It felt so much longer. 'You look lovely.'

'Asos and eBay,' Annis answered. She smiled, but it sat unsteadily on her lips. She was holding information that she had no idea what to do with. Would he recognise her when he turned up at the house? Her hair had been bleached and long then. She'd gelled it back today to wear with the hat. Maybe he would, maybe he wouldn't; she was dreading finding out.

'Warren's going to meet us at the church. He's stuck in traffic,' said Jolene. He'd texted ten minutes ago to say the M1 was at a standstill. She wasn't sure if she believed him or not and there was an intoxicating freedom in that. She wished he wasn't coming at all if she were honest. She wasn't alone.

A few moments of silence followed, then Jolene said, 'Thank you, Annis.'

'What for?'

'For coming back into my life. I can't tell you what it's meant to me.'

'Meant to *us*,' said Marsha, appearing at the door. 'I always hoped you'd come back and give me the chance to make up for being a shit sister.'

'I was shit to both of you,' said Jolene.

'There were seven years between us,' said Annis softly. 'We didn't have a lot of common ground. Maybe if we hadn't been the children of Eleanor and Julian Vamplew . . .' She didn't need to finish off her sentence for it to make sense.

'What I didn't expect was for us to find a way back to what we should have been,' said Jolene. 'It's been wonderful getting to know you at last. Both of you. Please don't disappear on us ever again, Annis.'

Annis's battered phone on the table vibrated and she jumped. Her nerves were taut this morning, and it was nothing to do with the funeral.

She picked it up and read a message from Daz.

Thinking of you. You know where I am 💋

And she knew he would be thinking of her and she wished she had told him to be here with her.

Marsha went to the cupboard, took out three glasses and a bottle of vodka bearing a gift label which she read aloud: *'To Eleanor, Merry Christmas from Wilf, Sheila and the Fur babies.'*

'Fur babies. Oh god, can you imagine her face?' asked Jolene with a bark of laughter. Her mother would have shuddered with repugnance.

Marsha handed the glasses out. 'No mixer, sorry, it won't kill us having a neat one. It's Grey Goose. Wilf and Sheila must have thought a lot of Mum.'

'You sure you should be having neat spirits after what they make you do?' Annis asked her.

'Shut up, brat,' was the reply, even though her sister looked anything like a brat. She looked lovely; she *was* lovely.

'Here's to the end of one era and the start of a new one,' said Jolene, holding up her glass. Her sisters touched it with their own and drank the generous measure down in one, coughing as it sank. Today was a day to be got through. Jolene was tempted to slip the rest of the bottle in her handbag.

'Where's Warren?' asked Marsha.

'Stuck in traffic.'

The truth of him rose up inside Annis, she opened her mouth to let it out.

'Jolene—'

There was a knock on the door.

'That'll be the car,' said Marsha, checking her watch and then adjusting her own hat, a much smaller affair than Annis's, but at her height she couldn't have pulled off the giant saucer look. She would have looked like a toadstool.

'What?' Jolene asked Annis.

'Nothing,' said Annis. It wasn't the right time. The

trouble was, there was no right time for what she was about to dump on her sister.

Their hands came out to each other instinctively.

'Let's give her all we have to give,' said Jolene. 'Let's say goodbye to our mother as sisters.'

The church was packed when they got there, a sea of reverent black. Anyone who knew Eleanor Vamplew would not have turned up in anything other than their funeral best. Father Gerard greeted them at the door, dressed in violet, for mourning, and his purest white. He was pure still, Marsha knew. Hers were the only lips his had ever tasted and he would have been tortured by forbidding himself the fruit of her, every bit as much as she had been forbidden the fruit of him. The difference was that his fruit had lost its bloom, but she had a whole fresh harvest festival waiting for her in the shape of Eric Granger – and she was going to dive into it head first.

The pallbearers slid the coffin from the hearse and lifted it onto their shoulders. A wreath of white trumpet lilies with golden throats covered the top of it, trailing down the side. The church was filled with the same lilies, dispensing their pungent scent into the chilled and sanctified air; a perfume that polarised opinion, just as Eleanor Vamplew had. As soon as she stepped inside, Marsha's eyes found Eric, standing with his grandfather. He was dressed in a black suit, black waistcoat, black tie and she felt a warmth spread inside her chest at the sight of him. He mouthed back at her, 'Are you all right?' and she nodded, smiled then followed her sisters to the front pew. They were the only family there. They hadn't tried to trace their uncles, they didn't even know if they were still alive, or if they had cousins. An elderly man leaned over from the pew behind and said, 'Sorry for your loss. Terry from the bridge club. Your mother was an excellent player.' Another one who failed to say, *Your mother was a good-hearted woman*.

They sang their mother's favourite hymn, 'Love Divine, All Loves Excelling', 'the song which had been played at her wedding, when her heart was full of love for the man she would soon be reunited with,' said Father Gerard when he introduced it. Then he read the twenty-third psalm and Jolene passed a tissue to Marsha, who was crying for more than the mother lying in the hideously-shaped box. She was crying for a young lonely Marsha Vamplew who used to come to this church, arrange the flowers, collect the hymn books, just to be in the orbit of that man in his perfect-priest robes standing there, that agent of God. She wished she could reach down through the years and give her a big hug.

Jolene ascended the pulpit and read a Bible passage her mother had chosen for herself: the ninety-first psalm, a passage about God's protection from fear, his assurances of comfort and care. *For he will command his angels to protect you.* And Marsha wondered why she had picked that. What the hell did their mother need protecting from?

Sally cried into her handkerchief until it was sodden. She was wearing her best black funeral suit. It had cost a lot of money but over the years she'd had her wear out of it. On the lapel was pinned the brooch that Norman had bought her on their wedding day and around her neck was Eleanor's locket.

She wished she had a penny for every time she had read the final words of her letter:

Please give my gold locket to Sally. She has been beyond faithful to me as a friend, I've never deserved her kindness. We did her a great wrong. It is nothing in relation to what I owe her but I hope it will convey something of what I would like to say to her but never will.

She had the letter in her bag to give it to Annis after the ceremony. She had been entrusted with the duty and must comply but she wasn't sure it was the right thing to do at all.

Chapter 42

The service was as perfect as it could ever be and when Father Gerard asked the congregation to rise as the coffin was lifted once more upon the shoulders of the pallbearers, the three sisters all breathed a collective sigh of relief. Though Jolene had overridden some of the more unnecessary extravagances, they were all sure that their mother would have agreed that her exacting standards had been met.

They followed the coffin down the aisle and at the hearse, Jolene placed her hand on the glass of the window.

'Goodbye, Mum,' she said. She thought of the mother she'd once had, the one who smiled, but she'd waved goodbye to her a long time ago.

Eleanor wanted to go alone to the crematorium. Her stipulation was that her goodbye to everyone and their goodbyes to her should end at the church door.

Marsha stood beside her sister. It was hard to imagine that her mother was inside that box; it made her a little claustrophobic to think about it. Her eyes were suddenly painful with tears at the thought that she couldn't remember one act of kindness that her mother had ever shown her. Just one would have carried her a long way, like a feather in a breath of wind. Over the years she'd come to realise that she would never have achieved all she had if the engine within her hadn't been solely geared up to nail her parents' approval. At the end of his life, her father had told her how brilliant a businesswoman she was, how proud he was of her. But it was her mother she needed to hear it from more.

Annis stood behind them, picturing her mother inhaling the perfumed lilies in her sleep. She would lie peaceful, knowing that she'd left her youngest daughter the bulk of her fortune and the apology had spoken for itself through the gesture. Her goal had been achieved, and its importance had been so great that it trumped being fair to her other two daughters. In their mother's screwed-up world, this was probably the nearest to affection she could gift.

The hearse slowly edged out of the drive, towards its ultimate destination.

'It feels wrong to let her go alone,' said Jolene.

'It's what she asked for, remember,' replied Marsha. 'Let her have her wish.'

Annis's arms came around her sisters. 'We did good,' she said. 'She might even have said *well done* if she'd been here.'

They walked towards the limo which would take them to the golf club where a banquet awaited the mourners. Jolene was about to get in when a car horn pipped and when she looked round, Warren was waving through the window of his Porsche.

Her heart lurched.

'Warren's here, you go on ahead, I'll see you there.'

Annis looked also, using the large brim of her hat as part cover; it was definitely him. The man who called himself Geoff. The man who had given her nightmares. She turned back quickly so he didn't see her but she wouldn't be able to avoid him for much longer. What the hell was she to do with what she knew about him? At least where her sister was concerned.

'Are you all right, Annis?' asked Marsha in the car, watching her younger sister watching her older sister walk towards her husband.

'I wish I was, Mash,' said Annis. And then she told her why the blood had shrunk from her skin.

Jolene walked over to the car, got in.

'Jolene, I'm so sorry. Some stupid bastard lorry had overturned on the motorway, closed off all three lanes. I've just this minute arrived.'

He leaned over to kiss her cheek and she inhaled his aftershave. It had once made her senses purr. He'd been everything she ever wanted – the full shebang, the jackpot. It would be much harder to let go of the man she thought he was, than the man he really was.

In the bar of the golf club, Annis stood near to a pillar which allowed her to see who was coming in while giving her a hiding place should she need it. Her eyes were so firmly fixed on the open doors that she didn't see Sally until she felt a tug on her sleeve.

'You look as if you're in another world, Annis,' said Sally.

She'd put lipstick on and it had bled over her lipline, giving her a look of The Joker from *Batman*. If her father had been here, he would have stored the sight to guffaw at later. Standing here, though, he would have taken her hands and said, 'Dear Sally, thank you for coming. You were so very important to my wife.'

'Hello, Sally. Thank you for coming.' Meant and said genuinely. Sally clearly had been crying a lot, probably more than anyone in the church; the tears had cut through the powder applied too thickly on her face, which was the wrong shade to match her skin. It was odd how her mum had enchanted this woman. Like fairylights in her staid, normal world. Mind you, there was a lot to be said for a staid, normal world.

'I have something for you,' Sally said, foraging in her handbag. 'Your mother asked me to give it to you.' She added the lie, 'After the service', to explain the timing.

She handed over an envelope. It wasn't the original one. She'd tried to restick it but it hadn't worked so she'd gone out and bought some high quality ones, the sort Eleanor would use. She'd also tried to replicate Annis's name on the front, but Eleanor's elaborate style defied copying so she'd left it blank.

'For me?' asked Annis for clarification.

'Yes, it's for you. Only you,' she said. 'A letter … she told me.'

Annis's hand came out for it slowly. The envelope looked quite bulky. If it was just a letter, it promised to say plenty.

'I can't stay, I have to get back.' Sally had given Norman a sleeping pill. It was a one-off but what else could she do? She had to be here today for Eleanor and she had to deliver the letter. She felt lighter by degrees as soon as it had left her hand, as if she were offloading a curse.

'I wish you well, Annis,' said Sally, knowing the truth would mangle her first before it would release her. Exactly as it had done with her.

Chapter 43

Annis put the letter in her bag; she was intrigued but there was a more pressing matter to deal with – and he'd just walked in. She could tell it was him even at this distance: his strong jaw, white teeth, his big square shoulders, the way he fitted a suit as if it had been cut precisely for him and him alone. He had a radioactive glow and she felt poisoned for being in the same orbit as him. And her sister had been married to him for ten years without knowing who he really was under that handsome shine.

'How do we do this?' asked Marsha, appearing next to her after doing a round of the room, making sure people had a drink, letting them say their 'Sorry for your loss's.

'Get her outside,' said Annis. 'I'll meet you there. Jolene is not going back with him today.' She was afraid that her sister had no idea how dangerous that man could be when crossed, and she didn't want her to find out.

Warren was blocking up the doorway so Annis pressed the lever down on the fire exit and got out that way. There was a small beer garden with a canopy above it. The air was hot and sticky, but she was shivering. The clouds had only given up some of their load in the night and they needed to drop the lot to relieve the humidity, but they were hanging on to it as if picking their moment.

Jolene and Marsha eventually came round the corner.

'What's the matter?' asked a confused Jolene.

'You'd better sit down,' said Annis.

Jolene looked from one sister to the other but neither was giving anything away. When Jolene sat, they did too, in a tight cluster.

'Do you remember me telling you about Geoff, the man who stalked me, who got nasty—'

'The widower, the paramedic, yes of course I do,' Jolene interrupted her.

'The one who blew a lot of money on presents and prostitutes. An *obscene* amount.' Annis's throat felt dry. She was not looking forward to dropping this bomb and blowing up her sister's world as she knew it.

Jolene's brow creased a little more. 'Where's this going?' There was a nasty little tickle at the edge of her thoughts, like a spider's sly approach on a web.

Annis took in a big breath to aid her, then she dived in with no more pussy-footing about. 'Jolene, it's Warren. He's the one I knew as Geoff.'

It didn't sink in immediately, Annis could almost see Jolene's brain resisting the information.

'Warren?' she said eventually. She couldn't believe it, but neither did she wholly dismiss it.

'Trust me, Jolene, if I had any doubt at all I wouldn't have said.'

Annis watched her expression change from incredulity to puzzlement.

'He used to talk about "speculation for accumulation",

he said it a few times when he was talking about money, which he talked about a lot. He gave me a necklace, a gold one, with a moon and a cat on it because he knew I liked animals. He told me his wife had wanted a dog but he was allergic to pet fur. Does this ring any bells?'

'I lost a necklace exactly like that three years ago,' said Jolene. Warren had blamed her for not taking care of it and did she realise how much it cost, because he talked about money a lot. She was wearing a crucifix today, for comfort and strength.

'The thing with Geoff happened three years ago. It's him. I'm so sorry, Jolene. I just started putting pieces together. I didn't want to find I was right, I really didn't,' said Annis softly.

'But he couldn't have passed himself off as a paramedic,' said Jolene.

'To be fair it wasn't medical stuff he'd bang on about in the bar, it was topping up his NHS pension with investments, stocks and shares, about how you have to take risks or not bother,' Annis answered that.

The biggest risk of all is not taking one. Another of his sayings, thought Jolene.

'When Denise did some digging on him, she found out that ... Geoff had been blowing money on escorts all over. He'd pay for them to go to Paris and Prague with him, splash the champagne, best hotel rooms, showing off on roulette wheels. He was the type who thought if he rented a woman's body, he owned them and he could do what he liked with them.' He'd taken his tastes a bit too far with three at least, a detail she spared her sister. 'There are some ... people very interested in the whereabouts of Geoff the paramedic, Jolene. It seems that they really did believe he was who he said he was and that's why they've been drawing a blank finding him.'

'Oh my god,' Jolene said eventually. The truth was too big for her to take in, it would choke her if she swallowed it in more than tiny pieces. Warren had had his mother rack up loans and remortgage her house just so he could blow the cash on getting his end away? All the money Jolene had thought she was pumping into his business had been pumped into a legion of prostitutes via his loins. So there was no one single mysterious, glamorous mistress, that was just a lie to keep her in desperate competition because the real truth would have had her running for the hills.

Annis picked up her sister's hand and held it; it was as cold as hers. Jolene looked as stunned as if Tyson Fury had just landed her one with a cement glove.

'I can't believe it,' she said, though she did. 'Everything I put up with for that . . . lowlife shit.'

There was a rumble in the sky, as if the ceiling of cloud was agreeing with them. 'We should get in,' said Marsha, as fat drops of rain started to plop onto the ground.

'I don't know what to do,' said Jolene, half-laughing at the absurdity of her situation. Her thoughts had frozen: she couldn't stay here; she couldn't go forward.

None of them knew what to do but being in a crowd would at least be safer until they did. They stood up, preparing to take the first step into the maelstrom, just as Warren rounded the corner.

'There you are,' he said, 'I've been looking for you, Jo.'

He was just as Annis remembered, though his hair was shorter. A commanding air, strong presence, confident. A man that took up a lot of space, who would make pupils dilate to let in more of him. You'd put your life in his hands if he was a paramedic.

When she spoke, Jolene's calm voice belied the trembling in her hand that was still clinging to Annis's.

'Geoff, you know Marsha but meet Annis, my young-est sister.' She used the name deliberately. His lips began to form a smile, ready to charm, then his brain caught up with his ears.

'Remember me?' said Annis, forcing bravery into herself. 'I've just been telling your wife about you. She didn't know.'

'Sorry?' he tried, head tilting, like a dog trying to make sense of a situation. Then he looked at her again – and this time he recognised her.

'You are quite the arsehole aren't you,' said Jolene. She laughed again. Shock, it had to be shock. 'So . . . let me get this right, you've spent everything I've earned in the last ten years on hookers and I'm in debt because you can't keep it in your trousers. Did your mother ever know what she was giving you money for? Did you go on a St John's Ambulance first-aid course with some of it, *Geoff*?'

He was winded, out-manoeuvred, his expression said he was a man clawing for an escape route but even a greased eel couldn't slip a sealed trap. The trouble was, that's when they got dangerous.

'Our marriage is absolutely over, of course,' continued Jolene, sounding a lot calmer and stronger than she felt. 'You'll be hearing from my solicitor as soon as I've got one.'

'You do realise she's one of the fucking hookers, don't you?' Warren said menacingly, extending his long arm towards Annis.

She remembered trying to get past him up the cellar steps, even though she didn't have a chance. She remembered biting down on the big hand over her mouth to make a moment in which to scream. The world was Warren Cattrell's personal sweet shop, he took what he wanted, one way or the other.

'Go to hell, Warren,' said Jolene. She turned away from him, not sure where she was going other than in the opposite direction to where he was standing.

For a big man Warren Cattrell moved fast. He lurched forward, grabbed his wife by the arm, ripping her away from Annis.

'We're going home, Jolene. We need to talk.'

'You're taking her nowhere,' cried Annis, wrapping her arms around Jolene's waist. Marsha locked onto Jolene's other arm, but such was Warren's strength, he was dragging them all the way he wanted to go, winning the tug of war. Until he suddenly stopped.

'Hello, Geoff.'

A wall of three men, as wide as they were tall appeared in front of them.

'We heard you was here and we thought we'd come and say hello.' There was a smile on the face of the middle man, but it wasn't the sort of smile you'd like directed at you.

Thank you, God, thought Annis. She'd rung Denise first thing that morning, told her that if anyone was looking for the infamous Geoff, where he'd be and when. Denise hadn't wasted any time.

'You're a hard man to find, Geoff,' said the man on the right. There was no smile on his face and his eyebrows were drawn down in an angry V formation.

'Now you let go,' the man on the left in a black leather jacket prised Warren's fingers from Jolene. His hands made Warren's look like a Ken doll's by comparison. '... and we'll all have a nice chat somewhere.' He addressed the three sisters: 'Sorry to interrupt such a solemn occasion, I do apologise. You don't mind if we borrow Geoff for a while, do you, ladies?' His voice was surprisingly gentle for such a wardrobe of a bloke.

'Jolene—' Warren shouted her name over his shoulder as he was propelled forward: he wasn't so cocksure now.

'Be my guest,' said Jolene.

'Sorry for your loss,' said the smiling man, with a reverent nod of his head.

'He's no loss,' Jolene answered.

Jolene sank onto the chair again. The rain was starting to really come down now, but they were sheltered under the canopied roof.

'Do you think he'll be all right?' she asked.

'No,' said Annis.

'Good,' said Marsha. 'I wish one of us had brought the rest of that Grey Goose with us. I wonder who they were.'

'People Denise knows. I rang her and told her he'd be here,' replied Annis, then she turned to Jolene. 'I'm sorry. I didn't know when to tell you. There was no right time.'

'This is exactly the right time,' said Jolene. 'No wonder the bloody businesses kept sinking. I was a soft touch from day one, wasn't I? I was a fish with my mouth open waiting for a line to drop in it.'

'Some people can smell vulnerability from a mile off. Like a shark,' said Marsha.

'I'm sure he did really like you, Jolene,' said Annis. 'Why wouldn't he?'

'From now on I'm sticking to fictional men,' she said.

'I said that and ended up having the time of my life in a

shed,' Marsha puffed out her cheeks. 'You don't get what I got from a printed page.'

'Eric is really nice.' Jolene smiled. 'You must fill your boots with each other and I'll write a book about it.'

'I think Lady Chatterley's already been written,' said Annis. She took her sister's hand and tried to chafe some warmth into it because she was shivering, whether with cold or adrenaline she couldn't tell. 'We'll help you. You'll be okay.'

Jolene nodded because there was suddenly too much emotion in her throat to speak, but she felt, in the moment, very much as if she would be.

'Have to say, I loved the line about the St John's Ambulance course, Dolly. He might be needing a few plasters soon,' said Annis with a grin, pulling her sister to her feet. 'Come on, let's see to our guests. Let's finish the day.'

They put on their Vamplew daughter faces and carried on where they had left off, spending time with everyone who wanted to tell them how much they'd miss Eleanor, how charitable she'd been. Father Gerard had shown up, his professional head on. He was a good priest, thought Marsha, watching him work the room. Maybe he became a better priest for having that blip and then being reconditioned in Rome. Looking at it objectively now, she didn't doubt that he'd fallen hard for her, that fragments of her would linger always with him but, like a married man, he wasn't free to give her the whole gift of himself and a part was not enough. The fantasy of them had burned for too long, not extinguished by the cold water of reality. She'd now snuffed it finally and forever by closing the door on what they might or might not have had, and opened another for someone who wanted to rush in and take full residence in her heart, not dangle by the doorstep like an uninvited vampire.

The first thing Sally did when she got home was to open up Norman's ancient laptop at the kitchen table. It still worked, even though it hadn't been switched on for ages. There was a Post-it note with his password stuck on the screen from when he had started forgetting it. She typed it in and looked for the Google symbol. He'd tried to give her lessons on how to use it a few times but she'd laughed and said when would she ever need to. But she'd had a go and could at least look for things.

She typed in the search bar: *Barnsley dementia help*. She wasn't going to go it alone any more. She'd wanted to be like Eleanor and do all the nursing, just as she'd done for Julian, but Sally wasn't her, they were nothing like each other. Thank goodness. Eleanor had nearly fooled her with those nice words in her letter: Sally the good friend, throw her a bit of gold for her troubles and hopefully the shine will distract her enough to make her forget everything else. *Nearly.*

She'd cried hard in the church and everyone probably thought she was crying for her friend, but she wasn't. She was listening to Father Bannen's fine words and thinking that he didn't really know Eleanor at all. Did anyone? He was talking about a bright light having gone out and Sally was thinking that's exactly what it felt like, because only when such a light has faded do you see what's crawling in the shadows. He eulogised Eleanor as a generous, church-going, marvellous bridge-player, a keen gardener, a pillar of the community and all Sally wanted to do was stand up and tell them all what she'd done to her marriage, done to her husband, done to her own girls. How many lives she'd soured and all in the name of love, an emotion the rotten so-and-so couldn't even feel.

She tapped in the number she'd found into her telephone. A voice said to keep hanging on the line and her call would be answered shortly.

As she was waiting, Sally opened up her locket and took out the oval photo of Eleanor with her skin-deep beauty, as thin as the polished wood veneer on her flower-covered coffin.

Sally thought then that if she really had been responsible for her dropping dead then she'd done them all a blooming favour, and she wasn't going to let Eleanor Vamplew reach through from wherever she was and haunt her conscience any more. She was dead and Sally was alive and she was going to take full advantage of her beating heart. She tore up the photo and snapped the locket shut just as the music on the phone stopped and a voice said:

'Barnsley Dementia Society, can I help you?'

And Sally answered, 'Yes, please.'

Later, at home, the three Vamplew sisters kicked off their black high heels, put on some comfortable clothes and sat around the kitchen table.

'Those people won't kill Warren, will they?' asked Jolene.

'No, but they'll give him a taste of his own medicine,' said Annis. 'They would have caught up with him eventually,' she added for her sister's peace of mind, even if she wasn't sure if that was true or not. He'd not been 'active' in Leeds, but Sheffield, Derby, Nottingham and it was presumed he came from somewhere between the points of that triangle, so Denise had told her.

'I think I might sleep tonight better than I have for years, and not because of this.' Jolene lifted the glass of Grey Goose to her lips. Today had been the end of so many things, too many really.

'Rock bottom makes a solid base for rebuilding,' said Annis, not letting Marsha refill her glass. She'd had one to be sociable, but she needed a clear head tonight.

Jolene smiled. That was the sort of thing one of her characters would say.

They sat in a peaceable silence for a few minutes, then Marsha asked, 'Do you think Mum and Dad will be reunited? Is that what they'd want? To find each other again?'

'I think they belong together, yes,' said Annis. 'Wherever they are now.'

'What do you think was the attraction for them with each other?' asked Marsha, sounding as if the question had been on her mind for a very long time. 'She was so … glacial. If you didn't know these people you'd picture Dad with someone … warmer wouldn't you? What was the glue that held them together?'

Annis shrugged a 'don't know'.

'I think she loved him more than she could love anyone,' said Jolene. 'I think she hoped he'd be the person who let her into this world of feelings that she could see but not get at. I even think she hoped to find it in us.' She stabbed her finger at Annis: 'Obviously not you because you were a mistake.'

'Cheers, Dolly.'

'But she didn't find it with me. Maybe she thought a son might be different, the bet she put all her gold on and that's why she was so upset when you turned out to be a girl, Marsha. It wasn't you she was disappointed with, it was much bigger than you. It was always about Mum and her wants. The only person she ever found any real connection with was Dad; it's terribly sad when you think about it.' Jolene sighed. She'd wished sometimes to be more like her mother and not feel so deeply, but she was glad she wasn't.

'She could appreciate him objectively, without emotion,' Annis added. 'He was a thing to be coveted, owned, guarded, like a diamond.'

'But what did he get out of it?' asked Marsha.

'Money, this house, sex. People envied their glossy lives. I think they fascinated each other and found common ground other than love. Look at all the people who marry for reasons other than that and manage to be quite content with their lot.' Jolene shook her head as her judgement on that. It wasn't for her. She wouldn't be marrying for companionship or security.

Marsha wondered, not for the first time, how two such people had produced them – three children who felt so much, who cared and loved and got hurt. It was as if the scales had tipped the other way, mother nature's counterbalance.

She yawned. 'They were well matched, weren't they?'

There was no need to answer that with words.

Annis waited until the others had gone to bed before she took the envelope Sally had given her out of her bag. She sat on the floor of the kitchen with John Abruzzi on her lap for comfort and then she read the words that her mother had written for her and her alone. The apology she couldn't deliver in person.

Chapter 44

Annis closed the door quietly and locked it, walked down the path and opened the passenger door of the blue Jeep.

'I'm sorry if I woke you up,' she said.

'It's all right,' said Daz. 'I was only just dozing off.'

He was lying and she knew it. It was two o'clock in the morning and his eyes told her he'd been rudely awoken from a deep sleep.

'Where do you want me to drive to?'

'You don't have to drive anywhere, I just wanted to see you.'

She was wearing psychedelic leggings and a green fuzzy top with rabbit hairs all over it. Her black eye make-up had run, her hair was stuck up, as if she'd had a recent electric shock and still his heart was tripping at the sight of her. She was holding a letter which was fluttering slightly in her hand because she was trembling.

'What's wrong, love?' he asked her, his voice a soft dart in her composure.

'There's something I haven't told you about me,' she said.

'Okay,' Daz said, nodding. 'Then tell me.'

It was the sudden ferocity of Julian's attack upon Norman that concerned me. I almost felt sorry for the vile little man, and poor Sally – the essential collateral damage. What father would not protect his child? But there was more in what he did.

That day, Julian deflected what he was upon Norman so he could openly hate it. I knew instantly. It was still inside him.

We destroyed them, we killed her trust in him. She tried to mend her marriage but it was never the same. There was nothing we could do about it, alas – it was them or us.

Annis wrapped her arms around herself.

'I left home because ... because of my dad,' she said and she waited for Daz to read into her words what she hadn't said. He got it immediately; he'd suspected something on those lines. Her front, her eggshell fragility behind it, why she'd left home so young. His arms came out and she shrank back. 'Please don't, let me finish.'

'Of course, okay.'

'I trusted my father, but I was confused. He said, *how can love ever be wrong?* He didn't even have to warn me not to tell anyone, because instinctively I knew that it *was* wrong, very wrong, and I felt ashamed.'

I put the pieces together. I could have forgiven him seducing Hilde Faulkender more easily than I could have forgiven him for grooming her. Grooming me. I had to be more than merely his attempt at normality, his hiding place. I had made myself much more than that to him, hadn't I?

'He played on my innocence and my ignorance to get what he wanted and made himself believe he had done it for love, not power.'

We had so much to lose. It was you balanced on one side of the scale and my whole world on the other. You have no idea what he meant to me.

'I hated my sisters. I thought it must have happened to them too and they hadn't protected me. But it was just me.'

My mother told me I'd never keep him. She knew about Hilde. She said he had a type, didn't he? Young. I fought the worm she put in my brain. I had no intention of letting him go. We were both victims of Mother Nature and we had found our haven in one another. We deserved to be happy.

'And when I was sixteen, my father asked me to go away with him, live some place where no one knew us or what we were to each other. He planned for us to go in the new year, so we wouldn't spoil Christmas for anyone. That's why I left. And that's why they never tried to find me.'

Daz swallowed before he asked the question he wasn't sure he wanted to know the answer to.

'Did your mum know?'

'I wanted her to guess. I wanted her to ask me why I was getting into trouble at school. I was waving a flag to her, because ... she was the only person I could talk to about it, but I didn't know what to say and there was no one else to turn to.'

You must believe me when I say I had no idea. When I saw the doll's house destroyed in your room, I suspected only then. I should have known: how besotted he was with you, possessive. I didn't think it was possible for me to feel anything like heartbreak. But when you went and he told me what he had done, there was a pain inside me the like of which I have never experienced before. I screamed at him, I hit him.

'She made him tell her when I'd gone.'

How could he have done this to us, risk destroying everything I had built? He said I had made him powerless, and that he wanted someone he could cherish and take care of. You would have given him all that: a fantasy constructed from aspects of me, youth, beauty, love. Love – what a pathetic abstract. And to think I once felt deprived of feeling it.

'She'd made herself enough for him, or so she believed. He was the only person she felt she could belong to and she thought he felt the same about her. It hurt her terribly that she was wrong.'

It was a relief when you went. I said as much in confession, but I didn't tell the priest why. Releasing the words would have made them real and I could not allow that. He was mine, and he had to stay mine, unsullied by scandal.

I have thought so much about you. It should never have happened, but he was ill. I was right to let you be cut adrift. We recovered as best we could and we were content, I think. I felt the loss of him greatly when he died. There was pleasure in nothing after he'd gone. I once thought that we were each other's reward, but maybe we were one another's punishment.

That is why I am leaving you the bulk of our money in the hope it will make your future life easier. There would be no advantage in not letting us lie peacefully in our graves.

Your Mother

'So, Mum left me her money to make amends. What do you think?' The letter was still fluttering in her hand.

'May I?' Daz held out his hand and Annis handed it to him. She waited until he read it all, watching his eyes follow the words, left to right, left to right. She watched emotions tweak his features, incredulity and astonishment. And at the end he asked, 'Why didn't she say this to you in person if she was sorry?'

'Because she wasn't. It's not an apology, it's a bribe. She's paying me to stay silent and not throw their memory to the lions.'

Her voice was strong but tears were leaking from the corners of her eyes and she dashed their irritating presence away with her fingertips. 'What a fucked-up family I come from, Daz. So I'm going to leave you now and I want you to walk away from me. Thank you for coming tonight and for your kindness to me. For obvious reasons I can't talk to my sisters about this and I had to talk to someone, but please don't feel used. You're a lovely man and I trust hardly anyone, but I do trust you.'

She turned to open the car door, but Daz Meynell's arms wrapped around her before she could. His hold was tight and warm and if he never let go, she didn't think she'd mind.

'The only thing that will be disappearing,' he said to her, 'is every rotten, shitty, memory you have. I'm going to do everything I can to make that happen, Annis Vamplew. I promise you.'

Chapter 45

Six months later

The three women stood on the cliff top and looked out at the grey, wintry sea.

'This the spot?' asked Annis.

'The exact spot,' replied Marsha. 'I don't think what we're doing is actually legal but this is where we let Dad go so maybe if they haven't found each other already, this is how it will happen.'

'Okay, here goes,' said Jolene, lifting the top off the urn and checking the wind direction before shaking it. The ashes lifted and spread, falling, rising, letting the breeze carry them where it chose. Annis reached into her pocket and shook more ashes from a small plastic bag.

'What's that?' asked Marsha.

'Just a note to follow her.' It was her mother's letter to her. No one else would ever read it. She would not tell her sisters what it said, she would not be the agent of more hurt and devastation. She would leave the few good memories they had intact. Not because she had been paid to, but because of the love she had for these two women standing with her. These two beautiful, fabulous women. Her shoulders were broad enough for them all.

Jolene's divorce was going through uncontested. Annis's recompense for helping reunite those who were looking for Geoff/Warren was that her sister got no hassle at all during the proceedings. It was in his best interests to comply, unless he wanted to join a choir as a castrato was the clearly delivered message. In five days exactly, Jolene would have her decree absolute. The remaining bottles of the Champagne Salon were already waiting on ice. She had been back to the marital home once with her sisters and Daz, Eric and a big van and together they had moved everything out that she wanted to keep and she had no reason to ever go back again.

She was broke and she had more chance of being impregnated by Brad Pitt than getting back any of the money she had given Warren over the years, but freedom was her temporary riches and her third share of the Vamplew estate would soon be hers to begin a new life. She'd live in hope of meeting someone as lovely as the men in her books, but for now she was content being alone without being lonely. She had plans for new books, a cottage to buy and make her own, a cat, a dog, maybe even a rabbit.

Marsha had sold her business. She was given an offer she couldn't refuse and so she didn't. For now, she was letting out her big house in Bakewell and had moved in with Eric. She discovered that sex in a king-sized bed with him was every bit as good as it was in a shed.

They'd talked about trying for a baby, maybe next year. A boy or a girl, they didn't mind which they were blessed with, one would be loved as much as the other. She could already picture them with a tiny wheelbarrow, planting seeds, baking, glitter and glue pictures. Marsha had finally found the acceptance that had been dangling like an unattainable carrot in front of her for too long, from a kind and very sexy gardener who looked like Eric Cantona – and also from herself.

Fox House was under offer. A couple with three children had just secured a mortgage for it. There were only four years between the youngest and oldest. They'd have thrills skidding down the polished hallway, Jolene thought, and picking apples from the trees in the orchard. The house needed some fun, some young energy to make up for too many unhappy years.

She had been staying with Annis in the house which strangely enough had lost its chill. Sometimes Jolene had gone to turn off the central heating to find out it wasn't even on. It was as if the house was getting to know them as much as they were getting to know each other. They felt protected within its walls. They'd part on fond terms. Then they'd all move on to better things.

Annis was doing a course on teaching adults how to read, at the local college. She brought a lot to the table through her experiences that she wasn't too proud to share. She'd open her school one day, nothing surer. She was on a mission to make that sad Vamplew money brighten a lot of lives. Redress the balance.

Daz Meynell had a new dog. Another bulldog, a poor little soul who needed some gentleness in his life and there was no better place to find it than in big Daz. 'Thug' took to his new name – Johnny Sack – as quickly as he took to his new owner. And Daz made good on his promise to do everything he could to make Annis happy, stamp over the years past with new memories full of laughter and love, office picnics and music by the Monkees.

Jolene put her arms around her sisters and felt the bond between them shared like a current. Their vulnerabilities had moulded them into women who loved and were loved, who had learned and created, succeeded and survived. They had escaped the confines of their own stories and become stronger for it. Together, again, always.

The ashes were gone now, the goodbye was complete, they were already part of the past, no longer visible, no longer relevant.

'We are only to look forward from now on us three,' said Jolene, pulling them close. She felt a lightness within, a joy rising like a morning sun. 'And do you know what? It's going to be good.'

Acknowledgements

Writing the acks of my book is always a treat I save until the book has gone to print. It's like the first cup of tea and an egg mayo sarnie after giving birth. And that's exactly what it feels like (give or take the morphine) because this book that you've just read is my creation, my baby, and there's a lot of blood, sweat and tears that's gone into it. Not just from me, but from the whole team behind me (sort of literary midwives). It's an absolute pleasure to give them a shout out.

Heading up my list on this one is Sally Partington, my copyeditor, because working with Sal is my joy. It's not hers. This book was a hard write, there was a lot to get spot on and Sal is always the perfect person to bat things back and forth with. And she's invaluable for giving you grammar lessons along the way, when your brain has frozen and you have lost all ability to decide if it's 'different to' or 'different from'. Sometimes it feels as if you are lifting up the *Mary Rose* from the quicksand when writing a book. You know what you want to say but you can't get it out and you just need to find the best grip for leverage. And Sal guided my hands on the rope and helped me pull this one up and put it where I needed it to be. She is so much more than a copy-editor. She is also nothing like drippy Sally in my book, by the way. But once the name Sally Lunn had landed in my head, it would not be changed.

Publishing is very different from how it was when I started off, there are so many ways to get your books out there and all are valid, but 'I'm glad to be trad'. Traditional publishing suits me and it means I have a gigantic team at my back – the best team. I've been with the same publisher since I climbed on this crazy ride and I have no idea how I've got to book twenty but I'm just glad that I rolled up my sleeves and gave myself a push even though it was laughable that this bird from Barnsley would ever get a book published, never mind end up in bestseller lists. Simon & Schuster have had faith in me from the off and they gave me my dream. So thank you Ian, Suzanne, SJ, Gill, Jess, Rich, Maddie, Dom, Kat, Sian, Pip, Louise, Francesca and all the rights team. I know how hard you work so I can stand on the stage and get the glory. And a special thanks to Clare Hey because having a good editor is so important and you are bloody brilliant.

Thanks to my agent Lizzy Kremer who is an iron fist, dunked in cement in a velvet glove. I'm beyond grateful this magnificent creature is in my corner.

Thanks to Emma Draude and Annabelle Wright at ED PR who are absolutely fabulous and go way beyond the call of duty for me. I'm so glad to have you. Although I am still waiting for a joint gig with Jason Momoa.

Thanks to Ian Anthony, the coroner's officer at the Medico-Legal centre in Sheffield. It's always great when you find people prepared to help you with the finest, stupidest details that nevertheless have to be right and I appreciate your time and patience in explaining the intricacies and details I needed to grasp. I'll be back.

Thank you to the reviewers, press and blogging community for spreading the word from your kind hearts. And to the Romantic Novelists' Association, which has brought me so much fun, support, wisdom and friendship.

Thanks to all the lovely bookshops who recommend my novels and do a great PR job – especially the Book Vault in Barnsley and Mike's Famous Bookstall in our lovely Barnsley market. And to Andrew Harrod, the editor of our local rag – the *Barnsley Chronicle* – who is a staunch ally as well as a friend.

Thanks to Stu, my website bloke, as per normal. A proper talent and a good mate.

Thanks to my lovely author friends who are there in times of writing worries and life disasters too. We may have bonded over the job initially, but our friendships have grown much deeper and dearer over the years. In particular: Debbie Johnson, Jane Costello, Lucy Diamond, Cathy Bramley, Veronica Henry and the beauts in the Shit Book Club: Judy Astley, Katie Fforde, Catherine Jones, Bernie Kennedy, Jill Mansell, Janie Millman, AJ Pearce, Jo Thomas and though Jane Wenham-Jones is sadly no longer with us, her name is included here because there are ten members of the SBC and there always will be.

Thanks to my readers for your loyalty and love. For your letters and your stories. Without you, I'd be nowt.

Thanks also to Daz Meynell of Meynell Mix Ltd who gave me a lovely fat donation for my affiliated charity Yorkshire Cat Rescue (yorkshirecatrescue.org) in exchange for naming a character after him. I hope you like Daz, Daz. He's one of my favourites.

Thanks also to the Monkees for being the Monkees, the group I loved most in the whole wide world from a very early age. This is how much I loved them. I used to run home from junior school on Wednesday to watch them on the TV and the class bitch made everyone send me to Coventry because I 'should have been a fan of the Bay City Rollers'. Did I fold? Nope. I carried on being a fan of the Monkees and I still am. And I gravitated to a new set of mates in the playground who are still my mates. Thank you Micky, Peter, Davy and Mike. I will always love you – and my pals.

And Kate Taylor was a real teacher, the best one I ever had. She has sadly passed but my god she was a hell of a woman. We were blessed to have her teaching us English. She was beyond inspirational.

This book has been one of the hardest and the antithesis of my last book about strong familial bonds. Not every family is the Brady Bunch, we all have our skeletons in the cupboard (despite what Instagram might tell you). I've had to do a lot of research for this, quite sad and challenging stuff but also what a thrill to write about narcissists and psychopathy, totally fascinating stuff and I gladly went down a lot of rabbit holes with it all. I relish getting into people's minds and must thank Dr Cliff Lansley from 'Faking It' for giving me some pointers. I love that programme – fascinating if you like drilling down into people's heads. Sadly some behaviours just defy logic. I hope you have all fared better with your parents than my three girls here.

To all the ladies I spoke to about some proper rotten childhoods – thank you for giving me your time, your feelings and your stories so freely. So lovely to see you are not defined by your battle scars and that you haven't been imprisoned by your past. You have moved on and have been determined not to repeat the patterns that could have destroyed you – but thankfully didn't.

Also a shout out to the staff and residents of New Hall Prison in Wakefield. Until I went there for a visit and to talk to people, I had no real idea of the negative impact that not being able to read has on one's life. Even being able to read a little instils confidence and the desire to go and read a little more and that is how a vocabulary is built up. Just take a minute to think about how many times a day we read something to get by: the TV guide, instructions on medicine bottles, train timetables . . . and then think how you'd manage if you couldn't read.

The world of someone who cannot read is so much smaller than the world of someone who can and their choices are fewer. Reading is a gateway to a bigger, brighter world because it impacts on *everything*: health, wealth, happiness. Readingagency.org.uk is a wonderful charity that promotes reading and, as they say, it doesn't matter what you read, only that you read. Do look them up.

I'm very lucky that I grew up safe and loved so thank you, Mum and Dad. Parents never get everything right and their kids try to correct their parents' mistakes with their kids and, in doing so, make fresh ones in their place. But if you give your children love, it goes a long, long way. One of my favourite poems is by Philip Larkin and it's called 'This Be The Verse'. Go have a gander, it's only short but it says everything. I would love to have used it at the beginning of this novel, but you'll see why I didn't if you read it.

And last, but by no means least: for Burny, in memory of Logan. I hope you can imagine him playing football up there, scoring goals with a big smile on his face and his red hair glowing in eternal sunshine.

Milly Johnson

Woman in the Middle

An emotional, uplifting and completely relatable new novel from the *Sunday Times* bestselling author

Shay Bastable is the woman in the middle. She is part of the sandwich generation – caring for her parents and her children, supporting her husband **Bruce**, holding them all together as best she can.

But then, when piece by piece, everything Shay thought of as certain in her life is taken away and disaster strikes, she has to put herself first for a change.

In order to move forward with her present, Shay needs to make sense of her past. And in doing so, she discovers that you have to hit rock bottom before you can safely say the only way is up.

**When you're doing it all
Who's there to catch you when you fall?**

Milly Johnson

My One True North

A gorgeous read full of hope, warmth and heartfelt emotion from the *Sunday Times* bestselling author

Laurie and Pete should never have met.
But fate has pushed them together for a reason.

Six months ago, on the same night, **Laurie** and **Pete** both lost their partners. Struggling to manage the grief, they join the same counselling group – and meet each other.

From their sadness, Pete and Laurie find happiness growing and they sense a fresh new beginning. Except, the more they talk, the more they begin to spot the strange parallels in their stories. Then Pete discovers a truth that changes everything.

But, as surely as a compass points north,
some people cannot be kept apart.

My One True North is a story of friendship and what love means, of secrets uncovered, teashops on corners and the northern lights.

Milly Johnson

The Teashop on the Corner

**The magical and feel-good novel from the
Sunday Times bestseller**

Life is full of second chances, if only you keep your heart open for them.

Spring Hill Square is a pretty sanctuary away from the
bustle of everyday life. And at its centre is **Leni Merryman**'s
Teashop on the Corner, specialising in cake, bookish
stationery and compassion. And for three people, all in need
of a little TLC, it is somewhere to find a friend to lean on.

Carla Pride has just discovered that her late husband Martin
was not who she thought he was. And now she must learn
to put her marriage behind her and move forward.

Molly Jones's ex-husband Harvey has reappeared in her
life after many years, wanting to put right the wrongs of
the past before it is too late.

And **Will Linton**'s business has gone bust and his wife
has left him to pick up the pieces. Now he needs to gather
the strength to start again.

Can all three find the comfort they are looking for in The
Teashop on the Corner? And as their hearts are slowly mended
by Leni, can they return the favour when she needs it most?

Milly Johnson

Afternoon Tea at the Sunflower Café

**The heartwarming and feel-good read from
the *Sunday Times* bestselling author**

When Connie discovers that Jimmy Diamond,
her husband of more than twenty years, is planning
to leave her for his office junior, her world is turned
upside down. Determined to salvage her pride, she
resolves to get her own back. Along with **Della**, Jimmy's
right-hand woman at his cleaning firm, Diamond Shine,
and the cleaners who meet at the Sunflower Café, she'll
make him wish he had never underestimated her.

Then Connie meets the charming **Brandon Locke**, a
master chocolatier, whose kindness starts to melt her soul.
Can the ladies of the Sunflower Café help Connie scrub
away the hurt? And can Brandon make her trust again?

Milly
Johnson

It's Raining Men

**A heartwarming and feel-good read from
the *Sunday Times* bestseller**

Best friends from work **May**, **Lara** and **Clare** are
desperate for some time away. In need of some serious
R & R, they set off to a luxurious spa for ten glorious
days. But when they arrive at their destination, it seems
it is not the place they thought it was. In fact, they
appear to have come to entirely the wrong village ...

May can't wait to get away from men after being cruelly
deceived. Then in Dullem she falls hook, line and sinker at
first glance for one of the inhabitants – but he's already taken.

Lara is living with James and his awful step-children
who taunt her with tales of his younger, prettier ex
whom they adored – the woman who Lara walks in
to find James in bed with. Reeling from the hurt, she
needs to heal. What she doesn't need is to be constantly
in battle with the owner of the holiday cottage.

Clare's kind, steady boyfriend Lud wants her to go
and live abroad with him for two years, but she's just
been offered the promotion of a lifetime. In Dullem
she finds some single excitement which happens to turn
up in the form of a very bad boy who is everything
Lud isn't – impulsive, wild and dangerous.

**Will this holiday be the break they all need?
Or will the odd little town with all its secrets
bring them all to breaking point ...?**

Milly Johnson

Sunshine over Wildflower Cottage

The perfect escapist read from the
Sunday Times bestselling author

*New beginnings, old secrets, and a place to call home – escape
to Wildflower Cottage for love, laughter and friendship . . .*

Viv arrives at Wildflower Cottage, a tumbledown
animal sanctuary, for the summer. Her job is to
help with the admin, but the truth is she is here
for something much closer to her heart.

Geraldine runs the Wildflower Cottage sanctuary. She
escaped from her past to find happiness here, but now
her place of refuge is about to come under threat. Can
she keep her history at bay and her future safe?

*Two women join forces for one shared
cause – with unexpected results . . .*

Milly Johnson

The Queen of Wishful Thinking

**A gorgeous read full of love, life and laughter
from the *Sunday Times* bestselling author**

When **Lewis Harley** has a health scare in his early forties, he
takes it as a wake-up call. So he and his wife Charlotte leave
behind life in the fast lane and Lewis opens the antique shop
he has dreamed of. **Bonnie Brookland** was brought up in the
antiques trade and now works for the man who bought out
her father's business, but she isn't happy there. So when she
walks into Lew's shop, she knows this is the place for her.

As Bonnie and Lew start to work together, they soon
realise that there is more to their relationship than
either thought. But Bonnie is trapped in an unhappy
marriage, and Lew and Charlotte have more
problems than they care to admit. Each has secrets
in their past which are about to be uncovered.

Can they find the happiness they both deserve?